DATE DUE

FE 18 99			
IY 19 00			

DEMCO 38-296

DAUGHTER OF
JOY

DAUGHTER OF

JOY

A NOVEL OF
GOLD RUSH CALIFORNIA

JoAnn Levy

A TOM DOHERTY ASSOCIATES BOOK
NEW YORK

DAUGHTER OF JOY: A NOVEL OF GOLD RUSH CALIFORNIA

Copyright © 1998 by JoAnn Levy

All rights reserved, including the right to reproduce this book, or portions
thereof, in any form.

This book is printed on acid-free paper.

A Forge Book
Published by Tom Doherty Associates, Inc.
175 Fifth Avenue
New York, NY 10010

Forge® is a registered trademark of Tom Doherty Associates, Inc.

Library of Congress Cataloging-in-Publication Data
Levy, JoAnn.
Daughter of Joy : a novel of gold rush California   /
JoAnn Levy.—1st ed.
p. cm.—(Women of the West novel)
"A Tom Doherty Associates book."
ISBN 0-312-86502-3 (acid-free paper)
1. Ah Toy—Fiction. 2. Norman As-sing—Fiction. I. Title. II. Series.
PS3562.E92718D38   1998
813'.54—dc21   97-35924
CIP

First Edition: January 1998

Printed in the United States of America

0 9 8 7 6 5 4 3 2

For Dan

AUTHOR'S NOTE

The story of Ah Toy and Norman As-sing is a work of fiction embedded in historical events. I am indebted to the California pioneers whose letters, diaries, and reminiscences provided both its inspiration and substantive details.

Those whose accounts of California between the years 1850 and 1854 proved particularly valuable include J. D. Borthwick, for his description of a bull-and-bear fight; T. A. Barry and B. A. Patten, for their descriptions of San Francisco, including Kearny street's sidewalks; Franklin Buck and John Carr, for the Weaverville War; and *Seven Years' Street Preaching in San Francisco* by Rev. William Taylor.

I am grateful to the Bancroft Library for copies of Sophia Eastman's unpublished letters, which include an account of the City Hospital fire; and for those of John McCrackan, a young lawyer whose letters to his family contained such wonderful details of gold rush San Francisco as the price and availability of cormorant eggs.

To the California State Library in Sacramento I am particularly indebted for its unfailingly supportive staff, for copies of the Vigilance Committee minutes, and for the library's excellent collection of pioneer newspapers, which provided descriptions of the Chinese Bible distribution of August 1850, President Zachary Taylor's memorial parade, San Francisco's statehood and Independence Day celebrations, fires, court cases, shipping news, the *Sagamore*'s explosion, Ah Toy's court appearances, Tong Achick's letter to Governor

Bigler, Norman As-sing's indictment for Triad activities in September 1854, and numerous lesser events.

Also valuable was the library's collection of early city directories, including San Francisco's first, published by Charles P. Kimball, a duodecimo pamphlet of 136 pages containing about 2,500 listings, including Norman As-sing and the Macau and Woosung Restaurant. Street names cited in this story are accurate for the 1850s. Some have changed. Dupont Gai today is Chinatown's famous Grant Avenue.

Especially useful secondary sources included George R. Stewart's *Committee of Vigilance: Revolution in San Francisco, 1850;* Curt Gentry's *The Madams of San Francisco;* and Maxine Hong Kingston's *China Men.*

For Chinese beliefs and customs, I relied on J. Dyer Ball's *Things Chinese,* Frena Bloomfield's *The Book of Chinese Beliefs,* and Henry Dore's *Chinese Customs.* Any failure to represent them accurately is genuinely regretted. This is the story of California's Chinese pioneers, and I hoped most sincerely to do both it, and them, justice.

1

San Francisco will one day be a half Chinese city, and it will certainly not lose by it.

—Etienne Derbec
San Francisco, 1850

Ah Toy drifted in and out of sleep with the ship's familiar rhythm. To avoid rolling against Wang Po, she grasped the bunk's edge. She relaxed her grip as the sea tilted her again toward the ship's timbers, fragrant with ancient cargoes of tea and spice.

She felt Wang Po's body echo the sea's cadence, falling against her back and away like a pendulum. She came slowly awake, hearing the ship's creaking timbers, the banging of a hatch cover, the shout of a crewman, the thud of a gust finding sail.

The ship leaned again into the sea. Wang Po silently spilled against her. Ah Toy's eyes flew open with sudden knowing. Breath abandoned her.

The sea relented, rolling Wang Po's lifeless body from her back.

Ah Toy leapt from the deathbed and clutched the bunk post. Her breath returned in gulps while questions flew through her mind like squawking gulls. What must she do? How would she live? Could she return to Hongkong? How? Who owned her?

That was a stopping thought: Who owned her?

That was a thing to think on, but first she must tend the old one. Ah Toy wrapped Wang Po's body in his bedding, tending him as his slave, not as a daughter as she had when Tsu Yen died.

Ah Toy clutched the post again, steadying herself, remembering Willow lane. She remembered clipping silver from Tsu Yen's earring and placing it in a tiny bag with a pinch of tea and a piece of candy. She had slipped the bag into Tsu Yen's mouth, so that she might have food to eat on her journey, and silver to buy what she needed.

When Tsu Yen died, the old mistress, Lao Tai Tai, still owned Ah

Toy. Who owned her now? she wondered, thinking on this new thing as she crouched between the bunks. Her terror had passed, and she realized she was not afraid.

Death was not fear. She remembered fear. Fear sucked breath from her mouth in the time of hunger and begging. When the famine came, her father with no face sold all the things from the house, even the cooking basin. There was nothing to cook. And he took the money for opium and had no face or shame. No face, no shame. These were the words Ah Toy remembered her mother throwing at him while she pounded a brick into grit for Ah Toy to eat. There was nothing else to sop hunger's gnawing pain.

Recollection of that hunger rose up now, old memories clinging to it like seaweed. Ah Toy and her mother, she remembered, left their house. At the gate her mother hid a stick up her sleeve, to beat off the dogs. She didn't want the neighbors to see her going out with it, she said. They would know she was begging.

Ah Toy remembered stumbling on her five-year-old legs, clutching her mother's sleeve. Few people would slam a door in a child's face, her mother insisted. So it was Ah Toy who tapped at doors and held out the begging bowl.

That was a time for being frightened, frightened by hunger, strangers, dogs, her mother's fear. And when her father sold Ah Toy to the dealers, she was frightened. And she was frightened again when they took her to the city and sold her to Lao Tai Tai, the old mistress.

Ah Toy was alone with her thoughts. The China men retreated each morning from the confining staleness to the deck above. In the gloom she saw only the untidiness of their bedding rolls, baskets, rice bowls, the odds and ends of limited necessities.

Perhaps she should yell through the open hatch, "Wang Po dead!" Someone would hear. Ah Toy tried to think of the Cantonese word for dead. The men all spoke Cantonese. She had heard no Hakka voice among them. She understood some Cantonese, learned on Willow lane, but spoke little of the dialect not native to her.

With Wang Po dead, who could tell her what to do? There was no high man aboard to say.

Ah Toy, sucking in the after-smells of dried shrimps and pickled cabbage, fingered the white jade dragon beneath her tunic. Tsu Yen, waiting to die, had given it with the promise it assured good fortune. Ah Toy turned the dragon with her thoughts. What must she do? Always someone had told her what to do. Wang Po and, before him, Mr. Buxton, the *fan qui* who taught her his language, and, before him, Tsu Yen and the old mistress. And far back, her mother and father, in a time so distant it seemed more story than memory.

With Wang Po dead, who owned her? Ah Toy considered the question, examining its possibilities as her fingers explored the dragon.

The ship's captain did not own her. He was a high man for the ship, but not for her. Wang Po had paid her passage, that was all the captain cared about. Ah Toy stroked the dragon, thinking on these things. Wang Po had no clan aboard, so she could not belong to any of these men. She clasped the dragon with a stopping thought. This was the new thing to think on: Did she belong to no one? Could that be? But all women belonged to someone, to fathers, uncles, husbands, families, masters, in-laws. But she had none of these.

The only woman she knew who belonged to no one was Lao Tai Tai, the old mistress on Willow lane who had bought her from the dealers. Willow lane was a far place in Ah Toy's memory. But she was certain the only men in that house were the mandarins who visited Tsu Yen and the other mist-and-flower ladies.

Ah Toy was certain Lao Tai Tai belonged to no man. Lao Tai Tai said things should be this way or that and so they were done. When Tsu Yen died, Lao Tai Tai said Ah Toy could not stay in the pretty house and entertain the high men. She was good enough to look on in the face, Lao Tai Tai said, but her shoulders were too square for real beauty. She was too tall, and her feet ugly. No one would want her.

Ah Toy had wept, but the old mistress said only, "You cannot choose your life, but you can choose your dreams."

And then the *fan qui,* the foreign devil with red hair on his face, came and bought her. He took her to the Thirteen Factories street, where she learned to dream.

Crouched now on the ship's planking, Ah Toy looked at her bare feet, embarrassed anew by their ugliness. She patted beneath the bunk, searching for her slippers. She could see little in the dim light from the hatch.

Now that light faded as someone blocked the hatchway. Ah Toy heard a man descending the ladder. From habit she averted her gaze. The men should see little of her face, Wang Po had instructed. Her fine-boned Hakka features, despite her height and big feet, might suggest her sex, he had said, and make trouble for him with the captain.

The man descending the ladder carried his bed mat from airing in the wind above. He spoke to her. Ah Toy kept her head down and said nothing. He spoke again, insistently. Ah Toy heard the smack of his corkwood shoes as he approached her. She stared at the slippers hiding her feet.

Now the man stood before her, speaking Cantonese.

She did not reply.

He grabbed her arm, hauled her to her feet, and gestured toward Wang Po's body. He said something in Cantonese Ah Toy did not understand. She saw it was Li Jin, the handsome scholar who had prepared rice for the spirits plaguing Wang Po. In confusion, she seized the first word to her mind, one of the *fan qui*'s words. "Dead," she said. "Wang Po dead."

Li Jin stared at her with astonished eyes.

As-sing, bent over his desk, scraped the doubloon with his fingernail. He watched a golden dot land on the rice paper. Except for "adobes," three-ounce octagons of unrefined California gold, doubloons were less uniform than other coins. One could "sweat" them with less risk.

He peered at the goldpiece, scratched its edge with a knife, plucked the wound again. A growing glitter peppered the rice paper. The coin, if not accurately weighed, would still be worth twenty dollars. As-sing swept its flaked progeny into a buckskin bag, balanced it in his hand, and mentally calculated its weight. At least three ounces. Enough to exchange for coins at Burgoyne's bank.

As-sing pocketed the pouch and returned the coin to a box in a locking drawer. As he stood, he admired the desk of carved walnut he'd bought at auction for freight fees.

The auction business in San Francisco was good this year. As-sing saw ships arrive daily, holds crammed with useless merchandise. So jammed was the waterfront that auctioneers now dragged cargo to street corners in town to holler the latest bargain.

The desk cost fifteen dollars, but the drayman charged twenty to haul it to As-sing's new restaurant and bakery, slapped up after the latest fire. It was the third disastrous conflagration in six months, but the city quickly bandaged itself with new buildings.

As-sing's desk was his new prize possession. It had come from New York, and As-sing loved all things New York. The desk made him feel like the "milliner" he intended to become. Selim Woodworth had laughed when As-sing announced his intention. Woodworth explained that *milliner* meant hatmaker, not a person of great wealth. He repeated the correct word several times, but to As-sing they sounded identical. The word was *milliner* and he intended to become one.

Beneath bricks in As-sing's bakery resided the golden evidence of his success. Whenever he hefted the flour barrel aside to deposit to his private bank, he afterward smoked a sweet pipe and contemplated his future as an American milliner.

Woodworth and the other Americans could laugh all they wanted. Were they clever enough to create gold dust, to earn a percentage on their money at no risk? As-sing closed his desk and went downstairs.

Han stood at the restaurant's rear door, examining cabbages. "A dollar each one? Sell to the pig farmers!"

Only six months ago, As-sing knew, cabbages had sold for two dollars apiece. Even so, Han, wearing indignation like a badge, scowled at the vendor. "Worm of a dog! Where is your respect? Is not this very place owned by the supreme leader of the Luminous Unity Society!"

As-sing, knowing Ignacio understood nothing of Han's Cantonese tirade, suspected the farmer endured the harangue because Han paid promptly and in cash. The French and Americans always wanted credit.

The Mexican stroked his donkey's nose. *"Sí, señor,"* he said, shrugging shoulders sloped beneath a colorful serape.

As-sing, listening to Han and Ignacio perform their predictable business play, scraped crisped rice from a pot. He slipped the morsel into his mouth and wiped the oil into his beard. He liked Han's noisy tirade and he liked the Mexican. Ignacio brought good produce and had provided everything for the big banquet in December.

As-sing had wanted to host his banquet on the same holiday observed by the French, Germans, Chileans, Californios, Americans, the English, everyone in fact except the Chinese and the Turks. As-sing remembered it as an important holiday in New York.

Ignacio had said no, explaining in broken English that the few vegetables available would be bought at high prices by the cooks at the St. Francis Hotel and Delmonico's. Better to have the feast before Christmas.

Accordingly, on December 10 the entire Chinese population of San Francisco had enjoyed Han's spring rolls stuffed with pork and cabbage. Licking his fingers now, As-sing recalled the fish with slivered ginger, soup of winter melon and another of shark's fin, pork ribs steamed with black beans. The feast lasted hours and cost As-sing a fortune. But he redeemed the gold in power.

As-sing had proposed to the China men the formation of a protection society like those in China. He had made a great speech. The ways of the *fan qui,* the foreign devils, were unpredictable, he said. A few acted respectful, but others tried to cheat them. Some bullied and ridiculed them, pulled their queues, frightened them with their great size. Therefore, the men of the Flowery Kingdom must join together for mutual protection.

As-sing, after his election as president of the Chao-i Kung-so association, translated the words for Selim Woodworth. He had persuaded Woodworth to act as the China men's adviser. "Luminous Unity Society," As-sing had said, "Chao-i Kung-so."

Woodworth had licked the end of a pencil and repeated, "Chew Yick Kung Chow," and written the fine words in his company ledger.

Now, as Han crescendoed into the conclusionary abuse that preceded the exchange of cabbages and gold, As-sing took his boots from behind the firebox. The heat kept the leather flexible. All the Chinese miners bought these boots. As-sing wore them because they were American, and he was an American now. He sat down on a kitchen stool, slipped on the boots, and wrapped a cord around their tops to help hold them on. Americans had such big feet.

While Han mumbled over his cabbages, As-sing lit three joss

sticks for the kitchen god that oversaw his restaurant. Americans understood money, but not luck. Then he lit three for Hwa-kwang, the god of fire. With the third eye in the middle of his forehead, Hwa-kwang could see a thousand miles and watch over the welfare of his friends even in the dark of night.

Confident the gods favored him, As-sing grabbed his stovepipe hat from a peg by the door. He had bought it in New York and always felt like a tall, rich American when he wore it.

Outside, As-sing glanced at the yellow silk fluttering above his restaurant. It warded off the five evils: centipedes, scorpions, snakes, poisonous lizards, and toads. He told Americans the flag symbolized a superior establishment.

They thought so. They jammed his restaurant daily, paying a dollar for coffee, two biscuits, and a plate of beans. Evenings they came for Cantonese food and throughout the day bought sweets at the New York Bakery next door, As-sing's latest enterprise. This month Han would bake mooncakes to observe the harvest festival.

As-sing's location across from the City Hotel assured constant good business. Even now the hotel's veranda teemed with red-shirted men in from the mines, businessmen in boiled shirts, and the ever-present loafers. The loafers waited patiently for someone to celebrate a business deal, a mining strike, a letter from home. Someone was bound to sound the invitation, "Let's all have a drink, boys!" Then the loafers would surge inside, past the billiard room with its nonstop clacking balls, and into the barroom for gin cocktails or "sulky sangarees."

As-sing's restaurant and bakery did good business from the loafers. Everyone had to eat, and the Chinese places were the cheapest in the city. Too, the Macau and Woosung Restaurant was only a block from the plaza, where half the populace milled day and night. Kearny street was the most frequented in town, and one of the first planked. Walkways fronting each business, however, remained the responsibility of individual merchants.

As-sing thought Kearny street's sidewalks a strange mosaic. Some stretches were paved with heavy iron shutters, others with packing cases covered with tin or zinc, or hatch covers. One merchant embedded in last winter's mud two dozen kegs set close. As-sing used rusted stove tops.

Stepping into Kearny street and looking north, As-sing could see the hilltop telegraph signal that announced ship arrivals. What most enlivened the populace was seeing the black pole flanked by two outstretched boards. That meant side-wheel steamer. All the Pacific Mail Steamship Company vessels were side-wheelers. Every two weeks the telegraph signaled the arrival of mail, always an occasion to suspend business, take a drink, then hurry to the post office.

The wind gentled at As-sing's back now as he peered at the signal. Only one arm up. No side-wheeler, but a ship was in. Perhaps it was the one he was waiting for.

Ah Toy saw that the scholar understood her words. Joy followed surprise, in this release from silence. To speak again, to ask the yapping questions, this was a thing she could do. Relief swept away uncertainty like leaves in a monsoon. She poured forth words, and more words, heard herself cascading words over the handsome man. She saw herself tug at his sleeve, felt her spirit lift in the excitement of speaking, asking.

But he was loosening her grip on his sleeve and saying, "No, no, much fast. Talk more slow."

Ah Toy, chastened, bowed her head. Submissive before a man's command, she swallowed her exhilaration. In English, bad Cantonese, and Hakka she saw Li Jin did not understand, Ah Toy explained how Wang Po had purchased her from the British trader who taught her English. She told how Wang Po had anticipated many taels of silver for selling her in Gum Shan, how he instructed her to be mute. He dressed her as a peasant boy to fool the shipping agent, she told Li Jin, and paid squeeze money to the ship's Hongkong medical examiner for his cooperation.

"Wang Po buy bury insurance?"

Ah Toy shook her head. "No. No money for this."

At that, the scholar was gone. Ah Toy slumped onto a bunk away from the body wrapped in the sleeping mat and covered her face with her hands. How she wanted to talk to this scholar, to ask how he knew English words, and whether he knew who owned her.

And then he was back with the ship's surgeon. The China men all trooped down the ladder, too. Noise and confusion surrounded Ah Toy. Words engulfed her, everyone talking at once. She joined in, pleading her questions. Li Jin ignored her, pressing his insistence to the ship's surgeon that Wang Po, a Sze Yup man, be embalmed and returned to his family. He, Li Jin, as a member of the burial society subscribed to by most Sze Yups, accepted the responsibility for the twenty-five-dollar fee for embalming, he said. The society would pay the cost and send the bill with the body to Wang Po's family.

Ah Toy understood Li Jin's concern. This scholar, trained in Confucian precepts, knew that the dead must be returned to their homes. A family's hopes for learning, wealth, even increased numbers, depended on a man's being buried propitiously. If Wang Po's body did not lie in the sacred grounds tended by his relations, his soul would wander as a hungry spirit bent on vengeance.

Despite the commotion, Ah Toy asked Li Jin her questions. He ignored her and left with the surgeon, taking away Wang Po's body.

Now the China men bunched around Ah Toy, gawking, grinning, snickering to each other. A man made a lewd gesture, and she felt heat rush into her face.

"You know nothing!" she yelled. "I no Tanka boatwoman!"

Laughter and obscene gestures greeted her outburst. Ah Toy spit Hakka curses into their grinning faces.

Someone shouted in a Cantonese she understood, "Wang Po's nephew with no speech talks like the wind!"

Ah Toy, backed against a bunk, didn't see the ship's first mate until the China men crowding around her fell away. The officer waded through them like a water buffalo through rice stalks.

"Now what bloody trouble is this?" he asked, planting himself in front of her, arms folded.

Ah Toy's anger spilled over. She yanked off the hat covering her coiled queue. "I no Tanka boatwoman!"

"Oh, blimey, we got us a China girl!" He turned to the men. "Out you go, boys, get yourselves abovedeck!"

Alone with the officer, Ah Toy explained she had no family and didn't know who owned her.

The first mate laughed. She saw how he looked at her. "No one I know, unfortunately, miss." He laughed again, then said, "You'll just have to see to yourself. Me and the captain'll have some words with the boys. They won't trouble you, and you see you don't cause any yourself."

Ah Toy felt her face flame. "You know nothing! I no Tanka boatwoman!"

The first mate grinned. "No, missy, anyone can see you're better than that."

Alone again, Ah Toy busied herself with packing Wang Po's things to send to his family. She tried to ignore the questions whirling through her head. Someone would tell her what she must do.

When the men returned, they looked at her and grinned. Then they ignored her for the gambling and gossiping that filled the long hours. She knew no one wanted trouble. The journey was perilous enough without angering the captain.

Li Jin spoke briefly to her about Wang Po's things, and Ah Toy listened politely. Then she pleaded for his help. She did not know who owned her, she said, or what she was supposed to do. No one was telling her what to do. She could feel herself filling up with uncertainty, and she tugged on his sleeve. "What I do? Where I go? Who tell me this thing?"

Ah Toy saw Li Jin contemplating her, his wide-set eyes appraising her. Finally, in halting English, he promised to speak for her to his ticket sponsor, a high man in Gum Shan. She must know the importance and power of high men, he said.

"Yes, yes," Ah Toy said, placing her hands together and bowing with them. "High man good. High man know right way." She felt relief wash over her. Perhaps she would be worth something to the high man to whom Li Jin was indebted.

Li Jin went to his berth then and lay there, fingers laced under his head. Ah Toy knew he watched her in the light cast from the lamp swaying above the mah-jongg and fan-tan players. She crouched on her knees in front of her bunk, feet hidden, unbraiding her hair, uncomfortable under his gaze. She searched her basket, retrieved an ivory comb, tugged it through her hair. She thought she saw him smile. She guessed he must be amused at how Wang Po had succeeded in fooling them by dressing a tall, big-footed woman in peasant's clothes and claiming her for a nephew with no speech.

Ah Toy, busy fashioning her hair into a knot at her neck, didn't notice the thick-shouldered missionary student until he hunkered down in front of her.

"I understand you speak English. I would like to talk with you."

Ah Toy looked up in surprise at the man who wore no queue.

Spiky hair framed his forehead. In perfect English he explained he had been educated in Dr. Speer's missionary school at Canton. He was accompanying crates of Bibles in Chinese ordered by the Jesus people in California.

Over the clacking of mah-jongg tiles and the shouts of men finding luck at fan-tan, Ah Toy listened to Tong Achik preach. She sat with her hands on her knees, feet hidden beneath her, aware Li Jin watched.

She glanced at him. Perhaps the scholar wanted to join them. "Li Jin speak English," she told Tong Achik. "Why not you tell him Jesus stories?"

The missionary shook his head. "Li Jin's belief is Confucianism, with many years, he has told me, spent in study. Unfortunately, his family could not afford the bribe money for the regional examination commissioners. He was forced to apprentice to a trader in Hongkong."

Ah Toy, from her years on Willow lane where the commissioners visited, understood. She understood, too, Li Jin's large disappointment. To be a scholar meant more than honor. Successful candidates received imperial appointments, by which even minor officials garnered substantial wealth and prestige.

Behind her thoughts, Ah Toy heard the missionary preaching. Annoyed with his Jesus talk, she burst out, "I know Bible woman on Thirteen Factories street pray this Jesus! She brag missionaries pay her three thousand *cash* a month! I know people listen missionaries to get food!"

Tong Achik smiled. "The food Jesus provides is also for the soul. That is why I was baptized."

Ah Toy shook her head. "I see baptize woman. She same like anyone."

"She is blessed with a place in heaven."

Ah Toy laughed. "To marry and bear many sons only blessing for woman."

Near the corner of Clay street a hand suddenly gripped As-sing's shoulder.

"Mr. As-sing!"

As-sing turned to see a big man with neatly trimmed whiskers. The stand-up collar of his white shirt framed a black cravat, and his waistcoat sported a double row of shiny brass buttons.

"Mr. As-sing," he said, brushing from his coat sleeves the dust raised by a passing stagecoach, "a moment of your valuable time, sir, for a business proposition."

How direct these Americans are, thought As-sing, holding the brim of his stovepipe hat as he nodded assent. He liked to talk business with Americans. China men never announced business; they fluttered at it like a moth. Americans snatched at it like pond carp at feeding time.

"Kimball, Mr. As-sing, Charles Kimball," the American said, leading As-sing to a stack of bricks where he positioned himself. His eyes level with As-sing's, he said, "Mr. As-sing, this town is growing fast." He leaned forward and, with a salesman's solemnity, added, "You've been here a long time, over a year. You know what I'm talking about."

As-sing smiled. Everyone knew As-sing.

"But all these people coming in every day, every day, sir, are lost here," Kimball said. "They don't know where to find DeWitt's store or Adams Express or your restaurant. They have to ask." Shaking his head as if sorrowed by the thought, he said, "And chances are, sir, chances are they'll ask someone else fresh off the boat who won't know." Kimball paused, then slapped his knee. "Well, Mr. As-sing, I've got just the solution to your problem."

As-sing waited. Pond carp, he thought, and hungry.

"A directory, sir, a directory!" Kimball slapped his knee again. "A listing, Mr. As-sing, of the town's citizens and businesses. Think of it! To know who is here and where they can be found." He smiled. "Invaluable, sir, for advising the location of your restaurant." As-sing plucked at his beard. "How much?"

"A trifle, sir. Unless, you want a half-page advertisement. Dr. May took one for his dysentery syrup. I'd venture half the men coming off the boats today could use a swallow."

As-sing shook his head at the Americans' idea of medicine.

"Ah, Mr. As-sing, sir, don't say no. A listing in my directory costs but one dollar. Mr. A-he bought one for his Canton Restaurant on Jackson street."

As-sing dug into his pocket. He thrust two dollars at the salesman. "One list restaurant. One, As-sing."

"Excellent idea, sir," said Kimball, pocketing As-sing's coins. He extracted a notebook and pencil from inside his coat. "Macau and Woosung? That right?"

As-sing nodded. "And name. Norman As-sing."

Kimball looked up and raised an eyebrow. "How's that again? Did you say Norman?"

"Norman. Norman As-sing."

"Got it," said Kimball with a grin. He clapped the notebook into his pocket and pumped As-sing's hand. As-sing could see him eyeing the crowd in the plaza. "Ah, there's Charley Elleard! He'll want a listing. Thank you and good day to you, sir."

As-sing watched Kimball dodge across the road to the plaza. He sidestepped a Chilean pushing a wheelbarrow full of nail kegs and nearly collided with the Irishman's goats.

The Irishman, As-sing had heard, had left in Ireland a wife and many children. Now, from loneliness, he lived with a horse, two dogs, and two goats in a shanty off Washington street. He was rarely seen in town without his substitute family in tow.

Many townspeople lavished attention on creatures that As-sing thought belonged in a soup bowl. Some even made pets of the rats infesting the town. These animal affections puzzled him. Charley Elleard dragged his black pony everywhere. Across the road As-sing saw Kimball clamping his hand on Elleard's shoulder, selling his directory. At Elleard's side stood the black pony arrayed in its silver bridle and saddle trappings. The wealth draped upon Gum Shan horses, particularly by the Californios, amazed As-sing. He supposed silver must be an offering and the horse a revered deity.

Everyone knew Elleard, whose profitable bar and oyster room on Clay street funded the silver extravagance dangling from his pony. He was the new constable as much for his pony's popularity as his own.

As-sing watched Kimball place a coin in the animal's mouth. He had seen the pony's trick often. The animal, adornment glinting in the sun, threaded its way between pedestrians to the bootblack stand on the corner. There, to the astonishment of newcomers and the delight of children, the pony dropped the coin in the bootblack's hand and placed a hoof on the boot-rest. The bootblack, familiar with their united performance, accepted the coin as politely as if a judge had given it. Then he whipped his buffing rag back and forth across the pony's hoof. When he paused, the pony withdrew its hoof from the boot-rest and delicately planted the other in its place.

As-sing, shaking his head at the strangeness of Americans, turned down the hill toward Burgoyne's bank. As he passed Elleard's oyster bar, he glanced in. A young woman waited tables. No wonder the business thrived. He, too, could make plenty of money if he had a woman in his restaurant.

Inside Burgoyne's bank, As-sing looked around. Blocks of gold-veined quartz awaited assay. Overworked clerks extracted black sand from uncleaned gold with a magnet. Slouch-hatted miners dropped bags of gold dust on the counter like muffled cannonballs. As-sing liked banks, liked being in the presence of wealth.

As-sing took his turn, plopping his pouch on the counter with a quiet thump. The clerk emptied it into the shiny brass dish suspended by a chain on the balance scale. He added weights to the opposite one until they leveled. As-sing's parings amounted to just over three ounces. The clerk, subtracting the fee for the exchange, handed As-sing one five-dollar and two twenty-dollar goldpieces, plus eight two-bit coins. As-sing pocketed his manufactured money with a smile.

Out on the Clay street wharf he was disappointed to learn that his shipment of Chinese houses had not arrived. A week ago, three had come on the *Hugh Walker,* which also carried several iron houses from England.

The merchandise shipped to California by Englishmen astonished As-sing, especially the iron houses. They came in bundles of plates, bent and rusted from the journey. They assembled into terrible stores and dwellings. As-sing had stepped inside one on a warm day. He still remembered the heat and the sickening smell of its anticorrosive paint baking in the sun.

The Chinese houses As-sing imported, however, with windows of translucent tortoiseshell, and delicately decorated inside and out, assembled beautifully. They sold readily at fifty to sixty dollars apiece.

As As-sing headed back up the wharf, he saw Selim Woodworth talking with a stranger. Woodworth was always genial to the China boys, as he called them after they bestowed on him the title "Mandarin of the Celestial Empire and China Consul."

"Mr. As-sing, good to see you!" said Woodworth. "I was just speaking of you."

Woodworth, hatless, wore a buttoned broadcloth coat against the wind. He extended an ungloved hand to As-sing and with a gesture indicated his companion.

"This is Mr. Taylor, a journalist from New York. He says he saw the *Kee Ying* you told me about. He wants to interview you."

At the mention of New York and the *Kee Ying,* As-sing smiled. He nodded to Taylor, clean shaven like Woodworth, and wearing a knee-length tweed coat.

Taylor said, "Mr. Woodworth tells me you were one of the three seamen who jumped ship from the *Kee Ying.* "

"Jumped ship" was not an expression As-sing knew. He stared his puzzlement. Taylor turned to Woodworth. "Mr. As-sing speaks English?"

Woodworth smiled. "Oh, yes, the Celestials quickly learn to speak our language with facility. Mr. As-sing picked it up from English traders in Hongkong and was more than a year in our Eastern states." He chuckled. "Some words give him a little trouble, though. Don't be surprised if he tells you he wants to be a milliner."

As-sing nodded. "Yes, Melican milliner."

"American millionaire," said Woodworth, smiling. With a wave he indicated his store. "Why don't you two gentlemen step inside where you can talk out of the wind."

Seated by Woodworth's stove, As-sing confirmed to the journalist his presence aboard the *Kee Ying.* The seven-hundred-ton junk had arrived in New York City from Hongkong in 1847. When it set sail for the Orient after four months touring the East coast, As-sing and two other crewmen stayed behind. Disliking New York's winter weather, As-sing drifted south to Charleston, South Carolina, where a storekeeper gave him his American name. A year later, word of gold in California galvanized Eastern shipping companies to launch anything in the yards that floated. Anyone with sailing experience found passage as a crewman. As-sing sailed from Charleston around the Horn and arrived in San Francisco the summer of 1849.

"All tent," he told Taylor. "No place sleep, no place eat." He looked at Woodworth for affirmation. Woodworth nodded.

"Me cook China food," As-sing said. "Good, cheap. Make plenty gold."

Taylor tapped his pencil against his notebook and asked, "Is it true you Celestials dine on rats? So I've heard."

As-sing hesitated, recalling the frequent scarcity of food even in the fertile Kwangtung province. These Americans knew little of poverty and misfortune. At last he said, "Hungry man not particular." He smiled. "As-sing prefer fish and duck."

Taylor looked up from his notebook. "Were you a cook in China, Mr. As-sing?"

"Merchant. Mandarin tax all time. Take too much."

"Then you intend to stay in California?"

As-sing grinned. "Me longtime Californ'. Be milliner here."

As-sing rose to leave just as the door swung open.

"Ah, excellent, good to see you, Mr. As-sing," said the Reverend Mr. Williams, entering. He smiled and removed his hat. "Woodworth, a ship arriving this morning reports having spoke the *Flavius* near the Sandwich Islands. She's the one carrying our Chinese Bibles and should be in within the month."

As-sing shook his head. He didn't understand why American preachers wanted everyone to believe in one god. China men worshiped family gods, kitchen gods, harvest gods, whatever necessary. That one god possessed time or interest sufficient to look after everything struck As-sing as absurd.

"You remember, Mr. As-sing, we talked about the Bibles," Woodworth said. "The Reverend Williams wants to give them to all the China boys. We're counting on you to help."

As-sing shrugged and reached for his hat from the rack beside the door.

"We intend a big ceremony, Mr. As-sing," said the preacher. "In the plaza, with the mayor."

As-sing turned. The mayor was important. A shrewd man never ignored important men.

"Luminous Unity China boys come see mayor," said As-sing, bowing with the authority of his Chao-i Kung-so presidency.

"Good, good," said Williams. "Oh, and, Mr. As-sing, you'll be interested to know that the *Flavius* carries several of your country-men. Perhaps more members for your society?"

In the days following Wang Po's death, Ah Toy tucked away un-certainty over her future and savored release from silence. For the pleasure of conversation, she let Tong Achik go on in his persuasive way about Jesus. Now, as she stood on deck, staring at the fogbank that blocked the ship's entrance to Gum Shan, he leaned against the railing next to her. A Hakka man, Hung Hsiu Chua, he was saying, claimed to be the younger brother of Jesus.

Ah Toy brushed her hair from her eyes and shook her head. "I no hear these things, and I Hakka."

"I suspected," Tong Achik said. "You are tall like them and have their look. And the Hakka do not bind the feet of women."

Ah Toy shifted a slippered foot, embarrassed, but Tong Achik talked on without notice.

"Hung has thousands of followers, most of them Hakka, and the women are equal. The women ride horses like warriors. They are promised in his kingdom they will learn to read and write and take the examinations the same as men."

Ah Toy looked at him and laughed.

"I tell you the truth," Tong Achik said. "Hung believes himself to be the deliverer of the Kingdom of Great Peace, as he calls it. The emperor, though, will crush Hung's rebellion, his *taiping*."

The missionary talked on. Ah Toy, politely pretending interest, waited for Li Jin to join them. The scholar nearly always did, to speak English, he said. But Ah Toy knew from the way he looked at her that language practice was more pretext than reason. The knowledge pleased her.

The next morning the fog lifted, allowing the ship's entry. At the shout "Gum Shan! Gum Shan!" Ah Toy hurried on deck with Li Jin and the other China men. Everyone hauled their few belongings, ready for the Gold Mountain.

Ah Toy leaned against the ship's railing and looked over. She watched a longboat pull close and a pilot solemnly climb the ropes. His dark cap and coat glistened with dew.

When the ship rounded a point, Ah Toy saw that the harbor spread beyond like a small sea. In one cove of the indented shoreline nestled the city. Curiosity overwhelmed uncertainty about her future. How incredible, she thought, to travel this great distance, to this strange place. She, Ah Toy, a slave girl with big feet.

Ah Toy pressed against the railing to see the fabled place. She frowned. No gold glinted from a mountainside. Surely, Gum Shan could not be these hills draped with tents and unpainted buildings.

The largest buildings clustered at the waterfront. Some of them had captured ships between them. To Ah Toy the city looked as if it had sneaked up on its harbor to enlist ships in urgent commercial enterprise before they could sail. Another curiosity was the roads descending down the hills. They ran into the water on top of long-legged wharves. The city appeared to be walking into the sea. In assistance, a steam engine at a pier's end thumped and wheezed a new piling into mud.

Now all thought fled as Ah Toy watched the *Flavius* skirt the tattered edge of ships nosed together like netted fish. There was so much to see. On one ship a boy on a stool milked a cow. On another a woman hung wash on a rigging line, the clothes flapping wetly.

Then the *Flavius* dropped anchor. Amid shouts, men on the

pier caught ropes thrown by crewmen and secured them to piling heads. Sailors clambered into the rigging, furling sails. Gulls squawked and wheeled overhead. It was all so much like a play, Ah Toy thought, absorbed by the excitement of arrival. A plank thrown against the wharf banged loudly, startling her back into her circumstance. This was the day the high man would decide her destiny.

The ship's first mate herded the Chinese passengers into a corner of the deck. Ah Toy found Li Jin. She stood silently at his elbow, watching. A customs inspector boarded and conferred with the supercargo. The European passengers debarked with their trunks and bags. Sailors hauled cargo on deck—cases of English ale and preserved meats, bags of lime and baskets of onions, writing desks and dining tables. A commission merchant counted nests of camphorwood trunks and rattan chairs. A black-coated preacher discovered the boxes of Bibles and hurried away with a paper attesting to the cost of their freight.

The sun had passed its zenith when the customs inspector at last motioned them down the ramp to the wharf. Ah Toy clutched Li Jin's sleeve as she felt, despite the firm planking beneath her feet, sensations from the sea. He smiled a rare smile. She felt awkward and clumsy under his gaze. One of the men chided the scholar in Cantonese. Ah Toy saw Li Jin shrug. That she had bound herself to him, having no owner, was apparent to everyone. It gladdened her that Li Jin permitted the attachment.

Ah Toy staggered after Li Jin and the China men clutching their bedrolls and baskets and bamboo carrying poles. Where the wharf met land, her throat caught at the stench of garbage submerged in green mud. Trapped in the muck were eggshells, cabbage leaves, fish heads, rotting clothing.

They filed into an open shed. The customs inspector formed them into ragged lines while an assistant counted heads and jotted numbers in a ledger. Those carrying a credit ticket for their passage showed it to a Chinese interpreter. He matched the name and home district to the sponsoring company's docket. The inspector examined every basket, pulling out packets of firecrackers and bags of rice, bricks of tea, a household god, bundles of joss sticks, dice boxes, paper fans, chopsticks, festival clothing. One man wailed at the confiscation of his opium pipe.

From Ah Toy's basket the inspector withdrew her green silk pantaloons. He stared at her, the bright silk dangling from his hand, then motioned she was free to leave. He dropped the pantaloons and moved on. Ah Toy repacked her things and looked for Li Jin.

She tried to imagine now what destiny awaited her. Li Jin, she knew, was going to the mines for gold to buy ricelands. Would the high man send her to the mines also? She was tall and strong. Or would he keep her for a slave? Or sell her as Wang Po intended? She didn't even think what she might wish herself. A woman didn't decide such things.

Ah Toy searched for Li Jin among the China men clustered in front of the customs shed. They surrounded a man wearing a *fan qui* hat. Li Jin told her to follow, that he would speak to the high man about her soon.

Seeing no high man, Ah Toy, confused, watched Li Jin vanish among the China men hoisting carrying poles to their shoulders. The swaying baskets looked like giant woven fruits. Clutching her things, Ah Toy followed their stooped, blue-coated backs up a hill. They passed stores and open-door saloons where rough-looking men leaned against long bars, drinking. She was glad to be dressed like a peasant, anonymous, just another China man.

At the top of the hill the road opened into a large square. It teemed with men in fantastic dress—sailors in red caps, officers in uniforms with sabers at their sides, dark-skinned men draped in brown and wearing black, flat-brimmed hats. Mules bawled. Boys chased barking dogs. A man with newspapers shouted their availability. A dark woman wearing feathers and beads sat on a blanket spread with squashes. A red-cheeked man played merrily on pipes fastened at his chin, pounding a drum on his back with sticks tied to his elbows, slamming cymbals with his hands. Vendors peddled cakes and sweetmeats. A man in black on a galloping horse draped with silver chased across the square after a wild-eyed bull, scattering the crowd.

To Ah Toy it looked like scenes from a dozen plays, all performed at once. She wondered if California might be the American word for pandemonium. Curiosity for Gum Shan pushed anxiety from her mind once more.

She saw that the square lay on the slant of a hill. At its upper edge stretched a low adobe building. In front of it stood a tall, stripped tree trunk. An American flag flapped from the top. The China men trudged toward it, climbing stairs cut into the hill. Ah Toy followed.

At the flagpole's base the men lowered their shoulder poles. They massaged wobbly legs, chattering their amazement. Ah Toy joined Li Jin at the elbow of the man whose thin beard glistened with oil. She had never seen a China man wearing such a hat. He stared at her now from beneath lids that looked too hardened to lift. He smelled of cabbage.

Ah Toy tugged Li Jin's sleeve. "Where high man please?"

"Stay here," he said, indicating the flagpole. "I must register for benevolence society."

Ah Toy watched Li Jin follow the strange man. She decided he must be the servant of the high man Li Jin promised to consult. Obediently, Ah Toy crouched at the base of the flagpole with her basket.

Within minutes, the sky clouded over. Ah Toy pushed her hands up opposite sleeves for warmth as a stiffening wind lashed sand against her ankles. She watched vendors close stalls. Men clasped their hats and ducked through the canvas doorways of nearby buildings.

Ah Toy looked around for Li Jin, but he had disappeared with the high man's servant. The pelting sand and cold wind decided her. Hugging her basket and bed mat, Ah Toy hurried across the square through the swirling dust. In front of a protecting building, she waited and watched. After a while, she succumbed to the warmth beckoning through a doorway.

Inside, Ah Toy drew a breath of amazement. Truly this was Gum Shan. Tables glittered with gold. Men surrounding them shouted to waiters for drinks and cigars. The air was thick with smoke and the sounds of clinking coins and tinkling dealers' bells.

Against one wall stretched a bar backed by a mirror and paintings of naked women. Behind the bar, Ah Toy saw a black-haired woman in an orange shawl. She laughed and poured drinks amidst a sparkle of glasses and bottles.

Music drifted from instruments played without interest by men in broad-brimmed hats. They sang mournfully.

The crowd at the tables was mostly men, but at one Ah Toy saw a woman. She sat on a stool, dealing cards with elegant boredom. She smoked a small cigar and nonchalantly slid a roll of coins from hand to hand, smooth as a collapsing golden telescope. She wore white pants, a blue coat, and blue kid gloves. Golden curls dangled over her cheeks from beneath a blue cap. Her eyes met Ah Toy's once, but she made no move to approach her. No one did.

Fascinated, Ah Toy watched the game at a nearby table where men held large picture cards. A man dressed in black with silver buttons withdrew a block from a box he twirled between two standards. *"Una elefanta!"* he announced, holding up a block with an elephant on it. Two men took chips from the table and covered a drawing of an elephant on their cards. At the shout of *"Un caballo!"* one covered a drawing of a horse. After more calls came *"Un hombre!"* Ah Toy saw him cover the drawing of a man, completing a row across his card. "Keno!" he yelled, and showed his card. The dealer nodded and the man scooped up the gold on the table.

Ah Toy was unaware how long she had stood inside the door, engrossed by the spectacle. She did not see Li Jin and the high man's servant enter. She started when Li Jin touched her shoulder. Beside him the high man's servant scrutinized her with narrow, appraising eyes.

"As-sing all over look you," Li Jin said.

As-sing took Ah Toy's arm. She pushed his hand away and cursed him in Hakka for his rudeness. When she threw at him the Cantonese word for servant, his lips and eyes compressed into slits. Ah Toy felt his anger like a heat. He looked as if he might strike her.

Behind him Li Jin paled. "High man, high man!"

As-sing grabbed her arm again.

Ah Toy, wrestling against As-sing's grasp, stared at Li Jin. "He no high man! Where embroider square on silk gown? Beads? Fur cuffs like horse feet? He no high man!" The thought flashed past that a scholar knew how high men dressed, and then she was struggling with As-sing. He was pulling her toward the door when a voice boomed, "Hey, there, Norman, what's the trouble?"

Ah Toy looked over her shoulder. A man with a bushy beard was looking past her at As-sing and grinned as As-sing released her.

"The coolie's just watchin' the fun, Norman," he said. "Plenty time to get to work. That right, China boy?"

The man slapped an arm around Ah Toy's shoulder, then stared at her in astonishment.

"Whoa, Norman, you got a lady coolie here!" He turned and hollered, "Hey, Henry! Come take a look at the China girl!"

Ah Toy bit her lip as men gathered around her. What did they want?

The one named Henry laughed. "Looks like Norman's got a new import business, hey, Norman?"

Ah Toy saw As-sing hint at a bow. "No, most honored friends to my restaurant," he said, his manner grave. "This bad woman."

Ah Toy felt herself redden with the insult. "You know nothing!"

"I take her," said As-sing, reaching for Ah Toy's arm.

Henry put out a hand, stopping him. "Hey, Norman," he said, looking at Ah Toy, "the lady don't have to go if she don't wanna. This here's a free country." He smiled and pretended a little bow to Ah Toy.

Ah Toy saw the man with the beard grin again. He waved As-sing and Li Jin out the door. She watched the scholar go. He looked at her with stricken eyes. And then she felt faint from a sudden fear. No high man would tell her what to do, she realized. The scholar was helpless in this place, too. A crowd surrounded her, everyone talking at once. She shut her eyes against her fright. She felt herself shaking.

"China lady she cold?"

Ah Toy, trembling, opened her eyes. The woman with the golden curls stood before her, one blue-gloved hand on her hip, the other holding a cigar.

The woman brushed a curl from her eyes and turned toward the bar. "Rosita! Sell to me your shawl."

Ah Toy looked from one face to another. The din of voices confused her. There were so many people. Everyone was looking at her, talking at once. She could not think what to do. She saw the shawl being draped around her shoulders, saw the woman's lips moving through words she suddenly understood were asking where she lived. Ah Toy shook her head. Panic captured her breath like a whirlwind. She had nowhere to go. She was alone. No high man would tell her what to do. She heard someone holler, "Hey, Simone, take her to your house!" Men laughed.

Now the woman was talking to the man with the beard. He shrugged and reached for Ah Toy's basket.

"Mine!" Ah Toy cried, finding her voice. She hugged her things to her.

"George, she afraid from you," Simone said, puffing on her cigar.

Ah Toy stared at the man's big hand wrapped around her bedroll. "It's okay, miss, you're comin' with me," he said. "I'm not trying to steal your stuff. I'm just goin' to carry it for you."

Simone put a hand on Ah Toy's shoulder and smiled. "Even miners are gentlemen in California. They take for you." She pushed back a curl and studied Ah Toy. Then she winked. "Men will be good to you here. You will be lucky Chinese lady."

And then Ah Toy, dizzy with confusion, was following the two men up a hill, away from the noise and lights of the plaza. She clutched the shawl and marveled at the sight of her bed mat balanced on George's shoulder like a fisherman's pole. Henry swung her basket, making jokes he laughed at himself. Ah Toy stared at her basket bouncing against his leg. No man had ever carried anything for her before.

At the top of the hill, George gestured her bed mat at a square of slatted wood. Above it, a moon hung in the darkness like a lantern. "Here's my house, China girl."

George threw open the door. Henry plopped her basket down inside and George touched a match to an oil lamp. The men stood like proud palace guards as Ah Toy entered.

To her amazement, the American's house consisted of one room. The floor was dirt. Each wall rose from a single sill laid upon the ground. Corner posts appeared to remain vertical only by the united efforts of each wall's horizontal boards. Their thin slats were so imperfectly joined, Ah Toy could put her hand through a dozen spaces into the night. A ceiling of dark twill sagged overhead.

A pair of three-legged stools flanked a stove of sheet tin sitting blackly in one corner. Next to the stove, shelves displayed tin utensils and canned foods. A blackened fry pan hung from a nail on the wall. Below it, congealed grease formed a white triangle.

Against the opposite wall, a canvas cot displayed two coarse blankets and a pillow. A pile of dust-covered newspapers loomed at the foot of the cot, next to a trunk topped by a washbasin and pitcher. Next to the door, where Ah Toy stood surveying the room in ignored astonishment, a mirror wired to the wall completed the furnishings.

"Only a hunnert dollars a month?" said Henry. "Shucks, I pay that fer a bunk on Jackson street in a room with no heat and twelve other fellers. This here's swell." He squatted on a stool, grinding it into the dirt floor.

"Yup," said George, stuffing kindling into the stove, "and paid up through the month. I told Simone the China girl can have it till then, seein's I'm headin' back to the diggin's tomorrow anyways."

"Ain't she the lucky one." Henry grinned at her.

Ah Toy returned a dumbfounded nod, and George gestured her toward the cot. Ah Toy sat, watching hungrily as he reduced a chunk of bacon to thick slices. He took the fry pan from its nail, set it on the stove, and tossed in the bacon. It sizzled with a smoky fragrance Ah Toy thought smelled delicious. George opened a can and poured beans over the bacon.

When he offered a tinware plate of the food, Ah Toy accepted it with two hands. "Yes, please, many thank you," she said, balancing the dish on her knees.

"Dig in, miss," George said as he filled plates for himself and Henry.

Ah Toy ate eagerly. The food tasted nothing like China food, but it warmed and filled her. Now, feeling suddenly too tired to think, she watched George pack a knapsack with clothes, canned food, a blanket.

"This'll hold me till I get back to my claim," he said, snugging a strap around his pack.

Henry looked at George in surprise. "Ain'tcha stayin' here tonight?" He wriggled a greasy thumb at Ah Toy.

"Naw," said George, hefting the knapsack to his shoulder. "I'll just stake me a place on the steamer."

"Oho!" laughed Henry, rising from his stool. "That filly back in Ohio got a mighty long leash on you."

George grinned. "I sent enough gold on the last steamer so's she can come out. Gettin' married soon's she gets here."

"Well, ain't you the lucky one," said Henry, wiping his hands on his trousers.

George turned to Ah Toy. "You'll be all right here, missy. That As-sing fella has got his restaurant down to the bottom of the hill. You can probably get ahold of your Chinese friends there and find out where you can live. Course, if'n you got a hunnert dollars, you can stay on here. The agent'll come lookin' for the rent in a couple weeks."

George shifted his knapsack. "Firewood's dear, 'bout forty dollars a cord. There's enough out back to see you through the month. Help yourself to the grub, too. Ain't much left."

He nodded and opened the door. "Good luck to you, Missy."

Henry flashed a grin and followed his friend out the door. It closed behind them with a thin bang.

Ah Toy sat stunned, the plate on her knees, staring at the door. She was alone in this place, with no one to tell her what to do. She could not recall being so alone before, although she had often been lonely.

She remembered vividly now that first loneliness, in the dealers' house where her father had abandoned her. She saw him, in her mind's eye, walking toward the moon gate. She had wailed and reached her little arms after him, but he never looked back.

She had been lonely, too, at Lao Tai Tai's house in Canton, until Tsu Yen made life there endurable. And after Tsu Yen died, when

Ah Toy lived in the *fan qui's* house and cleaned for him, she yearned still for the house of her childhood. She remembered every detail of it, from the *kang* where the family slept together to the courtyard tree she climbed with her brothers.

Ah Toy put the memory away, saving it for her dream. She dreamt often of a house blessed by sons and honored by daughters-in-law.

Dreaming was one thing, life was another. Ah Toy looked around the Gum Shan room, examining this aloneness, this new thing to think on. What she would do she did not know. Li Jin must tell her. In the morning she would find him.

The dimming stove fire drew her from her thoughts. She put her plate on the shelf and poked sticks into the stove's belly. The greasy fry pan stared at her like a large filmed eye.

This house was a sty. Beggars in Canton lived better than this California *fan qui.* Weariness fled as her disgust rose. From the pile of newspapers Ah Toy scrunched a fat wad, wiped the pan clean, and hung it on its nail. She threw the paper into the stove and watched it burst into flame. Orange shadows danced about the room.

Ah Toy drank in the room with her eyes. The poorest woman in Canton lived better, but Ah Toy didn't feel poor. She felt rich. This house was hers, however different from the one in her dreams.

She remembered still the girlish imaginings shared with Tsu Yen on Willow lane. Tsu Yen envisioned herself as the favorite wife of a powerful mandarin, a high man with a peacock feather and ruby button on his imperial official's hat, and twelve slaves to precede his palanquin and announce his many titles. Tsu Yen's imaginary house was all splendor and courtyards.

Ah Toy's dream was a clean, neat house well stocked with rice. Always in her youthful fancies she saw the house, but never the husband who would want her.

Now she imagined returning to China with the handsome scholar when he came with gold from the mines. Li Jin's family would accept her as a symbol of good fortune.

Seated next to the stove, the flame firing her thoughts, Ah Toy settled on this idea. Li Jin would marry her and take her from this dirty Gum Shan to live in a clean, neat house and she would bear him many sons.

She savored the thought, sweet as lichees. She decided on it. To-morrow she must find Li Jin. She would wear her green silk pan-taloons to show him she was no peasant and would be a good wife to own.

She looked down at the coarse cotton tunic she wore. Such ugly clothing, she thought. Excited by her plan, she grabbed her basket and spilled its contents on the cot. Imagining how she would look to Li Jin, she threw off her peasant clothes and pulled on the pantaloons. Over the cotton binding her breasts, she let fall her black silk tunic. From beneath it she drew out Tsu Yen's lucky white jade dragon on its silken cord.

Ah Toy peered at her reflection in the mirror. The wind had spoiled her hair. She started to pin it just as someone pounded on the door. Before she could think, the door flew open.

Henry lurched through it.

"Hullo there, Chinee girl!" He grinned, slapped the door shut behind him, and fixed reddened eyes on her. "Whooee! Ain't you the looker!"

He stumbled, then steadied himself on the trunk with one hand. The pitcher toppled to the floor with a thud.

Ah Toy backed away. The rank smell of whiskey drifted from him. Why was this drunken man here? What did he want from her? She watched him stagger and fall against the cot.

"Oops," he said, dropping onto the cot among her things. He grinned again as he focused on her. "Well, ain't you one purty China girl!"

Ah Toy felt anger rise like floodwater. She knew why he was here. "Me no bad woman!"

"Hey, hey, no need to git all riled up, Chinee girl." He hiccuped. "But a little fire in them bitty black eyes sure do look purty."

"You go!" She heard fright echo behind her rage. She was utterly alone. Who would protect her here? She watched Henry's grin fade.

"Now, don'tcha be so unfriendly, Chinee girl."

"You go, please." Ah Toy felt fear circle like a wolf.

Henry scowled. "I ain't goin' nowheres. Me and the boys got a little wager."

He pushed himself to his feet. "Some of the boys say China girls don't look like other women. So old Henry's gonna get a little look-see."

He stumbled toward her.

As-sing threw open the door to the Jackson street boardinghouse, swept aside the spirit banners, and clomped into the room. The newly arrived China men slurped tea at a long table, Sze Yup men at one end, Sam Yups at the other. These old alliances always aggravated As-sing. This morning he seethed at the sight, outraged still by yesterday's insult. A slave girl shaming him, and in a public place!

As-sing grabbed an empty tea bowl and banged it on the table. The China men fell silent and stared at him.

"Luminous Unity Society!" As-sing shouted. "All one here!" He glared at the Sam Yups from the three districts comprising Canton, then at the Sze Yups from the four Pearl River delta districts. Seeing Li Jin, the scholar he had sponsored from his village, As-sing slammed the tea bowl again. He would not forget who let him be shamed by a slave girl.

As-sing released the tea bowl. Retribution would wait. Business would not. "Luminous Unity Society! Not Sze Yup society! Not Sam Yup society! All China men same here!" As-sing shook his ledger at them. "Each man pays ten dollars to fund the Luminous Unity Society! Luminous Unity provides you boots and mining equipment on credit."

He slapped the ledger's cover. "Your debt is recorded. All debts must be paid before you leave Gum Shan. No ship will grant you passage without my certification that your debt is paid."

The room erupted into a babble of questions and objections. As-sing ignored them. "Li Jin! You go *sam fow* today," he said in English. "You lucky, talk English. Easy work, plenty money."

"Gold mines this *sam fow?*" Li Jin asked. He hurried to As-sing's side.

"No, no," As-sing said in Cantonese, impatient at the man's ignorance. "No mines in cities. *Sam fow,* third city, is Stockton. San Francisco is first city, *dai fow.* Sacramento is second city, *yee fow.* All important cities for business." A Mr. Capen owned a store in Stockton, As-sing explained. Stockton supplied the southern mines where hundreds of China men dug gold. Capen wanted their trade. For a diligent clerk and translator he would pay sixty dollars a month.

Li Jin bowed his appreciation over his good fortune.

As-sing nodded. "I accept generously ten percent from your wages."

"Uncle, such is proper. I am grateful." Li Jin hesitated, then said, "Perhaps, uncle, I may suggest a small thing to please you in return?"

As-sing listened as Li Jin told of hearing that a ship sailed soon for Hongkong. Since he had promised the woman his help, perhaps passage might be arranged for her.

As-sing squeezed Li Jin's arm hard. *"Mui tsai!"* he hissed. The intonation was unmistakably *slave girl.* "Do not dishonor my generosity!"

Li Jin hung his head and apologized.

As-sing glared. "The slave girl is not your concern. I will see to her!"

For two days Ah Toy kept her door barred, starting at every sound, fearful of Henry's return. Twice someone knocked. She heard men's voices and laughter, but they went away.

To avoid thought, she cleaned everything in the cabin, even the empty food tins. But worries still crept around the thing that had happened to her.

Henry, in his drunkenness, did not pillow. To pillow any man who forced himself was a woman's fate, ordained by destiny. But Henry wanted only to look at her, to see between her legs. Frightened, Ah Toy had slipped off her trousers as he insisted.

"Well, shoot, you jukst like any woman," he had said, peering at her nakedness, eyes bleary, hiccuping. "I told the boys differnt, you wuz differnt. Bet 'em a ounce."

Mumbling his disappointment, he had repeated, "A ounce, a ounce." He had squinted at her again and shook his head. "A ounce," he said, tugging a pouch from his pocket. He took out a gold coin and dropped it with a heavy clunk into the empty washbasin on the trunk.

Now Ah Toy stared at the goldpiece in her hand, marveling at its weight. Deciding, she dropped it into her beaded bag. If Henry returned, he would not find his gold. She was hungry. Both the tinned food and her rice were gone.

She dressed in her green silk pantaloons and black tunic to impress Li Jin. She was convinced that destiny intended her for him. She had "counted him" with the last of her rice.

In the past two days, Ah Toy had counted the rice over and over.

The simple divination required only the taking of a pinch of rice and saying Li Jin's name while she counted the grains. If they totaled an odd number, the answer was yes, this man was to be her true husband. An even number signified no, she was wrong. Each time she counted, the grains numbered odd.

Ah Toy pulled her hair into a knot at her neck, fanned it like a butterfly's wings, and secured it with an ivory comb. Then she picked up the orange shawl. She must return it before its bad luck affected her destiny.

Opening the door, she peered out. Seeing no one, she gathered courage and headed down the Clay street hill to the plaza. Men stared as she passed. She ignored them, concentrating on her errands. Seeing a fluttering yellow banner, she felt hunger bite. Her slippers gathered dust as she picked her way across a sidewalk of stove tops.

She smelled baking mooncakes and pushed open a door beneath the yellow banner. The shop was empty. Chairs rested upside down on the edges of tables. No crumbs littered the floor. She must be the first customer. Selling to her meant luck for the cake seller.

The door thumped shut behind her. The fragrance of mooncakes mingled with something familiar. She sniffed. It was the burned-sugar smell of her father with no face, of Lao Tai Tai's pipe. She shrugged. Opium smoke was no concern of hers. She was hungry. She rapped her coin on the counter.

A reedy voice called out, "I come, I come, friend New York Bakery." As-sing hurried from behind a partition.

Ah Toy stared at the bond servant Li Jin had mistaken for a high man. She laughed as his prepared smile abandoned amity.

"High man! Ha! Cake seller no high man!"

As-sing stiffened, and the sight emboldened her. She had not forgotten the indignity of his crablike grip on her arm. She had lived on Willow lane. She knew how to put a tradesman in his place.

Ah Toy waved the coin at him. His eyes snatched at it. "You sell mooncakes, high man?" She smiled, dropped the coin into her bag, and strolled toward the door. "Not hungry high-man cakes," she tossed over her shoulder.

"*Mui tsai!*"

Ah Toy whirled at the insult. "You know nothing!" Then she laughed at the rage contorting his face and sauntered out the door. Moments later, she heard the splash. Turning, she saw As-sing toss a second bucket of water into the street. Ha, she thought, try to wash away the bad luck of your first customer refusing to buy, high-man cake seller.

Inside the El Dorado, Ah Toy advanced toward the bar through the collective stares of stale-smelling gamblers. A naked woman in a painting gazed beguilingly upon the players from her majestic couch. Behind the bar, a man in a white apron polished a goblet and watched Ah Toy approach.

Ah Toy lowered her eyes politely and said, "I look pretty lady." She held out the shawl.

"Yes, ma'am," the barkeep replied, his words slack as syrup, "you do look a mighty fine pretty lady. A pretty lady's a real treat early morning, like dew on a peach."

Ah Toy stared at him, puzzled by his liquid speech, but he agreeably told her how to find Simone. She concentrated on his directions. She must return the shawl. Then she would find Li Jin.

Ah Toy turned south on Kearny street past the cake seller's yellow banner one block, following the barkeep's instructions. This would be Sacramento street, he had said. There, to her surprise, she discovered a scene plucked from Canton.

Bamboo hats spilled from a stall. Crates of vegetables and bags of rice cluttered the road. Sausages hung in aromatic bundles before a grocer's shop. Chickens squawked from cages, and throngs of China men hurried about their business of buying and selling.

Ah Toy picked her way between crates, inhaling the pungent

aromas of dried shrimps and cuttlefish. At a vegetable stall, she poked through baskets of yellow onions and green cabbages, sniffed brown knobs of ginger. The vendor filled a straw bag with her purchases, returning a handful of coins for her gold. With one of them she bought a bowl of noodles and ate.

Seeing an herbalist's signboard, Ah Toy ducked into his narrow, high-ceilinged shop. Tiers of drawers along two walls released musky odors. She smelled bat's dung and camphor, cinnamon, clove bark, lotus root. The familiar smells recalled old errands for Lao Tai Tai, when Ah Toy had bought the necessaries herbalists provided mist-and-flower ladies—the rare drug from bamboo joints that increased the mandarins' pleasure, and mercury for the mist-and-flower ladies to prevent conception.

The herbalist wore a cap banded with black satin. The sleeves of his gown concealed his hands. "Little sister," he said. Ah Toy watched him appraise her feet. With a sly smile he offered mercury.

"You know nothing," she said, inspecting his store and sniffing her disapproval. She bought a packet of pomegranate blossoms ground with iron for her hair. The herbalist urged her to return as she ducked out his doorway.

At the corner of Dupont street, Ah Toy saw Tong Achik distributing leaflets. She greeted him with a glad heart.

While Tong Achik thrust leaflets at passing China men, urging attendance at a Bible presentation, he told Ah Toy of Li Jin's departure for Stockton.

Ah Toy, disappointed, nodded her gratitude for the information. She continued up Sacramento street, thinking on this news. She concluded Li Jin's rapid advancement upon the Gold Mountain was an omen of good fortune. Destiny surely intended her for his wife. Then she stopped, lost in a new thought. How would she live until his return? She could stay in the house on Clay street until the agent came. How many coins made a hundred dollars? Certainly, more than she had. She shrugged, dismissing the concern. Life was decided, destined.

Near the corner of Pike street, Ah Toy saw the door with chalked numbers the barkeep described as Simone's. On the porch, two men quarreled. Ah Toy stood silent and unobserved at the bottom of the stairs, reluctant to interrupt.

A man in patent leather boots slammed a fist against a post. "The South just won't stand for it! Georgia will secede if the California bill passes the House!"

Ah Toy watched the other man pull himself tall. He wore his dusty trousers stuffed into worn boots as if he were a general. He jabbed the other man's chest with his forefinger. "The Union wants California, and it don't want slaves! We'll see California a state within the month, and the Southern senators can go pick cotton!"

The chalked door swung open. Simone, wearing a pink dressing gown, scolded the man in patent boots. "Go 'way! Go 'way! You finished here! Leave!" She shooed him from her porch.

The other man grinned at her. "Reckon it's my turn, ma'am."

Simone brushed a hand through her curls, then saw Ah Toy. "Come! Come!" she urged, waving Ah Toy up the stairs.

The man headed for her door. "Not you," Simone said, pushing him toward the stairs. The man watched Ah Toy pass him on the stairs, then shrugged and strolled away.

Inside, Ah Toy sat down in the chair of wine-red velvet Simone offered, astonished by the elegant room. Gilt-edged mirrors and paintings hung on red-papered walls. Damask draperies framed the windows. An etched-glass lamp burned sweet-smelling oil on a table draped with lace.

Suddenly, Ah Toy felt loneliness wash over her like ocean over sand, erasing fear, curiosity, even confidence in her destiny. She was so solitary in this Gum Shan.

Simone asked softly, "China lady have problem?"

Ah Toy's reserve dissolved. She covered her face with her hands to hide the unexpected tears.

Simone swept across the room and took Ah Toy's hands in hers. "So far from home. So strange a city. I know." She offered Ah Toy a lacy handkerchief and patted her shoulder. "Some brandy and you feel better."

Simone took two glasses from a silver tray and with a squeak of glass unstoppered a decanter.

Ah Toy, grateful, sipped the brandy. She recovered her face and explained her visit. One is an unlucky number because it is lonely, she told Simone in her slow English. Chinese people give gifts in even numbers, she added, for good fortune. She worried, but didn't say, that accepting the lonely gift might deflect her destiny with Li Jin.

Simone listened, sipping brandy. "This shawl she very beautiful for you."

Ah Toy put down her empty glass and pulled the shawl around her shoulders, stroking its tassels. "I like."

Simone refilled Ah Toy's glass. "So, I pay Rosita three dollar. You have three dollar?"

Ah Toy brightened. She poured coins from her purse and held them out to Simone.

Laughing, Simone counted out three dollars. Ah Toy laughed, too, from the warmth of the brandy. As she returned the remaining coins to her bag, she confessed the money was Henry's.

"How?" Simone looked puzzled.

Ah Toy considered. Should she tell? She felt ashamed, but Simone was so kind. The brandy loosened her tongue.

Simone stared as Ah Toy described her experience. Then she threw back her head and laughed until tears came. "The men are so stupid!" She clapped her hands as if delighted by male foolishness.

Ah Toy looked at her, uncomprehending.

Simone, laughing, explained. "These men believe Chinese

women not like other women. Go this way," she said, tracing short strokes back and forth on the table. "Not this way." She traced a vertical line.

Ah Toy suddenly understood. The brandy had made her head light, and laughter flew from her mouth.

Simone explained that the goldpiece belonged to Ah Toy. She had earned it. In California, women were rarer than gold, and worth a good deal of it. Several women from France had bettered their lives because of California's scarcity of women, she said. In France, they had been poor, forced to prostitute themselves on the streets. Here, they were admired and readily married. She, however, intended to return to France. "No civilize place San Francisco," Simone said, patting Ah Toy's shoulder as she passed to answer the door.

Throughout the afternoon, knockings at the door had interrupted their conversation. Simone told her callers she was not receiving. One irritably stubbed his finger at the chalked numbers, insisting he had called during the proper hours. Simone, soothing his impatience, invited him to return later. Ah Toy realized, admiringly, that Simone was a mist-and-flower lady.

Later, returning home along Pike street to Clay, Ah Toy sorted through her new thoughts. Now when men stared at her, she felt pride. She was more valuable than gold.

She thought of Li Jin and, as she walked, wandered into the familiar dream of her wedding. The groom would send a red sedan chair for her. Musicians in green uniforms and red-tasseled hats would play bamboo flutes and wooden horns. Serving women would dress her in bridal robes of red, with a headdress dangling beads and tassels.

In this dream Ah Toy had never before pictured the groom. Now she imagined him. He had the hollow cheeks and long fingers of a scholar. She smiled at the thought that even now Li Jin was earning gold in Stockton. She beamed her feeling of good fortune at a stranger, who stepped aside and watched her pass. Ah Toy nodded, envisioning herself as honored wife, the mother of five sons.

At Clay street, Ah Toy turned down the hill to her house. Her dream disappeared like smoke in wind. Before her door stretched a boisterous line of men, out to the walk and down the street.

She stared. Who were all these men at her house? She saw Henry. He saw her at the same time.

"There she is, boys!" he shouted, pointing up the hill at her. "I told you there was a Chinee girl here!"

Ah Toy marched on them. She knew her worth now. "What you want here?" she demanded of a youth clamping a faded hat against his shirt.

He flushed, then stared at his boots. "Well, H-H-Henry, uh, said you mi-mi-might, uh, let us loo-, loo-, look atcha, m-m-ma'am."

2

The Funeral obsequies in honor of the late
President Taylor, were celebrated yesterday. . . .
The China Boys brought up the rear of the
procession.

—*Alta California*
August 30, 1850

As-sing watched the loafers on the City Hotel's veranda congregate. The drivers of carts and wagons gawked, too, at the spectacle massing before the Macau and Woosung Restaurant.

In the doorway, As-sing smoothed the dog-fur jacket he wore for special occasions. He nodded as A-he arrived from the Jackson street boardinghouse with nearly a hundred marchers. A-he was gaining power. He would have to be watched.

Tong Achik had mustered every other China man in the city. They wore silk and satin tunics in rainbow colors and carried painted paper fans and umbrellas.

A-he and Tong Achik directed the men into marching formation, ten abreast. As-sing counted the rows. Nearly three hundred, an impressive demonstration for the mayor.

In the first row men held aloft a red banner announcing the Luminous Unity Society. It billowed in the breeze.

As-sing signaled and headed for the plaza. At the corner of Kearny and Clay, he paused the procession, seeing crowds surge from the arcade ahead. Nodding to A-he, As-sing proceeded ceremoniously, the footsteps of three hundred China men resounding against Kearny street's planking.

As they paraded into the plaza, people poured from doorways to see them. Horses ceased cantering as their riders gazed in astonishment. Men suspended their buying and selling to stare. In front of the El Dorado, As-sing saw the Frenchwoman in her jacket and trousers. She laughed and clapped her hands. The crowd picked up the clapping. Shouts and whistles echoed the smack of cork-soled shoes.

As-sing turned left at Washington street and led his parade up the hill. In front of the Bella Union, gamblers cheered the spectacle. Mexican musicians strummed an enthusiastic concordance as the marchers passed. The flute player tootled a cheery accompaniment.

At the *Alta California* newspaper office, where the dignitaries stood, As-sing, puffed with pride, signaled a halt. He could not remember a finer moment since arriving in America.

The Reverend Mr. Williams grabbed As-sing's hand. "A wonderful showing, wonderful. This is Reverend Dwight, and Mr. Buel here, he's secretary of the San Francisco Bible Society." As-sing nodded while the men congratulated him.

"Most impressive, Mr. As-sing," said Mayor Geary.

As-sing bowed. Geary looked more substantial now, in his boiled shirt and black cravat, than the first time As-sing had seen him. Then Geary was postmaster, sorting mail on the floor of an eight-by-ten room on Montgomery street. The post office, having no boxes, consisted of alphabeted squares chalked on the floor. People watched Geary sort the mail through a window with one pane removed for handing out their letters.

Following his postal appointment, Geary acquitted himself commendably as sheriff, magistrate, coroner, and judge. Then he organized the city's first police force. To everyone's relief, Geary's police quelled the "Hounds," a band of dangerous soldiers living by their wits and robbery after the Mexican War. Geary chained the criminals to an iron ball and put them to work improving city streets.

Now this important man was thanking As-sing for his assistance on the present occasion. As-sing bowed deeply.

A platform had been constructed in the plaza. As-sing followed the dignitaries up its rough stairs decorated with bunting and black rosettes. He remarked to Tong Achik the esteem the platform's construction signified.

Tong Achik shook his head. "It's for the memorial service tomorrow for President Taylor."

As-sing shrugged. "No matter. The China men have the honor of it first."

A-he and Tong Achik crowded the China men into a semicircle on the platform. As-sing looked out at the crowds gathering to watch. He saw several women seated on benches facing the platform. Ah Toy was among them. A thin smile found As-sing's mouth. This was a very good day indeed.

The crowd quieted as the Reverend Mr. Williams of the First Presbyterian Church acknowledged the dignitaries. Then, turning toward the China men, he began, "Citizens of the Celestial Empire . . ." As-sing translated the greetings into Cantonese.

Other speakers offered similar salutations. Then Mr. Buel told As-sing that he hoped more of his people would follow the example of the Celestial citizens gathered today and cross the ocean to this shore. "To your friends in China," Mr. Buel said, "we charge you with the message that, in coming to this country, they will find welcome and protection." As-sing bowed and translated.

The Reverend Mr. Dwight spoke next. Addressing the China men, he said, "Though you come from a celestial country, there is another one above, much better, much larger than your own. Here and in your country, you are sometimes taken sick and suffer and even die and are seen no more, and your fathers and mothers and brothers and sisters all die, but in the other heavenly country, all the good China boys live. They will meet there and never die!"

As-sing hesitated. He looked at Tong Achik, shrugged, and repeated the message in Cantonese. As his last syllable died, he saw the previously impassive faces of the Chinese register disbelief. Then they laughed. As-sing knew it was an absurd idea to all of them except the missionary. He watched Tong Achik hand around the

Chinese-language Bibles, ignoring his countrymen's amusement.

Mayor Geary delivered the closing remarks. He was about to take his seat when he appeared to reconsider. Turning a solemn face on the spectators, Geary said, "Tomorrow our city, the Queen of the Pacific, will march in tribute to the memory of our late departed president, Zachary Taylor." He turned to As-sing. "We invite the China boys to join the procession to honor our leader 'all the same like your emperor.' " Nodding to the China men, Geary added, "This will mark the first time that China and America join hands in such a demonstration of respect."

As-sing beamed as the crowd burst into shouts and applause. They stomped. They whistled. They cheered the mayor. They cheered China. While they cheered the deceased president and America, As-sing found Constable Elleard and his silver-draped pony. Someone put a coin in the animal's mouth. It trotted off to get its hooves buffed, and As-sing told Elleard what he had come to say.

Elleard looked at the bench where As-sing pointed and said, "I see her. The lady in the orange shawl."

Ah Toy followed Simone into the El Dorado, thinking on the cake seller. He had stood on the platform like a pretend mandarin, making speeches and shaking hands with Gum Shan high men. And no one objected to the imposture. Everyone, including the important-looking man with the pony, seemed insensible to As-sing's lowly position. She dismissed thoughts of the cake seller and his counterfeit status. Better to think on the man whose destiny entwined with hers, and the dowry she would present him.

Ignoring the noisy crowd celebrating the cake seller's Bible parade, Ah Toy examined the painting of the naked woman. In copying that pose, she saw she placed her arm behind her head differently. She had, however, duplicated the lifted leg and the drape of silk over her hip. She was astonished at how much gold men tossed into her washbasin in exchange for this exhibition. Each day, after the last look-see, she buried coins under her cot. She kept the nuggets and gold dust in the cleaned food tins on the shelf over the stove. While the men gawked at her, she stared at her gold-filled tins. By concentrating on the gold, she endured the humiliation. It was no greater than in her childhood begging.

Simone nudged Ah Toy's arm. "Our mayor handsome, no? A pity he adores his wife."

Ah Toy looked at the mayor surrounded by celebrants, then smiled politely at Simone, saying nothing. Li Jin was handsome. Americans had hairy faces and eyes set deep like devils'. She had seen hundreds of their faces as they trooped through her door for look-see. They all looked alike to her.

A woman drinking punch with Simone said, "Mrs. Geary has returned to Pennsylvania with her babies. Judge Baker said I might now persuade the mayor to attend one of my receptions."

Simone smiled and said to Ah Toy, "Irene's soirees *très chic*. Dance, food, wine, ladies, ooh la la!"

Irene greeted a dignitary passing with a plain-dressed woman. "Good afternoon, Alderman Gillespie. So nice to see you."

The man smiled and tipped his hat. "Mrs. McCready."

Ah Toy saw the woman on his arm stiffen.

Simone laughed and puffed on her cigar. "He will pay for that."

Ah Toy was puzzled. There was so much about Gum Shan she did not understand. "What you mean?"

"Ah, in China perhaps different," said Simone. Laughing, she explained that Irene McCready and the other elegantly dressed ladies who had sat in the plaza's first row were courtesans. Wives refused to acknowledge them. Simone shrugged and tossed a curl from over her eye. "We are fallen women, no?"

Ah Toy remained perplexed. In China, prostitution was a profession, not a disgrace. The mist-and-flower ladies of Canton were often honored as dutiful daughters who in times of famine saved the family. In hungry times, a salable girl meant one less mouth to feed. Sometimes selling her was the only way to keep her alive.

The girls whose destiny was Willow lane were not despised for it. One's destiny one could not foretell or change. Ah Toy was puzzled that in Gum Shan women such as Irene McCready and Simone were condemned for their destiny.

Ah Toy was suddenly aware that Irene was staring at her. "You know, my dear, you would look stunning in the European fashions." Irene took Ah Toy's hand and smiled. "Come, let's go to Mrs. Cole's shop and get you something to wear to the parade tomorrow."

In minutes, Ah Toy was standing in front of a brass-framed mirror. A spill of satin and ribbons trailed from shelves above a rigid dressmaker's form gowned in pink. To Ah Toy, the figure looked like a beheaded empress too astonished to topple. At the thought, unease enveloped her like a web.

Mrs. Cole, a birdlike woman in gray, held a dress to Ah Toy's shoulders. "A very nice day dress," she twittered. "Merino. A lovely fabric."

Irene McCready, circuiting the shop in a brittle swish of purple taffeta, glanced over her shoulder. Imperious as a queen, she shook her head. "Something gayer, Mrs. Cole. It's the president's funeral, not hers. We simply want her to see and be seen."

The reminder that the parade honored a high man's death lightened Ah Toy's foreboding. Perhaps her apprehension only signaled this sad event.

In the mirror, she saw Mrs. Cole cock her head like a curious wren, put a finger to her lips, and consider Ah Toy's reflection. "I believe I have something quite special," she chirped, eyes bright. "A French silk ready-made in the latest European fashion. It's a lovely shade of peach. It would be stunning with your coloring."

Ah Toy adored the dress, a confection of ruffles and lace. She slipped it on, then gasped as Mrs. Cole buttoned the tight-fitting bodice.

Irene McCready watched, one hand on her waist. The other held a furled purple parasol, which she tapped against her patent-leather boot. "You'll get used to it," she said, dismissing Ah Toy's discomfort with a wave of ringed fingers. "Turn around, let me see how you look."

Ah Toy felt the sensual swirl of silk against her legs. She wondered what Li Jin would think if he could see her.

"It's quite nice," said Irene, fingering a ruffle of lace. "In fact, my dear, you look gorgeous. You must have it. You'll come with me to the parade. I want to show you off."

That evening, Ah Toy pirouetted about her cabin in the French gown, imagining Li Jin's admiration. She posed before her mirror, trying to ignore the clinging sense of foreboding.

Suddenly, she thought she heard an infant crying. She strained to hear. Yes, she was sure she heard it. And then she heard a rooster crow. Her heart leapt to her throat. She rushed to the door.

Heart pounding, Ah Toy peered into the darkness. There it was! The infant cried again. The rooster crowed. And then a cloud drifted across the moon's face. She slammed the door against the misfortune the three bad omens prophesied.

Irene McCready hiked her skirts above her boots and daintily stepped across the sidewalk of sunken packing cases. Passing men grinned. To Ah Toy she said, "You can't imagine the mud we endured last winter. Pulled the boots right off your feet. Someone put up a sign near here: 'This street's not passable, not even jackass-able.' " She laughed at Ah Toy's polite, uncomprehending smile. "Don't worry, dear, you don't need to understand." Irene twirled her parasol and smiled as men doffed their hats.

Ah Toy saw how men admired Irene's exposed boots. This was a new thing to think on, that her feet might not shame her in this place.

They found places on the parade route just as drums and trumpets announced the procession. A uniformed man marched solemnly past. "That's Col. John B. Weller," Irene said. "He's the chief marshal for the parade. Behind him are the Masons."

The crowd applauded a formation of young men accompanied by a marching band. "And that's Colonel Stevenson." Irene pointed at a man in military regalia. "He came out years ago with a regiment of New York Volunteers to fight the Mexicans, and now he's got rich buying and selling San Francisco property."

Ah Toy nodded at Irene's observations on the wealth, marital status, civic standing, and California achievements of the members of the Odd Fellows or the First California Guard in blue shirts and black pants. Irene's chatter, the animated marchers, blaring horns, and banging drums helped quell the foreboding that stalked her.

"Look," said Irene, pointing up the street, "it's the funeral car for President Taylor!"

The crowd fell silent as four white horses draped in silver and black crepe drew an empty carriage past. The patient, steady clopping of the horses' hooves sounded small and lonely to Ah Toy. A riderless white horse, its saddle covered in crepe, followed the hearse. Men removed their hats.

Then, abruptly, they burst into applause. "Huzzah! Huzzah!" someone yelled. As shiny, brass-trimmed machines were hauled past, Irene said, "The fire companies have new engines."

The spectators' energy buoyed Ah Toy's spirits. She applauded a succession of city dignitaries, then uniformed marchers carrying a blue satin banner. Irene read the gilt words emblazoned on it. "It says, 'San Francisco Police Department, organised August 12, 1850.'"

Next came the judges of the courts, then an untidy collection of representatives from the various states, carrying banners. Irene read one as a somber group passed. "'Sons of New York. We measure the loss of our President.'"

Someone yelled, "Hey! Look what's coming!"

Irene squeezed Ah Toy's hand. "My goodness! Just look at that!"

The China men marched ten abreast, row after row of them resplendent in brilliant-colored tunics trimmed with fur and gold embroidery. The cake seller, strutting at their head, wore a scarlet skullcap with a gold button, a tunic of blue satin, leggings of yellow silk.

Ah Toy saw As-sing's eyes narrow as he recognized her. He skewered her with a dark look over the top of a painted fan. Then he lowered the fan and grinned. Ah Toy recoiled as if struck. It was the cake seller! He was the shadowy dread stalking her! The realization leapt at her like a bandit from hiding. The menace was real! The cake seller was her enemy and intended her harm.

And then she laughed with relief. She had feared some threat to Li Jin and her destiny. But As-sing was only a cake seller, a merchant, not a mandarin. The gold button on his skullcap was a charade, the costume of an actor on a stage. He was nothing.

With a swish of silk Ah Toy dismissed thoughts of the cake seller. She followed Irene McCready into the plaza for the funeral's concluding ceremonies, smiling politely as men tipped their hats to her.

The parade had spiraled through the city, circling the plaza in a great loop. On a front bench reserved for ladies, Irene and Ah Toy joined Simone, wearing her pantaloons, jacket, and cap. The

Frenchwoman surveyed Ah Toy's gown with amused admiration. "Ah, lucky Chinese lady, she has dress most beautiful!"

The women watched the procession arrive. A ragtag collection of gambling-hall musicians trailed the marching bands without invitation and joined them at the reviewing stand. Simone, pointing her cigar at a dapper-looking group of horn players, shook her curls in mock despair. "Such fine French musicians," she said, "but do not know proper music." She laughed at the French trombonist enthusiastically leading a tune learned in California. "He play 'Jim Crack Corn,' which not good for funeral."

Moments later the French musicians fell silent as the funeral car arrived. The government band that had marched with the procession struck up a dirge. Ah Toy saw the French musicians look questioningly at each other. The trombonist shrugged, raised his instrument, and commenced playing.

Irene McCready gasped and whispered, "I think 'Two Old Colored Gentlemen' hardly an appropriate air for so solemn an occasion." Suppressed laughter rippled through the crowd as other musicians smothered the government band's sacred piece. People named the refrains in disbelief. " 'Hail Columbia!' " "Oh, my, not 'Yankee Doodle'!" " 'Lucy Neal'?"

Suddenly, in a frenzy of outrage, a dignitary rushed at the French trombonist. He seized the instrument and wrested it away with a parting sigh from the player's lips. One after another of the impromptu players ceased midnote, with an effect even Ah Toy recognized as hilariously awful. The audience collapsed with laughter.

A dark-haired woman sitting next to Irene giggled. "Oh, dear, these Frenchmen, I suppose, presumed the tunes they learned here would do as well as any other."

From the bench behind, Ah Toy heard an indignant sniffle. "That's Belle Cora!"

A softer voice said, "Mrs. Richardson, we can sit elsewhere."

"Yes, Mrs. Royce, I agree we should."

Ah Toy heard the rustle of skirts as the women found other places.

On the platform, a clergyman announced, "Let us pray." The crowd hushed. "Almighty God, by the power of Whose word worlds are called into existence, Who in infinite wisdom ruleth over all, and without Whose knowledge not a sparrow falleth to the ground . . ."

Ah Toy, at the word *sparrow,* abandoned the preacher's droning. She imagined seeing a sparrow walk. A walking sparrow was a sign of good luck. After last night's bad omens she must be alert to good luck.

Following the ceremonies, Ah Toy found herself encircled with Irene McCready and Belle Cora by men eagerly paying their respects.

Suddenly, someone grabbed her elbow.

Ah Toy turned in surprise to see a man with a black pony draped in silver. "Hullo there, Missy," he announced. "I got a warrant here. You gotta come with me."

Irene McCready whirled on him. "Constable Elleard, you can't come up to a lady in the midst of these gentlemen with such an appalling announcement!"

Elleard dropped the pony's reins and dug into his coat pocket. "Got this here, and the lady's supposed to come with me." He thrust the paper at Ah Toy.

Irene plucked it from him, glanced at it, and looked at Elleard in disbelief. "This is absurd!" She waved the paper at a man in a silk top hat. "Look at this! This is nonsense!"

The man examined the paper. "What's this about, Elleard?"

"Just doing my job, sir. That there's supposed to be a warrant." He leaned an elbow on the pony's back and inspected the sky. "The China lady's supposed to follow me."

Ah Toy fought panic. She looked from the constable to Irene and then at the man holding the paper. She felt a chill, as though a cloud suddenly obscured the sun. In memory, she heard again the infant cry and the rooster crow.

Irene snatched the paper back and waved it at Elleard. "This is just a bunch of Chinese scribbling! Where do you think you're taking my friend with this nonsense?"

Elleard shook his head. "The lady supposed to come with me, says Mr. As-sing, over to Jackson street. Says the lady run off from her husband in China, and they gotta send her back."

Ah Toy stared in disbelief. "You know nothing! I no husband China! I no husband!" What was this man talking about? Destiny intended her for Li Jin. She had gold for her dowry. "You know nothing!"

She felt Irene's arm around her shoulders. "You see," Irene was saying to Elleard, "this is perfectly absurd."

Elleard rubbed his sleeve over some dust on his pony's bridle, concentrating his gaze on the task. "All I know is Mr. As-sing said this was a warrant and I was to bring the lady over to Jackson street."

Irene shoved the paper in Elleard's face. "Constable, if this is a warrant, then it's a legal matter for the courts, not for private citizens!"

Elleard shrugged. "Well, you know, ma'am, the China boys look after their own business. They don't bother our courts or police, and we don't bother them."

"Well, we'll just see about that, won't we?" Irene announced. "You can tell that Chinese puppet I'm taking this matter before Judge Baker!"

Elleard glanced in the direction of the reviewing stand. Ah Toy followed his gaze. The cake seller stood near the stairs in his fancy clothes, peering at her over his fan. He lowered the fan and examined it as though he had never seen one before. Then he folded it with disinterest and grinned at Ah Toy.

Ah Toy's anger exploded like a cannon. "You know nothing!"

This is no problem, dear," Irene said. "Judge Baker will take care of everything."

Ah Toy nodded, her thoughts in a turmoil. She knew As-sing was no mandarin, but the know-nothing barbarians did not. The cake seller might gain control over her, since she was only a woman, without status or power. In Canton, courts never found in favor of the person with no position.

At the door to Judge Baker's court, Ah Toy said miserably, "I no husband Hongkong."

"Don't worry," Irene said, pushing open the door. "We'll put an end to this silliness right now."

Inside, while Irene went to speak with the clerk, Ah Toy sat down near the door, next to a man whittling a stick. He grinned at her and winked.

Ah Toy looked around. The room was filled with men whittling, smoking, reading newspapers. She felt suddenly vulnerable among these *fan qui*. The cake seller might convince them he was a high man. She saw him now at the back of the room, puffed like a peacock in his blue coat and yellow leggings. He smirked at her from beneath his scarlet skullcap and she looked away.

Ah Toy studied Judge Baker at his desk, a rotund man in black. He glanced at Irene, then returned his attention to a young woman standing before him.

"At what point did you leave the ship, Miss Bryan?" he asked.

"Toboga, Your Honor, a small island off Panama City. I had expressly confirmed that if the ship's accommodations proved unsuitable, I should be put ashore and my passage money be refunded."

"Was this your understanding, Mr. Steffan?" asked Baker, turning to a bald-headed man in a purser's uniform.

"The *Johannes Christophe* was overbooked, Your Honor, due to the numbers of people demanding passage aboard her."

"I was denied my cabin," said Miss Bryan, "and expected to sleep unprotected upon the deck!"

"Is this correct, Mr. Steffan?"

"Judge, you understand the conditions prevailing—"

"Have you a receipt for your paid passage, miss?" asked Baker.

"Yes, sir, two hundred dollars." The woman handed him a paper.

Ah Toy watched the judge examine the receipt. Removing his spectacles and rubbing the bridge of his nose, he announced, "Judgment in favor of the plaintiff in the amount of one hundred and fifty dollars! Next case."

In wonderment, Ah Toy gazed at the woman who had prevailed over the man. This is a good omen, she thought.

The clerk called out, "The China woman Ah Toy!"

Ah Toy, aware that everyone watched her, approached the judge's desk with her head high. Her slippered feet padded softly over the floorboards.

"Norman As-sing!" called the clerk.

Ah Toy watched the simpering, confident manner of the cake seller as he hurried forward in his black satin shoes, their thick soles thudding in his haste. Suddenly, it seemed unthinkable that this common merchant should disturb her destiny. "He know nothing!" Ah Toy protested.

The judge looked at her sternly. "You'll have your turn, miss. The court will hear the complainant."

Ah Toy listened, anger rising, while As-sing poured falsehoods past an oily smile. He thrust a paper at the judge. "Letter from Hongkong husband," he said.

Ah Toy's anger burst from her in a gallop. "He know nothing! He no high man!" she cried, clutching fistfuls of her silk skirt.

As-sing glowered, but Judge Baker ignored her. He frowned at the paper As-sing handed him, examining it front and back. He tossed it aside. "This is an indecipherable document." He stared hard at As-sing. "Just what is your position in the matter, Mr. As-sing?"

"Chief all China boys. Send woman back to husband."

Baker looked at Ah Toy. "Have you left a husband in Hongkong?"

"I no married! No husband Hongkong!"

"Where do you come from, Miss Ah Toy?" Baker asked.

"Canton."

"How old are you?"

Ah Toy considered. "Year not same Canton and Gum Shan." In China everyone became a year older with the New Year.

"Are you twenty-one?"

Ah Toy looked from the judge to Irene McCready, who nodded almost imperceptibly.

"Yes, I twenty-one year," Ah Toy said, smoothing her skirts to hide her uneasiness.

"And why have you come to California?"

Ah Toy thought on Wang Po's intent to sell her or bind out her labor. She had no English words to explain such things to these people. She had only her new destiny. "Better life," she said softly, bowing her head.

"You mean you have come here to improve your condition?"

"Yes," she said, glancing up, "better life here."

Baker looked from her to As-sing, whose expression had frozen to impassivity. "Since you are not the husband, Mr. As-sing, and since we have no authority that this woman has left a husband, and since she denies the charge, I rule in favor of the defendant. One ounce for court costs, Mr. As-sing. Pay the clerk." To Ah Toy he said, "You're free to go, miss."

So surprised was Ah Toy by the judge's pronouncement, she barely heard As-sing's hissed *"Mui tsai!"* as he tossed a coin at the clerk.

Ah Toy clapped her hands in joy. She prattled her gratitude, telling the judge how pleased she was he had not kowtowed to Assing. "That man cake seller, no high man," she insisted, and saw that the judge was amused by her.

After her victory over As-sing, Ah Toy settled into a routine of waiting for Li Jin's return. Mornings she shopped on Sacramento street or strolled through the plaza, curtsying to admirers as Irene had taught her, and lifting her skirts to display her new calf boots. Afternoons, after the Sacramento steamer arrived, she exhibited herself for gold.

To escape the humiliation of raucous men gawking at her, she learned to hide in her mind. She imagined Li Jin's return and his surprise at the size of her dowry. With visions of the luxurious life she and Li Jin would enjoy, she erased the laughter of the men lined up at her door. The only sound she permitted herself to hear was the clink of gold.

The glittery metal soon filled the cans on the shelf over the stove and the chest buried beneath her bed. With some of it Ah Toy improved her cabin's furnishings. From the merchants on Sacramento street she bought bolts of silk in jade green and draped it over the rough wood walls. On her cot she spread a length of red satin embroidered with gold dragons. Atop her clean-swept dirt floor she laid a neat carpet of woven grasses. She replaced the wobbly stools with teakwood chairs and cushions of embroidered silk. She bought a table inlaid with ebony and ate with ivory chopsticks from dishes of red lacquerware. She bought a fine *fan qui* clock and learned to know when the Sacramento steamer docked. She liked to wind the key and watch the pendulum. The steady ticktock filled the empty corners of her cabin with passing time.

She lined her shelves with red paper to better display her abundance—bricks of tea and canisters of sugar, packets of spices and herbs, baskets of rice and dried cuttlefish, and rows of the tinned foods she had learned to enjoy.

Ah Toy's most treasured new possession was a statue of Kwan-yin, the goddess of mercy, a beautiful porcelain produced at the imperial manufactory in Kwangsi province. Lao Tai Tai, the old mistress on Willow lane, had prized the creamy white, crackle-glazed artistry.

Ah Toy arranged an altar for the goddess near her bed. When she exhibited herself to the barbarians and could not escape their lewd remarks, she gazed upon the goddess's merciful face for comfort. Kwan-yin held an infant, and Ah Toy imagined it as her own, the firstborn son she would bear Li Jin.

Sometimes she was filled with a terrible loneliness for the family she had lost, and an unbearable longing for the one that awaited her.

One evening, fleeing such feelings, she headed for the bright lights of the plaza. On a crowded corner a child smiled up at her. "It's the candy man," he said, displaying a handful of pink-and-white peppermints.

"Hore-hound—pep-per-mint—and—win-ter-green!" called the candy man. He wore a neat cravat and high, white collar as precisely pointed as his speech. "Large lumps! Strongly flavored! 'Ere they go!" he announced enthusiastically. "Judge Waller bought them! Colonel Frémont bought them! Buy 'em up! Everybody buys 'em!" He hesitated, surveyed his audience, then crowed, "Tom Battelle's sweetheart buys 'em!"

Ah Toy saw a well-dressed man leap from the crowd and grab the candy man's lapels. "Look here! You quit that or I'll horse-whip you!"

"All right, sir," said the candy man, withdrawing and bowing courteously. As his assailant walked away muttering to himself, the candy man hollered, "Tom Battelle's sweetheart does *not* buy 'em!"

Ah Toy wandered across the crowded, brightly lit plaza. At the

French confectionery on Washington street she bought an ice cream. From there she wandered into the Bella Union gambling hall. A boisterous music of drum and pipes clamored for attention over shouts and dealers' bells. Ah Toy saw a red-faced man blowing wildly upon a set of pipes fastened beneath his chin. His hands banged brass cymbals while sticks fastened to his elbows thumped a drum hung on his back.

Ah Toy remembered him. He had performed in the plaza her first day in Gum Shan. The entertainer seemed less strange now, and typical of Gum Shan's restless energy. Excepting the idlers whittling in court, everyone seemed intent on several spirited and simultaneous pursuits. Everyone was eager to make a "pile" with both hands.

Ah Toy edged out the door and into the bright night, remembering her first day in this vigorous city. In the distance, illuminated tents and campfires winked against darkened hills. The moon hung high as it had that first night. So much had happened to her in one month.

She crossed the street to the El Dorado. Inside, through the haze of smoke, she saw Simone perched on a stool before a felt-covered table. She clinked golden coins from one gloved hand to the other.

Simone's table was crowded with gamblers eager for the company of a woman. Before each of them lay a facedown card. Ah Toy watched the dealer deftly distribute a faceup card to each player. He dealt Simone an ace.

"Ah, *vingt-et-un,*" she observed, casually displaying a jack.

"Twenty-one!" called the dealer. He slid her a stack of coins across the table's green baize.

"Ah, my friend," said Simone, seeing Ah Toy. "Good, come eat with me."

Ah Toy followed Simone to the bar, where she gave her winnings to the El Dorado's owner, James McCabe. He counted the money and nodded approvingly. "Here's a double eagle for you, Simone," he said. He dropped a twenty-dollar goldpiece into her hand and smiled silkily at Ah Toy. "Take your dinner at Delmonico's and treat the pretty China lady on me."

On a darkened street two blocks off the plaza, Simone opened a door into a narrow building. "Do not come alone to here at night," she warned Ah Toy. "Too dangerous. Sydney men."

Inside, Ah Toy followed Simone up a flight of rickety stairs and into a long, low room. White muslin covered the ceiling and walls. Chattering diners glanced at Simone and Ah Toy as the steward seated them and offered the bill of fare.

Delmonico's restaurant delighted Ah Toy. In the brightness of oil lamps the room sparkled with glass and silver. On the table before her, several silver forks and knives lay each side of a serving plate. Ah Toy had eaten with forks and spoons when she lived in Mr. Buxton's house on Thirteen Factories street, but she had never dined in a *fan qui* restaurant. The array of eating utensils confused her. She picked up a stubby, thick-bladed knife and examined it.

"For fish," said Simone, smiling. "I teach you."

Simone ordered, and the waiter brought first a mock turtle soup with sherry, then a boiled salmon in anchovy sauce. Ah Toy liked it. "Taste salt, same like soy sauce," she said. Following Simone's example, she pushed a piece of the pink flesh onto the back of her fork with the fish knife.

After the fish, the waiter brought a sirloin of venison with capers, then a lobster salad. He apologized for the poor selection of vegetables. Coffee and sliced fresh pear completed the meal.

"Very good, *oui?*" Simone patted her mouth with a napkin. Ah Toy, contented, agreed the meal had been delicious. It had cost, including a bottle of wine, the whole of McCabe's twenty-dollar goldpiece.

At the door of the El Dorado, Ah Toy bid Simone good night and crossed the plaza. Despite the late hour, it remained lively. She understood now how the bright lights, music, and companionship of the town seduced lonely men from comfortless lodgings.

As Ah Toy climbed the Clay street hill toward her house, thoughts of Li Jin and her someday family returned loneliness to her. She turned to look again at the festive plaza.

Suddenly, north of the city, Ah Toy saw a startling crimson illuminate the dark. She gasped as it exploded into a frightening, flaring red. Horrified, she saw flames burst against the night in terrible beauty.

At the fire bell's first clanging, As-sing scrambled from his cot and threw on his tunic. He flung open his desk, searching frantically for his bag of gold dust. He stuffed it deep into his pocket with one trembling hand. With the other he fumbled a key into the drawer containing his box of gold coins saved for sweating.

His breath rasped in his throat. Outside, clanging bells echoed his panic. Men shouted and horses neighed. A pounding frenzy of wagons clattered past.

As-sing grabbed the box of coins and anxiously surveyed his moonlit room. There was the dragon-painted clay pot of preserved eggs. He would send Han for it if there was time.

He stumbled down the stairs. "Han! Han!"

The cook, holding a lantern, stood mute in the kitchen, his terrified eyes darting wildly about the room.

In Cantonese, As-sing shouted, "How near are the flames?"

Han shook his head.

As-sing grabbed the paralyzed cook by his shoulder. "Protect whatever you can carry! Take the kitchen god and Hwa-kwang!" The god of fire must need special offerings, As-sing thought desperately. He snatched his boots from behind the firebox, shoved his stovepipe hat on his head, and rushed into the street.

To the north, orange flames like dragons' tongues licked a ruby sky. Throngs of people laden with possessions fled past on Kearny street, away from the fiery glow beyond the plaza. Volunteer firemen shouted at the retreating horde. "We'll need a bucket brigade, men!"

One man hesitated. The crowd knocked him down and he disappeared beneath their feet. "The devil take you!" a fireman cursed. He shook his fist and hurried toward the blaze.

As-sing, gripping his boots and box of gold, pressed against his doorway. If the flames threatened, he would run. Until then, the building at his back was safer than the frenetic mob.

"As-sing! As-sing!"

The voice was A-he's. The owner of the Canton Restaurant stumbled from the crowd, wearing only his sleeping garments. His face was smudged with soot. "I've lost everything!" he wailed. "My restaurant is gone! The boardinghouse is gone!"

Against the noise of the carts and wagons jolting over the planked road, A-he gasped the familiar story. As-sing well knew the ten thousand crackings of falling timbers, the thunder of rushing flames, the tumultuous smashing of houses demolished to blockade the conflagration. Above A-he's frightened telling, As-sing heard the fire's distant devouring.

By eight o'clock the next day valiant volunteers had doused the flames. As the sun rouged the eclipsing smoke, As-sing locked his treasures away. Han, still shaken, calmed himself by preparing a bowl of noodles for the distraught A-he. As-sing went out to see the damage.

Dazed citizens filled the streets. Tearful women and children clung to remnants of their belongings in woeful camps. One confused man clutched a keg of gunpowder with one stave burned away.

On the east side of the plaza the five-story El Dorado, built of brick, still stood, as did most of the Parker House, under construction next to it. On the plaza's north side, the *Alta California* newspaper office, also brick, survived. So did the Verandah, an adobe gambling house at Washington and Kearny, damaged only where flames had snaked through windows. The French restaurant named Excellent remained, as did a few dwelling houses. Everything else on Washington between Kearny and Dupont lay in ruins.

As-sing picked his way north, past people numbly searching debris. Nearly every building on both sides of the street was destroyed. Amazingly, the city hall, on the corner of Pacific, had been saved. Its four balconied stories loomed ahead like a ship moored in a sea of black rubble.

Seeing it, As-sing tasted the bitter memory of the woman who had insulted his authority and stole his face. He sucked his teeth and savored vengeance.

As-sing turned west on Jackson to the blackened remains of the Canton Restaurant. He pulled the threads of his beard. Disaster offered opportunities. A-he needed gold to rebuild, so might others. As-sing had gold. The prevailing interest rate was 10 percent per month. He would profit.

As-sing, gazing at the destruction, wondered where the profit was for the incendiarists. Rumors, spreading fast as last night's flames, laid the blame on some Sydney men. It was said they started the blaze to divert attention from a theft.

For months, the foot of Telegraph Hill had swarmed with "Sydney ducks," sinister-looking men from Australia's penal colonies. They snarled their Australian slang and frequented low drinking places such as the Boar's Head, where they plotted pillaging forays. They lured strangers into their "Sydney Town" day and night and dazed them with a slung shot or the blow of a sandbag. If the unwary were lucky, the Sydney men robbed and ran. The unlucky they hurled into the bay.

Assault, robbery, and murder were on the rise. Sydney men sauntered through the city in midday now, ever on the lookout for the main chance. Already this morning As-sing had overheard renewed demands for a vigilance organization to protect citizens from this scourge on the city.

As-sing, heading back toward his restaurant, picked up the scorched remnant of a stovepipe hat. An acrid smell assailed him as the brim crumbled beneath his fingers. He pitched it back into the rubble and tugged his own treasured American hat over his ears. A responsible vigilance committee composed of the city's more substantial citizens, men such as Selim Woodworth, was not a bad idea. As-sing would favor ridding San Francisco of undesirables like the Sydney ducks.

He stopped with the thought. Banishment of unwanted newcomers was an interesting notion. He examined its possibilities as he wandered back to his restaurant.

On the first day after the fire, no one visited Ah Toy and she ventured out to see the devastation. On the second afternoon, when no one knocked at her door wanting to look at her, she walked down the hill again. The streets resounded with a tattoo of hammers and a steady rasping of saws. Parades of mule-drawn drays hauled off rubble, while sister processions delivered kegs of nails, stacks of boards, pallets of bricks.

Ah Toy, with amazed eyes, watched Gum Shan renew itself. It astounded her that the *fan qui* lavished money on shoddy construction, watched it dissolve into ashes, then industriously repeated the extravagance.

Within days the city returned to business as usual. Ah Toy did, too. She swept her floor and its straw carpet every morning of the dust left by the men's boots. She scoured her stove and kitchen things, brushed her silken draperies, smoothed the red satin cover of her bed, dusted her clock and teakwood chairs, polished Kwan-yin's porcelain image. She bought a likeness of Hwa-kwang and arranged an altar for the god of fire, away from Kwan-yin's honored position, lest either become jealous. She filled the hours and waited for Li Jin and her destiny.

On a visit to Sacramento street she purchased an apricot-colored tunic to wear with her green silk pantaloons, although, more and more, she favored European fashions. At Mrs. Cole's shop she bought another French gown, a blue silk the color of kingfisher feathers. Men on the streets stared when she wore it. They asked about her and word spread. Her business was good.

One morning, a month after the fire, Ah Toy scooped a double handful of gold from her basin. She filled a red silk bag with it. She had seen on Sacramento street a screen of the Eight Immortals she wanted.

At a stall she bought paper flowers for Kwan-yin's shrine and a jar of preserved ginger. These purchases would show the merchant with the screen that she was accustomed to buying. He was a dirty fellow with long nails and scholarly pretensions, but he spoke Hakka and Ah Toy enjoyed conversing with him.

With studied indifference, Ah Toy examined the screen of embroidered silk. The merchant hovered at her shoulder, extolling the eight genii of Taoist legend who had successfully attained immortality. "Such represent the essence of happiness," he said.

Ah Toy wished to fill her house with happiness. She coveted the screen, but sniffed her disapproval. She told the merchant shoddy merchandise was beneath her notice.

The merchant feigned affront. He insisted on the screen's rarity and fineness. Ah Toy parried his praise with disdain. The merchant, in turn, lauded the artistry as exceptional. Eventually, equally satisfied, they agreed on a price Ah Toy claimed was larcenous and the merchant moaned was robbery.

He filled one tray of his balance scales with weights equal to the gold required for the purchase. Ah Toy poured gold into the opposite tray. It failed to balance. She added more gold. The tray lowered only slightly. Surprised, she emptied the bag into the tray. It overflowed with glittery metal, but remained unbalanced.

The merchant, perplexed, examined the metal with a magnifying glass. "Half your gold is brass filings," he said, his tone accusing.

"You know nothing!"

The merchant frowned and poured the offending metal back into Ah Toy's bag. He handed it to her. "Brass filings."

Ah Toy knew gold was heavy. This metal was not. Her customers, she realized, had cheated her. Men had laughed and leered, then given her brass filings for the privilege. She felt herself redden with rage. She knew at once what she must do.

Judge George Baker's courtroom was filled with idle men reading newspapers, whittling, ejecting gobs of brown spittle at brass spittoons. Among them Ah Toy saw several men who had been to her house. One, a little man with pocked skin, she remembered as exceptionally disrespectful. He saw her staring at him and ducked behind his newspaper. A second man grinned at her with large, brown-stained teeth. He, too, she remembered as unusually coarse. These two had certainly cheated her with brass filings.

She marched toward the front of the courtroom and accosted the clerk. "Men cheat! No gold!" She smacked the red silk bag onto his table. "No gold! Brass!"

Laughter erupted from the courtroom.

"I say, miss," said the clerk, smiling, "you want to talk to the judge, you got to wait your turn."

For an hour Ah Toy fidgeted while petitioners and complainants and defendants recounted their grievances before Judge Baker. A woman accused of cowhiding a man for seducing her daughter received a reprimand and paid a token fine. Three instances of public drunkenness drew short terms of imprisonment. A matter involving squatters on a Californio's land grant was referred to a higher court.

At last the clerk called out, "The China woman!" Ah Toy leapt up and launched upon her ill usage, thumping her bag on Judge Baker's desk.

He smiled his recognition. "Hold on there, Miss Ah Toy, what is it exactly that you're trying to tell me? Where did this 'false gold' come from that you're complaining about? Did you sell something to someone?"

"No! No sell!"

"Then where did it come from?"

"Men come my house!" She opened the red silk and poured it over the judge's desk. She stabbed it with her finger. "Not gold! Brass!"

Baker peered at it and smiled. "I don't understand, Miss Ah Toy. Are you saying men come to your house and give you gold? Why do they do that?"

Snickers rippled through the spectators. Ah Toy turned a narrow-eyed anger on them. Seeing the two rude men she remembered, she pointed. "Those men come my house! Pay look-see! Cheat me!"

The men slunk in their chairs. Hooting laughter filled the room.

Ah Toy stared at the laughing men. "You know nothing!"

Judge Baker silenced the courtroom with a rap from his gavel. To Ah Toy he said, "Sorry, miss, but you don't have sufficient evidence to accuse those men." With his hand, he raked the metal to the edge of his desk and into the red silk bag. "Not enough evidence," he repeated, handing the bag to her.

Confused, Ah Toy looked at the bag. "Not enough? I get more!"

Ah Toy rushed down Kearny street and up Clay to her house. She grabbed the basin filled with gold and brass and hurried back into town. She fought through men in the streets staring at the signal on Telegraph Hill. "It's a side-wheeler all right!"

Ah Toy looked up and saw the signal's two black arms lifted wide.

Breathing hard from her errand, Ah Toy thudded the basin onto the judge's desk. "Evidence!"

Judge Baker and two men standing before him stared at the basin in astonishment. At length the judge said, "Mr. McCrackan, the court will hear your client's case against the ship *Sea Witch* following a brief recess."

To Ah Toy he said, "Listen, miss, you have no evidence who substituted the brass filings. This basin full of metal doesn't prove your case against the men you've accused."

Ah Toy heard men laughing. She whirled and pointed. "He cheat me!" she protested, pointing at the pock-faced man. "And him!" She pointed from one familiar face to another. "And him!"

The men she indicated cringed in their chairs. The others roared with laughter.

"You know nothing!" Ah Toy shouted. Just then a single loud boom sounded from the bay. To her surprise, the courtroom fell silent. Then a second boom echoed the first. No one moved or spoke. When a third boom sounded, every man in the room burst into whoops and hollers.

"Three guns! Three guns!" they yelled. "It's the side-wheeler *Oregon!*" Stomps and whistles filled the room.

Judge Baker pounded his gavel. "Court's adjourned!" Smiling, he handed Ah Toy her basin of brass and gold dust. "Statehood!" he said over the din. "California's been admitted to the Union!"

Ah Toy looked at her basin in disappointment.

"Get yourself a set of scales, Miss Ah Toy." Baker turned to his clerk and they slapped each other on the back. "Statehood!"

Outside, Ah Toy held her washbasin of metal, mystified equally by its insufficiency and the city's paroxysm of joy. Men fired pistols into the air, shook hands with strangers, danced in the streets. The stage for San Jose flew past with six horses lashed to breakneck speed, the driver shouting, "California is admitted!"

Rejoicing men surged toward the plaza, Ah Toy caught in their midst. In front of the El Dorado she slipped from them. Simone leaned against the wall, smoking a cigar and watching the excitement.

"*Très* gay, no?"

Ah Toy stared at the passing scene and hugged her basin. "I know nothing," she said, anger gone.

"You have problem?"

Ah Toy recited her courtroom confrontation. "Ah, yes, a problem the false gold," Simone agreed. Some zinc disguised as coarse placer gold, she confided, had been bet and lost at her table. Then the Frenchwoman laughed. "Not to worry. More gold come to us." She dropped her cigar and ground it beneath her boot. "Now you must be happy," she said, taking Ah Toy's arm. "Come, we will see some fun."

In the plaza, as celebrants exploded firecrackers and pistol shots, Ah Toy and Simone watched a man shinny up the flagpole with an American flag. Men shouted and waved their hats at him. "We're in the Union, thank God!" someone yelled. "Three cheers for the Stars and Stripes!" Hurrahs filled the air. Someone hollered, "Let's get him up a collection, boys!" Amid cheers, the crowd passed a hat from hand to hand.

Some men dragged a cannon to the flagpole. "Stand back, boys," one wheezed, "we're going to salute the thirty-first state to join the Union!" Ah Toy and Simone hurried back to the El Dorado.

Enthusiasm for the city's spontaneous holiday advanced

throughout the afternoon. Echoing booms reverberated from discharged ordnance. Every musician in the city joined his instrument to the din of pistol shots and firecrackers. Banners of red, white, and blue decorated nearly every building in the city, every ship in the bay.

The *Alta California* issued an extra edition of the day's news. Enterprising newsboys sold copies to eager buyers for as much as five dollars apiece.

As evening fell, music from a hundred bands filled the air. Light flowed from every anchored vessel in the bay and every window in the city. Bonfires blazed upon the hills.

Ah Toy, her distress forgotten, rejoiced with the city in their mutual golden expectations. Simone was right. There was more gold, plentiful as rice. Ah Toy watched patriotic citizens in the El Dorado collect more than two thousand dollars to celebrate California's admission to the Union. "We'll have a suitable response, boys, to the glorious news!" urged an organizer. "We'll have a parade and a grand ball!"

At the announcement, a pale man draped an arm around Ah Toy's shoulders. He leaned close to her face and whispered, "You will honor me with the pleasure of your company at the ball."

Ah Toy felt a shiver of dread as she looked into the man's flat blue eyes. His invitation was not a request. It was a declaration. She knew power when she saw it.

3

There has been great outcry in the gold regions here respecting the rapidly-increasing numbers of the Chinese miners, and it was proposed forcibly to stop their immigration.

—Frank Marryat

The pale man's lips stretched over a sound like a snake's hiss. "Sacksin," he said, "the name is Sacksin. Say it."

Ah Toy did as she was told.

He saw her home in his carriage, in which two large dogs lay waiting. "Hunters," Sacksin said, and commanded the liveried driver to Ah Toy's house without asking directions. She wondered when he had been there. The dogs stared at her with yellow eyes. Ah Toy stared back, remembering the begging bowl of her childhood and the stick her mother carried to beat off the village dogs. She was suddenly afraid.

The next day Sacksin sent his driver to fetch her for a theater matinee. The day after, it was horse races, shopping, lunch at Delmonico's. After that it was any event that Sacksin's curiosity fastened on. Ah Toy never declined. He was not a man to refuse. He was a high-man Englishman. He wore power as naturally as his well-fitted clothes.

He lived at the St. Francis Hotel in a set of rooms lavishly furnished. A manservant called him "my lord" and smirked at Ah Toy. Sacksin's wealth was attached to no visible employment. He amused himself by acquiring gold specimens in curious shapes, and by taking his dogs with their yellow, suspicious eyes to fine restaurants. He paid fearful waiters to feed them expensive chops beneath the table.

On a Sunday one week after Sacksin had invaded her life, Ah Toy dressed in a gown he had bought and told her to wear. "It's appropriate for a bull-and-bear fight," he had said, flinging the day dress atop her cot. He held a paper in front of her, pointing at the print.

"These top words," he had said, "they all say the same thing. 'War! War!! War!!!' Then it says, 'The celebrated Bull-killing Bear, General Scott, will fight a Bull on Sunday, at two P.M. The Bear will be chained with a twenty-foot chain in the middle of the arena. The Bull will be perfectly wild, young, of the Spanish breed, and the best that can be found in the country. The Bull's horns will be of their natural length, and not sawed off to prevent accidents. The Bull will be quite free in the arena, and not hampered in any way whatever.' " Sacksin laughed. "I believe we shall see some blood."

Ah Toy had nodded and said nothing. She had learned she was not expected to. But he liked instructing her.

Now, as Sacksin's carriage rattled over the planked road toward Mission Dolores, Ah Toy sank into new worries. This morning, shopping on Sacramento street, she had seen Tong Achik. No, he told her, he had heard nothing from Li Jin, but three returning miners knew of him. He had left the Stockton grocer, had been seen at Chinese Camp, Jamestown, Columbia. Bad stories came from the mines, Tong Achik told her. Americans at Columbia had published an agreement to forbid Chinese from mining in that district. Near Jamestown some Americans from a place called Arkansas had run Chinese miners off their claims and stolen their gold. Near Angels Camp, China men surrounded their tents with a twelve-foot trench and filled it with brambles to protect themselves from marauders. An expressman discovered the bodies of three China men in the Merced River, apparently murdered for their gold. No, Tong Achik assured her, Li Jin was not one of them.

Ah Toy had felt her breath squeezed from her by these bad reports. Li Jin was her destiny.

Now, following Sacksin into the arena, Ah Toy pushed thoughts of Li Jin from her mind. She must stay alert to whatever Sacksin wanted. If not, he might hurt her again.

Ah Toy simulated curiosity, mimicking Sacksin's interest, which pleased him. The arena, she saw, consisted of tiers of benches around a fenced area some forty feet across. She followed Sacksin up to the top bench, past brightly dressed Mexican women. They looked colorful as a bouquet of flowers as they chatted and puffed on their cigaritos. Ah Toy envied their freedom.

Sacksin sat next to a gray-bearded miner and pulled out his notebook. Ah Toy studied the arena. In its center was a large wooden cage on wheels. A chain trailing through its bars was anchored to a tree stump.

As she was staring, trying to glimpse the bear, some miners in dusty boots and slouch hats sat down in front of her. They hollered bets at one another. Ah Toy stared at them, wondering if they had robbed or killed China men.

"Twenty dollars says the bull wins!"

"I'll take that, and double! General Scott ain't lost yet!"

"I'll see that bet! The bulls before ain't been let at him. They was tied and had their horn points sawed off!"

Betting favored the bear. The old miner next to Sacksin leaned over and confided, "Nary a bull in Californy as kin whip that b'ar." Sacksin scribbled in his notebook.

Ah Toy watched two penned bulls kick dirt. They tossed huge heads with murderous-looking horns. How had the three China men found in the river died? Were they stabbed?

A gong hurrying straggling spectators to their seats pulled Ah Toy from bad thoughts. Across the arena two men removed the bolts securing one side of the bear's cage. As they rolled the cage from the arena's center, the chain anchored to the stump pulled taut. The bear tumbled from the cage's unbolted side.

Sacksin tapped his walking stick against his patent leather boot. Ah Toy sensed his excitement as the bear pulled against the chain anchored to a collar around its neck. It clawed the earth in frustration.

"That b'ar weighs twelve hunnert pounds," the old miner told Sacksin. "Watch'm dig hisself a shaller place to lie down in. That's how he fights. Seen 'im afore. That's what'n he'll do."

Ah Toy watched a man remove the bars between one of the bullpens and the arena. Another man climbed the railing behind the bear and waved a red flag. The first man prodded the released bull with a sharp stick. It dashed into the arena.

Seeing the bear and yelling people, the bull wheeled and raced back toward its pen. The bars had been replaced, but the bull ran at the fence and splintered it like matchsticks. Two men hurriedly goaded the bull back into the ring, then reinforced the pen to prevent further retreat.

Now the bull considered the bear, as though anxious to be done with the deed, Ah Toy thought. Lowering its head, it charged. The crowd cheered wildly. The bear, crouching low, received the bull's impact against his ribs. Ah Toy heard the thump. She pitied the bear as she pitied herself, chained invisibly to Sacksin, his eyes glittering now with bloodlust. Sometimes he looked at her in the same way, and she knew he saw her fear. She wondered if he ever pitted his dogs against each other, to see fear.

Ah Toy watched the bear catch his attacker by the nose. He rolled onto his back and grasped the bellowing bull by the neck. The bull stomped the bear with its hooves. The bear bit the bull's nose, then threw it to the ground. The bull struggled and regained his footing. To Ah Toy, neither animal, although both were bloodied, appeared near defeat. She wondered how long the agony would last. She didn't want to watch it. Did Americans torture China men when they robbed and killed them?

The bull retreated to the opposite side of the arena. The bear hunkered low in its hole, watching. The bull, its huge sides heaving, looked to be taking his enemy's measure. The crowd shouted encouragement. The bull charged.

Again Ah Toy heard a thud as the bull rammed into the bear's ribs. She cringed from the blow as if receiving it. The enraged bear, roaring with pain, seized the bull's ragged and bleeding nose with its claws. The bull bellowed and pulled free, but the bear caught him by a hind leg. Biting and clawing, he dragged the frantic bull around the arena, then released his hold. The bull limped beyond the bear's reach and dropped heavily. Did no one pity the wounded animals? Who pitied the China men beaten by robbers? Who would rescue them from their tormentors?

Ah Toy pushed such thoughts from her mind, for fear followed them into her eyes. She could not permit herself to appear fearful. It wasn't safe.

She watched two men jab the bull with sticks until they antagonized it into resuming combat. Twice more the animals engaged, with the outcome again favoring the bear.

The conductor of the performance climbed up on a railing, waving his hat for attention. He cupped his hands at his mouth and hollered, "The bull has had fair play, gentlemen!" The crowd booed and cheered. "There is no bull in California that General Scott can't whip! Anyone wants to put up two hundred dollars, I'll send in a second bull and the three can fight it out till one or all are killed. What do you say?"

Whistles and stomps greeted the proposal. Ah Toy watched three men tour the spectators with hats, collecting contributions. Next to Sacksin, the gray-bearded miner dug into a trousers pocket. "Finest fight ever fit in the country," he said, depositing five dollars in the collector's hat. "Mebbe that fella will let his bear git beat. Course, I doubt it. Animal like that's worth mebbe four thousand dollars. That's why they usually saw off the bull's horns. There's bulls a'plenty, but the bear's too valuable to risk."

Ah Toy saw Sacksin grin and drop a golden eagle into the hat.

The second bull entered the arena and appeared to Ah Toy to sum up the situation at a glance. He took the bear for the common enemy and charged. The bear, as before, absorbed the thrust and grabbed the bull's nose. After a brief but violent struggle, the bull freed itself. He spun, caught the bear on the hindquarters with his horns, and knocked him down. The first bull, as if emboldened by this action, charged the bear before it had time to recover, goring it deep in the ribs.

The bear howled its agony. Ah Toy covered her ears against the dreadful wail. The bear, standing, struck wildly with both forepaws in blind confusion while the bulls charged again. The bear fought valiantly, mauling the bulls until the conductor of the ceremony climbed on the railing and again cupped his hands to his mouth. "Is General Scott the winner?"

Stomps, whistles, and cheers awarded victory to the bear. Two shots rang out as the conductor put the bulls from their misery. Ah Toy glanced at Sacksin as he stood, striking his walking stick against the bench in front, joining the celebration.

He looked well satisfied. Perhaps the repulsive spectacle had spared her today.

They ride under the command of General Pico," Sacksin said in his clipped fashion. He gestured his walking stick toward the Californios parading past on prancing horses draped with silver.

"Yes." Ah Toy had learned to say yes to everything the Englishman said.

Another band of military musicians marched past, beating drums and blowing horns to celebrate California's statehood. Behind, six white horses drew a grand triumphal car. On it young boys in white shirts, black trousers, and red caps hugged lettered shields to thin chests. A little girl, dressed in white, her golden hair entwined with pink roses, held a white satin banner with gold lettering. Ah Toy flinched at the bad omen. Did Americans not know white was the color of death and mourning?

"The boys apparently represent the other American states," Sacksin said, "and the girl California. Her banner says 'California—The Union, it must be preserved.' "

"Yes."

A man seated on Sacksin's other side leaned over and said, "That little girl is the first child born in California of American parents. Her people came overland in '44."

Ah Toy watched Sacksin's mouth imitate a smile. He wore it like something borrowed that fit badly. He acknowledged the information with a nod, leaned his walking stick against his knee, and took a notebook from his pocket.

Ah Toy had watched him scribble in one of his notebooks the night he announced she would accompany him to the ball. "I shall amuse my chums with a record of this curious place," he had said. Then he lifted her chin with the head of his walking stick. "Not the least of these curiosities is you, my Oriental lily."

That had been but ten days ago, Ah Toy thought with a start. She felt as though Sacksin had owned her for years.

She watched a fire company march past, hauling its engine decorated with flags and ribbons. Flowers wreathed the bell. Another fire company followed with more equipment.

"Two suctions and three hoses," said Sacksin, pointing his stick at the carriages covered with flowers and flags.

"Yes." Ah Toy stared at the mahogany walking stick the color of dried blood. Its gold head perfectly fit the indentation at the base of her throat. Her voice still rasped.

She no longer recalled what had provoked her to tell him he knew nothing. But she would not forget his fury. "Never say that to me again!" he had shrieked. "Do you understand? Do you understand!" He jabbed his walking stick at her, pinning her to the wall. Then his face lost expression. In a whisper, he said, "Do you understand?" and pressed the golden knob into her throat. She remembered gasping "Yes" before she lost consciousness.

Another marching band banged drums past the reviewing stand. Ah Toy touched the bruise hidden by her diamond brooch. Sacksin had bought the jewelry for her with the taunting, mock enthusiasm of a child. "You want it, don't you? Say you do," he said, wearing his imitation smile. And she said yes.

Mrs. Cole had seen the mark on Ah Toy's throat and pretended she hadn't, flitting like a nervous bird around the rich man. Ah Toy realized then how defenseless she was. Conrad Sacksin was a rich and powerful man. She was a woman, nobody.

"I say, good show." Sacksin pointed his stick at four horses drawing a boat on a platform. An American flag flew from its mast, and marchers carried a white banner. Sacksin peered at it through his glass on the gold chain. " 'Watermen of San Francisco—United we pull more effective strokes—In Union we pull together.' " He returned the monocle to his pocket. "Splendid sentiment, don't you think, Miss Ah Toy?"

"Yes."

Behind her, Ah Toy heard the wives whispering disapproval. They had inspected her contemptuously when Sacksin handed her into the privileged first-row seats among the dignitaries. They looked away when Sacksin touched a kid-gloved hand to his beaver hat and said, "Ladies." It amused him that he could take her anywhere simply by the intimidation of his imperious manner and extravagant spending.

"Your countrymen, I believe, Miss Ah Toy." Sacksin gestured with his walking stick. As-sing strutted past with fifty China men banging gongs and cymbals. Sacksin laughed a thin amusement. "The banner says, 'China Boys.' "

Ah Toy heard derision in his voice and longed for a foe no

stronger than the cake seller. Against As-sing she had a chance. He was no high man. Sacksin was.

The China men brought up the rear of the parade. An oration followed, then cheers and gun salutes. The reviewing stand emptied, the wives swishing past Ah Toy with stiff necks and scornful looks.

Sacksin scribbled in his notebook. "A few thoughts I shall send off to London, to the *Times,* actually." He leveled a pale gaze on her. "Shall I read it to you, Miss Ah Toy?"

"Yes."

Sacksin held the notebook in one hand, the walking stick in the other, and read, "Forgetting for a moment the decorative features of this exhibition, let the reader consider the extraordinary character of the facts it symbolized. Here was a community of some hundreds of thousands of souls collected from all quarters of the known world—Polynesians and Peruvians, Englishmen and Mexicans, Germans and New Englanders, Spaniards and Chinese—all organized under old Saxon institutions, and actually marching under the command of a mayor and alderman. Nor was this all, for the extemporized state had demanded and obtained its admission into the most powerful federation in the world, and was recognized as a part of the American union. A third of the time which has been consumed in erecting our house of parliament has here sufficed to create a state with a territory as large as Great Britain, a population difficult to number, and destinies which none can foresee."

Destinies, thought Ah Toy, which none can foresee. She fingered the diamonds at her throat, wondering if Li Jin was safe. In the plaza, the boys who had hugged state shields to their chests tossed Chinese firecrackers, frightening little girls collecting fallen flowers.

Leaving the square, Sacksin's driver cursed the crowds choking the streets. "Sorry, guv'nor," he said, looking back at Sacksin, "it's all these folk come journeyin' up the river from the interior wantin' to see the festivities." Ah Toy heard steamboat whistles blasting departure signals.

It was nearly four o'clock when the carriage reached the St. Francis Hotel. Sacksin told the driver to see Ah Toy home. "I shall call at eight. Wear the red gown."

"Yes."

At her house, Ah Toy dropped, exhausted, on her bed. Sacksin sapped her energy as well as her will. And the long night still lay ahead, like a dark and fearsome road. Too wearied to remove even her boots, she escaped into the oblivion of sleep.

It seemed only moments later when Ah Toy woke, startled, heart pounding. The agonized voice called out again, "I shall die! I shall die!" She had thought she dreamed it. She could hear now the clatter of wagons in the road. The voice shouted again, "For mercy's sake! Don't take me to the hospital!"

Ah Toy threw open her door. Teams of struggling horses hauled a caravan of wagons up the hill. She heard the voice call again, "Don't take me to the hospital! I shall die! Take me to a good hotel and employ a good physician to attend me. I've got plenty of money and will pay for everything that's done for me!"

In the distance Ah Toy saw a dark-haired woman run down the hill, apron ties flying out behind like narrow white banners.

A man walking with the wagons called out, "Miss Eastman! We've so many injured here! We need help!"

The woman raced up and stared into the wagon bed. "Oh, he's terribly burned! This one can't live!"

Ah Toy stood at her door, horrified. The man saw her. "You there, miss! Please, help us!" He spoke quickly to the woman in the apron, then ran to Ah Toy.

Ah Toy recognized him as the preacher who sang up crowds in the plaza on Sunday mornings. "There's been a terrible accident," he said. "The steamer *Sagamore* exploded and we've dozens of dreadfully injured people here. We need help!"

Ah Toy wanted to close her door against the bad spirits hovering about these unlucky people. She lacked the will. The preacher pleaded, "Just walk with one of the wagons until we reach the hospital." He took her hand. "Please, miss?"

Ah Toy felt powerless against the preacher's beseeching. Since Sacksin's insinuation into her life, she had lost the will to decide anything. The preacher was pulling her to the nearest wagon toiling up the hill.

A badly scalded man lay in the wagon, his leg torn at the calf. He whimpered. The preacher put Ah Toy's hand on the injured man's and folded her fingers over it. "Just hold this young man's hand, miss. It'll comfort him," he said, and hurried away to another wagon.

"Bless you, miss, bless you," the young man murmured. "Don't leave me. Please don't leave me."

The wagon creaked up the hill, Ah Toy at its side, fearful and unsure. She watched the man's face, lest his spirit depart in her presence and endanger her with its escaped *chi*.

The American Hotel's ballroom was huge and spectacular. High ceilings glittered with chandeliers. Gilt-framed paintings hung upon the walls. Flags and evergreens adorned lofty pillars. Musicians sat on an elevated stage decorated with red, white, and blue banners. Above them was draped a painted vista of the city's waterfront, hills, and mountains, with views of its shipping and war weapons. At the center was a portrait of Washington, surmounted by an American eagle.

While Ah Toy watched the dancers, Sacksin and his friends murmured to one another the alarming facts of the tragedy. The *Sagamore* had just cast off from the Central Wharf for Stockton at five o'clock when her boiler burst. Witnesses claimed that steam had not been blown off for half an hour previous to the accident. An estimated one hundred passengers had been aboard. None escaped injury. Some bodies suffered such mutilation as to make identification impossible. The most gruesome task had been the collecting of limbs and body fragments found floating in the bay.

Ah Toy put from memory the wounded passengers disgorged from bloodied wagons into the hospital. She watched celebrants stroll about the ballroom, admiring the decorations and one another.

The *Sagamore's* tragedy had cast a pall over the evening's festivities. Despite the large gathering, possibly five hundred men and three hundred ladies, Ah Toy thought, only a few couples danced.

Most of the women of the town were present except Simone, who declined all invitations in favor of the profitable evening promised at the El Dorado. Belle Cora, wearing an emerald green gown draped with bugles of jet, swept about the dance floor with Charles Cora like a displayed treasure. Irene McCready, on the arm of James McCabe, was in azure blue. The demimonde wore bold colors. The wives wore genteel pastels of shot silk.

As midnight neared, gentlemen fortunate enough to escort ladies conducted their prizes to the elegant supper waiting across the street at the Union Hotel. Unaccompanied gentlemen, the Committee of Arrangements had declared, would not be admitted.

The Union Hotel, built of brick behind the Jenny Lind Theatre and the El Dorado gambling hall, rose an imposing four stories. Crossing to its entrance, Ah Toy sniffed sulfur in the fog that had, to everyone's disappointment, obscured the fireworks display on Telegraph Hill.

The Union Hotel's supper room glittered with silver, crystal, and chandeliers. Sacksin heaped Ah Toy's plate with salmon, roasted duck, ham in champagne sauce, almonds, raisins, and English walnuts. She nibbled apprehensively while he urged the Madeira. His polite public attentions would soon expire.

It was nearly two o'clock when Sacksin's carriage halted at Ah Toy's house. The horses stamped and snorted, breath steaming. Sacksin dismissed the driver with orders to return at dawn.

Inside Ah Toy's house he lit the oil lamp, then withdrew to a darkened corner. "So, my Oriental beauty," he said, voice husky, "are you pleased by your gown, your gloves, the diamonds at your throat?"

This was how it began, an enumeration of gifts bestowed, an accounting of what was paid, and what was due. Ah Toy knew the play and that she must perform her part. Reluctance agitated Sacksin, and she wanted no second encounter with his walking stick.

He could kill her. She saw it in his eyes. She was nothing, a Gum Shan souvenir, a trinket he might buy on Sacramento street, tire of, and toss in the bay.

She pondered her failure. Sacksin controlled her by assumption, with his position and power. Who dared oppose a high man?

Now, standing in the glow of the oil lamp, she said, "Yes." As the performance demanded, she smiled coyly into the dark. She stroked the satin dress, fingered with one gloved hand the diamond brooch on a ribbon at her throat.

"Say it!"

"Beautiful dress, most fine. Gloves, most fine. Diamonds, most fine."

"Take them off and show them to me. The dress first."

Slowly, for he objected if she hurried, Ah Toy unfastened the buttons on her gown. Impeded by the gloves, her fingers fumbled each one. He grunted approvingly.

The dress fell away in a graceful hush. Ah Toy stepped from the satin circle and knelt to pick it up.

"Leave it!"

Ah Toy stood uncertainly in the lamp's glow.

"The petticoat. Take it off."

Ah Toy tugged at the buttons at her waist. The pale silk slid silently to the floor. She stood before him in lacy underdrawers and chemise, expensively imported from France. Sacksin had bought them. The room was cool, and she shivered.

"Now the chemise." His voice sounded raspy.

Ah Toy unbuttoned the chemise. Her nipples tightened in the cool air as the warm silk fell away.

She heard Sacksin's unsteady breathing, the rustle of his clothes as he quickly undressed. She felt his eyes devouring her, his lacerating anticipation grinding against her.

"Now, the pretty pantaloons."

Ah Toy unbuttoned the undergarment. The pantaloons fell to her feet, and she stepped from them. She stood in the lamplight wearing only her boots and stockings, the gloves, the diamonds.

"Take the pins from your hair." His voice was breathy with excitement.

Ah Toy pulled out her hairpins. Her hair fell in black cascades over her shoulders.

"Gloves."

She tugged each finger free, one hand, then the other.

Sacksin stood just outside the circle of light. "On the bed. Show yourself," he said roughly. "Like you show look-see. I want look-see."

So he knew what she did for her living. Ah Toy obeyed. Lying down on the red satin of her bed, she raised her left knee, then opened her legs. Except for stockings and boots, and the diamonds on the ribbon at her throat, she lay wholly exposed.

With a lunge he was on her, like one of his dogs on a chop. He engulfed her, moaning gutturally. He wanted nothing more from her, she had learned, but for her to lie there. Waves of his acrid dampness washed over her. His hands plunged at her wildly, as though he might, if he tried, feel all of her at once. He grabbed at her, kneading her roughly, devouring her with his hands and body, seizing her with searching hands, probing fingers, digging at her, frenzied.

His hot mouth was a wet progression over her face, her breasts, stomach, thighs. He rocked with ecstasy, groaning his passion as he entered her. Thrusting against her, oblivious, gasping his delirium, his body arched and crushed, arched and crushed. And then with a strangled sob, he fell upon her, wet and breathless.

The dank smell of him assailed Ah Toy. Disgust rose in her throat beneath the purple bruise.

Sacksin called for her at eight the next evening to attend the opening night of the Jenny Lind Theatre. Ah Toy, submissively attentive, praised the entertainment, a performance of Italian arias by Madame Von Gulpen Korsinsky of Naples. Sacksin dismissed the program with a wave of his walking stick: "Nothing more than a music hall variety show."

Ah Toy detected agitation in his voice. Over supper at Delmonico's she picked at her roasted pork in raisin sauce, fearing the evening ahead. She saw no recourse from Sacksin's demands. Who would protect her? Not Gum Shan's China men. The only so-called high man was As-sing. Judge Baker and the courts offered no shield, for Sacksin had committed no punishable offense against her. For her to leave Gum Shan was unthinkable. Canton offered nothing. Big feet and square shoulders had no place on Willow lane. She had no home, no family. And to abandon the Gold Mountain without Li Jin was to abandon destiny.

These worries tormented Ah Toy's thoughts as Sacksin's carriage clattered up the Clay street hill. At her house, Sacksin took her hand to help her down.

"Thunderation!" the driver shouted. "It's a fire! Holy Mother Mary, it's the hospital!"

Alarm bells clanged a frantic confirmation.

Sacksin abandoned Ah Toy at her door and leapt into the carriage. "Drive on!"

Ah Toy, stunned, watched the driver lash his horses up the hill. A hook-and-ladder company rushed past, firemen shouting and waving their axes. Without thinking, Ah Toy pulled her cape close and hurried after them.

At the top of the hill a wooden house burned like a torch. A gathering crowd shouted encouragement to firemen as flames licked at the neighboring hospital. Dazed patients spilled from its blaze-lit doorway.

In the eerie firelight, Ah Toy surveyed the spectators. Sacksin was not among them. He had probably raced to his hotel to protect his dogs and gold. For now, she was safe from him.

The nurse stumbled out of the hospital, her nightdress torn. The dark-haired woman stood there, looking forlorn and confused, while sightseers stared at her. The scene recalled Ah Toy's first night in Gum Shan and the El Dorado's gawking gamblers. Remembering Simone's kindness, Ah Toy took off her cape and wrapped it around the bewildered nurse.

Sophia Eastman recognized her with distressed eyes. "Thank you." Then, seeing her patients collapsed in the road, she cried, "Oh, my heavens! What shall we do?"

Ah Toy watched, fascinated, while the nurse hurried among the injured, begging the crowd to shelter them. Someone shouted that a hotel on Pacific street was deserted. The hospital's doctor, Peter Smith, entreated bystanders to take his patients there. Litters and wagons and moaning patients acted a shadowy drama while firemen beat at the blaze. Another fire company arrived, hauling an engine.

"It's the Happy Valley boys from California Company Four!" someone shouted.

A man next to Ah Toy muttered, "For mercy's sake, what can they accomplish with that wheezy Yankee-Doodle engine?"

Ah Toy stood transfixed by the fiery tragedy. She preferred it to returning home and finding Sacksin there.

Dawn broke as firemen extinguished the flames. Below, on the bay, Ah Toy saw celebratory banners flutter from the masts of congregated ships. Somewhere farther east, Li Jin would be waking. She sent him good-luck thoughts on the morning breeze.

A hand on her arm startled Ah Toy.

"Please, miss," the nurse begged, her voice hoarse with exhaustion, "will you take this man to your house?" At her side a man blinked uncomprehendingly, his head wrapped in a dirty bandage.

"No, no!" Ah Toy said, backing away. "Bad luck! Man die my house bad luck!" The danger was *chi*. Sometimes a dying person's life energy took possession of a living person. Ah Toy wouldn't risk it. Life in Gum Shan was already too dangerous.

Tears leapt to the nurse's eyes. "He's not dying! This poor, unfortunate being," she said, looking at her nearly insensible patient, "survived the steamer accident, was with difficulty rescued from the flames, and must have thought it his destiny to be burnt alive."

Ah Toy stared in horror at the man whose destiny was to be burnt alive. The nurse put a hand to her own head, as if she might faint. "He has a head injury, but he will recover," she pleaded. "We need only temporary shelter for him until we can make other arrangements."

The nurse's disregard for her own safety struck Ah Toy as reckless. To expose herself to vengeful spirits, which necessarily occupied a place of dying, was foolish. Ah Toy suspected the nurse's boldness came from the strength of dead-body *chi* operating through her.

Ah Toy was about to protest further when the hospital's doctor staggered up, his coat stained with soot and blood. "Several of the cholera patients," he told the nurse, "died from shock and exposure before reaching safe quarters."

"What this chol-ra?" Ah Toy asked in alarm. She pointed at the man the nurse held by the hand. "He chol-ra?"

Almost instantly Ah Toy heard the word echoing back to her. It skipped through the crowd like a flat stone on water, alighting, rippling, glancing off a shocked voice. It sank in apprehensive murmurs as people disappeared into the pink morning.

Oblivious, the doctor told Ah Toy, "This man has only a head injury from the steamer accident, nothing more. A few cases of cholera have come here from upriver, but be assured the illness cannot exist here to any extent. The air up the river is very different from what we enjoy here. Please, you must help us."

Upriver, Ah Toy thought, upriver was where gold lay, where Li Jin was. She bowed her head beneath the weight of this new fear.

"Thank you, thank you," the nurse was saying.

Ah Toy looked up and saw that the woman had read despair as acquiescence. Ah Toy was too overwhelmed by dread to protest.

Ah Toy woke from a fitful sleep. She changed from her night garment to her old peasant clothes and padded silently across the room.

His eyelids twitched, and he moaned softly in his sleep. He still lived. Then Ah Toy remembered her greater anxiety. Cholera, the killing sickness, lay up the river where Li Jin labored. Fear settled in like a relative intending to stay.

A rapping on her door drew Ah Toy from ominous contemplations. She threw it open, expecting the nurse.

"Reverend Taylor, miss," the visitor said. "From the Methodist mission." He removed his hat. Soulful eyes stared from beneath a shock of dark hair. "I understand from Dr. Smith you have here one of our Methodist brothers. Mrs. Taylor and I can care for the boy, so I've come for him."

"Yes, yes! Come in!" said Ah Toy, gladly welcoming him in.

The preacher clutched his hat, studying the patient. "I'm reluctant to wake him from his healing slumber. Let's let him sleep a while longer."

Disappointed, Ah Toy offered the preacher tea. She wanted these men away. She needed to think. She worried that Sacksin had robbed her of the ability.

Taylor, accepting the tea, said, "I'll just sit here." He dragged a chair to the bedside.

Ah Toy fretted still that the injured man's *chi* might invade her house. "He no die?"

"Oh, no, not this one. He's young and strong. I can tell when they're dying, you know. I've been visiting the hospital for more than a year, and I know when the soul is about to depart. I've seen it often."

Dead body *chi,* thought Ah Toy, studying Taylor. Americans take such risks.

Taylor sipped his tea and smiled shyly. "Sick and destitute members of our church have generally been cared for by the brethren in San Francisco. I have no recollection of more than three Methodists who died in the hospital."

He cradled the teacup in his hands, watching the young man sleep. "When I first came here a year ago," he said, glancing over his shoulder at Ah Toy, "the cross of intruding myself into strange hospitals, and offering my services to the promiscuous masses of the sick and dying of all nations and creeds, was, to my unobtrusive nature, very heavy. But I resolved to take it up, a decision I have never regretted."

The preacher stared at Ah Toy with soulful eyes. "You cannot imagine, miss, the wretchedness and despair I've seen. The off-scourings of nations, the city patients, confined so closely as to barely allow room between their cots for one person to pass. I had thought filthy the pay rooms, the *choice* rooms, for the privilege of dying in which a man who had money might well afford to pay high rates. But the 'lower wards' of the city patients—for which the doctor received from public funds four or five dollars a day for each man—were so offensive to the eye, and especially to the olfactories, that it was with great difficulty I could remain long enough to do the singing, praying, and talking I deemed my duty."

The patient moaned.

"In those filthy wards men often died in the night," Taylor said, watching the young man, "without anyone knowing of their departure. In the morning the bodies were collected, laid into a plain coffin, and carried out to the dead cart, the driver of which was seen daily plodding through the mud to the graveyard, near North Beach, with from one to three corpses a load."

The preacher's talk alarmed Ah Toy. She imagined vengeful spirits hovering about. "He no die?" she asked again, pointing at the sleeping man. "No die chol-ra?"

Taylor smiled at her. "Oh, no. He won't die. But the cholera, I fear, is coming. I've heard bad reports from Sacramento and the gold camps."

Apprehension enveloped Ah Toy. She imagined Li Jin dying in some filthy place, his body condemned to the dead cart.

At last the young man woke. He asked for water. Ah Toy handed a glass to the preacher to give him, and she saw Taylor look at her, as if seeing her for the first time. Now he looked curiously around her room, at her silken draperies, at her fancy gowns hung on wall hooks.

He said suddenly, as if decision had bitten him, "Miss, that fire at the hospital started in the house of a strange woman. It was God's visitation upon evil that destroyed that house. Men and women of sterling integrity and purity steadily withstand the desolating tide of licentiousness that has swept over this land. I never give up a sinner this side the gates of perdition, for we are not saved by works of righteousness but by the mercy of God through the merits of Jesus. And if you will believe in the Lord Jesus Christ, I know of nothing to prevent your being saved from sin, and washed in the blood of sprinkling, and thus prepared for heaven."

Ah Toy looked at him blankly. Then realization swept over her. He had condemned her, like the town's whispering wives.

"You know nothing!" She flung the door open. "You go!"

Taylor hurried the injured man out the door and into a waiting wagon. Over his shoulder he assured Ah Toy his prayers were with her and entreated her to save her soul.

Ah Toy stood at her door, fists clenched. "You know nothing!" she yelled at the departing preacher. What did he know of her destiny, she thought angrily, of what survival required?

The sun was bright. Ah Toy held a hand against its glare and saw men straggling up the hill. "Go 'way!" she shouted. "No look-see today!" She slammed her door shut.

Ah Toy ignored the knocking until she heard the woman's voice. Recapturing graciousness, she invited the nurse in. The preacher had taken the patient, Ah Toy told her.

"Those men outside your house," Sophia Eastman asked, "who are they? What do they want? Where do they come from?"

The protest Ah Toy heard in the nurse's voice revived her anger at the preacher's insult. "Come see me, see Chinee lady! Pay me look-see!"

"I don't understand. Please. Where do they come from?"

"Steamer! Sacramento steamer!"

"Oh, dear," said Sophia Eastman, wringing her hands. "It must be the cholera."

"Chol-ra! Men die? No, not my house! Bad spirits!"

Ah Toy rushed outside. "Go 'way! Go 'way!" She fluttered her hands at the ragged line of men. "No chol-ra! No die here!"

Sophia Eastman was behind her. "Those of you who are suffering from unusual thirst," she called out to the startled men, "from cramps, dysentery, or vomiting, come with me to the Waverly House on Pacific street. There's a doctor there."

Ah Toy could think only of Li Jin. She must speak to the steamer captains. They would know the truth of the peril. She raced down Clay street.

At Sansome street a crowd sucked Ah Toy into their agitation. Mystified, she fought through them to the Clay street wharf. There, hundreds of people scrambled aboard ships. Runners shouted departures. Baggage spilled from drays. Men yelled. Women wept. Steamer whistles blasted. Bells clanged.

As Ah Toy tried to wedge through to the Sacramento steamers, she heard the word "cholera." It slithered through the crowd like a snake. Alarmed, she slipped to the shelter of a wharf building.

"They can't escape it," said a man coming out the door. "I've seen men who apparently were in the best of health so suddenly stricken that they died in public places."

Ah Toy turned to the speaker just as he looked at her. "Why, you must be Miss Ah Toy." He smiled. "My name's Woodworth, Selim Woodworth. Mr. As-sing mentioned the arrival of a Celestial lady, and I presume you must be she."

"As-sing no high man!"

Woodworth laughed. "No, I suppose not yet. But he's ambitious and fearless. Those traits go far in this country." With a wave he indicated the mob fleeing the city. "These folks, on the other hand, fear for their lives."

"Chol-ra?"

"That's what they're running from, yes. It came here on the *Carolina* from Panama three weeks ago, fourteen of her passengers dead from it. Another half dozen ill with symptoms entered the city. One of them died here and two physicians pronounced it Asiatic cholera of the most malignant type. We've had maritime quarantine laws since last April, but no one wants to enforce them. The *Alta's* editor is an anticontagionist, but the evidence is before our eyes. It's an epidemic."

A boy shoving through the crowd shouted, "Camphor balls, sulfur pills!"

Woodworth laughed sadly. "Quack nostrums. People will try anything. Brandy, chloroform, calomel, Dover's powder, poultices of red pepper and mustard. What is needed is sanitation. These open sewers must be banned. People must stop throwing garbage in the streets. I heard that Dr. Logan in Sacramento last week insisted on clearing that city's refuse, and the bonfires lit up J Street from Third to Eighth."

As Woodworth spoke, Ah Toy watched the evacuation. Drays toppled baggage onto the clogged wharf. People fought to board ships. The noise of whistles and bells, crying babies, complaining children, fretting women, and shouting men was deafening.

Suddenly, one person caught her eye. Only the sight of Li Jin could have gladdened her more. She was not mistaken. The familiar figure shouldered recklessly toward a ship. His two dogs strained at their leashes.

Ah Toy, hugging herself in gladness, surprised Woodworth with a happy laugh.

He looked at her quizzically, then followed the direction of her gaze. "Yes, I see. I've been expecting that ship and didn't think but that she carried passengers. Of course, you are pleased. As well you should be."

Ah Toy, puzzled, glanced at Woodworth and then to where he looked. She gasped.

On a docking plank at the wharf's end she saw a trio of brightly colored paper umbrellas. From beneath them gazed the rice-powdered faces of three Chinese women.

4

I passed to-day, in one of the streets, a Chinese
female, in rich silk attire, with the celebrated
diminutive feet. She was very pale, appeared to
be in bad health.

—J. Goldsborough Bruff
San Francisco
May 26, 1851

A'sing and Lipscom propose to put them in our
Custody pay all expenses in keeping them,
procure a passage for them.

—Papers of the San Francisco
Committee of Vigilance,
July 1851

As-sing pushed back his chair, stood before his guests, and raised a glass of wine. He looked around the room decorated with paper lanterns. He had observed all the New Year traditions possible in this place. Door-god posters fended off evil spirits from his restaurant for the coming year. He had hung twenty strings of firecrackers and watched them explode in climbing blasts. From a merchant on Sacramento street he had bought a half dozen kumquat trees, the orange fruit symbolizing the coming of money.

Han had protested As-sing's insistence on sixteen courses. "For barbarians? Give them a ten-dish meal!"

"Ten-dish is second-class," As-sing had said, and hired assistants for Han and given him an extra month's wages. The cook had outdone himself. There had been egg rolls with plum sauce, savory broth from shark's fin, bird's nest soup without a trace of feathers, pork dumplings with ginger sauce. Yes, As-sing thought, this is a most auspicious New Year.

"*Yum sing!*" he said, throwing back his head and draining his third glass of sweet plum wine.

"*Yum sing! Yum sing!*" echoed his guests.

Among the Americans were four city officials, three of them aldermen.

"*Yum sing,*" said Selim Woodworth, saluting As-sing.

"Bottoms up!" said John Lipscomb.

As-sing surveyed the guests at his tables, their presence affirming his position as chief of the Chinese in Gum Shan. Every important Sze Yup and Sam Yup man in San Francisco was present, including the power-hungry Sam Yup partners Ah Low and Ah Hone. The growing wealth from their import business might rival As-sing's personal fortune, and their two daughters of joy stuck in his throat like a fishbone, but the Sam Yups commanded no recognition from Americans like As-sing did.

Selim Woodworth rose, tapped his glass with the two-pronged steel forks Han had provided the Americans, and acknowledged his host with a nod. "Gentlemen," he said, addressing the room, "if I may say a few words."

"Hear, hear!" said Lipscomb, spilling wine on his coat. As-sing squinted at the contract-labor man who courted his favor.

"Gentlemen," said Woodworth, "there are many Chinese here in California now, and they are the most interesting class of foreigners in the country."

A-he, who understood English as well as As-sing, translated for the China men.

"To all appearances," continued Woodworth, looking around the room, "they are the most sober, honest, and industrious men in this country. Their deportment is grave and dignified. They seem never to interfere in any manner with the affairs of others."

While A-he translated, As-sing watched Ah Low examine the sleeve of his tunic, avoiding As-sing's gaze. As-sing expected acknowledgment from every China man present. Each knew the honor implied by the speech was As-sing's, that no other China man could assemble important Americans at his table. As-sing noted Ah Low's withheld recognition, its subtle assertion of autonomy. The man must be watched. As-sing would tell Wah Gae.

"We also have men from the Islands of Sandwich," said Woodworth, addressing the Americans, "and from all of the Pacific islands of note, from New Zealand and Holland, and from other Asiatic countries."

A-he translated as Woodworth concluded, "But of all the people of those countries I have seen, I am most favorably impressed with the Chinese." He drank off his wine and sat to enthusiastic applause.

A waiter brought in two huge platters, eliciting even from Ah Low exclamations of pleasure for Han's duck with eight-precious stuffing. The Sam Yup man plucked his scanty mustache in approval and nodded to his host. As-sing barely acknowledged the compliment.

The China men clicked their chopsticks and feasted. The Americans, as was their custom, talked while they ate, their conversation turning to business.

This talk of business propped up As-sing's attention. Buying, selling, investing, accumulating, these things interested him. His restaurant business prospered and he trifled in imports, the Chinese-made houses in particular. Occasionally he funded, at substantial return, the smart ideas of reliable men. He expected his investment in Wah Lee's laundry on Washington street to net a respectable profit. The washerwomen at the lagoon charged six to eight dollars for a dozen pieces and, by their labor, earned more than most miners. Wah Lee charged less and worked longer hours. He would do well.

As though reading As-sing's thoughts, Robert Wells, a commission merchant and a member of the Society of Pioneers, said, "That fellow with the tacks did well, didn't he?"

"Tacks?" asked Henry Gerke, another member of the California Pioneers. As-sing had invited all the officers, hoping for Sam Brannan, who declined. As-sing dismissed the disappointment like a bothersome servant. It was not important.

"Oh, a fellow from Boston," said Wells, spearing a cube of roast duck. "He purchased a consignment of carpet tacks from a greenhorn just arrived from Philadelphia. Bought the entire lot at ten cents a paper. 'What do people want of tacks who have no carpets?' he told the seller. Then he turned right around and sold the tacks at two dollars a paper to people putting up canvas houses. Did well."

As-sing was doing well, but of late his attentions focused on the

Luminous Unity Society. He worried about his diminishing influence over the increasing numbers of immigrants. The crack in his authority created by the large numbers of arriving Sam Yup men might well become a fissure if they formed a separate society. Ah Low and Ah Hone, he suspected, had such a plan in mind. If they succeeded, they would collect money As-sing anticipated. The record of credit extended to the hundreds of China men in Gum Shan was so valuable As-sing kept the ledger with his gold beneath the bricks of his bakery floor. Control over the Luminous Unity Society and its funds was critical to his power and fortune.

As-sing pulled his thoughts from the problem as a waiter presented a steaming platter of crab in black bean sauce. The China men exclaimed their pleasure, praising the food's aroma and appearance.

As-sing wanted millet wine for this course. The waiter confessed he didn't know where to find it. As-sing, irritated, scraped back his chair.

The kitchen was a jumble of food and boxes, chopping blocks, baskets, strainers, skimmers, buckets, and scoops. Han, pink from steam and labor, scolded his assistants. As-sing, pleased by this bustle of activity, the smell, the heat, the scurry and hurry and chatter, forgot his annoyance with the waiter. He found the wine himself in a crate next to the kitchen god.

He and Han, as was proper at the New Year, had turned the image to the wall while the kitchen god was away in heaven and smeared its lips with honey. The kitchen god's annual report to the jade emperor on what he had witnessed in the past year would be sweet.

As-sing spotted Wah Gae in a corner, watching him. As usual, the man had soundlessly appeared out of nowhere, eyes watchful beneath the red cloth tied about his head. Han had fed him. A rice bowl sat empty on a box next to the motionless man, the chopsticks arranged in the triangle that had first caught As-sing's startled attention in his restaurant. It was the sign of the Triad brotherhood.

As-sing nodded. Wah Gae returned no sign, but his hooded eyes said he would wait.

In the dining room, talk drifted from one business venture to another, mostly the arrival and sale of various commodities.

"We seem at present supplied with more than we need of everything," said Frederick Woodworth, sampling Han's lichee chicken.

"Except vegetables," said Charles Minturn, examining a shred of cabbage leaf on his fork.

"And women," said Wells with a grin. Everyone laughed.

"I heard that sixty French women arrived recently," Lipscomb said, wiping his mustache with the back of his hand. "Apparently it was a wild business. None had paid her passage, and the captain offered a girl to anyone willing to pay what she owed. He did not have a single one left by the time I got there."

An alderman named Van Ness banged his glass on the table. "We will never have a proper society in this city as long as these abandoned females continue to display themselves in our public saloons and streets!"

As-sing thought of Ah Toy, seen regularly now parading the plaza in her French finery. He clenched his jaw.

"It is my opinion," Van Ness was saying, "that these boatloads of shameless women should be shipped back where they came from. They are an affront to respectable women, and a crime against the hearth of home and family."

As-sing saw Lipscomb redden.

"The incidence of crime," Woodworth said, rescuing the conversation with a topic on which everyone agreed, "is quite astonishing."

As-sing was grateful. He wished no unpleasantness at his table.

But Van Ness's suggestion that shameless women be shipped back where they came from settled into As-sing's mind like a nesting mouse.

The subject of crime engaged everyone. Reports of robbery, murder, and mayhem, usually charged to Sydney men, filled the newspapers. Everyone knew someone victimized by robbers or sneak thieves.

"I myself," said Frederick Woodworth, looking around the table, "had rather a desperate encounter with two fellows last Monday night. I left the Union Hotel about ten o'clock, and on coming out, I saw two persons standing in the door and I imagined they looked very hard at me. I proceeded towards home, however, and when I reached the corner of Montgomery, I thought I heard steps. It being very dark and foggy, I stopped and loosed my sword in its scabbard and, standing, prepared to listen to see in which direction the noise came, when suddenly a blow from one of those slung shots descended, just touching the rim of my hat. Then quick as thought an arm seized me about the waist."

He scowled and drank his wine. His listeners urged him to tell the story.

"My first thought," he said, "was to get my pistol from my right-hand pocket, but the assassin's arm prevented my getting in reach of it. I managed to reach the handle of my sword, which had been sprung from its scabbard, and withdrew it with all my energy. The person with whom I was struggling hollered to his companion, 'Knock him on the head and be quick!' And it was this second fellow, just then coming to his accomplice's rescue, who received and partly stopped my blow. He uttered a most terrific 'Oh!' and the one with whom I struggled instantly loosed his grip and they both ran. I drew my revolver and sent six balls in their direction, although with what effect I never learned. It was too dark to follow them, which I would have done and given battle to all had there been half a dozen in number, so enraged and reckless did I feel. All fear had left me, and I thought only of punishing the villains."

"You must have got the one with your sword," said Minturn.

"I believe I disfigured him for life. I presume he received the blow on the face or neck, and if so, he will always carry a remembrance of the night. The blade is as sharp as a penknife, a beautiful piece of steel. As you may suppose, I shall never part with it since it has rendered me this service."

"I am of the opinion," Selim Woodworth said, placing a hand on his brother's shoulder, "that the city's law-abiding citizens must eventually take as their duty the assurance of peacefulness and safety for their community."

A sudden silence descended on the table. Into it Van Ness inserted the question, "Are you suggesting, Mr. Woodworth, the citizens of this new state reject and negate the law of the land?"

"I am suggesting, Mr. Van Ness, the necessity, in the absence of an effective police force, of the formation of a citizens' committee for safety, for vigilance, if you will." Woodworth looked balefully around the room. "And should such a committee be organized, I will consider it an honor to be the first to sign its register!"

As-sing aborted the argument by signaling a waiter to bring millet cakes and sweetmeats.

The China men, after politely smacking their lips over the last sweet, rose to depart. They bowed to As-sing, shaking their own hands inside their sleeves. Each offered his effusive appreciation for the fine dinner, which As-sing dismissed as unworthy.

The Americans followed. Outside, As-sing heard Van Ness accuse Woodworth of proposing lynch law. The Woodworth brothers argued with him, then disappeared into the night.

Lipscomb left last, expressing an inebriated gratitude for the meal. He again promised As-sing a fair return on the labor of Chinese workers if he would provide it. As-sing assured his sincere consideration, but his thoughts were on Ah Hone's and Ah Low's potential treachery. In the kitchen, Wah Gae waited.

For two months, the red-turban Triad had been As-sing's *boo how doy,* a hired thug whose dirk protected As-sing's business interests.

When Wah Gae had reported that Ah Hone and Ah Low controlled two profitable women, As-sing swallowed a bitter envy. But when he discovered that a third woman, a particularly beautiful girl, now resided with Ah Toy, he ground his teeth in fury.

The girl's name, Wah Gae advised, was Mei-Ling. She had arrived with the Sam Yups' two women during the cholera epidemic and contracted the disease. Since she was not expected to live, her owners had put her out of the house. The missionary Tong Achik, who had found her in the street nearly delirious, took her to the new hospital. The nurse told him to take the girl to the China woman on Clay street. This was all Wah Gae had learned, except that the girl had not died.

Tonight As-sing and Wah Gae would smoke and talk more. As-sing needed to know whether Ah Hone and Ah Low were plotting to withdraw the Sam Yups from the Luminous Unity to organize a separate society. And he wanted to know more about the girl Ah Toy kept.

In the kitchen, Wah Gae sat, unmoving, eyes and body alert. As-sing signaled and the red turban followed, silent as a cat.

February 22 fell on a Saturday, a day everyone usually worked, and Washington's birthday was not an official holiday. No China man wanted to close his shop for another parade. The refusal worried As-sing. It augured a weakening authority.

As-sing, though only a spectator at the parade, had plaited his queue with red silk in respect for the first American president. Without the China men marching, the two military organizations, the California Guards and the Washington Guards, made the largest showings.

As the parade concluded, the crowd suddenly enlarged, then surged up Kearny street toward the city hall. As-sing trailed like a kite on a string.

At the corner of Pacific street a mob shouted, "Hang 'em!" As-sing edged through the crowd, learning that the excitement concerned the Sydney men arrested for assaulting a man named Jansen who kept a store on Montgomery street. As-sing knew about the crime. The robbers had fled with two thousand dollars after cruelly striking the storekeeper with a slung shot. A blow from a two-pound lump of lead the size of an egg, tied into a handkerchief, could kill a man. The ruffians had left Jansen for dead.

The city's newspapers, detailing the outrage, had inflamed citizens, already disgusted by the boldness of criminals, and accused the police and courts of corruption.

Jansen had lived, although severely wounded, and then identified two men as his assailants. It was these men, held now in the city hall, who had aroused the citizens' bloodlust. They were for hanging the accused men at once.

"Now is the time!" someone shouted. The crowd pushed forward, intent, As-sing presumed, on taking the prisoners and administering their own justice. The California Guards repulsed the mob with a show of bayonets.

The crowd booed.

"The Guards," the captain shouted, "have merely done their duty! If the prisoners are found guilty, we will personally ensure their hanging!"

The crowd cheered.

"Ah, Mr. As-sing!" John Lipscomb, the contract-labor man, loomed at his elbow. "Exciting times, hey, Mr. As-sing? Did you see one of these?" he asked, waving a handbill.

As-sing shrugged.

"It's addressed to the 'Citizens of San Francisco,' " said Lipscomb. "Listen to this." He held the paper up, reading, " 'The series of murders and robberies that have been committed in this city seems to leave us entirely in a state of anarchy. When thieves are left without control to rob and kill, then doth the honest traveller fear each bush a thief.' "

As-sing nodded. That was why he employed Wah Gae.

" 'Law, it appears,' " said Lipscomb, reading the handbill, " 'is but a nonentity to be scoffed at; redress can be had for aggression but through the never failing remedy so admirably laid down in the code of Judge Lynch. Not that we should admire this process for redress, but that it seems to be inevitably necessary.' "

The handbill closed with a recommendation that all who wished to rid the city of robbers and murderers should assemble on the morrow, at two o'clock, in the plaza.

As-sing thought the proposal a most interesting one.

He was not alone. An estimated eight thousand indignant citizens, according to the *Alta California,* San Francisco's only Sunday newspaper, assembled the next day to protest any leniency for Jansen's assailants. When a man named Coleman, shouting from the balcony, proposed the people appoint twelve among themselves to try the accused, they roared approval.

As-sing thought the crowd looked dangerous. A sudden shout or forward thrust might transform them into a maddened mob. When a man pushing a cart through the crowd hollered, "Cronks sarsparilla!" As-sing was so startled he fled down Kearny street, nearly colliding with the driver of a two-horse tram hailing passersby with a shout of "Connecticut pies! Connecticut pies!"

The next day As-sing learned that the people's jury at midnight finally conceded disagreement and abandoned deliberations. Nine had been for conviction, three admitted doubts. A disappointed crowd had shouted, "Hang them anyhow! Majority rules!" Rumors flew that a party had organized to seize the prisoners and hang them at the nearest convenient place. The decision to turn the accused over to the proper authorities for a second, legal, trial eventually dispersed the frustrated citizens. Thirty-six hours of expressed outrage had, at least, helped dissipate months of suppressed fear and fury.

On March 5 a grand jury brought indictments against the two Sydney men, Berdue and Windred, and the populace returned its collective attention to the livelier attractions of commerce and amusement. But incidents of robbery and murder in the following weeks, As-sing observed, continued about as numerous as before. His own fear was incendiarism. Despite a generosity of joss sticks to Hwa-kwang, the three-eyed fire god, he remained apprehensive.

On April 13, at three in the morning, clanging bells and shouts of "Fire!" jolted As-sing out of sleep and into terror. He dashed into the street with hundreds of other frightened citizens, but the alarm proved false. The following night at eleven o'clock the fire bell tolled again, again mistakenly. Ten days later another false alarm sounded.

On Saturday night, the third of May, at a few minutes past eleven, the fire bell again clanged its warning. As-sing wrenched himself from sleep. These alarms were becoming a nuisance, he thought, tugging on his boots. He pushed his stovepipe hat over his ears and left to investigate.

Although people jammed the street, the recent series of false alarms had greatly reduced the atmosphere of urgency. As-sing followed the crowd toward the plaza.

On the south side of the square, to As-sing's dismay, he saw flames skipping brightly behind the windows of an upholstery and paint establishment. Suddenly the flames burst through the roof. People screamed as a ball of fire engulfed the building.

Volunteer fire companies pushed through the crowd, dragging their engines. "Make way! Make way!" they yelled.

As-sing, heart pounding from excitement, noticed a strong wind rising. Horrified, he watched it snatch the fire and send it blazing across Kearny street. The City Hotel's veranda erupted in flames. Then the road planking sucked the fire under its timbers like a funnel and dispatched it in four directions.

The fire whipped down Kearny street beneath the planks, bursting forth at one building after another. The broad road, with flames crackling and sparking beneath it, looked to As-sing like a terrible trail of gunpowder. People ran first one way and then another as fire cut off passage.

Screams and shouts and crashing timbers filled the hours that followed. As-sing wandered dazed in the tide of fear and escape as one building after another succumbed to the inferno. With fascinated horror he watched a man run back and forth on the roof of a burning four-story building. Adjoining rooftops blazed, preventing escape. As the fire ascended toward its captive, As-sing saw the man resignedly cross his arms and bow his head. The roof collapsed and he spilled into the flames.

The fire followed the shifting winds north and east, igniting every wooden structure as far as Pacific street. Insanity seized some of the populace. A hysterical man shot and killed a Mexican woman for no apparent reason. On Washington street another man, suddenly deranged, blew his own brains out with a pistol. In the same neighborhood, a man, in a moment of madness, shot his wife and child, then killed himself.

The fire headed east to the bay. Hundreds of people followed, alternately panicked and hypnotized. Near Washington street, a man surrounded by flames fell from exertion. No one could rescue him, or the three men burned inside the building of Wells & Co.

As-sing, dazed by disbelief, found himself standing in a vacant lot on Jackson street, watching the fire nuzzle the office buildings along Montgomery. Across the street, in Gothic Hall, the city's most beautifully proportioned building, As-sing saw a young man pathetically trying to save his possessions. The man, seeing a drayman, shouted, "A hundred dollars! Over here!" He loaded the cart with books and boxes and sent it to an address in the outskirts.

Through the open door of the lamplit rooms, As-sing watched the man stuff his pockets with keepsakes. He plucked a print from the wall, looked around uncertainly, put down the print, packed a box, peered out at the coming flames. Then, to As-sing's surprise, the young man paused, considered, and calmly pushed four chairs to his table. He set upon it four wineglasses and filled them with wine. At their sides he placed four candlesticks and lit their wicks. For a long moment he gazed upon his room as though upon the face of a departing friend. Then he closed the Turkish-red curtains, picked up the print, and left, gently shutting the door behind him.

Minutes later As-sing watched the curtains ignite and vanish into flame. Momentarily, through the naked windows, he saw the room illuminated, prepared as if for guests, wineglasses sparkling in reflected candlelight. Then the room exploded.

The conflagration eventually consumed nearly every building between Pacific and California streets, from Kearny to the Battery. Some people fled into the brick and supposedly fireproof buildings only to flee again as temperatures inside soared furnace hot. Most of these buildings burned from the inside. Their unshuttered doors and open windows invited passing flames that entered like ravenous guests to a feast. In others, iron fire doors and shutters glowed red and swelled with heat, cutting off escape for those trapped within. In one brick building rescuers found six men roasted to death.

Throughout the night, booming detonations signaled the fire companies' desperate attempts to halt the flames by pulling down and blowing up buildings. They leveled all of Kearny street between Clay and Sacramento.

In the morning, As-sing stood stunned before the devastation. He recognized the corner of Kearny and Commercial only by the sidewalk of warm iron stove tops beneath his feet.

All else was gone.

Ah Toy pulled her shawl close against the morning chill as the rising sun swallowed the last flames. She had joined her neighbors on the Clay street hill at the first alarm and watched with them through the night. Now the fire was relenting, weakened, finally, by the absence of anything left to consume. A wind lifted the canopy of smoke, revealing a city of ruins.

"The *Niantic* storeship is gone," said a man to no one in particular, pointing to the blackened bayfront. "The *Apollo* and the *General Harrison,* too. All three of them."

Ah Toy recalled her arrival in Gum Shan and her first sight of the three ships locked between buildings snugged alongside like sister vessels. In recent months the storeships appeared daily more incongruous. Steam shovels dumping sand hills into the bay inched the city steadily eastward, and the ships' permanent anchorage farther ashore. Their black hulks now looked as if they had been dropped amid the squares of flattened buildings simply to add interest to a monotonous scene.

"Looks like they saved the shipping, though," the man said. "See those big gaps in the wharves?" He pointed. "They smashed them at the Battery so the fire couldn't run out on the piers."

A boy climbed the hill and collapsed near Ah Toy. He was black with soot and smelled sour. A woman wearing a cape over her nightdress knelt beside him. "You all right, boy?" she asked, brushing his hair from his eyes.

"Yes'm, thank you, ma'am, just tired."

"Is that vinegar I smell, son?"

"Yes'm, ma'am. I clerk for Mr. Harrison and Mr. DeWitt," he said, dropping his head in exhaustion. "We saved the store. Spilled out barrels and barrels of vinegar and flooded it. Must have been eighty thousand gallons."

The watchers continued to point out sights among themselves. Five brick buildings survived on Montgomery, and perhaps a dozen others throughout the area of devastation.

"There's the pity," someone said. "Only one month ago we got streetlamps all along Montgomery from Telegraph Hill to Rincon Point. A person could finally feel safe to walk at night."

"Especially with the citizens' safety patrols."

"It's those Sydney boys, sure."

"Well, they got themselves in the soup now. There'll be a hanging next time the police catch one of them up to no good."

"You sure those Sydney ducks set this fire?"

"Sure enough. Saw some of them myself right after the fire started. They was stealing stuff from stores and folks' belongings right out of the streets and hauling it off to their boats."

"Looks like they hauled off the whole city," said a youth, hands shoved deep in his pockets. "I reckon this is the end. There ain't nothin' left."

"Ha! That's what you think!" said a man Ah Toy recognized. He lived across the street with his wife and daughters just arrived from the East. Ah Toy had talked with the little girls as they played in their garden, so enchanted was she to see children. But the mother always came out, pinching up her face and walking as if she had a board in her back, and hurried the girls inside. Ah Toy had complimented the flowers, but the woman narrowed her mouth and eyes and did not speak. When Mei-Ling was well enough to go out and the woman had seen her, she had whipped her curtains closed.

"Why, boy," said the man, slapping the youth on the back as though to prop him up, "you listen to me. I'm an old-timer, came out in '49. I've seen this city go down four times before this, and she always gets up again. This is the most gettin'-up city in the world."

"But look down there! There ain't nothin'!"

The man laughed. "This must be your first fire. You wait. There'll be fresh starts all over the place soon as tomorrow. There's all that shipping out there, boy. Full of tables and chairs and goods to sell. It'll come ashore before the week's out, and whoever owns it will make some money, sure enough. And what's more important is that the gold keeps comin' down the rivers from the mines. No one's going to count this town down and out with all that gold still flowing in. You watch. Inside of a month she'll look a regular city again." He scratched his chin. "Just wish I had me a boatload of lumber. Whooee! Whoever does is gonna get rich this month."

The man was right, Ah Toy thought. Lumber and carpenters would be expensive for the next month. She was lucky she had already added the room for Mei-Ling.

As the sun rose, people dispersed, their watchfulness over Clay street ended. The fire had burned no higher up Clay than the plaza, but it had snaked up Sacramento street, one block south, destroying everything as far as Dupont.

"The ladies in the house on that street," whispered Mei-Ling, pointing south with her chin, "I hope they are safe."

"You must go back inside," said Ah Toy.

"As you say, Elder Sister."

Ah Toy took Mei-Ling's arm as the girl teetered up the path. Tiny scarlet sleeping shoes peeped from beneath the hem of her black satin cape embroidered in five colors.

Ah Toy had known by the exquisite clothes in the straw case Mei-Ling clutched when Tong Achik brought her that she was a mist-and-flower lady of high rank. The case held gowns of choice Sou-chong silk, embroidered with threads of gold and silver.

It was, of course, not the clothing the girl feared losing from the case she gripped so tightly. It was the book.

"Your illness may only be hiding," said Ah Toy, leading Mei-Ling to a chair. "You must not invite the waiting bandit."

"Your kindness protects me, Sister."

Mei-Ling bowed her slender beauty, reminding Ah Toy again of her startling resemblance to Tsu Yen. She had the same frail fineness, perfect half-moon brows, and cherry-blossom lips. Although only fifteen years old, she dressed her hair as a woman, in sweeps that captured her face in a shining black picture frame. Dusted with rice powder, cheeks and lips rouged red, she resembled a porcelain doll.

Ah Toy had not been surprised when Ah Low, hearing the girl survived, demanded her return. Ah Toy refused. She told him a woman, even a China woman, was free in Gum Shan. It was the law. This she knew personally from the amazing scene she had witnessed in front of a nearby boardinghouse. A black girl who worked there was sweeping the porch when the white woman who owned the house came out, scolded the girl, grabbed the broom, and threatened to strike her with it. The girl shouted at the woman, and a man passing in the street rushed up the walk and slapped her so hard he knocked her down. Then he kicked her and called her names Ah Toy knew must be bad. "A nigger don't never sass a white lady!" he had yelled in the liquid way Ah Toy now knew indicated a place called the South. "You hear me, you ornery slave trash!"

A crowd gathered to watch. A man dressed like a miner shoved through, ran up the walk, and knocked the man down. "This is a free state, mister!" He had helped the girl to her feet and told her to leave if the woman mistreated her. "You're no slave here, miss. This is a free state. Nobody owns anybody in California. You remember that. Nobody owns anybody in California. It's the law."

The incident impressed Ah Toy with its implications. She recounted it to Ah Low, but he refused to comprehend. Finally, Ah Toy had said, "You know nothing!" and paid him for Mei-Ling.

Ah Toy had not seen him again, but she had seen the red-turban man loitering. She did not know if he came from Ah Low, but she knew he spied on her.

Now Ah Toy busied herself at the stove, stoking the fire and brewing a ginger broth to strengthen Mei-Ling's delicate spirit. She reflected for the thousandth time her good fortune in this girl, so much like Tsu Yen. She had not realized how much she missed such companionship.

Although the girl was not Hakka, she spoke the dialect and amazed Ah Toy with her accomplishments. Mei-Ling could read. She could write poetry. She could sing and play the lute. Ah Toy knew only mist-and-flower ladies of the highest rank attained such art.

Ah Toy, while shopping on Sacramento street, had bought a lute for the girl. Mei-Ling whiled away the stronger hours of her convalescence singing in her birdlike voice and plucking the instrument's silken strings. She had taught Ah Toy many songs.

"Mei-mei," Ah Toy said, "you must drink this ginger broth and rest." She offered a steaming bowl.

"Elder Sister, I thank your most generous courtesy." Mei-Ling took the bowl with two hands and bowed her head. "My wish is you should not serve me. May we not purchase a servant, Sister?"

For months Ah Toy had chased through her mind the several tails of regret, vexation, and reluctance. She had indeed become a servant to this girl, slipping back into the long-ago habits of her youth on Willow lane. It discomfited the girl, for she was indebted to Ah Toy for her life. And it discomfited Ah Toy. She was accustomed now to independence. In this place, she need be no one's slave or servant.

After Sacksin's departure, she guarded her Gum Shan freedom

zealously. The experience with him had strengthened her. No man since had so pressed himself into her life. She held her head high, remained aloof, permitted nothing to interfere with her patient task of accumulating gold and waiting for Li Jin.

And then had come the day when Tong Achik knocked at her door with the wilted flower that was Mei-Ling.

"No!" Ah Toy had said, seeing the sick girl. "Go 'way!"

He had pushed past her, carrying the nearly unconscious girl to Ah Toy's bed. There he pried from the girl's fingers the case she clutched and thrust it into Ah Toy's hands. "These are her things. She values them." He had stared at the girl as though beguiled. "She cannot be left to die on the street, and there is nowhere else to take her."

"She no die here! She no die in my house!"

"Perhaps not," he said with a rare smile.

Fearing the bad luck of the girl's *chi* escaping inside her house, Ah Toy had dedicated herself to her guest's survival. She purchased healing herbs from Li Po Ti, the Sacramento street herbalist, and manufactured medicines from them. Even so, for many weeks the girl's life spirit fluttered departure like a bird in an open cage.

So afraid was Ah Toy of the girl's dying in her room that she hired a carpenter to add another to the house. The added room was the first of a long list of expenses.

Hearing that a doctor had arrived from Canton, Ah Toy sent for him. His name was Chu-san, a serious young man of scholarly countenance and solemn conduct. He wore a purple gown with embroidered sleeves cuffed in the shape of a horse's hoof. He had felt Mei-Ling's pulse and scowled. The girl's pulse above the wrist, he told Ah Toy, was so weak that it had fled to the hollow beneath her thumb.

To Mei-Ling he had said, "The masculine and feminine principles are at war in you, interfering with the six passions and seven emotions. Sometimes you are hot, sometimes cold. In the day you are listless and low-spirited, and at night you dream ghosts misconduct themselves with you. It is very serious."

Ah Toy paid him well for his diagnosis and his medicine. Mei-Ling's appetite improved. Ah Toy bought her oranges just arrived from Tahiti, and strawberries from the Sandwich Islands.

The expense of the girl's room amounted to several hundred dollars to the carpenter and paperhanger. On seeing the addition, the agent for the house, deaf to Ah Toy's protestations, increased her rent to three hundred dollars. Ah Toy, fearing dismal surroundings might tempt the girl's spirit into fleeing, draped the walls with crimson-colored silk and jade green satin, bought camphorwood chests and screens inlaid with ivory, an intricately fashioned bamboo bed, sandalwood incense, and perfume boxes containing leaves of cypress and fragrant herbs. Still, Ah Toy knew the room must seem poor compared to those of the green, two-storied house in Canton.

"Very grand and large, Elder Sister," Mei-Ling had said, "with seven rooms along the street, and two wings as deep. With many courtyards and pavilions and gardens."

She had gone to the mansion very young, when her father died, she told Ah Toy. Her mother, having no resources, was forced to sell her. A Hakka slave at the mansion cared for her until her training commenced. She had known no other life than that of singing girl and mist-and-flower lady.

Ah Toy, worried that Mei-Ling's life force might depart in longing for luxuries, tempted her appetite with rare teas of chrysanthemum and wild blackberry.

These things Ah Toy did first from fear and then from affection. Like Tsu Yen, the girl was so sweet-natured and warmhearted that Ah Toy came to cherish her companionship. She was so earnest in her wish to become well and not be a trouble. She praised every gift and gesture and was so engaging that Ah Toy regretted not even the girl's great cost. The purchase price to Ah Low had been two thousand dollars.

"Mei-mei," she said, offering a second bowl of ginger broth, "a servant I myself desire. The cost for a servant in Gum Shan, however, is many pieces of gold each month."

The girl looked puzzled.

"Mei-mei, you understand my business," Ah Toy said, smoothing the girl's hair. "Before you and the two ladies on Sacramento street came, I earned much gold that way. But now because I am not the only China lady, my customers grow fewer. Also, for many days after the great sickness, during the time when your ship arrived, I had no business. And now, because of this fire, I know from before no one will come for many days for look-see."

"Elder Sister, I wish to speak." Mei-Ling placed the bowl of ginger broth upon the table and raised herself up on her tiny feet. Clasping her hands together beneath her sleeves, she bowed her head. "You honor me, Sister, with your gifts and your house. You must allow me to repay the gold that saving my poor life has cost you."

Ah Toy protested, but Mei-Ling silenced her with a gesture. "My unworthy self requires no further gifts, please, Elder Sister. Permit me."

"Mei-mei, we have before spoken of this. You are not strong enough. You do not understand the men in this place."

"I ask that you choose such as seem estimable."

"There are none who know your ways."

"Then I shall teach them."

"Mei-mei, you have not sufficient energy."

The girl giggled, hiding her merriment behind the drape of her sleeve. "Sister, it is the ivory scepter that requires the energy, not the flower."

Ah Toy laughed at the girl's mischievous wit, and Mei-Ling dropped her sleeve and looked up at her. The black wings of her hair barely reached Ah Toy's shoulders.

"I wish this, Sister. I will guide the barbarians into the true ways of pleasure. I will teach the joy of the meeting of clouds and rain."

Ah Toy looked doubtful.

"Elder Sister, I will show the book."

After the fire, As-sing paid one hundred and fifty dollars for a tent and erected it over the scorched brick floor comprising the remains of his bakery. That night, by the light of a lantern, he pried up the bricks and peered into his underground vault. Both the record book of the Luminous Unity Society and his gold had survived.

Ten days after the fire, walls again defined their former outline at the corner of Kearny and Commercial. As-sing wrestled a flour barrel atop his nearly depleted private bank and sold the tent. On Sacramento street, at the reopened stall of a silk merchant, he wheedled a triangle of yellow and hung it above his door. The New York Bakery and the Macau and Woosung Restaurant officially reopened for business.

Most of the city's new construction was a flimsy patch of slats and canvas, but plans were afoot for buildings more permanent. The most ambitious of these projects found its way to As-sing via Lipscomb, the contract-labor man.

He appeared one day at the restaurant, begging As-sing's attention. As-sing signaled Han to bring coffee, then sat on one of the packing boxes acting for chairs.

Lipscomb drummed knuckles on the table. "John Parrott just

bought property on Montgomery and proposes to erect the city's first stone building!"

As-sing shrugged. "So?" he asked, accepting a cracked cup of steaming coffee from Han. A crate of cups had cost him ten dollars, and half of them broken.

"From China!" said Lipscomb, slapping the table and splashing coffee from the cup Han had set before him.

"What from China?"

"The stones! Parrott intends erecting a perfectly fireproof building from granite. He heard he can get it quarried in China cheap. He's already interested Adams Express in leasing the completed building!"

As-sing sucked at his coffee and said nothing, knowing Lipscomb anxious to announce his business proposal, whatever it was. These Americans, he thought, they pounce on business like a cat on a mouse. He liked that.

"Of course, Parrott will need several China boys to erect the stones," Lipscomb said, pushing his coffee cup around in the puddle on the table. "According to the import agent, they'll be cut and numbered for ready building by masons familiar with the design."

"Ah, I see."

"Now, you understand, you'll get a percentage."

As-sing shook his head. He wasn't interested in a project a year off.

Lipscomb wiped his wet hand on his pants and leaned across the table. "I'd sure like to do John Parrott a good turn, Mr. As-sing. The bank won't give him the credit he needs to get the stones unless we can promise your China boys will put them up. You pledge me that labor, I'll be at your service, as we gentlemen say."

As-sing hesitated. The pledge Lipscomb wanted cost nothing.

"What service?" As-sing asked.

"Anything in my power to render."

As-sing offered his hand and they shook.

★   ★   ★

While San Francisco rescued its prospects from ashes, As-sing heard talk return to crime. The *Herald* published its conclusion that the fire appeared beyond doubt "the work of an incendiary." As-sing doubled the fire god's joss sticks.

After a new rash of robberies, slung shots, and quickly extinguished fires of suspicious origin, the *Alta California* published a proposal for the establishment of a "committee of vigilance." The committee should board every vessel arriving from Sydney, the editor opined, and prohibit the landing of passengers whose honesty and respectability seemed dubious. Furthermore, the committee should hunt out "hardened villains" and banish them from the city.

The evening of June 10, As-sing heard that more than a hundred prominent San Franciscans—merchants, ship captains, physicians—had crowded into Sam Brannan's storerooms at Sansome and Bush. They shut the door behind them and didn't disperse until nine o'clock.

Just before ten that night As-sing heard the fire bell. He sat still as a stone, waiting, breath ragged with apprehension. There it was again! He distinctly heard two strikes upon the bell. But now nothing. The pattern repeated. Outside, he sniffed the air, smelled no smoke, heard two strokes on the fire bell again.

Men gathered in the street, sensing excitement. Rumors blew through the crowd like a monsoon. Someone said that Sam Brannan had formed a "Committee of Vigilance" earlier that evening. Someone else heard that two members, after the meeting adjourned, had seized a Sydney man named Jenkins, caught stealing a safe, and brought him to Brannan's storerooms. Word filtered through the crowd that the fire bell of the Monumental Engine House, in a prearranged pattern, signaled a general meeting of the Committee. They had reconvened to try their prisoner.

As-sing followed the growing crowd to Brannan's storerooms.

In the bright moonlight he saw Selim Woodworth knock and go in. Minutes later, Ben Ray, captain of the city police, shoved through and pounded on the door, demanding the prisoner. The door opened a crack, releasing a narrow shaft of lamplight. Someone inside declined the order and closed the door.

As-sing, fascinated by this revolt against authority, waited and watched with the crowd. At midnight they heard a voice shout, "Shoot me like a man! Don't hang me like a dog!" The door opened and a resolute-appearing figure emerged into the moonlight. He climbed a small sand knoll and faced the suddenly silent crowd, his hands jammed in his pockets.

"The prisoner has been tried and convicted by a Committee of Vigilance," he said. "He will be executed in the plaza within the hour. I call upon you, as citizens who value the gravity of the occasion, not to interfere. The Committee has sent for a clergyman to assist the man in preparing for death." He paused. "Do the people find the Committee's actions satisfactory?"

The crowd shouted affirmation. Then someone yelled, "Who is the speaker?"

"I'm Brannan."

Someone else hollered, "Who are the Committee?"

Shouts rose from the crowd. "No names! No names!"

Soon after the clergyman arrived, the Committee emerged with pistols drawn. They formed themselves into a column four men wide and twenty long. In the middle of the phalanx As-sing saw the prisoner, arms tied at his sides.

In the plaza, someone readied a rope on the flagpole, but cries protested the desecration. The Vigilance Committee column pushed the prisoner toward the old adobe building, a relic of Mexican days, which As-sing saw was the intended gallows. A rope draped from the crossbeam bracing the roof revealed a noose on one end.

Just then the police rushed the column. Police captain Ben Ray shoved in and seized Jenkins, but fell back as one Committee member threatened him with a pistol and another with a club. Citizens jumped into the melee. Jenkins went down. Revolvers were drawn. Someone shouted, "To hell with the courts! Let's take care of this ourselves!"

As-sing saw a ship captain named Wakeman grab the rope. He yanked the noose over Jenkins's head. In an excited scuffle a dozen zealous men seized the dangling rope's other end. They pulled. Jenkins jerked from the ground, legs kicking and body contorting.

As-sing, with the now-hushed crowd, watched the man convulse in the moonlight until his tongue protruded and his eyes bulged.

Satisfied, As-sing drifted up Kearny street with the dispersing crowd.

As-sing's recovering business required too much time for him to concern himself with succeeding events, but he heard about them.

A public meeting in the plaza overwhelmingly sanctioned the Vigilance Committee's conduct. It adjourned with three cheers for their actions, and the Committee commenced its avowed purpose of protecting peaceful citizens.

From newly leased quarters on the west side of Battery, between California and Pine, the Vigilance Committee organized investigations, seeking out the retreats of known criminals. The keepers of such resorts received notices of banishment; they had five days to leave the city. Committee members arrested suspected burglars and felons. Others collected testimony confirming crimes.

To As-sing's ears came accounts of these interesting activities, and more. Wah Gae, arriving silent as fog one night, his queue bound high on his head by the red cloth, reported that Ah Low and

Ah Hone had survived the fire with fortunes intact, including the two daughters of joy. They had resumed their profitable profession in the second story of a rebuilt Sacramento street import business. Wah Gae also confirmed that increasing numbers of Sam Yups were joining the benevolence society Ah Low and Ah Hone had organized.

As-sing, to maintain power, knew he must cripple Ah Low and Ah Hone. For several nights he prowled his mind for a plan. When he found it, he crept upon it, circled it, examined it, grew convinced it could work.

June 22 handed him the opportunity to launch it.

That morning, fire erupted in a frame house on Pacific street, near Powell. Summer winds off the ocean fanned the flames south and east. Firemen's attempts to pull down buildings to halt the spread of flames were thwarted by owners opposed to the action. Thomas Maguire's newly rebuilt Jenny Lind Theatre went down again. The four-storied city hall at Kearny and Pacific, saved in the last fire, disappeared in this one. Fed by the shoddy structures erected after the May 4 blaze, flames ate their way through ten city squares and large parts of six more.

The Vigilance Committee emerged from this latest excitement more powerful than before. Public outcries urged them to stronger authority. If the people did not know who set the fires, they knew whom they suspected.

Sydney men departed the city in droves. Seeing this undesirable populace flee, residents heightened their demands that unwanted residents be compelled to depart. The Vigilance Committee obliged. By the end of June they had enlisted more than five hundred zealous citizens in their membership register. They worked seven days a week, morning and night, in the fertile field of improving San Francisco society.

And now, As-sing determined to act.

He would need the favor Lipscomb promised. In the regular

courts, laws governed who could testify. As-sing didn't know the Vigilance Committee's rules, but he knew an American's testimony was never discounted.

It was Lipscomb's idea to present As-sing's proposal on July 3, while most of the city prepared to celebrate California's first Independence Day as a state. The Committee, he said, would be anxious to finish business and participate in the festivities. They would be less exacting in their deliberations.

As-sing met Lipscomb at the Vigilance Committee headquarters. Lipscomb shared the good news that several members of the executive committee were busy interrogating a new prisoner. Four witnesses and a deputy sheriff claimed to know the man was guilty of serious offenses.

A sergeant at arms named McDuffee directed As-sing and Lipscomb to the benches installed for citizens bringing petitions of complaint and evidence. Within a few minutes, he called them before the executive committee.

Stephen Payran presided with a committee reduced, as Lipscomb had anticipated, by the holiday and the important prisoner. As-sing glanced at Lipscomb, who nodded his satisfaction at the group present.

Payran wrote out As-sing's statement, repeating some words, confirming others with Lipscomb, then read it aloud: "Norman As-sing—I know one Ah Hone. I know him to be a bad man— keeps a whorehouse here. He takes sailors and others and drugs them in their drink and when asleep robs them. He was known as a robber in Hongkong. Has been guilty of arson twice in Hongkong. He also has two women of bad repute with him known as whores and reprobates and who are accessory to the fact of his stealing. I also know one Ah Low. He is a partner of Ah Hone and of the same character."

Payran poured himself a snifter of brandy. "Is that your statement, Mr. As-sing?"

As-sing nodded.

"Sign here."

As-sing scratched the Chinese character for his name.

Payran examined the mark. "We'll consider your statement, Mr. As-sing. If you want to wait, we'll have a judgment for you shortly."

As-sing, his stovepipe hat in his hands, bowed.

Outside, Lipscomb congratulated As-sing on remembering the accusations they had agreed were most injurious. "Those were the right words, Mr. As-sing," said Lipscomb. "Arson, stealing, those are the things agitating people. The testimony went just fine."

In less than an hour, McDuffee called As-sing and Lipscomb back. Payran was alone. He dipped his pen into a bottle of ink and continued writing while As-sing and Lipscomb stood before him, waiting. At last he blotted the paper with a felt pad, looked up, and said, "I'll read you the Committee's report on your petition."

He swallowed some brandy and read, "Norman As-sing and John Lipscomb, respectable citizens of San Francisco, make report, as follows, that there are occasionally arriving in this city persons of desperate character guilty of arson and robbery at home. To keep the country clear of such, they would report that Ah Low and Ah Hone and two women are of such repute and that they refuse to leave the country. They further represent that it is dangerous to the community for them to go at large and desire that the said Ah Low and Ah Hone with the two women be taken in custody by the Vigilance Committee and be sent out of the country. As-sing and Lipscomb propose to put them in our custody, pay all expenses in keeping them, procure a passage for them, pay for it, and send them away under our direction."

Payran considered As-sing over his brandy snifter. "We'll send committee members to arrest these people in the morning. What is the address?"

As-sing gave the number of the Sacramento street building and felt his mouth explore a smug smile. Ah Low and Ah Hone's society would collapse like a tent deprived of poles when the two men departed.

"And where do the women reside?"

As-sing felt the blow of inspiration like a Sydney man's slung shot. The idea was blindingly brilliant. The complaint specified two women, but didn't name them. Ship them back where they came from, Van Ness had said. Now was the time.

For nearly a year the *mui tsai*'s insults had ulcerated his mind like sores. The shame in the El Dorado and in Judge Baker's courtroom, the offense of her flaunting presence in the plaza, the affronts still festered.

And now retribution was his at last. The taste of revenge was as sweet as bean-paste mooncakes.

"Clay street," As-sing replied. "Bad woman name Ah Toy."

To celebrate Mei-Ling's recuperation, Ah Toy hired a carriage to take them to the plaza to watch the Americans observe the Fourth of July. They sat on a bench Ah Toy selected for its conspicuous location. "We must see and be seen," she told Mei-Ling.

"Yes, Sister." Mei-Ling lowered her eyes and smiled shyly from beneath her paper umbrella.

Ah Toy watched passersby stare at the beautiful girl. Having reluctantly agreed with the girl's wish, Ah Toy decided to first display Mei-Ling on a public occasion. Then Ah Toy planned to attend the weekly balls gentlemen of the town frequented and there speak selectively to those she considered worthy of the girl. No *fan qui,* she supposed, truly merited the girl's talents, nor would appreciate them, but they would pay well. Ah Toy's funds had been badly drained by Mei-Ling's unexpected expense, and the fire had, as she expected, abated her own business.

"This is a poor parade," Ah Toy said, apologizing for the half-hearted observance. The fires of May 4 and June 22, she knew, had so depleted community resources that the city had no funds for a gala celebration. Most people had been burned out at least once, many twice. The flames, Ah Toy concluded, had consumed their spirit as well as their possessions.

The festivities had commenced well enough with the California Guards firing a federal salute of thirteen guns, but a fervorless parade followed. Firemen dragged flower-decorated engines, boatmen waved banners, draymen and the Sons of Temperance tramped behind. The only participants to rouse the crowd from indifference, Ah Toy observed, were two hundred marching schoolchildren.

The absence of China men in the parade amused her. She told Mei-Ling that the old cake seller must be losing his influence, but Mei-Ling only smiled her confusion. Despite Ah Toy's recitations of As-sing's offensiveness, Mei-Ling could not understand how any merchant, even in Gum Shan, supposed himself a high man.

A city dignitary was reading something announced as the Declaration of Independence. Ah Toy appreciated the sentiment, but the words confused her, and she could see Mei-Ling tiring. During the thirty-two-gun salute signaling the conclusion of observances, they left for Clay street.

An hour later, Ah Toy heard a hubbub of men's voices, then an insistent banging on her door. She opened it to see a half dozen well-dressed men with pistols. One stuck a paper in her face and told her she was under arrest. Two others took her by the arms.

Ah Toy felt her breath leave her when the man with the paper announced they were members of the Vigilance Committee. She had heard about the hanging in the plaza.

"What you want?" Ah Toy cried, trying to pull away. Wild thoughts rushed through her mind that they had come to hang

her. But then, beyond them, she saw the cake seller standing in the
street. He was grinning at her.

The man with the paper was reading it to her. "You've been
cited, Miss Ah Toy," he was saying, "as an accessory to acts of one
Mr. Ah Hone and one Mr. Ah Low, and you are to be sent out of
the country."

"You know nothing! You know nothing!" Ah Toy shouted. She
heard a wailing behind her. She turned to see Mei-Ling weeping
and stumbling toward her on tiny feet.

"That must be the other one, boys," the man with the paper
said. "Get her, too."

As-sing arranged his implements on top of the flour barrel in his
bakery: oil lamp, wire, jar, pipe. He warmed the wire's tip over the
lamp's flame, dipped it into the jar, and twisted. A gummy lump ad-
hered. He held the wire to the lamp, softening the substance. Again
he dipped the wire, warmed the clinging material until it expanded,
then pressed it into the bowl of his pipe.

In the distance he heard firecrackers and pistol blasts discharged
in holiday revelry. The sound mocked his failure.

Triumph over his enemies had been so brief. Only hours after
the arrest, Lipscomb had dashed into the restaurant, interrupting As-
sing's celebration dinner of roasted duck. "I just saw the two China
ladies heading up Clay street in a hired buggy," he gasped, "free as
birds!"

As-sing had rushed to the Vigilance Committee headquarters.
The clerk searched the day's orders, found the pardoning document.

Now, warming the bowl of his pipe and contemplating its vacant bliss, As-sing recalled his mortification at the clerk's droned words.

"It's a letter to the executive committee," the clerk announced. "It says: 'I have examined the evidence adduced on behalf of the defense of the prisoners Ah Low, Ah Hone, and the two females, and I am satisfied that there exists on the part of plaintiffs a conspiracy to deprive the above-named persons of their liberty, and reposing confidence in the wisdom of your body, I trust that the simple application for their release, here made, will meet with your ready assent, as I believe the above charge can be by me proven, should you be disposed to hear the evidence."

"Who wrote?" As-sing demanded.

"It says, 'I have the honor to be Very Respectfully Your Observant Servant, S. E. Woodworth, Mandarin of the Celestial Empire and China Consul,' and it's endorsed and filed this day, July fourth, 1851."

The clerk examined an attached sheet. "This is in Mr. Payran's writing, a mighty nice hand he has, and he signed it. Says at eight o'clock Mr. Woodworth appeared, and 'on motion and Mr. Woodworth representing himself as Consul for China he be allowed to appear for Ah Hone and Ah Low and the two women—report of Mr. Woodworth accepted and Chinese prisoners discharged.' "

As-sing inserted the rounded mass on the wire into his pipe, twirled it, removed the wire. He leaned against the wall and held the long pipe's bowl over the lamp's flame. Sustaining the necessary heat, he sucked deeply.

The warm, sweet smoke filled his throat and lungs. It curled into his mind, wrapping regret in solace. Disappointment retreated. An exquisite dreaminess lifted and drifted him in smoky embrace.

Through its succor he recalled the Vigilance Committee clerk saying, "Well, you can always get the brothel inspector to keep an eye on these folk."

A brothel inspector. So now the Vigilantes had an officer for inspecting brothels. As-sing inhaled deeply. Brothels, he thought, as his mind spiraled pleasantly into unseen clouds. A man might become a "Melican milliner" in such a business. And then he thought nothing more as his mind drifted gently away.

A week after her arrest, Ah Toy's anger finally faded. Once she had seen As-sing, she had not been afraid, only furious. The cake seller was nothing, an annoyance, ridiculous. She disdained his mock authority. She had spit her contempt at him.

At the Vigilance Committee headquarters, trusting experience, she demanded to see Judge Baker. She lost courage briefly when told the Vigilance Committee, not the courts, acted on behalf of the people now. She regained it when the executive committee arrived for the evening session. Selim Woodworth was a member.

Woodworth remembered their meeting on the wharf and listened with interest to her frenzied protests that As-sing had done this thing to her. Ah Low and Ah Hone asserted their innocence, too, and named As-sing responsible.

It was Mei-Ling's fright that most distressed Ah Toy. The girl had just regained strength, and this fearful experience had weakened her spirit again.

This gift will please her, Ah Toy thought, handing the merchant three dollars for a dozen cormorant eggs. Hen's eggs cost five dollars. These were three times as large. She watched as he carefully packed the blue delicacies into her basket.

In her basket, too, was a jar of costly cream for Mei-Ling's fair skin. Li Po Ti prepared it from powdered pink pearls, ginseng, and ginkgo leaf and scented it with the essence of almond seeds. The stale-smelling herbalist betrayed no smirking amusement now when Ah Toy requested a packet of crushed roots of the blood-tonic lily that prevented conception. Her trade was too valuable.

It was a fine morning for a stroll while Mei-Ling entertained the lawyer Ah Toy had selected at last night's ball. The only cloud on the day had been the fire bell's ominous clang just as the lawyer arrived.

The two of them had stood silent, listening. "It's not a fire, it's the Vigilantes," the lawyer said when the signal repeated. "They're calling up a general meeting. They've got through trying Stuart."

Ah Toy remembered seeing Stuart, a sullen man hunched behind bars in the Vigilantes' headquarters. The confessions of the star criminal, she suspected, eclipsed her infraction.

When the clanging ceased, the lawyer handed Ah Toy three hundred dollars. She was carefully competitive. French women demanded four.

Now Ah Toy meandered from the plaza to the dress shop. Mrs. Cole chirped a welcome and pirouetted. "It's the latest fashion. What do you think?"

Ah Toy had never seen anything like it. The skirt of the pink satin dress stopped three inches below Mrs. Cole's knees, exposing trouserlets of matching fabric.

"It's called the Turkish costume, and the design is quite catching on."

Before Ah Toy could think what to say, the door opened.

"No, no, no," said Simone, laughing, sauntering in, "bloomers not for lucky Chinese lady."

"Then, Mademoiselle Jules," said Mrs. Cole, "perhaps the fashion is to your liking?"

"Bloomers, no. Trousers, *oui.*" Simone laughed, thrusting her hands into the pockets of her sporting pants. A frock coat, silk hat, and kid gloves completed her outfit. She had worn men's clothing to cross the Isthmus of Panama on muleback, she once explained to

Ah Toy. After tasting the freedom of male attire, she adopted it.

"I go now to the hanging," said Simone, tucking an escaped curl into her hat.

"Hang?" said Ah Toy in alarm. "Who hang?"

"Oh, just Stuart, a Sydney fellow."

Ah Toy thought of the sullen man whose presence may have saved her and pitied him.

Simone drew Ah Toy's unresisting arm through her own. "I shall escort lucky Chinese lady to hanging, no?"

Ah Toy felt suddenly vulnerable, as though the hanging might have been hers were it not for Stuart. Weakly, she followed Simone into the throngs of spectators heading toward the wharves.

In front of the newly rebuilt Adelphi Theatre, they saw Irene McCready.

"How nice to see you again, Miss Ah Toy," Irene said. "I hope you enjoyed the ball. You were quite the belle."

Ah Toy smiled politely. Most of the women in town attended the fancy dress balls, even some wives. Americans, French, and Mexicans all joined in the waltzes, polkas, and gallopades. Ah Toy enjoyed watching the Mexican women dance; they moved with such languor and indolent grace. But it was, she saw, vivacious French women who had the eyes of American men. Excepting an occasional march or mazurka, American men preferred watching to dancing. She had found the lawyer among them last night, lounging against the bar filled with cut-glass decanters, drinking brandy smashes.

"Simone," Irene was saying, "you are just the person I want to see. Tell me, dear, what is this *tableaux vivants?*" She pointed to a posted playbill.

"Ooh-la-la," laughed Simone. "Mademoiselles make living picture, no?" The playbill advertised the theater's reopening under the management of Mademoiselles Racine, Adelbert, and Courtois.

Tickets for box seats cost five dollars. "Ooh, so good for French ladies, no? Twenty-five francs!"

Simone explained that the Frenchwomen assumed the costume and pose of well-known paintings and statues, primarily those displaying the female figure in various states of undress. An evening's entertainment consisted of several such artistic impostures, revealed teasingly behind slowly opening stage curtains. Her eyes sparkled. "So popular, to undress, no?"

The three women laughed. Irene unfurled a green silk parasol the color of her gown and nodded toward the theater. "Everything is being rebuilt so soon," she said. "Really, it is perfectly wonderful the recuperating aspect of California. I expect in another month or so the city will be finished again and ready for another fire."

"No, no," said Simone, leading the women down the hill toward the bay. "No more fire. Sydney men will go away or Vigilantes hang them."

Ah Toy felt her throat catch as Simone led them out on the California street wharf. Across from it, on the Market street wharf, loomed a derrick. It resembled a guillotine. Below, in the bay, men in small boats rowed toward it for a better view.

In the crowd, Ah Toy heard people defending the Vigilantes' actions. "The wretched state of things," she heard a man say, "with the law ineffectual, with lives and property constantly endangered by criminals, requires the desperate acts of desperate men." The Committee was composed, another said, of the city's most responsible men, good men, who patrolled the streets, guarding the citizens. From their own pockets they paid the Committee's expenses, five hundred dollars monthly to rent their meeting room, security for their prisoners, the cost of investigations and trials and deportations. "The proof is in the pudding," said someone behind Ah Toy. "We've had no robberies or murders since they hanged Jenkins."

The crowd suddenly hushed. Ah Toy saw a column of two hundred Vigilantes, arms linked, march onto the Market street wharf. Irene McCready spotted Colonel Stevenson in the front rank. Earlier in the day, she told Ah Toy, when the clanging signal drew a crowd to the Vigilance Committee headquarters, it was Stevenson who announced the imminent hanging of the Vigilantes' prize prisoner.

James Stuart, Stevenson reported, in the week since his arrest had confessed to numerous crimes. Stuart had beaten a ship's captain and his wife nearly to death, robbing them of a paltry one hundred and seventy-five dollars. Stuart had been the chief actor in crimes throughout the state, not least the February brutality against the storekeeper Jansen. The man had been fairly tried and found guilty. He would hang at two o'clock.

Behind the column of two hundred Vigilantes marched a phalanx of two hundred more, ten abreast and twenty deep. Between the two contingents walked a man with his hands tied behind his back. He looked grim, but his stride never faltered. No one tried to interfere. The Vigilantes had jammed the wharf, making rescue impossible.

"There's Stuart," someone said. "And there's Captain Wakeman. He's the one what put the rope on Jenkins."

The ship captain had been chosen executioner for this second hanging. He threw a stout rope across the derrick's uppermost beam. From the short end he solemnly fashioned a loop and snugged it tight. He offered Stuart a blindfold. Ah Toy saw the prisoner shake his head.

Wakeman handed Stuart's hat to a man nearby, then pulled the noose over the prisoner's head. The man holding the hat shoved it back on Stuart's head.

Wakeman fed the rope out to the massed Vigilantes. Without ceremony, he signaled. As one, they pulled.

Stuart's hoisted body jerked violently, then hung from the derrick beam as motionless as forgotten cargo. A breeze caught up his hat and it blew off into the bay.

Behind Ah Toy, two men whispered.

"The people up at Downieville hanged a woman last week."

"I don't believe it!"

"It's true. Five hundred people saw her pull the noose over her own head. She announced she had nothing to say except that she would do it again if she was so provoked."

"What'd she do?"

"Stabbed a man. Killed him."

"Hang a woman! Ain't that something, though!"

"She was only a Mexican prostitute."

Ah Toy felt faint. She grasped Simone's hand.

"Nonsense," said Simone. "Lucky Chinese lady not to worry such nonsense."

A woman in front of them pulled a shawl around her shoulders and cocked her head. "Serves them all right," she said to no one. "Now maybe we'll see some improvement in society in this town. Make this place decent for decent folks."

A vendor startled Ah Toy, hollering, "Boston pippins! Boston pippins! Just arrived! Packed in ice! Only twenty-five cents! Here they go! Here they go!"

Ah Toy forced a smile and bade Simone and Irene farewell. She bought four cold pippins and headed home with the dead man's image hanging in her mind. A knot of dread tightened inside her. She tasted old panic from the time of hunger and begging and the fearsome dogs. Not since Sacksin had she felt so threatened. The Vigilantes operated outside the law, she now understood. If Selim Woodworth had not released her and Mei-Ling, would they have sent her away? Or would they have hanged her like the Sydney man and the Downieville woman?

A vision of the woman placing a noose around her own neck trotted into Ah Toy's mind, dark as death. It snapped against her breath like the jaws of the dogs of the Great Dog mountain. Ah Toy hurried up the Clay street hill, fleeing the portent, clutching her basket of cormorant eggs, pippins, and the pink cream of powdered pearls.

A half block from her house she saw the lawyer. He leaned against her doorway, head down, hands in his pockets, scuffing dirt with his shoe.

He caught sight of her. "I want my money back!" he yelled.

Across the street, Ah Toy saw the pinch-faced woman peer from behind a curtain.

"I want my money back!" the lawyer repeated. "That girl's sick, and I want my money back!"

"Sick? What way sick!"

"She's fevered hot as blazes. She's too sick to do anything like you said she would. She couldn't barely even sing and play that silly lute. I've been waiting here for hours and I want my money back!"

Ah Toy grabbed his arm and pulled him inside. She had seen from the corner of her eye the skulking red-turban man. Her business was not for the eyes and ears of As-sing's *boo how doy*. She could take no chances in a country where cake sellers were high men and bankers hanged criminals.

Mei-Ling sat crumpled and sobbing on the red-dragon coverlet, her face flushed and damp beneath the rice powder.

The lawyer stared at her, miserable and silent.

"You wait," Ah Toy told him, helping Mei-Ling to her feet.

"Sister," Mei-Ling said, drawing a sleeve across her tears, "I can make the clouds and rain. I sang the songs of the moon-season flowers and the ninth-month asters."

"Hush," said Ah Toy, taking the girl's hand and feeling the heat of her skin. "You must go to bed. I will bring chrysanthemum tea."

Ah Toy told the lawyer to wait for her.

"I'm not going anywhere," he said, "until I get my money back."

Mei-Ling touched a hand to the wall for support, thumb and little finger spread, index and middle fingers together, fourth finger down. The girl's every movement, Ah Toy knew, was intended to please any eye beholding her. The foolish lawyer didn't appreciate such training.

Ah Toy felt Mei-Ling's forehead as she lay against the pillow. The fever was passing. "You will sleep, Mei-mei, and be well again. I will bring tea."

"No tea, please, Sister. I will sleep if you will forgive my failure."

"Sleep, Mei-mei. There is nothing to forgive," Ah Toy said, smoothing the girl's hair. "Mei-mei," she said in afterthought, "did you show the book?"

"No, Sister," Mei-Ling said, closing her eyes.

Ah Toy took the book and slipped quietly from the room.

That night, as Mei-Ling slept, her fever broken, Ah Toy sat before the open front door of her house. The air was balmy and the moon bright. She could see the silhouetted hills across the bay. They seemed close enough to toss a stone against. She wished she could see the mountains where Li Jin toiled.

It was a night bright like this that she first came to her house, Ah Toy recalled, with the moon hung in the sky like a lantern. She remembered her frightened confusion that night when the drunken man forced her to show herself. She could not remember his name, there had been since then so many like him.

But now the offensive look-see was behind her. Now she was, as Simone had always insisted, valuable.

In her lap, Ah Toy counted again the twenty-dollar goldpieces. Fifteen. Moonlight glinted from her three hundred dollars. The lawyer had kissed her shyly when he left and asked if he could visit again. "Not the girl," he said. "You."

The gold clinked dully as Ah Toy counted it again. The sound reassured her, calming the fear that seized her with the thought of the hanging woman. Money, lots of money, this promised protection. Money bought safety, comfort, freedom. Three hundred dollars. It had not been difficult. The lawyer was no experienced mandarin, wise in the ways of Mei-Ling's arts. The lawyer had never been to a house of peony flowers. Ah Toy showed the book, turned its pages, watched the man's eyes widen with arousal. Then, for herself, she pretended graceful shoulders and tiny feet. She pretended she was one of the lovely ladies of Willow lane, shyly teasing, tempting and caressing, admiring, stroking, whispering, at once coy and passionate, pretending.

Lucky Chinese lady, she thought, recalling Simone's prediction.

Ah Toy gazed into the distance. In Canton one saw no extended scenery. There, every visual charm was concentrated. But here, in this Gold Mountain place of her destiny, stretched this breathtaking panorama promising untold possibilities.

5

NUISANCE —Atoy, the Chinese woman, was charged with keeping a disorderly house on Clay st. She having removed, the charge was withdrawn.

—*Alta California*
December 14, 1851

CHINESE EMIGRATION. —The following table, compiled with great care, from the memorandas kept by S. E. Woodworth, Esq., exhibits the number of Chinese who have arrived at this port since the 1st day of January, 1852, from China. . . . It will be seen that the entire number is 18,040.

—*Alta California*
August 13, 1852

Elder Sister, you must not do these things for me."

Ah Toy placed the steaming chrysanthemum tea on the table next to Mei-Ling's bed and hushed her. "Do not concern yourself, Mei-mei. I shall engage a servant when I find someone trustworthy." She bathed the girl's brow with a cloth dampened in costly sandalwood perfume. She had money now, from the lawyer, from others. The food tins on the high shelf had filled again, as had the box buried beneath her bed. She accumulated steadily the dowry intended for Li Jin. He would come to her soon. She knew it.

A sudden pounding on the front door startled her from her reverie. A voice shouted, "Open up! You, in there, open up! Vigilance Committee!"

Ah Toy felt her throat tighten as though a noose had snugged around it. The Vigilance Committee! Was this more of As-sing's poison? Had they come to hang her? The figure of Stuart twisting from the derrick leapt into her mind.

"Come on! Open up!"

"Oh, Elder Sister!"

Ah Toy shushed Mei-Ling and hurried to the door.

"Name's Clark, John Clark," said a man in shapeless trousers and soiled shirt. "Vigilance Committee brothel inspector." He pushed past her. "No customer today, huh?" he said, tipping his hat up with a thumb and surveying the room.

"What you want!" One man alone, with no rope. She peered past him through the open door. No sign in the street of the cake seller. Did she see the red-turban man? She wasn't sure. She closed the door and turned to see stone-gray eyes appraising her.

"Like I said. Brothel inspector. Got a couple complaints on you, missy. You cheating your customers?"

"You know nothing!" Outrage shouldered aside her fear. The old look-see customers cheated her, she didn't cheat them. They got what they paid for, and so did the lawyer. He would not complain. He knew nothing of true mist-and-flower ladies. She was as good as the French women, and they had big feet, too.

"You know nothing!" she shouted, incensed by the accusation.

"Oh, I know a thing or two, I do," he said, staring at her with stony eyes. "I know I'm the Vigilance Committee brothel inspector, the *chief* brothel inspector." He leaned on the word.

Ah Toy had seen power. She knew when a man possessed it. This one wore it like a mandarin. Defeated, she watched the barbarian high man fill her house with his authority. He strolled among her things, fingered the screen of the Eight Immortals, the porcelain figure of Kwan-yin, the red satin coverlet with the golden dragon embroidery.

Ah Toy collected her fear into a small space and contained it there. This was a high man, but he was still a man. And she had learned her value as a woman. She knew what to do.

Ah Toy smiled coyly, offered a chair with a plump satin cushion. "You take glass wine, please?"

Clark dropped into the chair. "Sure, why not?"

Ah Toy felt his eyes follow her as she filled two wineglasses. She sipped from one as he drained the other in a swallow. She refilled his glass, smiling encouragement.

Clark had drunk three glasses of her claret when she slid the book onto his lap. His eyes widened as she opened the book's covers wrapped in crimson silk and showed the first painting.

Mei-Ling's rare book of thirty-six silk paintings mounted on heavy rice paper reflected the art and poetry of the Yuan dynasty. Opposite each painting a poem described the activity depicted. Ah Toy could not read, but she knew each picture's title. Every mist-and-flower lady on Willow lane did.

She watched Clark's eyes consume the silken picture. In colors of pink and cream, a beautiful woman sat on a rock with her legs apart. A man leaning over her directed his ivory scepter toward the delicate pink of her flower.

"Butterfly seeking fragrance," whispered Ah Toy, gently brushing Clark's hand with her own as she turned the page to the second painting.

"Letting bee make honey," she murmured breathily into his ear. The second painting showed a woman lying on her back, legs raised in wide welcome as she directed the man's scepter to the heart of her flower. The artist had painted her lover's expression as anxious and curious, but the woman's pretty face he suffused with ravenous appetite.

Ah Toy saw Clark's color heighten, heard his breath quicken. She turned the page. Trailing her fingers on his, she whispered, "Lost bird returns to forest." Against an elegant embroidered couch the painter had depicted a beautiful woman, her expression rapturous, legs lifted high, hands greedily grasping her lover's thighs and directing him to her.

"More wine, please?" Ah Toy asked, her voice velvet with promise.

Clark looked at her with hungry eyes. She lifted a glass and took wine into her mouth. Then she placed his hand against her neck and pressed, so that it was he who drew their mouths together. Ah Toy passed the wine slowly from her mouth to his. He swallowed with a gulp. With the tip of her tongue Ah Toy licked a drop from his lips.

She filled the glass again, watching Clark's eyes fasten on the book's fourth picture. Again he took wine from her mouth and with his eyes devoured the silken portrait.

"Starving horse," Ah Toy breathed into his ear. The woman's legs rested on her lover's broad shoulders, and her flower fully embraced his ivory scepter. The artist had captured on their lustful faces the moment of supreme ecstasy.

Clark turned to Ah Toy. Desire suffused his face. She smiled shyly as she unfastened her dressing gown. Head bowed, she dropped the gown from her shoulders and stood naked before him. She heard his quick breath and looked up at him. "What you like?" she asked with an enticing smile, drawing him toward the red satin embroidered with the golden dragon. "Butterfly? Bee make honey? Starving horse?"

Clark returned two days later. He staggered into her house as if he lived there, bragging he had just met the governor. Ah Toy smelled liquor on him and something else, something decayed.

"Yes, indeed, sure enough, 'His Accidency' came calling down to the headquarters," Clark said, helping himself to wine. "That's what we call Governor McDougal, you know, seeing how he got the job by accident, from Burnett resigning it. He's okay by me. Seems to approve the Committee. Course, we got us a couple of important criminals now. Stuart talked up a storm 'fore we hung him, and we got us some of his pals, a mean little weasel named McKenzie, for one."

Clark spit a reddish brown gob from the side of his mouth. Ah Toy watched it land on her floor like a large, wet bug. She sat on the edge of her chair, masking repugnance with a smile. Clark wiped his mouth on his sleeve. Ah Toy said nothing. She would give him no excuse to hang her. As-sing, she knew, had sent this plague upon her house. She would survive it. She summoned thoughts of Li Jin and her destiny to sustain her.

"McDougal's okay by me. His Accidency's a good drinker. Sergeant at arms brought in five gallons of brandy and ten cheeses."

That was the bad smell, Ah Toy realized, cheese. She could eat almost any barbarian food but their rotted milk.

Ah Toy brought Clark the book, but he pushed it aside. "Save your pretty pictures for another time, missy. Let's see the real thing." He grabbed her and buried his coarse beard against her neck.

Ah Toy tried not to breathe the barbarian's stink, but she did not protest. This was not a man to oppose. As long as the Vigilantes ruled, she must please him. He was her protection. They both knew it.

After that, Clark fell into a routine, sauntering into Ah Toy's house three times a week to brag about his Vigilante exploits and parade the names of big men he knew. He treated her familiarly, helped himself to her wine, to her food, to her.

He dropped onto her bed in his dirty boots. She took them from his feet and said, "Much dirt. Not like dirt my house."

Clark laughed. "Well, ain't that too bad! I been out patrolling on Battery street, and that's a mighty dirty job." He folded his hands behind his head and gazed at her ceiling drapery. "Course, if I had me some of them patent leather shoes like I seen on the fancy gents that visit you and your friend . . ."

After Ah Toy bought him the patent leather shoes, his demands increased. He wanted a gold watch. Ah Toy bought one for him. Then he wanted a pearl stickpin, a brocade vest, kid gloves, a gold ring with a diamond in it.

He helped himself to money. "Just a little pocket change for the barbering saloon," he said, grinning at her and taking two twenty-dollar goldpieces from her bag. "Get myself fancied up a bit like those lawyers getting rich off the land-commission cases." He laughed. "Course, they're the only lawyers working these days. Hasn't been a case of crime before the Recorder's Court in a week, thanks to the Vigilance Committee."

He poured himself a glass of wine. "We got plenty of lawyers favoring the Vigilance Committee now. Two of them come down to headquarters this afternoon with a fancy blue satin banner all stitched up pretty by the ladies of Trinity Church, a testimonial of their approbation."

Ah Toy listened politely and praised his exploits. She absorbed his presence in her life. For now, it was her destiny.

One evening, about a month after Clark first appeared at her door, he arrived with a half-consumed bottle of brandy. "Just come from a general meeting of the Vigilance Committee," he bragged, waving the bottle and grinning. "Going to be a hanging in the morning. You and your little friend ought to get down to the waterfront about eight o'clock, get yourselves a good view of the show. Going to hang that weasel McKenzie, and another of Stuart's pals, an evil character named Whittaker. Going to hang them from the yardarm of a ship in full view of Telegraph Hill. That'll send a message to the Sydney boys."

Ah Toy shut her eyes as an unbidden image of Stuart hanging from the derrick transformed into the Mexican woman.

The next day Clark arrived drunk and angry. "They got McKenzie and Whittaker!" he shouted. "Snatched the two of them pretty as you please right out of the Committee's rooms. Sheriff Hays and his deputy and that two-faced governor and the mayor."

He slammed his fist into Ah Toy's table. "Maybe some of your fancy friends was in on it, huh?" he said, glaring at her as though she had conspired with them. "Maybe some of the Law-and-Order gents you meet at them fancy dress balls over at the Exchange, huh?"

Ah Toy protested she knew nothing. Clark hit her. "Get me something to drink and shut up."

The next night was Wednesday and she attended the ball at the

California Exchange wearing rice powder and rouge to conceal the bruise. She flirted in the coquettish way of French women and invited a banker to visit Mei-Ling.

Ah Toy did not see Clark again until early Sunday evening. She and Mei-Ling had heard the fire bells that afternoon signally frantically. Ah Toy suspected their meaning and ignored them.

Clark burst into her house drunk on wine and victory. "Well, let's see those Law-and-Order boys steal McKenzie and Whittaker now! They'll have to cut 'em down to get 'em!" He laughed loudly and pranced an impromptu jig. "What did you think of them two dancing in the air, huh?"

He dragged Ah Toy into an improvised polka and galloped her around the room.

"No see," Ah Toy said, avoiding Clark's heavy boots as he thudded her floor.

Clark stopped. "Must have been fifteen thousand people down at the Battery. You didn't see us hang McKenzie and Whittaker?"

Ah Toy shook her head no.

Clark scowled, then took a long drink from the bottle he carried. Waving the bottle, he bragged how he and thirty others had recaptured the prisoners. "Snatched 'em from the city jail during a Sunday prayer service," he snarled, "and whisked 'em across town in a carriage. Hanged 'em from beams over the Committee's rooms."

Ah Toy saw the bodies in her mind's eye, twisting, turning.

"You shoulda been there." Ah Toy heard annoyance in his voice that she had not witnessed his triumph.

Suddenly he slammed his bottle onto her table. He glowered at her with bloodshot eyes. "You slant-eyed whore, I been five days on a lookout so's we could administer true justice, while you been entertaining your fancy gents!"

Ah Toy barely registered the threat in his voice before he hit her. After that, he beat her regularly.

Two weeks after the Vigilantes' double hanging, while Mei-Ling entertained a banker, Ah Toy strolled down Clay street toward the harbor. The talk at the ball last night was all about the *Flying Cloud,* one of the new California clippers. It had just arrived on the fastest voyage ever between New York and San Francisco. Ah Toy needed to see this special ship, to hold its image in her mind. During bad times with Clark, she could conjure it and imagine returning to China aboard it with Li Jin.

The North Beach wharf teemed with sightseers admiring the long, sleek hull. Atop one whiplike mast a blue, red, and white swallowtail house flag flapped in the breeze.

The *Flying Cloud* looked fast, even at anchor, but what interested Ah Toy was the story told at the ball. The ship's captain, she heard, fell ill early in the voyage. It was his wife, the ship's navigator, who brought the vessel around the Horn and safely to port on the fastest journey ever.

Ah Toy stared at the ship's figurehead, an angel holding aloft a trumpet, thinking on the Yankee woman's courage. Suddenly she heard the words of her childhood. Turning, she saw China men debarking from a ship at the end of the pier. They were speaking her Hakka dialect.

Impulsively, Ah Toy put out her hand to stop a passing boy. He was no more than fifteen years, tall like herself, and thin. "Where do you come from?"

He looked at her, amazement in his eyes.

Ah Toy laughed, realizing how strange she must look to him in European clothing. "Where do you come from?" she repeated.

Someone called out for Sam Yup men to register for the benevolence society.

"I must go," the boy said, looking at her warily.

"You have no hurry. Talk to me. You are Hakka?" Ah Toy interrogated him, but the boy was not from her village.

He had fled Kwangsi province, he told her, like most of the men just arrived. The countryside there suffered greatly now from the God Worshipers.

"Missionaries?"

"Not missionaries," said the boy. "These God Worshipers believe in the Eighteen Hells of Buddhism, make food offerings in the Taoist fashion to family altars, and read the Christian Bible during their ceremonies."

He described how Hung Hsiu Chua, the leader of these God Worshipers, had proclaimed a *taiping* state, the Heavenly Kingdom of Great Peace. His zealous followers, in the name of *taiping,* shattered idols, ransacked and burned temples, murdered monks, destroyed villages, slaughtered old men and women, and pressed young men into their service.

"Families have been utterly broken up," said the boy, "and husbands seek for their wives, wives for their husbands, children for their parents. Hunger haunts the countryside, and many flee to the cities and to here."

Ah Toy saw hunger in his face and tasted again the dry dirt of ground-up brick her mother had fed her.

She smiled at him. "You will eat here, and you will be safe."

"I must register with the society, lady," he said, looking toward his shipmates and the man they surrounded. "There is a *wui kun* for Hakka people?"

Ah Toy followed his gaze and saw Ah Hone. "That man is Sam Yup," she said. "Many Sam Yups have come here, many Sze Yups. At first there was only the Luminous Unity Society, one *wui kun* for all China men, but now the Sam Yups have organized their own, and the Luminous Unity is mostly Sze Yup. There is no *wui kun* for Hakka men."

As Ah Toy explained the formations of the Chinese companies, she glimpsed a drunken sailor lurch from the crowd surrounding the *Flying Cloud*. He took a knife from his belt, and suddenly the Hakka boy's head jerked back. *"Aaiii!"* he screamed.

"Dog! You dog!" Ah Toy yelled. The bleary-eyed sailor grinned foolishly. In one hand he held his knife, in the other the boy's severed queue.

"Got me a souvenir," said the sailor with cheerful effort. He held up the black braid to admire.

Ah Toy snatched the queue from him.

"Hey, lady!" he bellowed. "Why'd you go and do that? I want me a China man's pigtail."

"You know nothing!" Ah Toy screamed. The stupid barbarian had visited an evil omen on the boy. The boy's hair was his glory and his manhood. Without his queue he would be looked upon with contempt by his countrymen.

She handed the boy his lost dignity. He took the queue in two thin hands and looked at her with open anguish. Tears streamed down his gaunt cheeks.

Ah Toy grabbed the sailor by his jacket. "You know nothing! You stupid dog!"

The sailor grinned sheepishly as Ah Toy dragged him down the pier. The weeping boy followed, carrying his hair.

Ah Toy knew where to go. The Vigilance Committee offices were on the west side of Battery, between California and Pine, just two blocks from the Central Wharf. In minutes they were there.

Ah Toy glanced at the twin beams projecting above her, where the dead men must have hung. She put the image from her mind and rapped on the door.

To the sergeant at arms who opened the door, she said, "Arrest bad man!" She pushed the confused sailor forward. "Bad man cut hair! Very bad!"

The Vigilante looked at the sailor with amusement. "Well, ma'am, I'm sorry, but this ain't no concern of the Vigilance Committee."

"You know nothing! Where John Clark? He here?"

"Clark? Why?"

Ah Toy thought quickly for the word Americans used. "I Clark mistress!"

The Vigilante laughed. "Well, that may be, and you can bet we'll be asking him about it," he said, grinning at her, "but the Vigilance Committee don't concern itself with sailors what slice pigtails. You'd best haul your prisoner down to the Recorder's Court."

Still laughing, he shut the door in her face.

Ah Toy countered the courtroom spectators' stares with the unflinching self-regard she had learned in Gum Shan. She sat down near the door, her back stiff with dignity.

No one laughed as they had yesterday when she dragged in the grinning sailor and the weeping boy.

Ah Toy did not know this recently elected Judge Waller, but she considered him good luck. Yesterday he had gaveled silence from amused onlookers, listened patiently to her complaint, and surprised the sailor with a fine of one hundred dollars.

Judge Waller's attention now was on two women who stood before him, both talking at once. Ah Toy listened. She learned much about Americans from their courts.

The dispute didn't interest Ah Toy, since it involved only a Dutch oven, but one of the women did. Her face was badly bruised, one eye nearly purple. Ah Toy winced at the beating the woman had endured. The other woman, looking healthy and strong, complained to the judge that Mrs. Kenny had borrowed a Dutch oven from her and refused to return it.

"Och, and did ye not keep me bonnet trimmings!" shouted Mrs. Kenny. She turned her bruised face to the judge and rattled off her grievance. "In she come to me room, with no please or by your leave, Yer Honor, thunderin' about her blessed oven. And me doin' me wash, a pot in one hand and a shirt in t'other, wid her carryin' a pistol! Ye see what she did me, Yer Honor, she hit me wid that pistol butt!"

"Well, this one owed me seven dollars! And I told her I'd shoot her if she ever set foot in my house again!"

"And where ye 'spect me to live, old woman? Me just married and me husband gone to the mines! Ye'll be gettin' yer blessed rent money!"

"Old woman, ha! You think you're such a young duck, just in your honeymoon!"

Spectators burst into laughter. Waller hammered his gavel, muffling guffaws into sniggers.

Ah Toy wondered what was funny. The woman had been beaten. Ah Toy touched her own bruised, rice-powdered cheek and winced. These do-nothing men would laugh at her, too.

"Mrs. Thompson," Judge Waller was saying, "the court finds you guilty of aggravated assault and imposes a fine of two hundred dollars."

Ah Toy recalled Judge Waller's decision in the case she had witnessed yesterday while waiting to haul the sailor before him. The defendant, a woman, had been charged with assault with intent to kill, the complaint brought by a man asserting he was her lover. The woman testified they had quarreled, and she demanded he leave her house. When he tried to force an entrance to her room, she stabbed him with a dirk, injuring him but slightly.

Judge Waller, after eliciting these facts, had dismissed charges against the woman, astonishing Ah Toy. The woman had injured a man and this Gum Shan judge had forgiven her.

Ah Toy was in his courtroom today because Clark had beaten her in a fury for saying she was his mistress. Now, seeing these sniggering men, Ah Toy reconsidered. Better not to complain of the beating. Clark was a high man. He would beat her again, perhaps deport her, even persuade the Vigilantes to hang her.

The risk to her destiny was too great.

As she hurried down the street, noisy with scraping saws and pounding hammers as workers slapped down more planking, she thought of Mei-Ling. The girl had been feverish this morning, her fragile spirit unsettled by Clark's brutality. And now Ah Toy also had the Hakka boy, Chan. Fearing the contempt of his countrymen in the mines, and swearing his indebtedness for her aid, he refused to leave. This morning, his wounded hair bound in a cloth, he had begged to do her a service. She handed him the broom as she left and told him he could sweep her house.

Ah Toy worried now, hurrying past her board-backed neighbor clucking disapproval, whether the boy knew how to sweep properly.

She discovered he did not, but he learned quickly. Ah Toy showed him how to make the heavy side strokes of the foreign broom. And he must never, she admonished, sweep from the back of the house toward the front. Sweeping dust out the front door drove wealth and good fortune from the household. The proper way, she instructed, was to collect the sweepings on a paper.

Ah Toy, watching the Hakka boy sweep with industrious gratitude, realized that the servant she had promised Mei-Ling had found his way to her.

After Chan mastered the household chores, Ah Toy took him to Sacramento street to teach him to shop. He followed her through the stalls, watching her bargain for rice, vegetables, sausages.

Ah Toy explained Gum Shan's currency. The English shilling, she told him, the American quarter dollar, French franc, and Mexican double real were all the same. Of equivalent worth, too, were the English crown, French five-franc piece, and American or Mexican dollars. Smaller silver coins, whatever the denomination or country of origin, were all considered *bits* and would buy almost nothing.

Chan frowned. Ah Toy smiled, recalling her own confusion when her first Gum Shan goldpiece fathered a handful of strange coins.

Now she sniffed the air, catching a familiar fragrance. "Mooncakes! Come, Chan, we will buy mooncakes! Mei-Ling and I shall observe the moon festival!"

Along the crowded and aromatic length of Sacramento street Ah Toy shopped, adding to Chan's basket fruits and groundnuts, mooncakes and joss sticks, red candles and gold-leaf joss paper. When she discovered a solemn-looking figure with long white ears, she exclaimed with delight, "Moon hare!" She bought the likeness of the god who lived on the moon, pounding the elixir of life in a mortar beneath a cassia tree.

Ah Toy planned in her mind the altar she and Mei-Ling would honor in the night. The moon festival belonged to women. In the center she would place the long-eared moon hare, a dish of thirteen mooncakes, the fruits for fertility and longevity. Perhaps she would slip away with some incense sticks, to wish for marriage to Li Jin, and listen for the words of the first passerby to tell if her wish would be fulfilled.

At Li Po Ti's shop, Ah Toy bought cosmetics to place on the altar. After the ceremony they would be endowed with the secret of beauty. As Ah Toy counted coins into the herbalist's palm, she heard shouts and laughter in the street.

"Lady!" cried Chan from the doorway. "Come see!"

A crowd had gathered around several men roped like yoked oxen to a cart. Breathing hard, they bent their backs, pulling it up the hill. Inside the jolting cart, heads down, hands grasping the wooden sides, stood six girls.

Gawking men shouted offers as they trailed the cart up Sacramento street. Ah Toy, curious, followed with Chan.

On Dupont street, Ah Toy saw a round-faced man waiting, his queue sleek with oil. He directed the harnessed men and their cart into an alley next to a joss house, then hustled the girls through a basement door.

Ah Toy saw Tong Achik just as he saw her. The missionary spoke without greeting. "Good. You will be permitted. Go in. You will tell me who takes them."

Ah Toy looked at him, puzzled. "Who these girls?"

"Slave girls! It is not Christian! I must tell Dr. Speer what happens here, but only those with wealth to buy may enter. Everyone knows you. You will be allowed."

Ah Toy remembered the black girl beaten on the porch, the man helping her up insisting no one owned anyone in this place. "No slaves Gum Shan. Against law."

Tong Achik shook his head. "Law in Little China means that if Chinese make no disturbance outside it, Americans won't interfere inside it."

Ah Toy considered. "Woodworth good man. Tell Vigilance Committee."

"This is no thing for Vigilantes! Besides, the Vigilance Committee disbanded."

"What you mean!"

"Just that. They disbanded themselves two days ago."

Ah Toy absorbed this astonishing news like a blow from Clark's fist. Her face betrayed no surprise, but her mind staggered with it like a heavy treasure, caressed it, danced with the joy of it. She must think on what to do.

For now, from curiosity, Ah Toy, Chan behind her, descended stairs into a room with unpainted walls and a dirt floor. The round-faced man greeted her with a deep bow. She did not know him, but everyone in Little China knew her. They talked of her when she passed on the street, pointing at her with their chins, respecting her wealth and station. She was a famous courtesan with important connections.

The basement's only furnishings were a wooden box painted green and an oil lamp. The six girls huddled in a corner.

Chan said, *"Taiping,* I think, lady. Many girls from Kwangsi province sold by families burned out from villages. Very cheap. Five dollars sometimes, maybe fifty."

Ah Toy recognized Ah Hone, Ah Low, several wealthy merchants. She saw the stealthy red turban, As-sing's *boo how doy.* The cake seller must be here, too, she thought, recalling bitterness. As-sing, she knew, had inflicted the Vigilante brothel inspector on her like a disease. But she had survived. She smiled to herself at the victory.

The round-faced man gestured for attention, drawing Ah Toy from her thoughts. *"Shou-ma!"* he announced. The selection of concubines had begun.

Ah Toy knew the age-old ritual. Tsu Yen, in the long-ago time of Willow lane, had told Ah Toy how the old mistress had purchased her in this way.

Now, here in this Gum Shan basement, this joss-house barracoon, the old ways continued.

The dealer directed the girls to walk forward together slowly, turn around, walk back. Two of them, the prettiest, moved haltingly.

Their graceful rolling gait, which men found so seductive, announced bound feet.

The man told a sad-looking girl, her face scarred with the heavenly blossoms of the smallpox, to stand on the overturned box for inspection. Ah Toy watched the girl lower her head and endure the examination, while noisy men demanded she show her face. Some gestured their lack of interest, dismissing the girl like an animal unworthy of notice. Others wanted to see her hands. The girl pushed up her sleeves, showed her hands and arms. The round-faced man told her to display her feet. The humiliated girl lifted the wide legs of her trousers to show her big feet.

Men shouted offers. Ah Toy saw they were not experts. Knowledgeable buyers of girls sampled the vital scents, sniffing the mouth and under the arms for pleasant aromas. Masters of this business demanded that girls demonstrate the fragrance of their flower by inserting a small fruit, usually a red date. A pretty face could not compensate for an odor that displeased the client. Tsu Yen had said that the date aromatic with her flower's fragrance had been passed among the buyers to sniff and lick.

The sad girl, destined for a mining camp, sold for three hundred dollars.

The next two girls sold quickly, one for five hundred dollars, the other for six hundred, both to Ah Hone and Ah Low. The remaining buyers waited impatiently while the seller prepared the white-paper contract. Ah Low and Ah Hone had come prepared to buy and they put gold in the girls' hands. The girls accepted the gold, signifying their agreement, and passed it to the seller. Then each girl dipped her left thumb in ink and pressed it to the white-paper contract, which specified the number of years she must work to repay her cost. Ah Toy knew such girls rarely freed themselves from these contractual arrangements. The contract's value was to the buyers, should they need to prove ownership or resell the girls.

The fourth girl, younger and more attractive than the first three, stepped up on the box for examination. Inspecting her, two men suddenly broke into an angry argument, shaking fists in each other's face and gesturing signs with flashing hands. As their sleeves fell back from their arms, Ah Toy sensed Chan stiffen at her side. The light of the oil lamp revealed strange marks burned into the men's arms.

As-sing's *boo how doy* shouted at the quarreling men. With fierce looks, they abandoned the fight.

Ah Toy turned to Chan, who had ducked behind her, deeper into shadow. "What is this?"

Chan stared at the men. "Secret society," he whispered. "Those Sze Yup men from Hongkong, Kwan Duc secret society. Marks on arms show convicted Triads."

Beneath the noisy bidding for the girl, Chan said, "Red turban secret society, very high." He indicated with his chin As-sing's *boo how doy.* "He is number four three eight, Assistant Mountain Lord, deputy head of lodge here. Other two are number four three two, Straw Sandals, messengers, organizers of battles or meetings with other societies. Head man remind Straw Sandals of number eight oath, brothers must not quarrel over prostitutes. If this law is broken, may the brother be chopped in a thousand pieces."

"How do you know these things?"

The boy looked frightened.

"Tell me."

Chan bowed his head. "I have drunk the bloody wine, lady."

"You are Kwan Duc?"

Chan gestured away her question. "I say too much, lady."

Buyers' shouts drew Ah Toy's attention back to the auction. The fifth girl daintily stepped up on the box, then looked demurely down at her hands folded within her sleeves. Ah Toy recognized her for an experienced mist-and-flower lady. Every motion confided her training. She tilted her head first to one side, then the other, smiled winsomely. A low forehead and flat nose deprived her of prettiness, but she compensated with a seductive demeanor.

She was smart to show herself to good advantage, thought Ah Toy. The higher the investment in her, the better she would be treated.

The sea journey had robbed the girl's hair of luster and it needed dressing, but Ah Toy saw in her, as did the now loudly bidding buyers, carefully calculated attractiveness. The girl knew her value.

The bidding was at seven hundred dollars when Ah Toy offered eight. She bid with no thought of the cost or of the girl. She bid from revenge.

As-sing glared at her and shouted, "Eight hundred fifty!"

Ah Toy smiled, bemused with her power, surprised by her impulsive participation. The cake seller wanted something, and she could take it from him. She owed him retaliation. Whatever this girl cost, Ah Toy would gladly pay. Defeating the cake seller sweetened the bitterness of her arrest at his instigation.

"Nine hundred," she said with a nonchalance that implied unlimited wealth. She intended to prevail regardless of the cost and by her demeanor disclosed her intent. This triumph would not compensate for Clark, but it was a beginning.

As-sing retired from the engagement with a shrug that suggested the prize was unworthy of his interest. The *mui tsai,* said his manner, accepts second best. Ah Toy smiled her amusement. She enjoyed the contest.

The last girl was young, no more than thirteen years, Ah Toy guessed. Despite her frightened expression, she was startlingly pretty. Standing on the box, the girl shrank from observation as if hiding inside her yellow tunic, its long, wide sleeves banded in black satin.

This girl was no mist-and-flower lady. Her tunic and trousers were elegantly fashioned from silk of the best quality. Pearls decorated her ears, and gold hairpins fastened the braids coiled above them in the fashion of virgins.

The girl stood still as death as the rude buyers plucked her hands from inside her sleeves and caressed her fingers with their old men's hands. After repeated demands from the round-faced man, she meekly displayed her feet.

Embroidered, four-inch black satin shoes, the toes curled up to a point, covered the girl's tiny feet, dainty as lotus buds. Ah Toy remembered the excruciating pain of foot binding. The dealer who bought her as a child had soaked her feet in warm water, then turned her toes under and bound them tightly in wet binding cloths, arching the foot like a bow. Ah Toy could not endure the pain, regardless of how valuable and beautiful lotus-bud feet would make her. She had screamed in agony day beyond day. After a month the old woman abandoned the effort and sold her for a slave instead.

Ah Toy was certain the girl on the box was the daughter of a wealthy family, intended to bring a rich dowry to her parents and honor to her future husband's family.

Ah Toy realized, too, that the cake seller was determined to have her. She watched him resolutely counter every offer. He would, Ah Toy knew, use the girl first himself. She imagined the girl's terror and repulsion when he scrabbled at her with his bony hands, engulfing her in his lust and the smell of cabbage. Then he would sell her youth and beauty again and again for large money. A girl of this quality was rare in the brothels of Canton. Here her value was incalculable—if she lived. Such girls rarely survived long.

"Twelve hundred."

As-sing glared his malice. "Thirteen!"

Ah Toy ignored him. His hatred lay beneath her notice like an ugly beetle. "Fifteen."

She intended to save this girl, whose fright she sensed as if it were her own. The old fear of dogs and hunger and her father with no face enveloped Ah Toy like a stink.

"Sixteen!"

Ah Toy heard As-sing's greedy rasp of a voice. Outrage seized her. These men, buying girls in this grimy Gum Shan barracoon like goats or sheep, these men were all the fathers with no face, were all the men who sold daughters, all the men who mistreated, abused, and beat women.

"Three thousand dollar!"

Ah Toy stunned everyone with her offer, including herself, but she did not flinch from her bid. She could not save all the girls. But she could save this one.

The round-faced man, already amazed, looked perplexed as Ah Toy pushed away the white-paper contract.

"Red-paper contract," she demanded.

The seller's expression collapsed in disbelief. Ah Toy understood his surprise. She had paid an enormous sum to adopt a daughter.

By the time Ah Toy returned to the barracoon with nearly four thousand dollars of her gold, she knew the next purchase she would make. She sent Chan and the girls home in a carriage and headed for the Washington street baths. It was Wednesday, and Clark, at her expense, indulged himself there on Wednesdays.

Whether women ever entered the sacrosanct interior of a men's shaving saloon Ah Toy neither knew nor cared. She threw open the door. Barbers, customers, and black attendants stared at her. She stared back at each surprised countenance, seeking the familiar stone-gray eyes.

One man, his head frothy with soap, gaped at her from his stooped position beside a marble washstand. His black attendant, with soapy hands suddenly immobile, as though caught trying to steal the suds, blinked his astonishment.

Men in various stages of shaving and barbering reclined in crimson velvet chairs, their legs stretched out on crimson velvet stools. Ah Toy surveyed them as coolly as if they had been arranged for her selection, like barracoon girls.

She marched to where Clark sat openmouthed and flung Hakka curses at him, her voice rising in rage. English left her. She could only think "Dog!" She punctuated her fury with it.

"Dog!" she shouted, and Clark cringed. He cringed, she quickly realized, not from her but from the laughter resounding from the marble floors and walls.

Let him be embarrassed, she thought triumphantly. That is what he feared and hated, why he had beaten her for saying she was his mistress.

Ah Toy caught her breath, listening to the laughter fill the shaving saloon. Now she focused her anger into careful consideration. Earlier, she had decided to buy Clark off with two hundred dollars, the way a Canton merchant might pay off one protector to employ another. But she needed no protector except the courts, and she need give Clark no more gold. There was no more Vigilance Committee, and he was no high man.

Calmer now, she regained her English. She opened her bag and shook out a handful of worthless coins accumulated during her morning's shopping. "You protect me, high man? I pay you." She tossed coins at him, none larger than a franc.

Clark ducked, raising an arm to protect himself as if she might shoot him. Ah Toy laughed as the coins tinkled onto the marble floor.

The barber standing behind the chair grinned. "Excuse me, Mr. Clark, I believe I'm in the way here." He stepped aside as Ah Toy pitched another dozen coins. Their ringing against the marble floor was lost in the laughter enveloping the room.

Now Ah Toy started flipping silver coins at Clark one at a time, with a studied nonchalance. "You like patent shoes, high man? Buy shoes. I pay." She tossed a coin.

"Like gold watch? Yes? I pay." A coin landed on the towel covering Clark's chest. He stared at it as though it might attack him.

"You like gold ring? Yes? I pay." A coin tinkled loudly across the marble floor. Laughter had ceased. The men in the shaving saloon stared at Clark in silence.

"Like wine? Yes? I pay."

Ah Toy tossed more worthless coins at Clark. He winced, shrinking from them as though they burned.

"Like go barber? Yes? I pay." Ah Toy dropped a coin to the floor. It rolled crookedly, struck the base of a marble washstand, spun drunkenly, and collapsed.

"Like beat China lady? Yes?"

Clark closed his eyes as if to disappear.

Someone said, "Oh, I say, Clark, with women so scarce as they are in California, they ought to be better treated."

Ah Toy held her bag upside down over Clark's head, his eyes squeezed shut with mortification. A final silver coin fell with a tiny plop and rolled to the floor.

"No more," she said.

Ah Toy turned and walked with measured dignity past the men on their crimson velvet chairs, out the door, and into Washington street. It was a bright, sunny day.

In his Macau and Woosung Restaurant, As-sing sucked steaming tea from a cracked cup and listened to Tong Achik's idea with disbelief. "Acrobats!"

"The people of Han," interjected Hab Wa, "fascinate Americans."

Especially our women, thought As-sing, recalling for the ten-thousandth time in the past two months his loss to the *mui tsai*. The memory of his defeat in the joss-house barracoon burned like salt on sores.

Tong Achik said, "Americans spend gold like it was dirt. They will pay to see our performers."

While Tong Achik argued the cultural and economic desirability of importing Chinese theatrical troupes to Gum Shan, As-sing sucked at his tea and watched Hab Wa. As-sing saw ambition in his rigid jaw. With his excellent English, he should do well. Beyond that, As-sing dismissed him. Let this one spend his gold on circus acrobats for Gum Shan, he thought. True wealth lay in the needs of men. And men wanted women and the solace of the pipe. Supplying these needs promised wealth, and his own best hope for becoming an American millionaire now that the Luminous Unity Society threatened collapse. With the formation of the Sam Yup and Sze Yup societies, the Luminous Unity consisted only of the few men emigrating from Kwangtung's remote Sun Wui and Hok Shan districts. As-sing still had his restaurant, bakery, and import business, but his power over the China men flooding Gum Shan like the waters of the Pearl River was no more.

While Tong Achik and his friend discussed their theatrical ideas, As-sing's thoughts strayed like straw in wind. He watched Li Jin absently drinking tea behind a perplexed expression. The scholar had come into the restaurant with his friends talking only of how unrecognizable the city was. What had been bayfront when he left was now Front street and the Battery, lined with brick warehouses with iron shutters. Tents and shanties had disappeared, and the Jackson street dormitory, too. The Sam Yups and the Sze Yups had their own large brick houses, he observed with surprise, as though As-sing were ignorant of the fact. The scholar sat down at his tea wearing astonishment like a hat.

Tong Achik was talking of acrobats still. As-sing was annoyed. "Americans don't want our acrobats," he interrupted. "They want our women!"

As-sing saw the scholar look up as though jolted from sleep, heard the words fly from his mouth. "What happened to the woman?" he asked, looking from Tong Achik to As-sing. "You remember, the Hakka girl? What was her name? Ah Toy?"

As-sing spat his tea. *"Mui tsai!"* He slapped the table, glaring at Li Jin. Had the scholar forgotten the face lost in the El Dorado? "What do you want with that one?" he demanded, eyes narrow and hard. "Is that one the reason you come to the city, abandoning your responsibility to your family? Do you think you can buy her? You do not speak? Speak!" As-sing smacked the table with his cracked cup. It fractured, releasing rivulets of tea. He whipped a hand over the wet table as though slaying cockroaches. "Speak!"

Li Jin hung his head, cowed. No one spoke. After a long moment, Hab Wa broke the silence. "Li Jin returns to his family."

As-sing put his wrath away. A departing sojourner meant money. "Ah, then," he said, wiping his hands on his tunic and bestowing upon Li Jin a wiry smile, "you come to pay your debt, I see. That is good. I will tally them," he said, rising.

"Debt?" Li Jin asked. "What debt?"

As-sing, heedless of the panic in the scholar's voice, hurried away.

Surprise still registered in Li Jin's eyes when As-sing returned with his abacus and record book, its cover a dull, smoky brown. As-sing sat, licked a finger, and turned pages.

"Ah, yes, I see you repaid the cost of your ticket from Hongkong. Also your costs to the Luminous Unity Society. Good. We have just the monthly remittance due for your employment with the Stockton storekeeper. You paid, I see, two months, which leaves thirteen months at six dollars a month—"

Li Jin protested. "I was mining, not storekeeping!"

As-sing flicked the black wood balls of the abacus with a thumb and forefinger. They clicked lightly into place. "Our agreement was ten percent of your wages of sixty dollars each month. You do not abandon your agreement when you abandon your responsibility." He considered the positions of the counters, then flicked more balls. "You must pay also the departure fee." He smiled thinly at Li Jin as he returned the black ball counters to their upper and lower positions. "One hundred eight dollars."

"I have only gold enough for my passage! You shipped all my gold to my family last month!"

As-sing shrugged. Most miners sent their gold by express to San Francisco now, rather than risk being robbed of it. It was a small part of his business to transfer the gold to China-bound ships and send it to waiting families. He earned only 1 percent on such transactions.

"One hundred eight dollars," he repeated.

Li Jin protested. "Where am I to get such a sum?"

As-sing smiled and shrugged. It was not his concern.

Hab Wa placed a hand on his friend's arm. "You have heard what the Americans say: 'There is always more where that came from.' About gold, they are right."

As-sing stood, his business finished. "The Yuba River mines are reported rich. Many Sze Yup men go there now."

Tong Achik nodded. "Yes, Li Jin, so I have heard also. But you have no need to go at once." He rose, holding a hand out to his friend. "Come, we will visit someone you remember. You will be surprised."

The noon meal was Ah Toy's favorite part of the day. The men who came late at night to visit Mei-Ling and Chow Lai had left, and the men who would come for the afternoon had yet to arrive. Through the screen of crimson silk that divided off the sleeping space she shared with her daughter, she could hear Chan placing rice bowls and chopsticks on the table. Ah Toy, fastening gold hairpins into the coiled braids above Xiao-li's ears, smelled ginger and sesame.

Chan's devotion never flagged, and Ah Toy accepted his intention to stay. She had hired a carpenter to build a lean-to against the side of the house for him and a room for Chow Lai. Ah Toy marveled at the size of her household.

"Pretty," Ah Toy said, tucking another hairpin into Xiao-li's braids.

"Tank-, dank-, thank you, Mother." The girl stumbled over the difficult sound while Ah Toy smiled encouragement. She wanted all the girls to learn English, especially the orphan Xiao-li. The *taiping*s had slain her family and sold her to slave dealers. She had no home to return to in China. Ah Toy knew the girl's only hope for safety and happiness lay in marriage. And Ah Toy, after long thought, had decided on Tong Achik.

Ah Toy knew the missionary adored Mei-Ling, since he came often to inquire about her ever-fragile health. From his visits Ah Toy knew him to be a good man. He would be a good husband, but he could never afford Mei-Ling and she could never be a poor man's wife. When the time was right, Ah Toy would offer him Xiao-li, with a generous dowry. The girl would have a safe home and the honor of being first wife.

"Go," said Ah Toy, kissing Xiao-li's cheek, "go help lazy Chow Lai dress."

"Yes, Mother," said Xiao-li, bowing her respect.

Ah Toy watched the girl totter away without envy. She knew how impossible would have been her own survival in Gum Shan, and through hers, that of these girls, had she been crippled like them. Sometimes she wondered whether the beauty of bound feet was not a false one, disguising as desirable an ancient subjection. She saw how the Americans who visited her girls stared at their tiny feet with curiosity for their strangeness, not with admiration for their beauty.

She had asked the lawyer why he did not prefer Mei-Ling for her beautiful feet. He said something Ah Toy had since thought on often, that beauty lay in the eye of the beholder. And to her great embarrassment, he had kissed her bare toes. She had been sorry when he left for a place he called Connecticut. The barbarian was a decent man. Since his departure and the coming to her house of Xiao-li and Chow Lai, she had taken no visitors for herself. She had whispered her prayer to the moon hare.

Ah Toy sat down at the table and Chan served a platter of shrimps sauced with sesame and ginger. Chow Lai, poking a shrimp with her chopsticks, yawned.

Mei-Ling laughed. "Did my sister not sleep well?"

Chow Lai giggled. "Well enough, despite the noise from your room. Were you entertaining a banker or an elephant?"

Ah Toy captured a shrimp with her chopsticks and scolded affectionately, "Talk English."

A rapping on the door startled everyone. "Chan," Ah Toy said, "go tell no visit now."

A moment later, Chan announced, "It is Tong Achik. And . . . ?"

"Hab Wa," said a voice Ah Toy did not know. Then another, which she did:

"And Li Jin."

Ah Toy, stone still, her chopsticks poised above her rice bowl, felt his presence like an embrace.

"Mother?" Xiao-li asked, putting her hand on Ah Toy's arm. Ah Toy stared at the hand holding the lilac sleeve of her dress. This dress was not how she had imagined he would see her. This dress was old. She owned much better.

Chow Lai dropped her chopsticks and clapped her hands. "It is the one!" she said to Mei-Ling. "The one she spoke of the night of the moon festival!"

"This is true, Elder Sister?" asked Mei-Ling. "Happiness for you comes to our door?"

Xiao-li pressed Ah Toy's arm. "Mother?"

"Hush!" said Ah Toy, rising. "Eat."

At the door, she nodded to Tong Achik, acknowledged Hab Wa, and with her eyes drank in the scholar. "Have you eaten?" she asked, remembering politeness. "Chan," she called, "more dishes. Bring wine."

The afternoon flew away in a happiness Ah Toy had never known. Li Jin, she saw, followed her every movement with his eyes, as if she were a strange and curious creature he had never seen before. It was to her he told the stories of the gold mines, of the bandits he had escaped, the tax collectors, the citizenship judge who demanded fifty dollars in gold for a paper Li Jin sent to his family. She listened enraptured, aware she basked in his gaze like sunshine.

Ah Toy was aware but could not today summon concern that Tong Achik sat entranced by Mei-Ling, who, when evening fell, sang and played upon her lute. Ah Toy saw, too, how Chow Lai flirtatiously paraded herself, and how the one called Hab Wa resisted with amused detachment. And she saw how Xiao-li smiled and chattered with everyone, as though she had her family again. All of it Ah Toy saw through a haze of happiness.

The day felt like a festival. She gave Chan money to buy more wine and good things to eat. She sent away the afternoon visitors with apologies, promising that Mei-Ling and Chow Lai should entertain them another time. She laughed with the joy that filled her noisy house.

Only when Li Jin told her he had come to San Francisco intending to return to China did she feel a sudden uncertainty. Was this the time to go back? She looked around her, at her lovely daughter, at frail Mei-Ling, at the devoted Hakka boy with his chopped hair, at clever Chow Lai. She had collected so much responsibility in this place. How had she allowed herself to be so unprepared for her destiny?

"But first I must pay As-sing my debt," she heard Li Jin saying, explaining his need to return to the mines.

Ah Toy sent a prayer of gratitude to the goddess Kwan-yin for this time in which to arrange for her substitute family.

Chan offered a dish of red melon seeds, interrupting her thoughts. She took a few to nibble and Chan held the dish to Li Jin.

Li Jin looked at the boy. "In the mines, Chan," he said, taking a handful of seeds, "some men intentionally cut their hair. They appear fierce with hair growing low to their eyes. Barbarians look on them with greater respect than those with shaved heads and queues, who look so harmless and amiable. To cut the hair is no bad thing for those who wish to adopt the fashion of Gum Shan."

Ah Toy, watching Chan's face brighten, felt a love for Li Jin's kindness to the boy. This man of her destiny was a good man.

Chow Lai laughed saucily. "Gum Shan fashions please me. I like French dresses, silver forks, and choosing husbands."

Ah Toy reddened. "Chow Lai!"

Ignoring the reprimand, Chow Lai spoke boldly, as though

women always discussed marriage in the presence of men. "Not for me old ways with go-betweens and three covenants and six ceremonies and tea presents. I intend choosing husband. I know fortune-telling. I choose right person with lucky eight ideographs, and I choose lucky wedding day."

Ah Toy clapped a hand to her mouth, but Chow Lai only laughed. Hab Wa laughed, too, and raised his wineglass. "To Gum Shan's dispensations!"

Tong Achik joined the toast, bestowing a laughing approval on Chow Lai's audacity.

Emboldened, the girl announced she could demonstrate her skill and hurried on tiny feet from the room.

"Ah Toy," Tong Achik said, "you intend permitting Chow Lai's marriage?"

Ah Toy understood his question. Even as he spoke, his eyes adored Mei-Ling.

"My arrangements for Mei-Ling and Chow Lai are not secret," she said, brushing a strand of hair from her face. She felt untidy from embarrassment, laughter, wine. "I offer my sisters half what they earn. From that, if they choose to repay me their cost, they may do as they please. Or, if a man offers to repay her cost, she is free to go with him. But this I agree to only if it be her desire. These girls are not for sale."

Mei-Ling had bowed her head, averting her eyes from Tong Achik's admiration. Now she looked at Ah Toy with gratitude. "Elder Sister is most kind. I wish always to stay with her."

Ah Toy smiled her appreciation. Mei-Ling had, by her sentiment, announced to the missionary the futility of his suit.

Chow Lai burst into the room, laughing, teetering on her pretty feet, waving a sheaf of rice paper, a brush, a block of ink. "Sister," she said to Mei-Ling, "help me collect the name and birth-time ideographs of these handsome men. One might be lucky for me." She laughed at her own impudence.

Ah Toy sat helpless, amazed by Chow Lai's outrageous behavior. The girl was indelicate, but utterly charming. She collected ideographs from the men and wickedly promised to marry them all if her analysis willed it.

Mei-Ling, who adored Chow Lai's unruly spirit, laughingly helped write the characters with graceful brushstrokes. Chan poured more wine, and even Ah Toy laughed as Chow Lai flirted disgracefully, making charming sounds of surprise and pleasure over each character filling up the paper.

Even Chan, usually so dour, joined in the fun, insisting Mei-Ling record his ideographs, too. "Maybe Chow Lai like my fierce hair," he said, grinning at Li Jin. "You make extra character show fierce hair," he instructed Mei-Ling, and everyone laughed with him.

Ah Toy ignored the Gum Shan clock ticking away the late hours as her house filled with joy and laughter. She wondered if this must be something like Irene McCready's gay parties where important men drank wine and danced with beautiful girls.

She laughed at the thought, and Li Jin turned to her. "Silver music," he whispered. "You laugh like silver music."

Ah Toy, embarrassed, hid her eyes. She felt awkward, as though once again hiding her feet from him in the dark ship that had brought them to this amazing place.

Just then, over the laughter and Chow Lai's coquettish yelps, Ah Toy heard an insistent rapping on her door. She looked at her clock. The hour was late for visitors.

She opened the door prepared to scold whoever had come so late to visit Mei-Ling or Chow Lai. The lamplight escaping from her door glinted off a silver star pinned to the man's uniformed chest.

He stepped in and looked around. "We got a complaint against this house," he said. "Disturbing the peace."

Ah Toy felt happiness fly away like a bird. Fear settled into its nest. Across the street a triangle of light leaked from a window. Then it disappeared.

In the midst of her testimony, Ah Toy saw Judge Waller shake his head and turn to the bailiff. "Miss Ah Toy does not understand the charge. If we are unable to proceed, the court will require an interpreter."

"Understand, yes!" insisted Ah Toy. "I know word!"

"Miss Ah Toy," said Judge Waller, pulling at a collar point above his cravat, "the word *disorderly* apparently confuses you."

"No! I know what mean! My house no disorder! My house clean, always clean! Chan sweep morning, night. Clean house!"

Ah Toy turned on the courtroom's laughing spectators. "You know nothing! My house clean!"

A man rose and approached the bench. "A point of information, Your Honor." They conferred briefly, and the man sat.

Judge Waller, looking embarrassed, cleared his throat. To his clerk he said, "Note for the record that Mr. C. A. Johnson, a noted attorney of this city, advises that keeping a disorderly house is not an indictable offense at common law here."

"That's absurd!" said the pinched-faced woman. She wore a plain bonnet and gray dress over the stiffest back Ah Toy had ever seen.

"That woman," she was saying, stabbing a finger at Ah Toy, "keeps a common house of ill fame, where men go drinking and tippling and whoring and misbehaving themselves at all hours, disturbing the peace of decent folks and—"

"Mrs. McKibben," said the judge, "the court acknowledges your complaint."

"Do you, sir?" Mrs. McKibben glared at the judge and then at the laughing spectators. "Do any of you men?" She drew her chin against her collar and narrowed her mouth to a slice of disapproval. "Are you not the same men who spend your evenings, like dogs, smelling out the vile excrescences of evil places?"

Ah Toy saw men's heads drop before the woman's baleful survey, as though their newspapers and whittling sticks suddenly demanded attention.

"Is it not wonderful the liberties men take?" Mrs. McKibben continued in her acid voice. "Is it not passing strange how they seek the society of virtuous females, there to discourse upon the charms of domestic life, and the solace of home and hearth, and virtuous associations, and directly upon leaving cross the street and enter a house of ill fame!"

"My house no ill! All my house well!"

Judge Waller shook his head. "Miss Ah Toy, the complaint against you has nothing to do with sickness or cleanliness—"

"Oh, yes, indeed it does, Your Honor, indeed it does!" Mrs. McKibben punctuated her words with firm-fisted raps on his desk. "The issue here is moral health and purity! The good must drive out the bad to make this city a suitable residence for the virtuous and the pure!"

Ah Toy stood helpless before the woman's onslaught.

"Your Honor, consider the children," Mrs. McKibben was saying. "Think of them, exposed to this evil influence, seeing a constant stream of men coming and going at this woman's house! Decent people with families live on Clay street!"

Judge Waller silenced Mrs. McKibben's harangue with a crack of his gavel. "Mrs. McKibben, the court is not unsympathetic, but Miss Ah Toy's establishment, however distasteful to society's sensibilities, does not at present violate the statutes of this country."

He turned to Ah Toy. "Miss Ah Toy, you are charged with disturbing the peace. I will delay my decision in this matter until court reconvenes on Monday morning. Until then, I advise you to consider how to restore harmony with your neighbors."

Ah Toy followed her neighbor's board-stiff back from the courtroom, nursing her own outrage. What did this woman who talked so hard of "ill fame" know of Mei-Ling's long sickness? She knew nothing! She knew nothing of Xiao-li's vulnerability. She knew nothing of the humiliation of survival. No hunger exposed her body to lewd, laughing, drunken barbarians. She was a wife.

Irene McCready had warned about Gum Shan wives, but not how to deflect their rare power. China wives possessed no authority, no influence. A man visited the mist-and-flower ladies of Willow lane or the singsong girls of the flower boats as he wished. A wife's objection or interference was unthinkable. From where did Gum Shan wives gain such power?

Ah Toy knocked at the door of the Pike street house, and a black man bowed her in with a sweep of a white-gloved hand. "Mrs. McCready is receiving," he said.

"My dear, how nice to see you," said Irene. "Jeffers, bring tea," she told the black man. She sat opposite Ah Toy in a puff of blue silk the color of cornflowers. "Oh, do take off your bonnet, dear. It hides your lovely eyes and beautiful hair. If you don't mind the advice, avoid bonnets. Dress your hair in the Chinese fashion, so exotic. Very becoming, really. I know all the men think so."

"Most kind." Ah Toy nodded politely. She removed her bonnet of pink satin flowers and patted into place the escaped strands of her hair. She must look as harried as she felt, rushing here from Judge Waller's courtroom. But she could not think what else to do. Irene

McCready understood Gum Shan wives. Perhaps she could say what to do.

By the time Ah Toy finished her story and confided her alarm that Judge Waller would sentence her to the prison brig, the silver teapot had grown cold.

Irene had listened with encouraging smiles, sipping tea from a cup painted with rosebuds and rimmed in gold. "You are in luck," she said.

"Luck? How luck?" Ah Toy feared her luck had run away.

"Quite simple, really, dear." Irene placed her cup on its saucer. "You must move to a more congenial neighborhood. In this country—I don't know about in your country, of course—so-called houses of 'ill fame'— Now don't let those words bother you one little bit. They have nothing at all to do with health, unless"—she laughed—"one counts the health of one's purse." She laughed again. "As I say, in this country it is altogether better for, how shall I put this?" She hesitated, one ringed finger at her chin. "Umm, sporting ladies, you understand, yes?" she asked, raising an eyebrow.

"Mist-and-flower ladies?"

"What an agreeable expression. I believe Mr. McCabe told me another he had heard." She paused, thinking. "Daughters of joy? Is that right?"

Ah Toy nodded.

"Yes, well, gentlemen have their own perspective, don't they?" She examined her teacup, then looked out the window. "In any event, one had best avoid wives."

Ah Toy heard metal in Irene's voice. She recalled hearing that James McCabe bragged he could take Irene anywhere until they were asked to leave a fund-raiser organized by church ladies.

Irene clattered her teacup onto its saucer. "Jeffers! This tea is cold!"

While the black man removed the tea tray, Irene stared out the window. When he left, she leaned toward Ah Toy, as if reading her thoughts. "On one occasion, which I would very much like to forget, a brood of affronted wives prevailed upon a delegation of men to advise Mr. McCabe that Christian women declined to welcome into friendly association any—and I remember the words precisely—any 'who trampled upon institutions which lie at the foundation of morality and civilization.'"

Irene sat back with a sharp laugh. "Morality! Ha! Deceiving their husbands, divorcing in droves, jealous lest some other woman receive better presents, that's their high-and-mighty morality for you! Of civilization, I say nothing. This city's most civilized institution is my house! I offer the best wines, finest suppers, ladies of wit, intelligence, and talent. An evening here is the most civilized affair in San Francisco!"

Jeffers returned with tea and almond cakes. Irene poured. "My dear," she said, offering Ah Toy a cake, "the wives are a tiresome but untiring force. Avoid them. Move. I have a house to let here on Pike street, one of my own investments. You may take possession immediately, as the tenants left somewhat abruptly for Australia."

When Ah Toy saw the number 36 on the house, she knew luck had not deserted her. *Three* was the same word as *living; six* was a good-fortune number because it shared tone variations with the word *longevity;* and *nine,* which the numbers equaled, meant *eternity.* No computation of these numbers formed the unlucky death numbers of *four* and *seven,* nor the lonely number, *one.*

The house was perfect, with sleeping rooms upstairs, a kitchen with piped water at the back door, a dining room, and parlor. Ah Toy considered furnishing it like Irene's, with a Brussels carpet and rosewood furniture. She dismissed the idea. Visitors to her Clay street house admired her Oriental things.

Ah Toy ordered her driver to the salesrooms of Duncan and Tobin.

The importers offered the finest Oriental merchandise in the city. Ah Toy was amused to see an entire carriage from Japan, exhibited like a museum piece. There were shawls from Tibet, inlaid brass workboxes of rare woods from Bombay, embroidered silks and satins threaded with gold filigree, and a thousand ivory-carved curiosities: animals, pagodas, junks, chessmen.

Ah Toy, a plan forming in her mind, wandered among scented sandalwood and carved camphorwood indicating her choices to Mr. Duncan: two low tables inlaid with ebony, three settees in red satin, four chairs with arms carved like tiger paws, rice-paper scrolls painted with mist-shrouded mountains, the carpet of royal blue sculpted with yellow peonies.

On Clay street, Ah Toy propelled her household into a whirlwind of packing. Xiao-li wrapped the household gods in silk. Ah Toy cradled in cushions the *fan qui* clock that had ticked away her lonely hours. Mei-Ling directed Chan's packing of the kitchen things, the bricks of tea, baskets of rice, the dried cuttlefish Ah Toy loved to nibble, the dishes painted with flying cranes. Chow Lai, in a pretense of busyness Ah Toy found more amusing than annoying, teetered from room to room giving counsel everyone ignored. By Saturday afternoon, Ah Toy, to keep the indolent girl from getting underfoot, had settled her in a chair at the door to advise disappointed visitors of the new lucky address.

Boxes piled up for the drayman. "Down two block, 'round corner, number three six," Ah Toy told him, and watched the accumulations of her Gum Shan life move down Clay street behind his clip-clopping horses.

Sunday morning the drayman returned, tying with stout ropes

to his wagon her teakwood chairs, her table of inlaid ebony, the screen of the Eight Immortals wrapped in the red satin coverlet embroidered with the gold dragon.

By noon everything from the Clay street house was gone, the wicker and camphorwood, silken draperies from the walls, Ah Toy's French gowns and calfskin boots. With the wagon's last trip, Ah Toy sent her family.

Now she stood alone, in the doorway of the place she had come to dressed as a peasant. Chan had swept the dirt floor and piled newspapers by the old stove for kindling. The shelves, still covered in red paper, displayed two new cans of beans. No one in her house understood why, and she chose not to explain.

Except for the two doors cut to the rooms she had added, the house looked as it did the first time she saw it. The walls, robbed of their draperies, revealed their imperfectly joined slats. The twill-cloth ceiling sagged overhead. The fry pan hung on the wall. On top of the trunk was the old washbasin. For a moment Ah Toy saw again the goldpiece that had lain in it two days, until her hunger took it. She had never been hungry since. She put from her thoughts what defeating hunger required.

Ah Toy looked down at the old green silk pantaloons she wore, dusty from her morning's work, remembering. How eagerly she had dressed in them once, anticipating the scholar's approval. The time seemed distant as China.

Now, walking down Clay street toward her new lucky-number house, Ah Toy smiled. She had thought through exactly what to do. Li Jin remained a poor man and could not seek her consent to marry. But she had gold, lots of it. The gesture was hers to make. It must not wait.

In her new parlor Ah Toy sat for a moment, imagining Li Jin in one of her new chairs, his hands on its tiger-paw arms. A silver tray on the table beside him would display the red-paper envelope with a few dollars inside. Seeing it, he would understand at once. She would call Chan to bring tea. Mei-Ling would sing and strum her lute. Ah Toy would pour tea and offer it in the proper way to the man to whom she wished to betroth herself. Li Jin would drink, then hand the red-paper envelope to Mei-Ling. She, as go-between, would accept the ceremonial bargain money.

Ah Toy decided. She would do it now. "Chan!"

"Yes, lady?" he said, hurrying from the kitchen.

"Go to the place where the Sze Yup men stay. Tell Li Jin he will honor my new house if he will take tea with me this evening."

Now Ah Toy prepared herself. She bathed with scented soap, perfumed her body with sweet oils. She dressed her hair with pomegranate blossoms, fashioned it into wings ornamented with golden hairpins. In her ears she fastened pearls and painted her face with rouge and rice powder.

When Chan had not returned by twilight, Ah Toy insisted the girls take their evening meal. For the first time in her life she could not eat.

Ah Toy sat in the parlor, in a chair with arms carved like tiger paws, waiting. She wore a dress of red satin.

The red-paper envelope lay upon the silver tray next to the empty chair opposite. She stared at it, waiting.

She listened to the *fan qui* clock tick toward her destiny and waited.

But the scholar did not come.

When Chan at last returned, he would not look at her. "I go all place, lady," he said, staring at his feet. "Li Jin gone."

Ah Toy looked away, sparing him the sight of her disappointment. Through tears, she stared at the red envelope filled with money and hope.

Chan shuffled uncomfortably. "Lady," he mumbled, "I see red-turban man, Kwan Duc, As-sing's *boo how doy.*"

Ah Toy whisked away her tears and looked at Chan. His eyes questioned whether she wished to know more.

"Yes?"

"As-sing sent his *boo how doy* to Li Jin with message . . ." Chan hesitated. "Message—message to be gone."

"That's not what he said, is it?"

Chan scuffed his corkwood sandals against the new carpet. "No, lady."

"Tell me exactly what the red turban told you."

Chan stared at the carpet.

"Tell me!" Ah Toy saw the Hakka boy bite his lip. "Chan, I have no anger for you. Tell me what the red turban said!"

Chan hung his head. "He say to Li Jin that As-sing want his money now, to 'stop sniffing around the *mui tsai* like a dog' and go at once to mines at Foster's Bar on Yuba River." Chan looked up. "I very sorry, lady, to say this thing."

Ah Toy stared at him. "Why does As-sing's *boo how doy* tell you these things?"

Chan shrugged. "For Kwan Duc brotherhood." He pulled a red cloth from his sleeve and showed it to her.

"Chan, throw that away! This is not Canton! On the Gold Mountain is no need for secret society!"

"Lady, they are here. They are all here." Chan pushed the cloth back inside his sleeve. "I keep to be useful to you. I learn many things." He stared at his shoes.

Ah Toy felt fear close her throat. In a whisper, she asked, "What else should I know?"

Chan looked up, dismayed. "This place Foster's Bar, this very bad place for China men."

Ah Toy covered her face and wept for her destiny.

6

Where their interests have come into conflict
with those of the Chinese or Mexicans, the
Yankees have evinced a brutality which does
them little honor.

> —William Perkins
> Sonora, California
> 1851

CELEBRATION OF THE ANNIVERSARY OF OUR
NATIONAL INDEPENDENCE. — . . . The great
and principal feature of the procession was
the *Celestials.* . . . The whole was under the
command of Norman Assing, Esq.

> —*Alta California*
> July 7, 1852

THE CHINESE THEATRE. —This "Celestial"
temple of the Muses . . . will be thrown open to
all who are curious to witness the peculiar
performances of the Hook Tong Dramatic
Company.

> —*Golden Era*
> December 19, 1852

Lady," Chan said, his voice gentle, "all dust and dirt has fled this house like peasants from Manchu warriors. You warrior lady, but nothing remain for fight."

Ah Toy reluctantly surrendered the broom. Chan left, closing the door quietly behind him. On the bed Mei-Ling slept deep within fever.

Ah Toy blamed herself. She had neglected her family in her constant worry for Li Jin. Chan collected news from the streets, from every returning steamer carrying China men back from the mines. No one reported Li Jin among the men injured by the attacking Americans at Foster's Bar. After many months Ah Toy hung fear into a back place, like an old gown, and ignored it.

While Ah Toy's attention wandered elsewhere, the cold, damp winter attacked Mei-Ling's ever-delicate health. Ah Toy had not seen the old foe lurking. Discovering it, she defended with every weapon, with prayer, potion, and broom. She remembered how Mr. Buxton, on Thirteen Factories street, assuaged her lament for Tsu Yen by explaining that malevolent ghosts killed no one. Tsu Yen died of the plague, he said, and made Ah Toy understand that filth was the cause, cleanliness the prevention. Dirt had ever since offended Ah Toy like the breath of death.

But her house, Ah Toy knew, gleamed from cleanings and still Mei-Ling weakened.

Ah Toy drew a chair next to Mei-Ling's bed and watched the girl's life spirit tremble toward flight.

Ah Toy had summoned the doctor, Chu-san, who came in his

purple tunic with sleeves shaped like horses' hooves. He examined the girl's wayward pulse and said, "She must have a carp to eat. Nothing else will bring the eyes, which have sunken, to their forward position again."

Ah Toy bought the carp, boiled it, coaxed broth between Mei-Ling's lips. Still the girl's spirit receded like a tide.

Li Po Ti's remedy likewise availed nothing. The herbalist prepared a rare curative of ginseng root, dragon's heart blood, preserved lizard, bird's claws, black dates, rattlesnake's tail, ground reindeer's horns, lotus leaves, and willow cricket skins. Ah Toy urged a spoonful of the potion between Mei-Ling's lips every three hours until it was gone. And still the girl's spirit fluttered toward escape.

When Li Po Ti's treatment rendered no improvement, Ah Toy had sent for the Taoist priest at the temple on Dupont street. He rang bells and burned yellow paper covered with incantations to frighten away the evil ghost. But despite incense, ghost money, food offerings, and prayers, Mei-Ling continued to weaken.

Tong Achik had brought the American woman doctor whose office was on Dupont street. "Typhus," she had said, one grim word for Mei-Ling's chills and fever and terrifying headaches, and prescribed laudanum.

Now, as Ah Toy coaxed a few drops of the watery opium between Mei-Ling's lips, she heard the door curl open. Xiao-li peered in. "Mother," she whispered, "visitors inquire for sister's health. They wish that you speak with them."

"Who visits?" asked Ah Toy, smoothing Mei-Ling's damp hair.

Xiao-li slipped into the room. "It is him, Mother, the one you chose for me. Also the one who visits Chow Lai. I will stay with sister. I am not afraid."

In the times since Ah Toy had sat long into the night of her failed betrothal, she had talked often with Xiao-li of the future. When Li Jin returned again, Ah Toy explained, all must be prepared. Destiny required readiness.

She talked to Xiao-li about the barbarian beliefs Tong Achik shared. During Mei-Ling's long illness Ah Toy had explained that the God worshipers believed the body's spirit, its *chi,* ascended to heaven, a glorious place free of hunger and vindictiveness. Mei-Ling's *chi* would never wish to stray from this beautiful cloud garden and therefore was not to be feared.

Ah Toy kissed her daughter's cheek. "When Mei-Ling wakes, offer the bamboo tea. It will cool her."

In the parlor, Tong Achik said, "She is no better?"

Ah Toy shook her head and called Chan to bring her guests tea. She spoke with Tong Achik of Mei-Ling's illness, while Hab Wa scanned a newspaper. "Here it is!" he cried.

Ah Toy, wondering at his excitement, watched Hab Wa's finger trace through columns of type. The English words looked to her like trails of ants.

Tong Achik leaned forward, anxious, hands on his knees as though ready to rise and run. "Did they print it all?"

"I think so," said Hab Wa, his finger tracking through the column of type.

Ah Toy sipped her tea. "What say this paper?"

"Hab Wa and I wrote a letter to Governor Bigler," Tong Achik said, "and sent a copy to the newspaper, which has published it. You remember, I told you the Committee on Mines and Mining Interests complained to the legislature about the increasing numbers of Chinese miners."

Ah Toy shook her head. If Tong Achik had before spoken of this matter, she had forgotten it.

"Governor Bigler, in a message to the legislative committee," said Tong Achik, "called the Chinese 'contract coolies' dangerous to the welfare of the state. The committee recommended that Chinese be excluded from the mines."

Ah Toy's thoughts flew to Li Jin. "This happens? When?"

"Not yet. The committee wants to avoid any policy that could disturb commercial relations with China."

Hab Wa looked up from the newspaper. "The Chinese must stop being so separate. The barbarians do not understand us because they do not know us."

Ah Toy recalled her first night in Gum Shan and the barbarian who insisted she was different from other women. "They know nothing," she said.

Tong Achik said, "Hab Wa and I tried in this letter to explain the truth about Chinese immigrants."

Ah Toy sipped her tea. "Read it to me."

"It is long," Hab Wa said.

"Read," said Ah Toy.

Hab Wa began: " 'Sir: The China men have learned with sorrow that you have published a letter against them. Although we are Asiatics, some of us have been educated in schools and have learned your language, which has enabled us to read your message for ourselves, and to explain it to the rest of our countrymen. We have all thought a great deal about it, and, after consultation with one another, we have determined to write you as decent and respectful a letter as we could, pointing out to Your Excellency some of the errors you have fallen into about us. You speak of the China men as 'coolies,' and in one sense the word is applicable to a great many of them; but not in that in which you seem to use it. 'Cooly' is not a Chinese word; it has been imported into China from foreign parts, as it has been into this country. What its original signification was, we do not know; but with us it means a common laborer, and nothing more. We have never known it used among us as a designation of a class, such as you have in view—persons bound to labor under contracts which they can be forcibly compelled to comply with. The Irishmen who are engaged in digging down your hills, the men who unload ships, who clean your streets, or even drive your drays, would, if they were in China, be considered 'coolies'; tradesmen, mechanics of every kind, and professional men would not. If you mean by 'coolies,' laborers, many of our countrymen in the mines are 'coolies,' and many again are not. There are among them tradesmen, mechanics, gentry (being persons of respectability and a certain rank and privilege), and schoolmasters, who are reckoned with the gentry, and with us considered a respectable class of people. None are 'coolies,' if by that word you mean bound men or contract slaves. The ship *Challenge,* of which you speak in your message as bringing over more than five hundred China men, did not bring over one who was under 'cooly' contract to labor. They were all passengers and are going to work in the mines for themselves.' "

Hab Wa sipped some tea and continued, " 'The poor China man does not come here as a slave. He comes because of his desire for independence, and he is assisted by the charity of his countrymen, which they bestow on him safely, because he is industrious and honestly repays them. When he gets to the mines, he sets to work with patience, industry, temperance, and economy. He gives no man offence, and he is contented with small gains, perhaps only two or three dollars per day. His living costs him something, and he is well pleased if he saves up three or four hundred dollars a year. Like all other nations, and as is particularly to be expected of them, many return home with their money, there to remain, buy rice fields, build houses, and devote themselves to the society of their own households and the increase of the products of their country, of its exports and imports, of its commerce and the general wealth of the world. But not all; others—full as many as in other nations—invest their gains in merchandise and bring it into the country and sell it at your markets. It is possible, sir, that you may not be aware how great this trade is, and how rapidly it is increasing, and how many are now returning to California as merchants who came over originally as miners. We are not able to tell you how much has been paid by Chinese importers at the Custom House, but the sum must be very large. In this city alone there are twenty stores kept by China men, who own the lots and erected the buildings themselves. In these stores a great deal of business is done; all kinds of Chinese goods—rice, silks, sugar, tea, etcetera—are sold in them, and also a great quantity of American goods, especially boots, of which every China man buys one or more pairs immediately on landing. And then there are the American stores dealing in Chinese articles on a very large scale, and some with the most remarkable success. The emigration of the 'coolies,' as Your Excellency rather mistakenly calls us, is attended with the opening of all this Chinese trade, which, if it produces the same results here as elsewhere, will yet be the pride and riches of this city and State. One of the subscribers of this letter is now employed as a clerk in an American store, because of the services he can render them as a broker in business with his countrymen; he has sometimes sold ten thousand dollars a day in Chinese goods.' "

Ah Toy looked at Tong Achik. He nodded. "Read more," she said, thinking that Tong Achik's growing wealth and powerful position was a good omen for her daughter.

Hab Wa drew his finger down the column of ants. " 'If you want to check immigration from Asia, you will have to do it by checking Asiatic commerce, which we supposed, from all that we have ever known of your government, the United States most desired to increase. What Your Excellency has said about passing a law to prevent coolies, shipped to California under contracts, from laboring in the mines, we do not conceive concerns us, for there are none such here from China, nor do we believe any are coming, except a small number, perhaps, who work on shares, just as people from all other countries sometimes do. We will not believe it is your intention to pass a law treating us as coolies whether we are so or not.' "

Hab Wa paused and looked at Tong Achik. "I don't know if this is as convincing as we hoped. The letter is so long that perhaps no one will read it."

Tong Achik shrugged. "Go on."

Hab Wa read, " 'In what we here say we have most carefully told Your Excellency the truth; but we fear you will not believe us, because you have spoken in your message of us as Asiatics, 'ignorant of the solemn character of the oath or affirmation in the form prescribed in the Constitution and statutes,' or 'indifferent to the solemn obligation to speak the truth which an oath imposes.' It is truth, nevertheless, and we leave it to time and the proof which our words carry in them to satisfy you of the fact. It has grieved us that you should publish so bad a character of us, and we wish that you could change your opinion and speak well of us to the public. We do not deny that many China men tell lies, and so do many Americans, even in courts of justice. But we have our courts, too, and our forms of oaths, which are as sacredly respected by our countrymen as other nations respect theirs. We do not swear upon so many little occasions as you do, and our forms will seem as ridiculous to you as yours do to us when we first see them. You will smile when we tell you that on ordinary occasions an oath is attested by burning a piece of yellow paper, and on the more important ones by cutting off the head of a cock; yet these are only forms and cannot be of great importance, we would think. But in the important matters we are good men; we honor our parents; we take care of our children; we are industrious and peaceable; we trade much; we are trusted for small and large sums; we pay our debts and are honest; and, of course, must tell the truth—"

"*Aaiii!* Mother, come!" Xiao-li stumbled into the parlor. Tears spilled over her cheeks.

Ah Toy moved as if through fog, unseeing, intent on tasks that masked her grief.

The funeral was on the fifth day. Ah Toy had hired a geomancer to determine the propitious times for encoffining and for burial. Throughout the night before, as Mei-Ling lay sealed within her cypresswood casket, Ah Toy had wept while musicians played their doleful instruments.

Everything that could be done, Ah Toy had done. Outside her house she replaced the red paper lanterns with white ones. She posted a white paper in a bamboo frame, giving notice of the spirit's departure. Inside the house, the strips of red paper pasted above doorways were replaced with white ones.

Ah Toy had wept as she bound Mei-Ling's hair with a red cord and dressed her in new trousers and a coat lined with red satin. Into the coat's buttonhole she fastened a tiny red bag containing a silver earring Mei-Ling could use for money, and pieces of candy and salt vegetable to make her food more palatable. In Mei-Ling's mouth she had placed a few grains of rice for her farewell meal. Around her neck she tied wisps of cotton wool that she might bear away with her the misfortunes of the house.

Ah Toy lined the coffin with packets of dry lime, ashes, and earth. Over them she laid cotton wool for a mattress, and for Mei-Ling's head a pillow of red cloth with crescent corners.

Then Ah Toy announced she would have a procession, with professional mourners and two bands of musicians.

Chow Lai had said with surprise, "No one who has not been married is entitled to a funeral procession!"

Ah Toy was adamant, determined to dispatch Mei-Ling's spirit with all the observances within her power and purse to provide.

"This Gum Shan is a new place," she told Chow Lai, "without old rules. People make new rules here, and my rule for Mei-Ling is that she shall have a procession."

Now, in the street, Ah Toy heard musicians banging drums and gongs. It was nearly noon, the time named by the geomancer for departure to the cemetery. She sent Chan and Xiao-li to the second carriage and called, "Chow Lai? Where are you?"

"Here, Sister."

Chow Lai, in white satin pantaloons and a blue jacket that matched her earrings of kingfisher feathers, posed provocatively in the open doorway. Her cheeks and lips were bright with rouge.

Ah Toy saw people in the street staring at the saucy girl. "Chow Lai! You show yourself like a grocer displays vegetables!"

Chow Lai smoothed her hair. "For the same reason, Sister. The grocer who sells no vegetables buys no meat."

The girl spoke truth, Ah Toy knew. Mei-Ling's illness and burial, and the loss of her earnings, cost dearly. Ah Toy knew that she, too, must soon display herself to recoup the losses.

The procession started south down Pike street, led by two men carrying streamers of white paper. A man scattering mock money from a basket filled with paper coins followed, purchasing the right of way for Mei-Ling's spirit. The entourage turned right on Sacramento street to Stockton street, then south toward the plank road that led to the Yerba Buena Cemetery.

Behind the man tossing mock money, two bearers carried large paper figures on bamboo poles. A black figure of a fierce-looking soldier would frighten away malignant spirits. The red figure of a woman with a teacup and teapot would serve Mei-Ling in the spirit world. Next came bearers with a paper sedan chair for Mei-Ling's comfort there, and two miniature mountains of gilt and silver paper, that she should have an inexhaustible supply of money. Mourners in subdued colors followed, displaying scrolls, banners, flags, and silk umbrellas with three flounces. Behind them eight bearers carried an empty green sedan chair, a mourner marching on each side. A two-horse wagon filled with noisy musicians preceded horse-drawn carriages with the chief mourners, Mei-Ling's coffin, and food offerings of rice, fruit, fish, chicken, and a whole roasted pig the color of mahogany.

Three Taoist priests in blue gowns promenaded behind, clanging cymbals, murmuring prayers, perfuming the air with incense. A trail of wailing mourners with lighted joss sticks followed on foot, a band of musicians endorsing their cries with shrilling flutes, thumping drums, and the reverberating brass of gongs.

The procession passed down Stockton street and along the plank road toward the mission, collecting the respectful and the curious, who followed like streamers on a kite.

The Yerba Buena Cemetery lay where McAllister street intersected the plank road. It was bound into a triangle by Larkin street. Beyond stretched the unmapped sands of the city's western reach. The cemetery's sand, dotted with chaparral and sagebrush, lay bleached beneath the noonday sun. Untidy mounds declared the resting places of those who had died upon the Gold Mountain. As the procession entered, a hare raced toward the bloodred branches of a solitary manzanita.

The geomancer selected a suitable spot in the section reserved for Chinese. He indicated to the diggers the direction the coffin must lie. Ah Toy urged care. Unlike the bones of men—which would in time be unearthed, the remaining flesh dissolved with vinegar, and the bones packed in clay jars for return to China and proper burial—Mei-Ling's bones would remain on the Gold Mountain. A woman's bones merited no reverence.

Chow Lai and Chan supervised the setting out of tables and mats for the pyramids of pears and oranges, trays mounded with colored pastry, bowls piled high with rice, plates with fish and duck, and the board on which reposed the roasted pig.

Wails greeted bearers bringing forth the coffin. A Taoist priest struck the box with a large kitchen knife and, with a second blow, broke an empty bowl to alert Mei-Ling's spirit for its approaching journey.

As gravediggers lowered the coffin, musicians pounded gongs and drums. Loudly lamenting mourners set fire to the paper soldier and servant, the paper sedan chair, the paper mountains of gold and silver, and all the mock money, forwarding to Mei-Ling's spirit their usefulness on clouds of smoke.

The priests placed in the grave the streamers carried in the procession. The diggers anchored them with sand. Through her tears, Ah Toy watched a breeze lift the lengths of white paper. They fluttered from Mei-Ling's grave like trapped wings. Ah Toy looked up into the blue sky and sent prayers. Go to heaven, my friend, and be happy in the cloud garden.

Now she looked around at the festive gathering paying respect to Mei-Ling. Ah Toy saw with a glad heart that Tong Achik had accompanied the procession. Such honor was unusual, she knew, when in China even a husband was under no obligation to accompany the corpse of his wife to the gravesite. When the time was right, she would present Xiao-li to this good man.

Many more people than Ah Toy had expected attended Mei-Ling's funeral. Some were curious foreigners, but she saw, too, Assing's red-turban *boo how doy.* He slipped in and out of the crowd, swift and silent as a cobra strike. A flash of red caught her eye now and she saw him again. He had pinned against a wagon, Ah Toy saw with surprise, two China women.

Several China women, Ah Toy knew, had come to Gum Shan recently. So Chan advised her from the gossip collected on Sacramento street. A secret society, the Hip Yee tong, imported and controlled the women, he said, confining them in tiny rooms in Little China's alleyways.

Ah Toy watched Wah Gae coil about the two women trapped

against the wagon. Just then, a noisy knot of Ah Toy's hired mourners distracted him as they trooped around the wagon with trays of
food to return to the city.

In the confusion, the two women escaped. On satin-slippered
feet, their heads bowed low beneath ornately dressed hair, they
scurried toward Ah Toy.

At As-sing's direction, seven China men unfurled the crimson silk
and hoisted it on bamboo poles. The banner's gold-thread dragon
flared into the sunlight, flashing glittery looking-glass eyes. The
dragon banner, twenty feet long and twelve high, had cost As-sing
two thousand dollars. He looked at it, bucking and dancing in the
morning breeze, and didn't care. The investment assured him lead-
ership of the parade's China men.

Nearly four hundred agreed to march. Carrying elaborate paper
fans, they had organized into district groups. Men from Kwangtung's Heungshan district would soon outnumber the Sze Yups,
As-sing suspected, surveying the men in carriages, on horseback,
and on foot. With the increased immigration from China—nine
hundred on just one day in April—membership in Gum Shan's
three Chinese companies had swelled, especially with Hakkas and
Heungshan men. Fortunately for his own recent investment with
the thriving Sze Yup society, neither group possessed the financing
necessary to establish separate companies.

Two men unrolled a purple satin banner inscribed in English:
"The 4th of July hereafter and forever a festival day for the Chinese."

"Well said, As-sing." Tong Achik, holding the reins of a chest-
nut horse, nodded his approval.

As-sing acknowledged him with a bow. Tong Achik had gained
much face from meeting Governor Bigler at the state government

offices in San Jose. As-sing, Sam Wo, and other wealthy merchants had sent gifts of Oriental shawls, rolls of the best silk, and seventy embroidered handkerchiefs. Tong Achik had presented the gifts to the governor, but Bigler remained resolutely anti-Chinese.

Emissaries and diplomacy accomplished nothing, As-sing thought. Americans respected wealth and power and those who possessed it. He shared such practical views.

Ahead, at the corner of Broadway and Stockton, the First California Guard fired a thirteen-gun salute, announcing the parade's commencement. As-sing climbed into the carriage behind the winking silk dragon. The four matched gray horses pranced restlessly, jingling harness bells. Sam Wo nodded. As-sing's new wealth depended on Sam Wo's Hip Yee tong connection. Both men knew it. An honored place in the processional carriage was the latest cost the man exacted.

As-sing ignored the man's sleek presence and savored anticipation. Ahead, the California Guards, marching at the fore in red-trimmed blue coats and trousers, pivoted into Stockton street. The forty-member Eureka Light Horse Company and sixty men of the Marion Rifles, wearing green uniforms with black velvet trim and yellow buttons, followed.

The Society of California Pioneers took up the march. Behind them, an association of French citizens, carrying banners of tricolored silk, tramped in steady concordance with the rat-a-tat tapping of three foppish drummers.

As-sing's driver clicked his horses' reins. The Chinese delegation moved forward. At Stockton street, the banner men whirled their swirl of crimson silk and its flashing-eyed dragon into a roar of approval. As-sing beamed and tipped his stovepipe hat to the shouting, cheering spectators.

The procession looped its splendor around the city's center, along flag-draped streets jammed with applauding onlookers — Stockton to Clay, down to Montgomery, over to Bush street and down to Battery, from there to California and up to Sansome, and then to Washington. Amid whistles and cheers, the strutting China men exploded firecrackers, thumped wooden drums, and beat a brassy thunder of gongs.

As-sing knew he had mounted the finest spectacle ever to grace the streets of an American city. Even the sight of Ah Toy, watching from the corner of Pike and Clay street with her women, failed to diminish his triumph.

He owned many daughters of joy. The *mui tsai* was nothing.

As the parade passed down Clay, Ah Toy nodded to the American lawyer who rode with the National Lancers. They wore uniforms of blue and orange and carried steel lances.

"Honored Sister," said Chow Lai, laughing, "these men all look the same to me. I cannot tell one barbarian from another except by the color of their excessive hair."

"Barbarians pride themselves much on their hair," said Ah Toy, her thoughts flying to the smooth-faced Li Jin. She had hoped to see him today. He should have returned from the mines by now. Chow Lai and Xiao-li had searched with her the faces of marching China men. They saw Chan strutting with the Hakka men and Tong Achik on a prancing horse, but not Li Jin.

Chow Lai had said, "Look, Xiao-li, your bridegroom!"

Xiao-li had hidden her face. "Mother, is this proper?"

"You and the bridegroom have seen each other many times," Ah Toy said. "It is not improper here to gaze upon the one you shall marry. Everything here is different. Remember the words of the Reverend Speer."

Xiao-li had returned from the Presbyterian mission house in-trigued. "Mother," she had said, "it is a strange thing to think on, but the earth and all the creatures could not create themselves. Such things cannot just happen, there must be a creator. Dr. Speer says this creator is a god, and this one god created and governs everything. Those who obey him will go to heaven where there is everlasting food and happiness, and no sickness or famine or death! Dr. Speer says that people in every country revere this god. They worship only him, no other gods, and this god needs no temple or statues."

Ah Toy had smiled. There was, she concluded, no harm for Xiao-li in this god belief. Confucianism, Buddhism, and Taoism served women no better. Even so, the girl would never abandon the old thinking. None of them could. Ancient ways endured.

Ah Toy had permitted Tong Achik to send Xiao-li to the missionary. In return he promised to observe the old ceremonies. Lacking a professional marriage broker, Ah Toy sent Chan with the first document, making the proposal. Tong Achik, as evidence of acceptance, returned a draft of the eight characters representing the year, month, day, and hour of his birth. Then he called on Ah Toy with gifts of jeweled hairpins and silver bracelets for Xiao-li. He agreed to send Ah Toy the traditional second document, fixing the marriage day.

Now, as a procession of native Californians pranced past on silver-draped horses, Xiao-li leaned against Ah Toy with a soft sigh. "You are unwell?" Ah Toy asked with quick concern.

"Only a little tired, Mother." Xiao-li rested her yellow paper parasol on her shoulder.

"It is the fatigue of the feet, Sister," said Chow Lai, rocking on the satin-cased buds peeking from beneath her skirt. "We must return to the lucky-number house now."

Chow Lai rarely ventured from the house, where she reigned like an emperor's favorite. When Ah Toy remarked on her customers' devotion, Chow Lai confided, "Chan buys for me in Sacramento street the Indian monk's red powder."

Trained mist-and-flower ladies possessed secrets unknown to Ah Toy. "What is this powder?"

"Ancient assistance. Only small amount," Chow Lai cautioned, pinching rice powder from her cheek for an example. "Place in horse's eye," she said, dabbing the powder against the end of her finger to demonstrate. She stiffened her finger to illustrate the powder's potency. "Small horse," Chow Lai giggled, looking at her rigid finger.

Ah Toy laughed.

"Red powder make ponies gallop like stallions," Chow Lai said. "Men pleased so strong. Give plenty gold." She grinned and gave Ah Toy some of the rare substance.

Ah Toy preferred Mei-Ling's book of bound silk pictures, which urged visitors to swift pleasure. She had no wish to induce the prolonged rigidity the Indian monk's red powder ignited. The strength and capacity of powdered stallions required much time.

With the exception of the disfigured lawyer, she permitted no man more of her time than Mei-Ling's book encouraged.

After the parade, Xiao-li helped Ah Toy dress for the celebration events the lawyer insisted they attend. Fastening the buttons of Ah Toy's gown, Xiao-li said, "Wear the white jade dragon, Mother. It is so beautiful and promises good fortune."

Ah Toy smiled at the words heard first from Tsu Yen in a life she once knew. She placed the pendant around her neck and fingered the jade in the old way. She hoped soon to return to the land of the good-fortune dragon, for honored years as a mother of Li Jin's sons.

A knocking on the door downstairs interrupted her reverie. She tucked it away in the place she kept dreams and went to greet Elbridge Austin.

Ah Toy had met Austin at a ball hosted by the Monumental Engine Company, and it was to its merrily crowded headquarters that he whisked her now for the Independence Day celebration. "For a collation," he said, handing her out of the carriage.

Inside, next to a brass pump engine decorated in ribbons of red, white, and blue, he filled two glasses with champagne. He showed her the label. "Grizzly Bear," he read, chuckling at the crudely designed beast papered on the bottle. "Some smart Boston bottler has got the pulse of the California market."

He handed her a glass. "To independence," he said, clinking his glass to hers, "and the Fourth of July."

Ah Toy sipped. "Cold!" she said in surprise.

Austin laughed. "Yes, my lovely, we have ice again, our elusive luxury." He held the bottle to her cheek to feel the unfamiliar chill. "Only thirteen days from Sitka and fifty cents a pound," he said, refilling their glasses. "California gold brings the world to its port, and never mind the cost."

Ah Toy sipped and put a finger under her nose. The champagne's bubbles tickled.

Austin took her hand. "Such a pretty and dainty hand. Such a lovely hand deserves praise, laurels." He lifted her hand to his thicket of mustache and kissed it.

Ah Toy smiled. She liked this big, funny man whose profuse face hair masked but slightly the purple gash sliced across his countenance. A saber scar from the war with Mexico, he told her. His damaged face made him shy with American women and grateful to her for her indifference to it.

Austin had for several weeks come regularly to her house, sweeping gentlemanly bows to giggling Chow Lai and shy Xiao-li. He brought preposterous gifts of California-grown vegetables that amused him with their gargantuan size. A seventy-five-pound squash defied Chan's every effort to reduce it to meals. A single radish too large for its half-bushel basket even now lounged in her kitchen like a cannonball.

What Ah Toy most appreciated was Austin's encouragement that she talk to him. He listened when she did. Eventually she told him about A-Ti and Gee Sing, and he promised to help them.

"This comely hand," said Austin, turning Ah Toy's hand in his own while he peered at it as if through a jeweler's glass, "merits ornamentation, adornment, embellishment." He kissed it again and winked at her. "Perhaps I have just the thing."

Ah Toy laughed. "Long green bean?"

"Aha! The lovely lady jests! Such banter, such wit! Forsooth," he said, filling her glass with a flourish, "the lovely lady shall be rewarded with a gift for her wit and her wrist. At dinner, I think, in candlelight, where baubles gleam most radiant." He winked and handed her the glass.

It was their unspoken agreement that he paid her with gifts, a gesture he preferred to placing gold in her hand. His gifts were generous and easily sold, and Ah Toy did not object.

The evening was a festive whirl. Austin flaunted her through a blur of happy toasts at the fire companies—Monumental Engine, Howard Company Number 3, California Number 4, the Sansome Hook and Ladder Company.

At half past eight, he escorted her to the plaza for the fireworks display. It began with an exuberant discharge of rockets and Roman candles. Nearly fifteen thousand spectators had gathered for the extravaganza, and with the exception of some disappointing "Maltese suns" that failed to ignite, the show was a great success. Ah Toy thought the finale a splendid display. Full-length figures of Minerva, George Washington, General Scott, the goddess of liberty, and a miner had been painted on canvas and mounted between two columns. Over Minerva's head were the figures "1850," over the miner, "1852," and between them, " '76." Above the whole was a high arch. A match was applied and the structure glittered with stars. A piece of firework shot like a meteor over peoples' heads, burned briefly at the far side of the plaza, and shot back. Ah Toy gasped in amazement, but Austin pointed out the almost invisible wire on which it was mounted. It shot back and forth several times, each time more brilliantly.

The odor of saltpeter hung in the air as Austin led Ah Toy to the Franklin House for supper. The candlelit glitter of crystal and silver gracing the city's restaurants no longer dazzled Ah Toy, but she still appreciated a bountiful meal.

San Francisco lacked for nothing now. Clipper ships delivered the world's delicacies to the tables of gold-rich California, and farmers harvested a bounty of vegetables and wheat from the fertile interior valleys. Game and fowl filled the city's markets and meat dealers' stalls. Chan told of seeing on the streets whole cartloads of geese, ducks, quails, quarters of bear and antelope, haunches of elk and deer, fish of every description. The recent salmon season was bounteous to the point of waste. The price on Sacramento street plummeted from forty cents a pound to three.

Ah Toy had long since lost her fear of famine. Gum Shan remained crude, dirty, incomprehensibly unmannered, but it overflowed with things to eat. She murmured her pleasure now as a white-aproned waiter presented a platter of oysters.

After she swallowed the last strawberry, Austin laughed heartily. "Lovely lady, you refresh my spirit! You are a joy to witness! American women pick at food as though they had no need of it." He winked. "They are, by comparison to your lovely self, remarkably reluctant in many ways."

Ah Toy smiled and accepted a candy mint the waiter offered.

"Sweets for the sweet," said Austin. From his pocket he took a diamond bracelet and dangled it in the candlelight.

"Cost much gold!"

"Actually, my lovely, it cost five dollars for lottery tickets to Duncan's grand raffle," said Austin, fastening it around her wrist, "which in no way diminishes the bauble's worth, I assure you."

Ah Toy calculated its value at eight hundred dollars.

"Smart fellow that Duncan," said Austin, accepting two glasses of dessert sherry from the waiter. "He's had great success on steamer day, auctioning off fancy silk shawls to departing miners to take to their sisters and sweethearts. So he decided to go himself one better and hold a grand raffle."

"What this raffle?" asked Ah Toy, sipping the sherry. It tasted like candied sunshine.

"Like a lottery. Californians love a lottery. For most of us California *is* a lottery, isn't it? Well, we've become proverbial for throwing away a few dollars upon a chance and think nothing of it. So Duncan printed twenty-five thousand tickets and sold them for a dollar apiece. The prizes were one thousand items of merchandise he claimed worth, in all, twenty-five thousand dollars. I'd guess more like fifteen, and he pocketed ten thousand dollars as tidily as if he'd sold the stuff. Anyway, he displayed the goods and announced there'd be a thousand numbers drawn. Half the city must have bought one or more tickets. The drawing was a big event, I assure you, held at the American Theatre with all the ceremony of an election. A committee of gentlemen selected by the ticketholders superintended the affair. They pulled a thousand slips of paper from the twenty-five thousand in a great revolving wheel and called the numbers as though each one matched this beautiful bracelet." He turned it on her wrist. "Only the first and last numbers drawn won the most valuable prizes. Most holders collected shawls and silk hangings, although some ivory and jade carvings may have been worth two or three hundred dollars."

"You hold first number or last?"

Austin laughed. "You think the last number not as lucky, don't you?" He folded his arms across his chest and grinned at her. "Well, the last number won a gorgeous painting of Diana and her maids preparing for the chase, the figures rendered exquisitely life-sized."

Ah Toy wrinkled her nose and shook her head.

"No, you would not have wanted it. Neither did the ticket-holder, in fact. Duncan bought it back for eight hundred and fifty dollars. He, at least, prized it."

Ah Toy patted Austin's hand. "You number one lucky man. Win best prize."

Austin took her hand and kissed it. "Yes, the best." He smiled at her, his scar hunching into a purple rope beneath one eye. "So, now. Where shall we take you to show off your lucky jewels? The New Orleans Serenaders are at the Adelphi Theatre. Mrs. Stark is performing at the American. Elisa Biscaccianti is singing at the Jenny Lind. Which shall it be?"

The Jenny Lind Theatre, on the east side of the plaza, next to the El Dorado, rose in spectacular beauty like the phoenix it was. Twice destroyed by fire, the theater in its third incarnation boasted a facade of finely dressed, yellow-tinted Australian sandstone. A luxurious interior seated two thousand.

The cost ruined its owner, Austin told her. "Maguire, to pay his creditors, has sold the beautiful thing to the city for its offices," he said, guiding Ah Toy to pink velvet box seats with gilded fronts. "The city council, for reasons apparently known only to themselves, paid him two hundred thousand dollars for it. The people and the press are justifiably indignant."

Ah Toy nodded her indifference. A government's imperative, whether barbarian or Chinese, it seemed, was excessive taxation for foolish expenditure. She thought it a shame, though, to sacrifice this golden pink elegance to such misguided requisition. The third

Jenny Lind was the most magnificent theater yet built in San Francisco. Even its act drop, featuring a picturesque ruin, was exquisite. It was just now being withdrawn. The audience, seeing Elisa Biscaccianti, burst into applause.

The diminutive songstress smiled, and the audience cheered. She bowed. They cheered louder. Ah Toy was mystified by such a display when the woman had yet to sing a single note. The entertainer seemed to share Ah Toy's wonder, for she bowed again with an imploring look that begged an end to this exchange of civilities.

At last she sang. Biscaccianti was, Austin explained, a coloratura soprano. "Not equal to Jenny Lind, the critics say, for fullness and inspiration," he whispered, "but surpassing the Swedish nightingale in pathos, melody, and artistic finish."

To Ah Toy's ear the patriotic songs sounded dull and lifeless. "Not like Chinese opera," she told Austin at intermission.

"I should like to hear a Chinese opera," he said, pouring them wine.

"Perhaps come soon this place." Hab Wa, she knew, was contracting to bring Chinese entertainers to Gum Shan.

"If and when, I should be honored to escort you to a performance."

Ah Toy smiled at the unattractive barbarian behind his blanket of red hair. "I go with you."

"I will hold you to the promise." Austin clicked her glass with his. "Incidentally," he said, promenading her among the crowd, "I am holding you also to your promise to appear as a witness for those two women. We have been in court once, you know, and they reversed themselves, utterly denied anyone extorted money from them. They promise me now, to the extent I can trust the interpreter's credibility, they will tell the truth. Your presence, I am hoping, will give them courage."

"No China high men this place!"

"I believe you, but that sinister-looking fellow with the red bandanna intimidates them."

"I no afraid cake seller's *boo how doy!*"

"Lovely lady, I doubt you are afraid of anything, unless it's my two left feet."

Confused, Ah Toy looked down at Austin's patent boots.

He laughed. "A figure of my speech, lovely lady. I suggest we adjourn to the Jackson House where the Empire Engine Company is hosting a ball. I was assured it shall be numerously attended by the wit and beauty of San Francisco, which shall be an utter lie without your appearance."

The ball lasted past midnight, and dawn was approaching when Austin opened Ah Toy's door for her. He took her hand. "Forgive, my lovely lady, but I regret I must take my leave."

Ah Toy tugged his hand as if to lead him upstairs.

"I fear, dear lady, neither your own undeniably desirable charms nor your tantalizing picture book can overcome sweet slumber's call. I have, unhappily, expended myself on wine."

Ah Toy, wine-weary with fatigue, craved to creep into her bed alone and summon sweet dreams of her future. But her obligation encircled her wrist, sparkling in the lamplight.

"Lucky number, lucky bracelet." She pressed Austin's hand to the white jade dragon suspended between her breasts. "Lucky dragon. Much luck this house."

She kissed Austin's scarred face. "You come with me," she whispered seductively, pulling him by the hand up the stairs behind her. "I make you strong like stallion."

The American Theatre, built on the fill comprising Sansome street, on its opening night sank several inches under the weight of its audience. Ah Toy detected no unsteadiness in the building's foundation now, however, as Austin led her to their first-tier box seats decorated with gold-banded pillars and red velvet curtains suspended from gilded eagles' beaks.

"I should enjoy seeing more of the acrobats," said Austin, draping Ah Toy's cape over her chair, "especially that double-jointed dwarf. And those Chinese magicians put Occidentals completely in the shade."

Ah Toy smiled as she recalled the lawyer's enjoyment of the Chinese tumblers and jugglers with their flying knives and balance plates. That troupe had moved on to New Orleans and the East, she told him. Tonight's performers, imported as an investment by Hab Wa and Tong Achik, would stay. Following their engagement at the American, the company intended erecting their own theater; they had brought the portable framework with them from China.

"No acrobat tonight," she said. "Famous Chinese play tonight. Many actors this company, Hook Tong."

"Tong? This is a tong! Are these people more Triads!"

Ah Toy hushed him with a shake of her head and put a finger to his lips. His voice had carried, and she saw people turn. The fires of anti-Chinese sentiments burned bright enough; they needed no fuel from the secret societies.

"*Tong* mean all kind people together," Ah Toy whispered. "Some tong people this, some that. Not bad only. Hook Tong actor people."

She knew Austin was disappointed by his failure to indict Wah Gae for extorting protection money from the two women A-Ti and Gee Sing. Ah Toy's court appearance accomplished little. The women still refused to testify despite confessing to her and Austin that Wah Gae and other Kwan Ducs demanded money from them for protection. Competing tongs, the Hip Yees and Ong Sungs, trying to drive out the Kwan Ducs, also forced the women to pay. It was regrettable, but inevitable, they confided, that secret societies supported their criminal activities by extorting protection money from prostitutes and storekeepers.

The women gained courage when Ah Toy argued that Gum Shan customs deplored such tactics, but the tongs again frightened them into silence. Twice the judge recessed while Ah Toy and Austin cajoled the fearful women. Entreaties proved fruitless. Eventually, the judge, angry and frustrated, dismissed the case.

Austin, incensed over the injustice, urged Ah Toy to expose in the courts the criminal element preying upon the Chinese community. To protect Chan, she had declined.

Chan had confided to her that in his home village he had been forced to drink the bloody wine. He joined the Kwan Duc secret society to protect his family, he said, and to escape death. He feared reprisal if Ah Toy exposed the Triads.

Ah Toy suspected now that A-Ti and Gee Sing never intended to testify in court. They wanted only the sanctuary of her house, safe because Ah Toy remained outside the pale of the Chinese community. She had exempted herself from the old ways by her knowledge of English, her ready resort to American courts, her associations with judges and lawyers.

Ah Toy had finally acceded to their pleas to move into her house. Since the women entertained only China men, they represented no competition to her or Chow Lai, and the lucky-number house was spacious.

Austin stared at the stage. "Is that strange thing part of the action?" he asked, pointing at a statue.

"No, no," said Ah Toy, smiling. "That theater god, Han Shang-chu, one of eight immortals. He patron god for musicians."

Just then the Chinese musicians took up their instruments. The clashing sounds of flutes, lutes, flageolets, gongs, stone chimes, and wooden drums assailed the audience.

"Good grief," said Austin, covering his ears, "that Han Shang-chu fellow must be an impostor! No god in his heaven could foster that impertinent racket and call it music!"

A man in the adjoining box laughed. "Sounds to me like a band of cornstalk fiddles," he said to Austin, "strained up to a double-G key with an occasional blast from a pumpkin-vine trombone breaking in by way of variety."

Cymbals crashed as the stage curtain opened. A magnificently dressed actor sat on a chair on top of a table. His gown of red and blue satin shimmered with gold embroidery. Its dozens of tiny mirrors flashed reflections from the theater's lights.

Ah Toy heard the man in the next box chuckle. "This dandy has solved for himself the city's rat problem," he told Austin. "My wife gets up on tables, too, but she's yet to take her chair with her. Now, if this gentleman can get those black-faced fellows galloping around on the stage to carry him through the city in that counterfeit sedan chair, he has solved the mud problem, too. These Chinese are an inventive lot, aren't they?"

Austin's beard tickled Ah Toy's ear as he whispered, "I would appreciate your advices, my lady, on those prancing fellows with the painted faces and that splendidly dressed gentleman who has got his chair up on the table. This style of theater had not reached Baltimore by the time of my departure, I assure you."

"Chair on table same like mountain," Ah Toy said. "Important commander watch from top." She explained that the prancing actors masked with black paint represented rough but honest men on horseback. When actors with faces painted green entered the stage, she said, "Green men demon. Big war come now."

A noisy and energetic engagement ensued between the black-

faced actors and the green-faced. Following the vigorous interces-
sion of actors with faces painted red, which Ah Toy explained signified courage, the actor on the mountaintop chair climbed down.
Musicians banged a brassy clamor of cymbals. Tossing the loose
front panels of his robe over his shoulders to reveal a different costume, the actor strode to the side of the stage. A plain-dressed man
handed him a cup of tea. Another man removed the chair from the
table and placed it to the side of the stage.

Austin pointed at the man with the chair. "Now who is that fellow, and what does that signify?"

Ah Toy smiled. "No need mountain now. Chair is chair. Man is
man who move chair, that all." She explained that in Chinese theater, little was considered necessary to invoke meaning. The audience was expected to understand that a man carrying an oar and an
umbrella was rowing a boat across a river in a rainstorm.

"But what about the cup of tea? What does that mean?"

Ah Toy smiled at the perplexity twisting Austin's scar into a
purplish gnarl. "Mean actor thirsty!" She laughed.

Austin laughed, too. "Very well, then explain why the fancy-
dress commander flung his gown over his head."

"He no commander now."

"What happened? I must have missed something."

"No miss anything. New play now."

"How do you know?"

"First one finish."

Austin's booming laugh turned heads and Ah Toy cautioned,
"Not funny this part. We see now story about how Soo Tsin made
high minister by six states."

"How do you know that?"

"All China people know these story. You listen down there," she
said, indicating with her chin the China men in the orchestra seats
below. "Hear words same like actors."

"I've been hearing all the babble down there. I just thought they were talking to each other."

"Some people talk. Some say story word."

"It's all right to talk during the play?"

"People pay money. Do what want."

"I see that." Austin looked over the gold-banded pillars at the orchestra seats. "They seem to be doing a lot of eating, too."

"You want eat? Boy sell melon seed, candy." Ah Toy watched a Chinese boy plow through the orchestra seats selling sweets.

"I'll wait for the intermission. We should have a break soon, shouldn't we?"

"No. No break Chinese play."

"But it seems very long."

"Yes, Chinese play long, sometime two, three day."

"Three days! You mean people are expected to sit three days through this prancing and tea-drinking and fiddle-scraping and cat-yowling that passes for singing!"

Ah Toy laughed. "No, no! Some go, more come. Play go three day, not people." She directed Austin's attention to the theater door where playgoers continued to arrive. "See . . ." She tugged at Austin's coat sleeve. "That man, that man I tell you command Wah Gae."

As-sing stood between the front row and the orchestra pit.

"The fellow in the stovepipe hat?"

Ah Toy nodded.

"He's the one you call 'cake seller'?"

"Yes, very bad man."

"I know who that is. That's Norman As-sing. He's in a heap of trouble with John Parrott."

Ah Toy exulted over As-sing's shame. Everyone knew of As-sing's failure to provide laborers for the erection of Parrott's building on the northwest corner of Montgomery and California streets. The foundation had already been laid when the ship arrived from

China with the dressed granite blocks. At the site, As–sing's crew examined the blocks chiseled with Chinese characters and refused to construct the building. No threats from an enraged As–sing could sway them.

Parrott, in desperation, sent to China for the building's architect. Months later the wizened little man arrived with his own workmen. When shown the building site, the architect explained through an interpreter that the owner was placing the building on the wrong corner. The stones had been cut and marked for the opposite corner, where no evil influences resided. The northwest corner was a bad-luck location, he explained, where evil spirits ruled. It was understandable, he argued, that no Gum Shan China man wished to defy such spirits.

Parrott, exasperated past endurance, protested that he didn't own the opposite corner. He demanded the building be erected immediately. The architect and his stonemasons had conferred, with much muttering and shaking of queues over the malignant location. Finally, after burning much yellow paper and drenching it with tea to drive off evil spirits, the workmen raised their bamboo scaffolding and commenced building.

Parrott paid them a dollar a day plus a half pound each of rice and fish. They worked from sunrise to sunset, with an hour for rice and fan-tan. In ninety days they completed the imposing three-story edifice. On the ninety-first they boarded the ship that had brought them and sailed for home. The express agents, Adams & Company, and the banking house of Page, Bacon & Company, moved into the building. No China man would go near it.

On the favorable corner across the street, Sam Brannan erected a brick building with green iron shutters for Wells, Fargo and Company. Ah Toy was one of hundreds of Chinese customers of the good-luck building. She always saw processions of China men walking in one door and out the other. They came to pay their respects to the god of wealth dispensing blessings on the bank with the auspicious *feng shui*. No China man doubted the long life and bountiful future of Wells, Fargo and Company.

Now, in the orchestra pit, a clash of cymbals signaled a change of acts. Next to Ah Toy, Austin cracked beechnuts and exchanged opinions on the drama with the man in the next box.

Ah Toy stared at As-sing. The cake seller's continuing loss of face pleased her. For the memorial parade honoring statesman Henry Clay, As-sing assembled so few China men they were relegated to the procession's last position. As-sing, pretending importance, carried an unimposing banner proclaiming "The China men of San Francisco." Everyone knew it was a poor showing.

For the great autumn festival, a thousand China men marched from Sacramento street to Dupont street, then around the plaza and up Kearny toward the cemetery to honor the dead. As-sing was just one of a dozen other high-man pretenders following the musicians. Ah Toy exulted over his diminishing importance.

On the stage, several actors converged menacingly on a man with his nose painted white. Austin said, "Explain the nose business, if you will, my dear. I'm at a loss here."

"White nose mean villain."

Austin cracked a beechnut, offered it to her, and asked, "Why is he lying down and placing a handkerchief over his face?"

"Villain dead now," Ah Toy said, then nibbled on the beechnut.

The white-nosed actor rose, removed the handkerchief, and left the stage. Austin said, "I don't suppose we are seeing a variation on the resurrection here. Where's the villain going?"

Ah Toy shrugged. "He dead. Not in story now."

Austin laughed, cracked another beechnut, and said, "I don't think this will play in Baltimore."

In the orchestra pit, cymbals crashed and dozens of actors streamed onto the stage. "Good grief," said Austin, "I don't think there are that many Yankee actors in the whole city."

The man in the neighboring box said, "You know, these people represent an unprecedented foreign immigration. According to shipping notices in the *Alta,* more than two thousand Chinese arrived here recently in just forty-eight hours. The *Cornwall* alone brought five hundred, and a half dozen other ships carried anywhere from two hundred to four hundred."

Austin nodded. "I fear for their reception in the mines."

The word *mines* snatched Ah Toy's attention. The mines meant Li Jin. What happened in the mines happened to Li Jin. She pulled at Austin's sleeve. "What you mean? What you know?"

"About the mines?"

"Yes! What you know!" She peered into Austin's gashed face and felt anxiety knife her.

It was Chow Lai who discovered why Ah Toy had fled to her room with the statue of Kwan-yin. Chan knew only that Ah Toy ordered him to bring her some bricks, a piece of bamboo, a wood chip, a string, a small stick. A-Ti and Gee Sing, who kept to their rooms, knew nothing.

Chow Lai stood now in the doorway to Ah Toy's room. "Sister, this is a peasant's method. Do not be sad from it. I do not believe it reliable."

Ah Toy stared at the wooden chip lying on the floor beneath the string stretched from the statue of Kwan-yin to the bamboo pole held upright by bricks. "I have asked many times," she said, tears in her eyes. "The chip falls toward me one time and away the next. I do not know whether Li Jin is safe or dead."

Ah Toy had lived with dread ever since Austin told her about the lawless gangs preying upon Chinese miners. So many bad stories. Was Li Jin beaten with a pistol by the white man who sold a claim to Chinese miners and three days later demanded it back? Or was Li Jin robbed and murdered in the counties where it was now considered a sport, like a deer or bear hunt, to rush into Chinese camps at night, yelling and discharging revolvers?

A Mexican, Austin said, admitted upon his arrest that he had robbed and killed several Chinese, and then protested, "But Christian people ought not to hang me for that."

Was Li Jin among the unlucky whose destiny had sent him to Gum Shan for this Mexican man? The gods would not tell her. One time the vibrating string pitched the chip toward her, an affirmative answer, and the next away, the gods saying no.

Was Li Jin among the men struck, stabbed, or shot by tax collectors? Or tied to a tree and flogged? Or perhaps chased by a collector on horseback and lashed with a whip as he ran? The string method of divination refused to say.

Was Li Jin's neck placed in a noose while robbers drew the rope across a beam overhead until he confessed where his gold was hidden? The gods remained silent.

Xiao-li and Chan joined Chow Lai in Ah Toy's doorway. She saw her distress mirrored in their faces. She saw Chan glance at the fallen chip, disapproval in his eyes. He hesitated, looked as if to speak, said nothing.

"My fear is no secret," Ah Toy said. "Speak as you wish. You are my family."

Chan brushed his spiky hair from his forehead. "Lady, for truth, trust those who see the gods' designs in darkness."

Chow Lai looked at him in surprise. "In this place is a fortune-teller with no sight?"

"Yes," said Chan, "from the mines, where he discovered his talent after losing his eyes."

Ah Toy put her hand to her mouth to catch the cry escaping her throat. So many bad things happened in the place Li Jin traveled.

"How came this blindness?" she asked, fearing more terrible stories about barbarians tormenting China men.

"The gods willed it," said Chan. "This man, Yun Feng, fell asleep with his head under a harmful plant the barbarians call poison oak. Yun Feng, when he awoke, washed sleep from his eyes with its leaves. Now he sees what the gods intend."

Ah Toy leaped at the news of a seer from the place where Li Jin had gone. "Chan, take me to this fortune-teller!"

The Hakka boy looked doubtful and shook his head. "Lady, this fortune-teller live deep in Little China."

Ah Toy knew danger lurked in the dense huddle of lean-to shacks and sheds of San Francisco's Chinese quarter. The risk meant nothing. She had to know her destiny. "We go at once," she said.

Ah Toy, dressed in peasant clothing, ducked beneath a low doorway, then followed Chan down another dark and narrow passage of the bewildering maze that was Little China. She could see little from beneath the slouch hat Chan had insisted she wear.

Ahead, in a doorway, she saw Chan beckoning with his chin, his spiky hair a fierce defiance wrapped in red cloth.

Ah Toy had objected when Chan tied the red badge of the secret society over his forehead. "For safe passage," he said, and insisted she wear peasant clothes and the hat. She was known to be As-sing's enemy, he said, a valuable ransom to any *boo how doy* daring enough to kidnap her. Many such reckless men lived by their wits in the confusing tangle of Little China's alleyways.

"Through here." Chan led her across a dirt courtyard toward an opening shielded by a strip of canvas. Inside, a heavy-lidded man sat on a packing box dipping stained rice paper into a bowl of murky water. Ah Toy recognized the faint sweet smell clinging to the paper. It was the paper in which opium was wrapped. She remembered a slave in Lao Tai Tai's house who begged for such paper. He soaked it for its residue and drank the cloudy beverage. Poor man's opium it was called. The man on the packing box ignored them.

"This way," said Chan.

Ah Toy followed him into a windowless room. Thin shafts of gray light seeped through the cracks between slats. A dark-robed man sat in the corner, his open, sightless eyes restlessly wandering the unseen droop of calico ceiling. He smelled of incense and opium.

Chan engaged the fortune-teller in the conversation preliminary to business, then bowed his departure. "I wait in courtyard," he told Ah Toy.

Yun Feng stretched two gnarled hands toward Ah Toy, vacant eyes searching the ceiling. "Give me your hand," he said.

Ah Toy extended her right hand. Her left one she kept to her side, the sleeve rich with gold coins and the scroll of rice paper, Li Jin's ideographs.

Chow Lai had remembered them. Squealing her recollection, she had hurried to her room. She rushed back on tottering feet, waving the paper covered with the eight characters of Li Jin's birth. "From the time in the little house!"

Ah Toy recalled that happy night and the coy game Chow Lai had played, collecting the men's birth ideographs.

Chow Lai beamed. "Fortune-teller examine ideographs, say Li Jin's future!"

Ah Toy shook her head. "This man sees only the intents of the gods, not characters on paper." She uncurled the paper to look at Li Jin's future as if she could read it.

Chow Lai sniffed in exasperation. "Not that one! The blind one tells answers only. In the temple is one who reads ideographs for the future. You must go there also!"

"If the blind one fails," Ah Toy had said, patting Chow Lai's plump cheek in gratitude.

Yun Feng pressed his fingers against the bones of her hand, feeling the length of her fingers. *"Mo ku."*

Ah Toy understood. In English the words would literally mean "touch bones." The blind one was reading her bones. This ancient art of touch permitted him to foretell her future, but Ah Toy wanted only to know whether Li Jin remained safe. She asked, but Yun Feng said only, *"Mo ku,"* and drew the tips of his fingers along the bones of her hand.

Ah Toy, blessing Chow Lai's scroll, tried to withdraw her hand. The blind man gripped it and said, "With regard to your fortune for the present year, this year for you I read from your bones a coming calamity." His eyes roamed the ceiling as if seeking words to drop on her. "You know very well what you are about, and that you attract men." His lips curled into a grin.

Ah Toy pulled her hand from him. "You know nothing!" she shouted, ducking through the doorway.

"Give money to my man!" Yun Feng called after her.

Ah Toy plucked a coin from her sleeve and dropped it in the dirt in front of the man on the packing box. As she flung aside the canvas strip, he slurped his drink and retrieved the coin without looking at her.

The courtyard was empty. She called out, "Chan!" No one answered. She called again, waited. No one came.

Ah Toy felt confident of the first two turnings, but now the passage terminated at two doors. She did not remember which one she and Chan had come through. She opened one. It looked familiar. The light of a single window at the far end revealed several doors. She pushed open the nearest one.

She knew at once they had not come this way, but Chan might be here now. The room was crammed with noisy gamblers, their eyes pinned greedily to the dealer's stick. Chan, she knew, like most

China men, was addicted to games of chance. Perhaps he had come here for a quick bet on the fan-tan game.

Some thirty men surrounded a table where a dealer raked a whalebone stick through a mound of brass coins, counting them out in fours. Chan was not among the men.

Through the second door Ah Toy found only singsong girls chirping to the music of a bamboo harp and moonfiddle while China men leered at them.

A third door was locked. A fourth opened into a smoky anteroom. Beyond, she saw men reclining on bamboo bunks with their pipes. The room reeked of opium.

Ah Toy reached the end of the corridor just as Chan entered. He no longer wore the red cloth. Before she could speak, he gestured silence, then whisked her through the maze that led to Dupont street. Furtively, he looked around, then motioned her to a tea shop.

In a low voice, his eyes raking the street as though calamity might leap in and grab him, Chan told how two Kwan Duc men seized him from the courtyard. "Ong Sung man insulted Kwan Duc man," he whispered. "Grievance of one tong member is grievance of every tong member. Kwan Ducs are hungry for a fight. They posted a *chun hung,* a challenge to the Ong Sung men, on red paper. They called them a group of missionaries if they were afraid to fight and demanded to meet in one hour. Two Kwan Duc men saw me in the courtyard and commanded me to join them for this war."

"How did you escape?"

"Many men come, with much confusion. Then a messenger from the Ong Sung men arrived with an offer to settle the insult. I heard it announced. A commotion followed and I slipped away."

"No war now?"

"I don't think so. It was a good offer. Twenty-five dollars, a roast pig, and five strings of firecrackers of ten thousand crackers to the string."

Ah Toy sipped her tea and felt in her left sleeve the crinkle of rice paper with Li Jin's ideographs. She refused to be deterred by foolish men. "Drink your tea," she said, "and then we go to the temple."

Ah Toy hurried Chan through the hubbub of China men industriously buying and selling, past restaurants with white-coated cooks boiling dumplings, smoking shops with customers puffing at small metal pipes, stores selling porcelains and palm fans, stalls filled with squawking chickens and bulge-eyed fish. A bronze dragon mounted above a doorway advertised the trade of a Chinese goldsmith. Next door, men knelt with their heads in the laps of barbers who drew sharp, narrow blades over their patrons' skulls and braided their queues with silk.

Six paper lanterns marked the temple. Inside, Ah Toy looked curiously around. Colored lamps illuminated mysterious furnishings. Silk umbrellas with long handles, and poles topped with bronze emblems, reclined in corners. Flags with suns and moons and dragons hung from the walls. On a low, wide table two silver dragons two feet high were surrounded by offerings and prayer tokens—oranges, a tobacco pipe with a jade ring hung in the middle, scrolls tied with red ribbon. Porcelain vases with half-burnt incense sticks littered the altar with soft droppings of gray ash. The air was spicy with joss.

Beyond, in the innermost part of the temple, a large bronze statue of the great Buddha loomed behind silk curtains. Ah Toy and Chan watched a worshiper, on his knees before this main altar, rattle a container of bamboo sticks until one fell out.

A Buddhist priest stooped to retrieve it. He examined the Chinese character carved into it, then withdrew a scroll from a shelf below the altar. He consulted it for the number corresponding to the fortune stick. "Kwan Tung, the respectable and the good," said the priest, reading from the scroll, "helped to send his two sisters-in-law to meet his brother safely."

The petitioner pondered the message, accepting responsibility for applying its riddle to his concern. He rose, bowed, offered a few coins of contribution, and slipped from the room.

The priest offered Ah Toy the container of fortune sticks. She declined.

"Bamboo blocks?" he asked.

Ah Toy considered. The blocks, whether of bamboo, horn, or split oyster shells, spoke simply. A person threw them in front of the temple altar. If the convex sides both landed up, the answer was yes. If the planed sides, the answer was no. The ritual required only three throws.

Ah Toy accepted the blocks, mentally asked whether Li Jin lived, and threw. Both convex sides landed up. If the next throw landed the same way, Li Jin surely lived. But on the second throw the blocks turned planed sides up. One chance for a definitive answer remained. Ah Toy tossed the blocks hopefully. One block turned up, the other down. Ah Toy shook her head. For some reason the gods chose not to reveal to her their intent. They answered only with paradox.

Ah Toy pulled the scroll from her sleeve and handed it to the priest. A skilled reading of Li Jin's ideographs should reveal his future, without variance or conundrum. "Is this man alive?" she asked.

The priest examined the paper. "These are the eight ideographs of his destiny?"

"Yes. He himself wrote them, the ideographs of the hour, the day, the month, and the year of his birth."

The priest studied the characters. "I must make calculations." He left her to consult his books.

Ah Toy waited at the feet of the great Buddha, while Chan watched at the street for any tong disturbance.

After several minutes the priest returned, his face impassive. "This man's fate is the earth fate for the year and time. The earth element covers him. He is surely dead."

Ah Toy felt dizzy. She stumbled, caught herself. Tears filled her eyes. "Please reckon with your books once more," she begged. "Perhaps there is another interpretation."

The priest looked doubtful.

Ah Toy fumbled gold coins from her sleeve. She offered them with a trembling hand.

While the priest pored over Li Jin's ideographs, Ah Toy prayed to the Buddha.

The priest concluded his calculations.

Ah Toy watched him roll the scroll upon which was written Li Jin's destiny, and by extension, her own.

He handed the scroll to her. "He is dead."

7

REPORT OF THE GRAND JURY OF SAN
FRANCISCO COUNTY. —We find in existence in
this community a society of Chinese . . .
established for the purpose of . . . punishing with
fines and bastinado all who may transgress their
laws. . . . So great is the dread entertained for this
society that the sufferers are unwilling to
complain or certify before the proper authorities.
—*Alta California*
May 30, 1853

THE TRIAD SOCIETY. —Ah Sing and about
forty members of the Triad Society, went a few
nights since to a Chinese house of prostitution
kept by Ah Luck, and demanded the quarterly
payment of $10 a head. . . . Atoy informed the
court "that all the China men were fools, and
didn't know nothing, and when some man came
in and demanded $10 a head for the women, the
China men paid out the money because they
were fools, and didn't know nothing." It was
proved that
Ah Sing was the regular collector of the Triad
Society.
—*Daily Herald*
September 24, 1854

Ah Toy fastened pins into the black butterfly of her hair, enjoying the familiar midmorning stillness of her house. A-Ti and Gee Sing always slept until noon. Across the hall she heard the satisfied sounds of Chow Lai's untroubled slumber. In the next room, Xiao-li repeated softly the Jesus words from her mission school lessons. Downstairs she heard only Chan's muffled kitchen noises, wafting up with the fragrance of ginger.

Into this quiet she heard a knocking at the front door. She listened, fastening her hair.

"Lady! Lady! He is back!"

Ah Toy, hearing the excitement in Chan's voice as he bounded up the stairs, felt her breath quicken. Thought darted like a hummingbird. Could it be?

"Lady! He is back!" Chan said, standing in her doorway. "Now we prepare Xiao-li!"

Ah Toy rescued a smile from her plummeting elation. "Prepare tea."

In the parlor, she greeted Tong Achik.

The missionary launched his excitement without preliminaries. "Judge Barbour permitted the swearing in of *five* Chinese witnesses in Nevada City!" He raised one hand, fingers wide. "The court accepted the burning of yellow paper as a pledge to truth! Dr. Speer, who served as interpreter, agreed that the judge, jury, even the attorney for the defense found their testimony convincing. For murdering the Chinese miner, the court declared George Hall guilty of murder in the first degree!"

Ah Toy smiled over her tea at Tong Achik's discovery of Gum Shan's justice. It was not always readily or fairly dispensed, but, like the dragon upon whose back rested this fortune-favored city, justice resided deep within the country's foundation.

"The killing was witnessed only by China men," said Tong Achik. Ah Toy realized this was indeed the telling point. Five China men so impressed the judge and jury of their veracity, even though sworn by burning yellow paper, that they found an American guilty of murder.

Tong Achik pulled a newspaper from the pocket of his American-style coat. "Judge Barbour's statement is a great victory for us," he said, smoothing the paper.

Scholar's hands, like Li Jin's, thought Ah Toy, inviting, as she often did, the name into her memory. "Read. I share your happiness."

Tong Achik explored the paper, found the passage. " 'Many persons here have supposed it is less heinous to kill a Negro, an Indian or a China man than a white person. This is a gross error. The law of our country throws the aegis of its protection upon all within its jurisdiction. It knows no race, color or distinction.' "

Tong Achik folded the newspaper. "Judge Barbour sentenced Hall to hang in three months."

Ah Toy pondered Tong Achik's words. Her mind drifted on them to the sorrow of the murdered miner's family and then to her own sorrow. In the year since the temple priest had shattered her destiny, she had felt like a hungry ghost, lost, angry, and vengeful. Although she licked like a satisfied cat the triumph of her vengeance against As-sing for Li Jin's loss, sorrow never left her.

As though reading her thoughts, Tong Achik said, "I spoke with many who knew him, remembered him well." He looked away from her. "It is believed he lies buried in a collapsed mineshaft."

Ah Toy bowed her head, felt twin tears quit her eyes and find her hands folded in her lap. The earth element covers him, she thought.

Tong Achik rose. "I will send the red sedan chair."

The bridal chair was carved of wood, painted red, ornamented with kingfishers' feathers. Hab Wa, acting as friend of the bridegroom, accompanied it. Bowing, he presented Xiao-li the letter written on red paper tinged with gold. It urged the bride, Come.

Ah Toy, seeing her daughter into the bridal chair, wept for her own never-to-be wedding.

Xiao-li, behind her veil of red silk, whispered, "Mother, be happy. I go to my destiny."

Musicians banged drums and gongs, screeched horns, and exploded firecrackers. The procession commenced. Ah Toy and Chow Lai rode in the forward sedan chair sent for the bride's attendants. Chan, honored with the position of bride's brother, followed in a chair behind Xiao-li's. Attendants marched behind, displaying carved wooden pavilions piled with good-luck pastry buns decorated with red mottoes wishing the bride prosperity in her new life.

The noisy bridal parade spiraled through the city. By the time it reached Tong Achik's rooms on Washington street, Ah Toy felt bright as polished gold. She, Ah Toy, a Hakka woman with big feet and a father with no face, had rescued this girl in a filthy barracoon and bought her happiness on the Gold Mountain. For Xiao-li, at least, Gum Shan promised all its possibilities.

The bridegroom stood before his door with a large paper fan. He walked to the bridal chair, closed the fan, tapped it on Xiao-li's door.

As Ah Toy and Chow Lai helped Xiao-li from the chair, Tong

Achik smiled. He gestured with the fan at his groom's clothing. "You are pleased, mother-in-law?"

Ah Toy smiled. She was pleased.

At the doorway, Ah Toy and Chow Lai placed a heavy veil over the bride's head. Chow Lai said in theatrical admonishment, "Xiao-li, you enter now the dark future. Place implicit faith in your husband to guide you and you need not fear a misstep." Giggling, she guided the girl across the threshold.

Inside, strips of red paper festooned the walls with Chinese proverbs for marriage. Trays of fruits, sweetmeats, and tea had been prepared for guests. Ah Toy removed Xiao-li's veil, and the bride knelt before the bridegroom in ritual obeisance. Strands of pearls cascading from her headdress tinkled musically.

The bridal couple next sat on the bed together. Tong Achik intentionally sat on part of Xiao-li's gown. The bride, by not objecting, declared herself captive and willing to submit to her husband's orders.

Chow Lai tugged at Xiao-li's captured gown. Giggling, she said, "When I marry, I shall never permit my husband to sit on my skirt. I shall obey only if inclined."

Ah Toy spanked Chow Lai's hand. "The day you were born the gods must have forgotten submission. No one doubts your unlucky husband's destiny as your slave."

While guests remarked on the bride's beauty, Ah Toy poured tea into two cups bound by a red thread. She gave one to the bride, one to the groom, bade them sip. Retrieving the cups, she mixed the contents and told the couple to drink again. "Draw inspiration from this mixture of two souls," she said.

In the absence of ancestral tablets, Tong Achik had inscribed a red paper with the words "The ancestors of Tong Achik, for generations back." Now the bridal couple worshiped all the ancestors of all the generations of the Tong surname.

With formalities completed, the wedding party and guests, amid fusillades of firecrackers, adjourned to a restaurant on Jackson street. The wedding feast waited.

Tong Achik's friends and business associates, including officials of the Six Companies, had donated wedding money wrapped in red paper, securing an invitation to the sixteen-dish feast. Among them Ah Toy saw the Reverend William Speer. In three days he would unite Tong Achik and Xiao-li in the colorless ceremonies of his faith. He bowed to Ah Toy as she paraded the bride.

Before each guest, Xiao-li lowered her fan three times and bowed three times. Each guest returned a bow or recited a proverb, to which Xiao-li replied in the proper fashion.

She fatigued quickly, and after two hours, as was customary, was permitted to retire.

Ah Toy left, too. She had not yet seen her building.

For more than a year Ah Toy had cloistered herself on Pike street. Austin had left for Baltimore, and Simone for Paris. Ah Toy never left her house. She had welcomed with false affection men she seduced with Mei-Ling's book. She had created stallions from ponies with the monk's red powder. She had amassed more gold than she imagined existed. And she had plotted vengeance.

Now Ah Toy directed the driver to the south side of Telegraph Hill. In front of a conspicuous building painted light blue and fronted by an airy portico, she said, "Stop here."

The horses snorted and stomped while she gazed on her revenge. She liked it. A pair of lions, carved in wood, guarded the wide doorway. Above hung gilded tablets proclaiming the *wui kun* of the Ning Yeung benevolence society.

Ah Toy, admiring it, thought on how much had changed since that long-ago day on the wharf, where she had gone to admire the famous clipper ship. She had told Chan there was no *wui kun,* no hall, for Hakka people.

There had been then only the cake seller's company, the Luminous Unity, limping along with few members, while the Sam Yup and Sze Yup companies flourished. Then men from the Heungshan district organized the Yeong Wo company, and after that the Hakkas formed their company, the Yan Wo. Five companies.

Chan, through his complex connections of eyes and ears on Sacramento street, informed her of the business of all of them. When As-sing abandoned his crippled Luminous Unity Society and clambered to power over the Sze Yups, dissension followed. Members from the Hsinning district, the most powerful group in the company's roster, nursed serious grievances with the company's management, Chan reported, chiefly Norman As-sing.

Ah Toy had delighted in her steady, secret funneling of gold to the disenchanted Hsinning men. They splintered the Sze Yup company and formed their own.

The Chinese had six companies now. The Ning Yeung building, *her* building, stood before Ah Toy, evidence of As-sing's plunging influence.

Chan had brought news of the cake seller's continuing fall—the Triads had ensnared him.

Ah Toy followed every new rumor of As-sing's descent into criminal activities.

She was not yet finished with the man who had sent Li Jin back to the mines and destroyed her destiny.

Evening nibbled at the long shadows of late afternoon as As-sing dragged himself up Jackson street, jostled by unknown China men hurrying to and from their unknown business. Once he had known nearly every China man in the city. Now they numbered in the thousands, their presence almost daily increased by ships unloading them like blue-coated bulk cargo. Their unfamiliar faces displayed curiosity, diffidence, bravado, wariness, all the expressions of the China men for whom he had organized the Luminous Unity Society.

Despite their immense presence in Gum Shan, China men still turned to the benevolence societies for support. The secret societies, too, As-sing thought, ruing his destination. Triads infested Little China like ticks, sucking blood from each other in the old ways.

As-sing identified the house to which he had been summoned. A blue lantern marked it. He climbed the stairs.

Inside, he removed his hat and coat. From the sleeve of his black robe he withdrew a red cloth. He wrapped it around his forehead, draping its ends forward over his shoulders. The guard directed him upstairs.

The number of China men jamming the room surprised As-sing. The Kwan Ducs were more established than he had suspected. He stood at the door flanked by flags signifying the East Gate. Ahead he saw the traditional first entrances, the arch of swords, and through it the second and third entrances, and beyond them the symbolic Heaven and Earth Circle, Fiery Pit, Stepping Stones, even the Two-Planked Bridge. Behind the altar hung banners symbolizing the West Gate. The room was complete—banners, flags, secret insignia, even the yellow umbrella and green-painted tub of rice.

As-sing frowned. Rice, he thought, rice had failed him and the powerful Joshua Norton. Rice had plummeted him to a reliance on the red cards pasted in the shop windows of Dupont Gai.

He edged through the black-robed men to an inconspicuous place away from the initiation path. He lowered his eyes, not pleased to be seen. In his mind he retreated from the sound of the doors banging shut to represent the East Gate being slammed and locked. Better his memories of the disagreeable past than this dangerous present, these ceremonial beginnings of ancient rites.

He leaned against the wall, recalling how easily accomplished the rice plan first appeared.

With his contacts and Norton's money, capturing the rice market looked as easy as taking feathers from dead birds. Norton had nearly a quarter of a million dollars to invest. Between them they secured the cooperation of every importer in San Francisco. They succeeded in purchasing, down to the last pound, all the rice in the city. Demand almost immediately raised the price to unheard-of heights, thirty-six cents a pound in bulk, unloaded. As-sing had begun figuring his profits, flipping the black balls on his abacus, imagining the realization of his longtime dream, an American millionaire at last.

Then, unexpected as snow, there arrived in port two huge unanticipated ships full to bursting with rice, immense cargoes that neither he, Norton, nor any of the cooperating importers could take up or control. Suddenly rice was plentiful, and cheap, far cheaper than the cost of the huge quantities he and Norton held. Some of their associates, to protect themselves, sold out, ruining Norton completely.

The failure snapped Norton's mind like a stick. As-sing had seen him roaming the city mumbling nonsense in majestic postures, acting as if he were emperor of California. No, As-sing thought, California was merely one of a union of states, and could not logically create emperors. Crazy Joshua Norton would likely settle for nothing less than emperor of the United States.

As-sing was all but ruined, too. Except for his new plan, he had only his restaurant, bakery, and an inconsequential position with the Sze Yups' benevolent society.

A familiar chant pulled him from his thoughts. He looked up to see again the old-fashioned swords, the yellow umbrella. It was all here. Looking at the banners and flags, he remembered every detail of his own initiation. He thought he had left the old failures of his people behind. But they, his people and their ancient ways, had followed and found him, ensnared him again, caught him in their old ropes.

Wah Gae, when he had first displayed the sign of brotherhood with his chopsticks, had seemed useful. Now he stood by the altar, dressed in the red robe of lodge leader. He surveyed with glacial indifference those he had commanded to attend Gum Shan's first Kwan Duc initiation ceremony.

The summons came to As-sing on the familiar slip of bamboo inscribed with the local lodge name, Wide Gate Society. As-sing had read the bamboo slip with bitterness. Wide Gate, Kwan Ducs, Hung League, whatever they chose to call themselves, once a man belonged to the Triads—as all the lodges were called from the triangle character *hung,* representing the union of heaven, earth, and man—he belonged forever. There was no escaping.

As-sing recognized Sam Wo, wearing the prayer beads and white robe of incense master. Sam Wo, with his indispensable contacts for opium in foreign ports, owned a piece of As-sing now, as did the Triads.

Both Sam Wo and Wah Gae, as officers, had rolled their trousers up three folds. Both wore a grass sandal on the left foot. As-sing could not recall the meaning of these arcane symbols. Triad mythology accumulated like barnacles, an impenetrable crust of secret signs, passwords, banners, obscure symbols, mysterious ceremonies and rituals.

The candidates for initiation huddled near the locked door. Wary, barefoot, their tunic lapels flopped open, each clutched his five incense sticks. This initiation would take hours.

The herald called the recruits' names. As-sing wondered how many of these young men had come willingly, responding to posted notices or solicitations. And how many had come reluctantly, objects of menace and intimidation? In Canton, Triads commonly recruited by threatening destruction to property or families.

The ceremony commenced. The recruits bowed and walked

under the arch of swords, thereby "passing the mountain of knives." There followed a steady chanting of verses, a demand for the three red stones, with permission granted to proceed to the second entrance, the symbolic Hung Gate guarded by two generals. The recruits knelt there three times, chanted, were led to the guards of the third entrance, the Hall of Fidelity and Loyalty.

As-sing lost track of time. His attention strayed. He thought again on his new plan, nurtured from a seed sown by Tong Achik. During a meeting of the officials of the Six Companies, Tong Achik had exploded his resentment over the absence of a consul for Gum Shan's twenty-five thousand China men. "Mecklenburg-Schwerin, a country no one ever heard of, has a consul here!" he said, smacking the table for attention. "No one knows even where that place is! San Francisco has twenty-seven foreign consuls, but none for the Chinese!"

As-sing had ignored the outburst. Tong Achik was naive. China's imperial government would never recognize either the barbarian country or the defection of its citizens. Their departure from the Flowery Kingdom was, after all, illegal.

Still, the idea of a consul was interesting. A consul was a public official, a high man.

As-sing knew of a building available on Sacramento street, between Kearny and Dupont. Why should he not rent it and place above its doorway a red signboard, with gilt lettering, proclaiming the office of the consul of China? Why indeed shouldn't Gum Shan's China men have a consul like other foreigners? And why should that man not be Norman As-sing?

As-sing looked around, examining the faces of the Wide Gate brotherhood, seeing mostly Sze Yup men. It was undoubtedly true, as he had heard, that several Triad lodges had been established in the city, dividing along familiar district allegiances, recruiting on a regional basis. Offshoots of the Kwan Ducs included the Hsieh I, the

United Righteousness tong, and the Tan Shan, the Red Mountain tong. The Sam Yups had the Hip Yee tong. Yeong Wo company men joined the Ong Sungs.

The chanting continued as recruits were led before the generals guarding the Heaven and Earth Circle, and from there to where the Vanguard stood. As-sing heard Sam Wo ask the familiar questions, examining each recruit's knowledge of the society. It was at this point, As-sing remembered, that recruits who agreed to continue the initiation performed the ceremony symbolic of cleansing traitorous hearts. Those who did not agree were taken to the West Gate and their heads chopped off, a powerful argument for membership.

Preliminaries concluded. At the front of the room, before the altar, recruits recited the quatrains preparatory to the taking of oaths. The altar was a jumble of emblems and relics, red papers inscribed with characters proclaiming the Hung family in ten thousand cities, brass lamps representing the First Five Ancestors, a white cock in a bamboo cage, a pot of wine and five bowls, a pot of tea and three cups, a dish of red dates, an incense pot, a bowl of fresh flowers, joss sticks, a needle strung with red thread. As-sing shook his head at this array of supposed significance.

Now each recruit inserted three sticks of incense into the censer. The silver wine jug was brought, and wine passed among the brethren. As-sing drank. Everyone drank, chanted, watched the lighting of the seven-starred lamp and the Hung light, knelt at the signal to offer reverential prayers. On their knees they recited in ragged chorus the eight salutations to the heaven, earth, sun, moon, the Five Founders, the brethren, the renowned amongst their companions.

They stood when an officer at the altar began reading the thirty-six oaths that bound recruits to the society. "First," he said, "after entering this gate to learn the regulations of the society and keep the secrets, a brother must honor his parents and his brothers. If he breaks this law, he shall be drowned within one month in the Great Sea and his flesh and bones will be separated."

As-sing leaned against the wall, exhausted by the late hour. His head throbbed from the incessant chanting and the suffocating scent of sandalwood. The oaths continued.

"Third, a brother must not molest the chief or injure the brethren. If anyone shall do this, he shall be killed by ten thousand knives."

The voice droned on. As-sing wanted to leave. As if mocking him, the officer declared, "Ninth. No brother may interrupt a ceremony or walk in or out of the lodge during a ceremony. If this law is broken, may he be struck by five lightning bolts and his blood gush forth."

The oaths continued, an inventory of rules and retribution—if a brother gives away the secret ceremonies of the society may he be eaten by a tiger or have his eyes bitten out by a snake; if a brother fails to hand on money given him by another brother for that brother's family, may he be struck by arrows and knives; if a brother starts a street riot, may he die of poison; if a brother causes trouble by slander within the society, may he die the death of a thousand cuts; if a brother introduces into the society anyone who wants to discover its secrets, he shall be punished by seventy-two blows from the Red Pole.

As-sing watched the recruits finally rise from their knees for the conclusionary acceptance of the thirty-six oaths. Wah Gae filled a bowl with wine. Sam Wo took the squawking cock from its cage. He chopped off its head. The smell of fresh blood mingled with incense.

Wah Gae held the quivering, headless cock over the bowl. Its blood drained into the wine. A third officer pricked each recruit's finger with the silver needle strung with red thread. The blood was added to the wine bowl.

"The white cock is the token," Wah Gae announced ominously, "and we have shed its blood and taken an oath. The unfaithful and disloyal shall perish like this cock."

Wah Gae burned symbolic yellow paper. He added the ashes to the wine and blood each recruit had to drink. It would be midnight before this repetitious rite concluded, As-sing thought.

Suddenly a great noise rose from the floor below. Alarmed, the recruit holding the wine bowl stood transfixed, the bowl at his chin, lips crimson.

Downstairs, a guard shouted, "A draft of wind! A draft of wind!"

As-sing felt blood drain from his face. It was the Triad message for a spy in their midst.

It could only be the police.

As-sing, faint with apprehension, watched Triad guards abandon their banners, run to a window, and clamber onto the overhanging roof. Others followed in a frenzy of escape as the door burst open and police rushed in.

As-sing, trapped against the wall by the press of frightened Triads, heard overhead the scampering feet of fleeing men.

He longed to be among them.

Judge Waller rapped his gavel. "Bailiff, clear the court of spectators so we can seat these men."

As-sing hunched into a corner, hopeful that in their black robes and red headbands the China men all looked alike. He felt confident that Marshal Seguine, now being sworn to tell the truth, had not identified him as anyone important. With luck, he would escape this dishonor unrecognized.

Judge Waller looked around his overflowing courtroom and then at the witness. "What are the particulars here, Marshal?"

"Judge, about five o'clock last night I was told that something was going on at this big house on Jackson street. After collecting all my available force by about ten o'clock, we went to the house where we found a China man watching and we went up and burst the door open. The room of business appeared to be upstairs, where there was a table with eatables and flags on it. The room was decorated in fanciful style, and one of the men was dressed in gorgeous robes and armed to the very teeth. There were about two hundred China men in the room and about fifty were armed with swords, and there were fifteen to twenty knives in the room. Many of the China men tried to get away, and some escaped through the roof. We arrested one hundred and fifty-nine men. They were all taken with the exception of those who escaped in the confusion."

As-sing knew he would never erase the memory of his humiliation. The police had tied his queue to another man's, and that man's to another. They were collected in half dozens and hauled to the station house like fish on strings.

"Some of the Chinese have reported to me," Seguine was saying, "that there was a large company of robbers who were trying to get from the Chinese prostitutes ten dollars a month from each one. Every fifteen days five dollars were to be paid, and the first payment had been already made. I have since heard that the same party had demanded one hundred dollars each from the merchants in Sacramento street."

Prostitutes. As-sing tasted an old bitterness. During the long night behind bars, listening to the China men bleat their anxiety, he concluded the *mui tsai* had done this thing to him. He was certain she had snaked secrets into barbarian ears with her unblunted tongue.

A familiar voice hooked his ear. He clicked to attention.

"I have heard," Tong Achik was saying to Judge Waller, "that there was a secret society in existence here among the Chinese, who have been in the habit of collecting taxes from the Chinese brothels. I have seen the flags and insignia which were found in the room. They are the same as the flags used in illegal societies in China."

One of the marshal's men dragged into the courtroom the green-painted tub of rice, in which had been stuck a dozen or so flags and banners.

"That flag," Tong Achik said, pointing, "represents the arms of the Chinese general. The mottoes read: 'The national flag of the palace,' and the one beneath is 'Bravery and strength of heart.' Another is 'The unity of thousands,' surrounded by the words 'Virtue, honesty, and politeness.' "

The marshal handed Tong Achik a red cloth covered in Chinese characters. Tong Achik examined it. "This contains the oaths and regulations of the society."

"I object!"

The voice belonged to a lawyer hired by Wah Gae to represent the arrested men.

The judge acknowledged him. "State your objection, Colonel James."

"I object to the contents of this document being made known. Unless it has been proven that a criminal offense was committed by a secret organization, the court has no right to inquire into the secrets of the organization."

"You are, I presume, suggesting a parallel with the Masons and similar societies," said Waller. "Such societies as the Masons are recognized by law. The society in question is not. The witness may read the document."

The lawyer objected. "Judge, it is our contention that the soci-

ety in question is a benevolent society, and that its rules and regulations are confidential."

Waller shook his head. "It is the opinion of the court that the
document should be read." He told Tong Achik to proceed.

As-sing stared. It was unthinkable to reveal such secrets.

"This is, essentially, a constitution for the society," Tong Achik
said, studying the cloth. "The preamble states that the members
would form themselves into a society to take care of each other and
that the members were to be as though of the same bone and flesh.
It says, 'Whoever enters this Wide Gate Society must change his surname to Hung and is to respect the father and mother of the society. The present chief has not acted rightly, having oppressed the
weak, and we who live freely join the Hung Society, and those
who oppose it and protect the reigning dynasty, may the spirits
come about them.' "

Judge Waller looked perplexed. "Can you explain for the court
this reference to dynasties?"

"Yes. The society's original purpose was political. It was formed
to resist Mongolian conquerors who seized the Dragon Throne
and set themselves up as the Ching emperors. At that time, the aim
of the secret societies was to drive out the invaders and restore Chinese rule."

"And when was this?"

"About two hundred years ago. Since then, unfortunately,
the followers have degenerated into bands of rebels and robbers."

As morning dissolved into afternoon, As-sing's conviction grew
that the police raid was the woman's doing. For one thing, Tong
Achik's ready testimony indicated prearrangement. And the parade
of Sacramento street merchants, testifying they had heard a secret
society levied taxes, suggested a deliberate design.

Now As-sing gleefully watched the design unravel like a cheap

rug. Each merchant swore under oath he knew nothing of this secret society by his own knowledge.

Judge Waller at last announced his decision. "From the evidence presented, there is nothing to connect this society to the
party of Chinese who have been guilty of illegal practices. All present are discharged with the exception of the man whose name was
found attached to a receipt for money said to have been extorted
from a Chinese woman. Dismissed."

Tong Achik protested. "The object of this society is to extort
money! The constitution, oaths, and ceremonies are mere cloaks for
this purpose!"

Heedless, As-sing fled the courtroom into a gray San Francisco
fog, grateful to escape the Hakka woman's scheme.

He smiled as he hurried toward Jackson street to retrieve
his New York hat. She underestimated the old ways. Few China
men possessed courage sufficient to defy the Triads. It was a
rare person who abandoned the customary to embrace the unfamiliar.

For a brief moment he felt a bond with the *mui tsai*.

Then he spit in the street.

The man bowed clumsily, then jammed his hands in his pockets.
"Thank you for coming, Miss Ah Toy. I'm Mr. Evans, representing
the prosecution. We will very much appreciate your testimony since
we can count on, I think, after all, only two Chinese gentlemen to
testify, in addition to the police. I fear Miss Wing may lose courage.
Mr. Tong Achik assures me that you will not."

Ah Toy, ignoring As-sing's glower from across the courtroom,
assessed the young attorney. Everything about him suggested neat-

ness, from his starched collar to his polished boots. He smelled of soap and fresh tobacco.

"All China men fools," Ah Toy said crossly, and seated herself in a rustle of taffeta. She was annoyed at wasting her time over the slippery cake seller. He had slithered into her life like an eel, and he wearied her. He sat with smug assurance now in the midst of accused Triad defendants.

Ah Toy knew that the court's failure to indict the Triads following the police raid on the initiation ceremony had emboldened the secret societies. Newspapers regularly reported their outrages. The court just as regularly dismissed complaints brought before it, and always for the same reason: the refusal of witnesses to testify.

So brazen were the secret societies that they all but abandoned secrecy. In early March, it was the Triads who organized the grand procession to the cemetery for the spring offering. Leading the musicians banging gongs and drums, the undulating dragon, the creaking carriages filled with rich merchants, the two hundred tramping China men with paper umbrellas, were banner men carrying a huge red flag emblazoned with the secret society's insignia.

Ah Toy, Chow Lai, and Chan, attending Mei-Ling's grave, had watched the procession arrive. On the graves of departed Triads were placed such extravagant offerings as whole roasted hogs, whole boiled goats with the horns on, platters of crabs ornamented with gilt.

Having publicly revealed themselves, the secret societies demonstrated their strength. A China man who failed to repay a loan of four hundred dollars was found chained inside a house in Happy Valley. He had been imprisoned and whipped for days. The police who rescued him had been alerted only by the crowd gathered around the house to listen to his cries. In court, the accused secret society members asserted that the man could not or would not pay his obligation. The lender had obtained satisfaction by whipping the debtor. The beaten man, in fear for his life, refused to testify against his tormentors.

In all cases brought against the secret societies, victims routinely reversed their testimony. The failure of one witness to recognize the miscreant or to recall the crime so infuriated one jury that they voted to dismiss the defendant and jail the witness.

Ah Toy expected no better from the witness now under examination. She appraised Wing San. The girl's moon face bore the shadows of hard usage. Her tunic and trousers of cheap silk hung awkwardly. In response to a question by the court's interpreter, she prattled nervously.

Ah Toy knew her story from Tong Achik. She had been brought from China two years ago and sold to the herbalist Li Po Ti. She lived with him only briefly. Li Po Ti owed a man some money, and she was given in part payment of the debt. Soon after, that man sold her to another, Wong Choy, who intended making a courtesan of her. She was then fourteen years old. One of her first customers asked to buy her, and she was sold. She lived with this man, Fong Wang, as servant and wife. He put her out to work at two washhouses. She received no pay for her labor, and Fong Wang frequently whipped her. After a particularly bad beating, she ran away to live at one of the washhouses. Fong Wang found her there and accused her of receiving some men who worked at the washhouse. He beat her again. Afterward, a man from the washhouse came and asked her if she wanted to live with him if Fong Wang would sell her. Fong Wang refused, and when he threatened to whip her again, she ran out into the street where a policeman found her.

Ah Toy, upon hearing this tale, felt pity for the girl. She and Tong Achik both knew this story might have been hers if Wang Po had not died on the voyage to Gum Shan. At Tong Achik's urging, Ah Toy agreed to testify against the Triads the girl had identified as selling her to Li Po Ti. Wing San was one of several witnesses summoned in an attempt to bring charges against the Triads for various criminal activities.

Evans, the prosecuting attorney, questioned the girl now. "Miss Wing, did you consider yourself the wife of any of your purchasers?"

The court's interpreter repeated the question and then her answer. "She says it was hard to tell, that perhaps her last owner considered himself her husband, but he never told her so."

Evans asked if it was customary for a husband to keep such information from his wife. The girl replied that a husband never told his wife anything and never allowed her to interfere with his business.

Ah Toy saw the girl look at the China men in the court, then lower her eyes. In the voice of obedience Ah Toy remembered from her own enslaved youth, the girl said in rapid Cantonese, as though competing for a scholar's prize, "The Chinese are not like white people. A Chinese woman is supposed to obey her husband, or owner, without asking reasons for anything. And if she chooses to be indiscreet enough to hesitate to do as he commands, she must expect to be punished as he sees fit."

Ah Toy watched Evans pace anxiously back and forth in front of the witness as the interpreter translated. The attorney's fear that Miss Wing would fail as a witness was evident in his demeanor. He looked like a gambling man watching his horse finish last.

"Miss Wing," he asked, "should a woman not protest such punishment?"

Wing San thought so long after the interpreter placed the question that Evans urged him to repeat it. The moon-faced girl finally spoke, so quietly that Ah Toy strained to hear her. "A woman does nothing by protesting," the girl said. "She receives no sympathy from men, because they all act in the same way toward their women, and women recognize their inability to help themselves." Wing San looked around the courtroom and found Ah Toy. To Ah Toy the girl said, in a voice heavy with acquiescence and grievance, "The attempt of any woman to overstep these rules only brings more trouble upon all of them. As a consequence, we must regard unfavorably a troublesome woman."

Ah Toy jumped to her feet, face flaming. She would tell this stupid girl that she knew nothing, nothing!

Evans turned abruptly to look at Ah Toy. "I have no more questions for the witness," he said loudly. His expression begged Ah Toy's forbearance. Judge Baker is impatient enough with the Chinese cases, his eyes implored. Don't provoke him into barring you from the court for contempt.

Had Ah Toy not promised Tong Achik this favor, she would have swept from the courtroom. Instead, she bit her lip lest she yet call the girl a fool. From across the courtroom she sensed the cake seller's oily amusement. She briefly turned her anger toward the absent Tong Achik, provoked anew at his request.

Tong Achik was convinced the Chinese could find justice in the courts, despite the crushing decision in the Hall case. The American George Hall had not been hanged for his crime. His attorney was appealing the conviction to the California Supreme Court, arguing, to every China man's astonishment, that the Chinese were Indians. The logic of the strategy was, of course, Tong Achik had explained to Ah Toy, that the law barred Indians from testifying against white men. If the court decided the Chinese race was related to Indians, then the testimony of the five China men who saw Hall kill Ling Sing was inadmissible.

"We must hope for justice," Tong Achik told her. "The courts can protect our people from exploitation by the Triads and show that the ways of Gum Shan are not the ways of China."

Ah Toy shook her head at his folly. To change the Chinese, Tong Achik would need patience sufficient to push rope uphill. And there was the *Libertad*. That tragedy only assured the Chinese of the Americans' indifference to their welfare.

It was to attend to that calamity that Tong Achik had prevailed upon her to testify in court in his stead. "Word has come of terrible mistreatment of the passengers confined on Goat Island," he had said. "A dead China man was thrown into a wheelbarrow and trundled to the boat landing by the nautical man attending them. Ah Sam had just arrived at the landing with rice sent for the sick men. He saw with his own eyes the nautical man dump the China man's body from the wheelbarrow like a load of garbage. The dead body rolled over and over down the hill and into the bay."

The arrival of the *Libertad* with ninety of its four hundred Chinese passengers dead had distressed the entire Chinese community. Inspection of the ship revealed only two sacks of rice remaining among the meager provisions supplied them, and short water. When surviving passengers continued to die at five to ten a day, city physicians, fearful the illness was pestilent, quarantined them on Goat Island. Ah Sam reported that the sick men lay upon the bare floor of open sheds, with no protection from the weather.

"They suffer from cold and exposure," Tong Achik told Ah Toy. Securing her promise to testify against the Triads, he had hurried away to contend with more pressing misfortune.

And so it was left to her to observe these senseless proceedings. She watched now as a burly man in a gray uniform rested his left hand upon the Jesus book, raised his right hand, and swore to tell the truth. Evans asked him to state his name and occupation.

"My name is Richard Monks, and I am chief of police of the city and county of San Francisco."

"How long have you resided here?"

"Since June, eighteen hundred and forty-nine."

"Are you familiar then with the so-called secret societies of our Chinese residents?"

"Yes."

"Can you tell the court how these societies derive their revenue?"

"Through means of extortion, and houses of prostitution."

"How do the secret societies extort money?"

"Well, almost any way they wish to. The people are so entirely under the control of these societies, and are so dominated by fear, that any demand that is made upon them, they pay without question."

"Can you give an example?"

"Of course. There was a Chinese butcher on Washington street. One evening he threw out a little clean water onto the street. A Triad member who was standing near got water on the sleeve of his coat. I happened to be passing by as this Triad demanded one hundred dollars of the butcher for the offense. The butcher didn't have the money, and the Triad said he would call again later. I told the butcher not to pay the money, but to make an arrangement to meet him at a certain place and I would be there. He promised to do so, and would you believe it, before I got there, he had paid the Triad one hundred dollars. That will show you that anything these Triads demand, they get."

Evans examined some papers, then asked, "Chief Monks, in your prior experience as a witness in cases against the secret societies, would you say that the Triads are much given to securing perjured testimony?"

"It is impossible to rely on Chinese witnesses. For instance, a man is killed. I am sent to investigate. A man is pointed out to me as the murderer, positively identified as such, and I have evidence that man was not within five blocks of the scene of the crime at the time of the murder. I arrested the man, as my duty as a police officer compelled me to, but I knew the man to have been in a shop on one street when the man murdered was on another."

Ah Toy was growing bored by the police chief's droning examples of what everyone knew, and she could see, so was Judge Baker. She watched him examine his gavel as though wondering what it was. He removed his spectacles, rubbed his eyes, replaced the spectacles. Finally, he leaned over the desk and said impatiently, "Mr. Evans, unless this line of questioning reveals to the court that our esteemed chief of police has actually seen with his own eyes the crimes to which he alludes, it may not continue. The court requires witnesses, Mr. Evans."

Ah Toy knew what she was expected to testify to, and she knew it was futile. The stupid girls who had taken refuge in her house, A-Ti and Gee Sing, had, while Ah Toy was out, received as customers two bold Triads. Ah Toy had returned just as the girls were paying the men protection money. Despite her outrage, the girls refused to testify in court.

"Torture! Torture!" they had squealed.

"You know nothing!" Ah Toy had shouted at them. "Gum Shan court not same like China court!" But neither threats nor entreaties could persuade them they would not be tortured for their testimony. They feared China's five authorized punishments for both prisoner and witnesses, the prisoner to make him confess, and the witnesses to make them divulge what they were supposed to know and were holding back. Ah Toy could not convince the girls they would not be flogged, cudgeled, struck upon the lips, put in stocks, or suspended by their thumbs and fingers.

Now Evans was questioning a frightened boy no older than Chan, his queue neatly oiled.

The interpreter repeated the questions and the judge demanded he answer. The witness haltingly responded. He previously claimed that one of the defendants in the courtroom had fought with him so that another might steal his pocketbook. "He now says," explained the interpreter, "this was not so and knows nothing about it at all."

The judge lost patience. "Mr. Evans, I am tempted to have your witness arrested for perjury! These Chinese cases are a great deal of trouble. It is impossible, in my experience, to get at the truth of them!"

The interpreter repeated the warning, and the witness, who looked near tears, babbled something Ah Toy could not hear.

"Now what is he saying?" demanded the judge.

"He is changing all the time," replied the interpreter.

Judge Baker slammed his gavel into his desk. "Is there not some system of bastinado to compel the truth from these people!"

Ah Toy expected Evans to collapse like a folding fan before the judge's wrath, but the attorney respectfully asked the court's indulgence, dismissed the witness, and called another.

A composed young man, his blue tunic and trousers clean and pressed, took the chair. He had a thin, intelligent face. Like a scholar, thought Ah Toy wistfully. After he was sworn by the burning of yellow paper, Evans asked, "Can you speak English?"

"Yes."

"How long have you been in California?"

"Two year."

"What do you work at?"

"Cooking."

"For white people?"

"Yes."

"Do you know whether any paper is ever put up offering money to kill China men?"

"Yes. I saw them." Ah Toy watched the witness bravely point at several Triads sitting in the court.

"Have they threatened to kill you if you testify?"

"Yes. I am a little scared."

"What are you afraid of?"

"Afraid shoot me."

"Do you know of anybody being killed?"

"Yes."

"What for?"

"One boy he testify before, and they kill him with a knife."

The young man's courage saddened Ah Toy. How could he now save himself from a knife thrust into his back, or a quick hatchet chop to his head?

Ah Toy grew angry again. These men had come so far, risked such danger, only to stupidly kill one another perpetuating old brutality. Gum Shan suffered no famine, no crippling taxation, no uncorrectable government. Why were the China men blind to the possibilities here? Why did they not see they need not prolong ancient injustices here? Her anger rose up bright as a stove fire fed fresh kindling.

She heard her name called. At the bench she waved away the yellow paper. "This place not China!" She pointed at the Bible. "I swear say all true same like you."

Evans smiled encouragement. Ah Toy reined her outrage, answering his questions as calmly as she could. As she related the events witnessed at her house, however, she felt heat rising in her again. When Evans asked her if the men who had demanded money from A-Ti and Gee Sing were present, she looked into the faces of the defendants. Her eyes met As-sing's. He smirked. Suddenly her anger was away from her, racing like a horse.

"All these China men fools! They know nothing!" She pointed at As-sing. "Some man say he high man, demand money. Other men fools and pay him! They know nothing!"

Judge Baker slammed his gavel. Evans pleaded with her to be

calm. Ah Toy spit her fury. "No high man this place! China men fools! Know nothing!"

She ignored everyone, including the young China man who threw open the door and rushed toward her. She did not see Chan until he shouted, "Lady, he lives! Li Jin lives!"

8

ILL FAME. —The *San Francisco Courier* says that
although a few Chinese brothels have been shut
up under the new ordinance for the suppression
of such establishments, in the higher walks of
lewdness, it is remarked, that no change has been
effected. Let us have no partiality in the
enforcement of the law.

> —*Alta California*
> June 1, 1854

The first I knew of the impending war came
from one of the China bosses, who came into
the shop with a pattern similar to the iron of a
pike-pole, and wanted to know how much I
would charge to make one hundred like the
pattern, out of steel.

> —John Carr
> Weaverville, California
> 1854

The main thing was that there had been a war
and what a war! In memory I can hear their
voices yet mingled with the fierce battle cries of
the enraged armies backed by the white miners.
"Give 'em hell, China Boy! We've come to see a
fight!"

> —Jake Jackson

All Chan could tell her, from reports of the Weaverville war received in San Francisco, was that two Hakka men and six Sze Yup men had died. Twenty more had been injured, a dozen seriously, Li Jin among them.

Ah Toy knew she must go to him.

She rushed home. In a frenzy of joy and fear, she pulled pantaloons and stockings from bureau drawers. She shouted at Chan to bring a valise.

Chow Lai teetered to her doorway. "Elder Sister, what are you doing? Where are you going!"

"Li Jin lives!" Ah Toy felt inflated with achievement, as though she had plucked his departed *chi* from the sky and restored him to earth by the strength of her yearning for him. She tossed clothing into the valise. "I go to him now!"

She dashed to embrace Chow Lai. Distress furrowed Chow Lai's moon face. "Be happy for me," Ah Toy said, watching tears cloud the girl's eyes. "I must go." She resumed her packing.

"Sister," Chow Lai cried, "police will come!"

Ah Toy opened a bureau drawer, took a chemise from it. It was true, the police would undoubtedly come again.

Chow Lai sobbed. "Police arrest us! Close lucky-number house!"

A-Ti and Gee Sing, overhearing Chow Lai's cries, howled from the hallway in alarm. "No police!" they screamed. "Torture! Torture!"

"Be quiet!" Ah Toy commanded. The girls wailed louder.

"You cannot leave us, Sister!" Chow Lai cried.

Ah Toy leaned against her bureau, covering her head with her arms. She tried to block out A-Ti's and Gee Sing's wailing, tried to think. Chow Lai was right, of course. Since passage of the ordinance prohibiting disorderly houses, the police had arrested Ah Toy several times. She thought nothing of it. She was not afraid of courts and judges. She appeared as ordered, agreed to cease business, paid the fine, and returned home. But anything might happen to Chow Lai and the terrified A-Ti and Gee Sing without her protection.

The dilemma paralyzed Ah Toy. In the looking glass above the bureau she saw her reflection robbed of decisiveness. She stroked Tsu Yen's white jade dragon hanging around her neck. She must be resolute.

Turning, she said, "It is my destiny. I must go."

Chow Lai's tears tracked her gown with tiny footprints of grief. "Do not leave us, Sister."

Ah Toy's energy to resist, to counsel, to consider, had deserted her. "If you will not be left, then you must come," she said in resignation. "I do not know what else to say."

Chow Lai, overjoyed, called Chan to bring her a valise. Hearing her, A-Ti and Gee Sing responded with fresh wails.

"Then come! Come!" Ah Toy shouted at them, thoughts reeling. What she would do with all of them, she did not know. She trusted destiny to guide her.

This here's Chinadom," the driver called over his shoulder.

The four women peered from the carriage. The Chinese presence in Sacramento was substantial, extending in thick settlement up I Street from Second Street as far as Sixth.

The driver stopped his horses before a doorway decorated with a familiar signboard. He looked around at Ah Toy. She shook her head. She had told him to take them to a hotel.

"Uh, ma'am," he said, "this here's the Sze Yup house, where the Chinese peoples stay."

"No, no," said Ah Toy. "Not this place."

The driver shrugged, slapped his horses' backs with the reins, and trotted them up the street. In front of another large building, he called out, "Whoa, Daisy! Ginger!" He twisted around toward Ah Toy, who inclined her head from the carriage and looked at him quizzically.

"Well, ma'am, I don't know as how, uh, well, uh, you fancy ladies might mean to stay here. This is a gambling hall, but I seen plenty China ladies here." He looked confused and embarrassed, then hopeful. "I seen a big room in the back of here, where opera troupes and puppet shows come. Got seats for a hundred people. Lotsa white folks come to see them."

Ah Toy, vexed, shook her head. "No opera, no singsong girl," she said, exasperated. "No stay this place. Go hotel, please," she said, and flashed a double-eagle goldpiece.

"No place like that in Chinadom," he said, his eye on the gold. He shook his head and shrugged. "You got good money, I guess you want maybe the Orleans."

"Yes, Orleans," said Ah Toy, feeling provoked. "Go Orleans."

On Second Street, the driver stopped his horses before a three-story brick hotel. A balustraded, second-story terrace shaded its promenade. "This here's the Orleans," he said, handing the women out onto the boardwalk. "Finest hostelry in the city. Got a reading room, billiard room, saloon, real nice parlors and chambers for guests."

Chow Lai, gazing up and down the street, purred her approval. During their impromptu tour, Ah Toy had watched the girl admiring this riverfront *yee fow,* this second city. Its three-story buildings sported fancy facades and lacy ironwork balconies. They stood shoulder to shoulder like decorated soldiers. In front of the Orleans Hotel now, Ah Toy watched Chow Lai smile, satisfied as a preening cat. The pillared boardwalk was crowded with men, noisy with their clomping boots.

By the time Chow Lai crept beneath the Orleans Hotel's fleecy blankets, Ah Toy saw that the girl had decided. With the excitement of a cat preparing to pounce, Chow Lai whispered her intent. She would rent a house on Second Street, she told Ah Toy, and take A-Ti and Gee Sing into business with her.

Ah Toy sensed destiny's favor. With the girls settled upon a new life, she was free to pursue her own. To the north, Li Jin waited. She dared not think more than that, lest her fears invite some malignant ghost to snatch him from her again.

The next morning, in the crowded vestibule of the Orleans Hotel, Ah Toy stood anxiously with her valise at her feet. She clutched the stage ticket purchased at the California Stage Company office in the hotel lobby and listened with distracted affection to Chow Lai's chattered reassurance.

"*Yee fow* good place, I think, Sister." Chow Lai rocked on her tiny feet, hands clasped within yellow satin sleeves. "A-Ti, Gee Sing, we stay here. This our destiny, I think." She giggled. "Make much gold like Elder Sister."

And so it was decided, Ah Toy thought, acknowledging with a smile Chow Lai's respectful bow.

"Stage 'bout be leavin', ma'am," said the runner. He hoisted Ah Toy's valise to his shoulder.

Ah Toy kissed Chow Lai's funny face and whispered, "Good

fortune." With a rustle of taffeta she turned and followed the runner through the hotel's front door toward her destiny.

Outside, Ah Toy saw dawn lick a pink edge across the distant Sierra Nevada. The nearer foothills still lay in purple shadow, as did much of Sacramento despite its tumult of activity.

Two dozen conveyances lined Front Street, each joined to four impatient horses. They crowded against the boardwalk fronting hotels, tent stores, the steamer and stage offices surmounted by huge white signs lettered black. Boys held the fidgeting, snorting animals in check, while passengers elbowed through the confusion toward waiting vehicles.

Many of these vehicles, Ah Toy saw, were only light wagons with four or five board seats nailed across. Their destinations were lettered crudely on the side. Others on the same design had been improved with paint and an awning overhead. And some were regular coaches, big high-slung things, extravagantly ornamented, their tops trimmed with baggage rails.

Stage-line runners shouted a bewildering list of destinations. "All aboard for Folsom, Mormon Island, Mud Springs, and Hangtown!" "This way for Nevada City! Who's agoin'? Only three seats left! Take you there in five hours!" "Last chance today for Coloma, Georgetown, Auburn, and Yankee Jim's!"

It seemed to Ah Toy, as the runner led her through the crush, that for everyone going somewhere, someone else had been hired to see that he got there.

The runner pointed. "Over there in front of the Elephant House hotel, just past that round tent next to the Eagle Theatre. That big Concord stage, that's the one. Be like riding in a rocking chair."

Four white horses stamped and snorted before the stagecoach, a huge green affair slung close to the ground between high, spoked wheels painted yellow. Elaborate scrollwork decorated the carriage sides. The painted doors depicted distant-mountain views.

The stage runner stowed Ah Toy's valise in a hinged leather boot at the rear. The driver, a rough-looking fellow in a canvas coat that covered his boot tops, eyed her from her boots to her bonnet. "Reckon you'll sit inside," he said at last, shifting the plug of tobacco that plumped his cheek. He drew words from his mouth like a slowly pulled string. "Seein' as how you ain't wearin' them Chinee pajamas."

Ah Toy stepped from the hanging steel plate into the coach. Inside were three wide, calf-covered seats. "You wanna take a seat there in the back with them other two ladies," said the runner, directing her. "Ladies don't fancy sittin' in the middle. Gents facin' 'em got nowheres to put their legs, ya see, 'cept to dove-tail 'em."

The two women stared at Ah Toy. She felt as though she were a surprising new specimen of fashion from Mrs. Cole's dress shop. On the front seat three men faced the rear. One young man, just opposite, Ah Toy thought about to speak to her. She saw the women silence him with thin lips.

The driver shouted at people, "Hurry up, there! Let's go! Let's go! Move on!" His horses snorted and pranced, eager to be off. He flicked his reins against their backs and cracked his whip. The stages moved out four abreast across the width of Front Street, wheels creaking, coaches rattling, horses' hooves thudding in clouds of dust. Beyond town, they spread out in all directions and thundered off toward their diverse destinations.

Ah Toy, daring to think no thoughts, watched the rising sun illuminate the plain stretching north of Sacramento City. The road lay like a broad, flat ribbon unwinding into the distance. The stage raced up it, the driver slapping his reins against the pounding horses.

The journey became a familiar repetition of relay stations and hostlers and steaming horses exchanged for fresh. At Rancho Chico, a green oasis of stately oaks, the coach took a new driver, a "famous whip," she heard a passenger say. The two thin-lipped women departed, replaced by a shy schoolteacher, hired by the people of Shasta City, she said.

The next stop was Red Bluff, a cluster of tents and cabins perched above the Sacramento River. Ah Toy glimpsed the wide green water through bordering trees while the innkeeper's wife showed her to a room. It was furnished with a washstand and narrow bedstead, its rope bottom covered with a worn quilt. Exhausted by the journey and her anticipations, Ah Toy fell into a heavy, dreamless sleep.

The next morning, with the horses again pounding north, Ah Toy feasted on the landscape. To the west rose occasional spare brown buttes. To the east, the Sierra Nevada receded into a cloud-capped azure blur. Ahead lay the brown and narrowing Sacramento Valley, relieved by the green that marked the river's course. The triangular beacon of a mountain loomed in the north.

By noon, Ah Toy felt the sun's crushing heat like a stone. Only one passenger, a man with a monocle, remained immune to lethargy. He had boarded at Red Bluff and introduced himself as Anton Roman. He owned the Shasta Book Store, he said, and poured speech like spirits from an upended cask.

To distance the worries for Li Jin that drew her north like a magnet, Ah Toy listened to Roman catalog his merchandise. He described sets of Shakespeare and Milton and Byron and other names that impressed the schoolteacher.

Ah Toy saw relay stations and stage stops pass in a stifling tumult of steaming horses and sweating hostlers. The swaying stagecoach swirled dust into the overheated day. The bookseller discoursed like a lecturer. Tiny towns of tents and cabins blurred past: Jelly Ferry, Readings Bar, Horsetown, Igo, Muletown.

Then suddenly the bookseller was pointing through the raised canvas curtain of the stage window. "Here we are, Queen City of the North. That's my store, miss," he said to the schoolteacher. "You be sure to come on by."

As the driver halted his horses, a runner threw open the stage door. "End of the line, folks," he announced. "Ever'body out. Welcome to Shasta City."

Bewildered, Ah Toy climbed out. She stood on the boardwalk fronting a hotel, valise at her feet, and watched the stage driver turn his team. The town's Main Street was a hundred feet wide, designed for turning the dozens of teams of horses and mules crowding the town.

The bookseller hovered at Ah Toy's elbow, enumerating the uses of the two dozen brick buildings lining the street. All the other passengers had departed. Ah Toy remained his only audience.

"That's the bowling alley," Roman said, pointing across the street, "and next to it there's the jeweler, and over there's my store. And we've got two other bookstores in town," he said, earnest as a salesman. "We have us a regular educated population here. Course there's a good-sized Hongkong at the southeast end of town, too, where I expect you're heading. We have civilization here fine as San Francisco: five hotels, two drugstores, a public school, three doctors, four attorneys, a public bathhouse, a dry goods store with fine fabrics and fancy clothing, and—"

Ah Toy turned on him, suddenly frantic. "I not go this town! I go Weaverville! Where stage for Weaverville?"

The bookseller adjusted his monocle and looked at her in surprise. "Weaverville? Well, ma'am, there's no stage goes to Weaverville." He laughed. "Shasta City is end of the line, the head of 'whoa' navigation, as it were."

The mule skinner's name was Pete. "Oh, you'll like Weaverville, miss," he said, eyes twinkling through the bush of hair covering his face, "right purty place, just tucked up like a bowl in them Trinity Mountains." He was a big man, with dirty red sleeves rolled up over arms like tree trunks. He loaded his mules with flour barrels and tobacco boxes, then plucked Ah Toy up by her waist like so much more freight.

Ah Toy held her breath, as much from surprise at the unexpected maneuver as from the smell of Pete. He stank of whiskey, sweat, and mules. He deposited her neat as a package on the back of a mule. "This here's Peaches. Real sweet-natured. You'll like her."

Ah Toy, holding a parasol in one hand, grabbed a handful of the animal's coarse mane with the other. She had come so far, and now Li Jin was so close. She felt a rope snugged around her waist.

"You ladies insist on sittin' sidewise, got to tie you on," Pete was saying. Ah Toy smiled to herself in sudden amusement, remembering how Simone told of abandoning French dresses for men's trousers to ride astride a mule crossing the Isthmus. Ah Toy had come to Gum Shan in trousers. Now she was wearing a French gown and holding a parasol over a mule named Peaches. How extraordinary, she thought, as the mule stepped daintily behind the bell horse leading the train. Ahead, the trail wreathed the edge of a mountain in a narrow cut.

"Never took me no China lady afore," Pete said, walking along by her side, a hand on Peaches' rump. The other brushed at flies buzzing his face. "Mostly the China men they walk."

"You know China men Weaverville?" Ah Toy looked at Pete from beneath her parasol, suddenly feeling closer to Li Jin. Perhaps this bad-smelling man was a friend.

Pete shrugged. "I know the fella what works for my friend Buck

at the general store. Name's John. And he knows 'em all. Got hisself hurt purty bad in that China war they had a few weeks ago.
That was somethin', I guess. Sorry I missed it. Last time I was up to
Weaverville the China boys was just gettin' it up, havin' the blacksmith forge 'em up some wicked-lookin' three-pronged instruments. Put me in mind of an overgrown salmon spear, somethin'
more'n a foot across and the center tine just as long, too. The boys
was out in the woods cuttin' poles and dressin' 'em up for them
spears. Some of them poles was maybe fifteen feet long."

Ah Toy, seeing the weapon in her mind, felt anger rising up like
a convulsion. The stupid men, she thought, dragging old quarrels to
Gum Shan like strings of firecrackers saved for a holiday. Chan had
said that the Weaverville war rose out of a mining dispute between
a Sze Yup man and a Hakka man. A new argument always unearthed buried ones. Here in Gum Shan, as in China, it was still the
native Cantonese against the Hakkas, ever the strangers, despite
their arrival into Kwangtung from the north nearly six hundred
years ago. These clan and district allegiances seated men at one another's complaints like at family meals. Every Hakka man chewed
every other Hakka man's grievance, every Sze Yup or Sam Yup
drank his brother's wrong with his tea. The men were fools, she
thought, and knew nothing.

"I seen one of these Chinese musses before, though," Pete was
saying. "That one promised to be a real hullabaloo, too, but it never
come off. Two big parties of Celestials, all drawn up in battle array
they was, hollerin' their heads off, threatenin' each other with picks
and shovels and river rocks. Looked to be a real set-to, so all the
miners gathered up to watch. But them China boys just stood
there yellin' at one another and shakin' fists. Pretty soon the miners was cheerin' them on, tryin' to get them into it, but it was no
go. After about an hour of threats, with the excitement all on the
rise, the hostilities ended, with nary a stone thrown nor a blow
struck. The boys just suddenly put down their weapons, frater-

nized a bit, and moved off to their tents. What the row was about, or how peace was struck, was a mystery to us outside barbarians. Disappointin' to some of the boys who was hopin' to see a general engagement."

Ah Toy gazed up the trail, watching the bell horse lead the string of mules into the Trinity Mountains, thinking of the unnecessary harm men did one another. "Hurt bad, your China man friend name John?"

"Pretty bad, but he's come around. 'Bout as many lives as a cat, that John. He come into Weaverville jist like yerself, must be close on to two years ago. Angelita had 'im aboard. Angelita's this Mexican lady runs a string a mules clear from Marysville north to Weaverville. Anyways, she was comin' up through Nevada City, I think it was, through one of them coyoted hills north a town." He looked at Ah Toy. "You know what coyotin' is?"

Ah Toy shook her head.

"It's a kind a tunnelin' into the ground, shaft minin'. Plenty dangerous. Folks gettin' themselves killed in 'em all the time, from timbers collapsin' and stuff." Pete scratched into his beard. "Anyways, accordin' to my friend Buck, Angelita was comin' outta Nevada City right early in the mornin' and her little boy heard a swallowed-up kind a hollerin' comin' outta this shaft. He took a gander down and, Lord A'mighty, there's a fella down there look to be 'bout dead. Angelita's skinners hauled 'im up in one of them buckets. Turned out to be a China man and he just passed out cold at her feet. Well, she couldn't just leave 'im, 'cause Angelita's a real nice lady, but a course she didn't have no time to go traipsin' around Nevada City with 'im, neither. She was headin' on up to Weaverville and figured that's a good place for a China man. Plenty a China men in Weaverville."

Ah Toy stared at Pete, her fingers tight on Peaches' mane. "What name?"

"The China man? John, like I said. Works for my friend Buck

at the general store. Probly knows 'bout ever' China man in Trinity County. Kind of a big shot in Weaverville's Chinatown. He can help you find this scholar friend a yours, I reckon."

Ah Toy sent a prayer into the mountains as the bell horse trudged up the trail with its bells jingling, drawing the mules behind with their dainty feet puffing dust.

To Ah Toy, the town of Weaverville, although nestled into a green bowl cradled by the Trinity Mountains, looked much like any other mining camp she had passed in the stagecoach. It had a few planks and boardwalks thrown down for when rains came, some cabins and tent houses, two or three fancy-front hotels.

Pete deposited her and her valise in front of one of them, the Metropolitan. He pointed out to her Buck's store, where he was headed with his freight. She could find the China man named John there, he said, and wished her luck.

Ah Toy wanted to follow Pete, to find Li Jin. What would he say when he saw her? What would she say to him? She had not dared think past finding him alive, and suddenly she was here, on the edge of her destiny. Ah Toy looked down at her dress soiled with trail dust. She could not go to Li Jin looking like a Mexican-woman mule driver.

The room shown to Ah Toy on the second floor of the Metropolitan Hotel looked like a garden. On the floor a carpet bloomed burgundy-colored roses. Slender vines of the same blossoms twined a design on the wallpaper. A bed ornamented by curled iron, its coverlet a patchwork of tiny calico flowers, absorbed one side of the room. A mirrored oak washstand held a porcelain pitcher and washbasin. A plain oak chair and table completed the furnishings.

Ah Toy bathed and perfumed herself and dressed in her gown of cream-and-crimson stripes. Austin had once said that the gown's belled skirt, dipped waist, and tight bodice reminded him of a vase exhibiting a single perfect flower. She would show herself to Li Jin as a fragrant blossom from the Flowery Kingdom. She fastened pearls into her ears and beneath her chin tied the pink satin ribbons of her bonnet. In the washstand mirror she examined her reflection. She remembered the morning she first sought Li Jin, thinking then how splendid she looked in her green silk pantaloons and black silk tunic, her hair fashioned into a black butterfly at her neck. How much had happened since then, Ah Toy thought, closing the door behind her. Only her destiny remained unchanged.

Ah Toy saw Pete's mules still lined up in front of the store, ears twitching, tails flicking flies. Their hooves puffed clouds of red dust. It drifted like powdered sunshine in the afternoon heat and settled on the boardwalk. Beyond, his back to her, a China man in blue swept dust from the boardwalk through shadows angled by a late-afternoon sun. He worked clumsily, holding the broom handle against one side like a crippled man's crutch.

At her footsteps, he turned.

Ah Toy stared, still as stone. Li Jin stared back in silent disbelief. He gripped the broom as though it might flee its new responsibility to prop him up. Then she ran to him, feeling surprise and gladness and shyness all at once, her eyes filling with tears. Now she stood before him, drinking his image as though he were water and she thirsted. Her eyes traveled him, discovered the diminishment beneath one sleeve. She reached out, touched his arm, bowed her head as a tear fell and darkened a crimson stripe on her bosom.

"I have come for you," she said at last, looking up.

Li Jin touched a hand to her cheek, as though to assure himself she was real. "Yes," he said.

Ah Toy's questions tumbled from her. What had happened to him? How had he lived? Was he rescued by the Mexican woman? What of his injury?

He had got work near Nevada City, he told her, digging out a mine collapsing from winter rains. The weight of waterlogged earth had twisted and skewed the shoring, Li Jin explained. In places the tunnel permitted a man's passage only by crawling. His job was to clear the shrunken tunnel and haul the dirt to the windlass rope dangling in the shaft's column of telescoped daylight. The foreman, a Cornishman, directed Li Jin's digging, took measurements for new timbers, then abandoned Li Jin to his labor.

The ideal shaft miners, Li Jin learned, were either England's Cornish tin miners or Americans from Wisconsin's lead mines or Pennsylvania's coal mines. They were as at home under the earth as moles.

"I was not." Li Jin told how he scooped dirt by the light of a flickering candle and choked on the suffocating smell of the earth's bowels.

Ah Toy imagined the steady rain of crumbling dirt onto Li Jin's back. Like rats scampering over him, she thought, feeling his terror as though it were her own.

Li Jin explained how the smothered, sucking sound of his digging and his own gasping, oxygen-hungry breath filled his ears while he waited out the ominous creaking of twisting timbers. "Occasionally," he said, "somewhere in the blackness, a supporting pillar ruptured and exploded like a gunshot. Each time, I swallowed my breath, as though rehearsing the cave-in that eventually trapped me."

Ah Toy felt her own breath depart. "Please, let us sit." Li Jin sat with her on a bench in front of the store. Timidly, she placed her hand on Li Jin's. "The fortune-teller said the earth element covered you."

Li Jin took Ah Toy's hand in his. "A woman rescued me. She said her name was Angelita, but I think she must have been mistaken, that it was Ah Toy." He smiled, then continued his story.

"Sometimes I hear in my mind again the horse's bell and the mules' passing overhead." Before that, he said, he had heard only his own wheezing panic as he clawed through the collapsed tunnel, gulping oxygen from air pockets the gods had left to sustain him. Dirt gritted against his tongue and teeth and choked his throat. He clawed his way to the shaft, called out, and fainted. When consciousness returned, he discovered himself tied on a mule, secure as a flour barrel.

Ah Toy put a hand to Li Jin's injured arm. She asked the question with her eyes.

Li Jin shook his head. "And so I am come to Weaverville," he said, standing. He pulled Ah Toy up to him with his one good arm. He smiled at her. "I want to show you something."

As they walked, Li Jin told Ah Toy that Weaverville was a good place for China men. They were tolerated here. More than a thousand worked abandoned claims without persecution. The four dollars' monthly mining tax each China man paid the county helped protect them, of course. Trinity County officers discouraged attacks on the county's chief source of revenue.

They followed a footpath lined with towering pines. Ah Toy saw in a clearing ahead what Li Jin had brought her to see.

"Our joss house," he said. Weaverville's five family associations had constructed the temple of wood and painted it blue. They painted darker lines to resemble the mortar joinings of stone, out of which such buildings were constructed in China.

To Ah Toy, the little temple with its ornamented, upturned roof corners looked as delicate as porcelain. Around it, wispy trees, brought as seed from China, Li Jin said, had leafed into thin, green umbrellas.

The path also led to the barbarians' cemetery, Li Jin explained. The China men had fenced the joss house to protect it from evil spirits accompanying barbarian funeral processions. The spirits traveled only in straight lines, and low to the ground, so the gate had been offset from the temple's entrance, and stairs added.

He led Ah Toy inside, past the spirit screen designed to deflect any errant soul determined upon entering. Ah Toy stood silently while her eyes accommodated the dim interior.

"We came here first, the day of the great battle," Li Jin said, his voice low. "I carried a trident twelve feet long. I placed my weapon with those of the other Sze Yup men leaning by the temple door. I lit three joss sticks for the temple god, Dai Tze."

Ah Toy felt a sudden chill.

Li Jin pointed with his chin to the corner. Ah Toy saw the glinting cylinder of the King's Umbrella.

"We procured it from China for our processions."

Ah Toy admired the intricate design of gold thread woven into imperial yellow silk. Hundreds of tiny mirrors had been stitched to it to drive away evil spirits with reflections of their own horrible appearance.

Inside the temple's main room was a carved teak altar, painted red and elaborately gilded. Within it sat likenesses of the gods of wealth, luck, and courage. A table was strewn with offerings. Mounted against a banner-draped wall were two tall, red signboards depicting the sojourners' brave enterprise. Li Jin translated, "I came. I sought. I found. I returned home safely."

Ah Toy contemplated the signboards. She yearned to return home with this man destiny had sent her. That Li Jin should travel this long way to risk dying at the hands of another China man was senseless. Why did men haul old quarrels behind them like plows, constantly invigorating ancient differences? But she knew this was not a question she could ask.

"The day of battle," Li Jin said, as though reading her thoughts, "the Taoist priest led the Sze Yup leaders in the ceremony for a great undertaking. He circled this room many times, first ringing a bell, then banging a gong, and last, tapping a wooden box. Each time he passed before the gods he bowed low and rapped his forehead. Having captured the gods' attention, he paraded the room with a lighted candle, raising and lowering it in tempo with his chanting. He struck a gong, lit several joss sticks, then placed rice cakes and vegetables on the altar. He sent us from the room so the gods might partake of their meal unobserved. After a few minutes he declared the gods not hungry. We congratulated each other on this fortunate circumstance. The gods were more likely to grant petitions when sated than when ill-natured by hunger."

Ah Toy stared at Li Jin. She saw no regret and said nothing.

"We offered the gods fresh, unlit joss sticks and, at the priest's direction, removed and extinguished the burning ones. The priest collected them, mixed in the unburned sticks, and tied them together. He reversed this bundle, so only unburned ends were visible, and withdrew one stick. We stood silent, anxious for a sign of the gods' support. We had petitioned for victory over our enemies. If the priest should withdraw an unburned stick, the gods' reply would be negative. When the priest pulled out a stick and showed it, the end was charred. We rejoiced. We outnumbered the Hakka men, but victory was not certain. They are tall and determined warriors. Five days before our ceremony they had charged up and down Weaverville's main thoroughfare with hideous yells, led by a barbarian named Sites. He rode a horse decorated with military regimentals. The Hakkas offered him five hundred dollars to fight for them, but he wanted a thousand and they didn't have it."

Ah Toy wanted to tell Li Jin to stop, that she didn't want to hear more of this stupid thing the China men had done, but she knew she must.

Li Jin led Ah Toy back along the footpath toward the lower end of town. "I will show you where two hundred and fifty Sze Yup men assembled for the fight at Five-Cent Gulch."

Ah Toy said nothing. A man must talk of these things, she thought, and bit back words she knew he would not hear.

"Weaverville swarmed with spectators," Li Jin said, reliving the excitement. "Hundreds of barbarians came from all over the county, having heard of our preparations. We had bought all the hatchets in town and contracted with the blacksmith to forge our weapons and shields and helmets. The barbarians roamed among us, cheerfully examining our weapons. They whistled at the fearsome two-handed swords the strongest warriors carried, five-feet long and mounted on six-foot handles. I was proud of the Sze Yups' appearance. Pikes and three-prong spears mounted on twelve-foot poles all fluttered crimson streamers."

Ah Toy saw in imagination the noisy gathering of warriors and sightseers and said nothing.

"Spectators cheered us as our commanders ushered us into ranks. There were two groups. The commanders' strategy, should the challenge culminate in battle, was a pincers maneuver to encircle the ferocious but outnumbered Hakkas. I was assigned to the first group, in the third rank, behind the men with short swords and shields. The sun's heat beat upon us. My metal helmet felt heavy and hot. Then I relinquished all thought of self. I became one with the collective intensity of men fated for war. Over the cheers of spectators, I heard the crashing gongs and blaring horns as we moved out behind the waving red and black flag emblazoned 'Canton City Company.' "

Ah Toy imagined how Li Jin had proudly held aloft his weapon, watching its streamer from beneath his helmet. She could contain herself no longer. "Why did you do this thing? Is life so valueless?"

Li Jin looked at her, Ah Toy thought, as if he didn't know her. "The Hakkas challenged us!"

Ah Toy said nothing.

Li Jin led her to Five-Cent Gulch, flats of washed gravel east of Weaverville, the place designated for battle. She watched him look around, as though seeing again the hundreds of spectators.

"When the commander halted, we stood still as clay statues," Li Jin said, "our pole weapons upright as trees. Then, at his signal, we lowered our spears and swords and, with terrible yells, ran a hundred yards. When we stopped, the front ranks with their short swords dropped to one knee to form a rampart. We arrived here in a furious charge, gravel crunching and flying from beneath our boots. Across the gulch the Hakkas waited, massed in a compact body, as our strategists had predicted their smaller numbers compelled. They stood still as death, foreheads wrapped in red, beneath a scarlet and gold dragon banner. Their weapons flashed a thousand points of light from the sun."

Ah Toy, against her will, envisioned the scene Li Jin painted with his words.

"Our plan was to separate at the battle site. Warriors of the second group trooped away through the gravel, taking positions at a distance. Should the Hakkas charge, our group would hold the flat. Then our second group would attack the enemy from behind to cut off escape. While we were maneuvering, Sheriff Lowe rode onto the battleground. His horse's hooves sprayed gravel as he dashed back and forth before us. He shouted at spectators to stop this war.

They laughed at him. Some hissed and booed. They hollered they had walked miles to see 'this scrap,' that Lowe was a meddling fool who could watch the fun with them or go to hell."

Ah Toy watched Li Jin gaze into memory. His voice became distant with the telling.

"I remember the sheriff standing up in his stirrups. 'Damn you all!' he yelled. 'You're worse than these heathens! If one Chinese or one white man is injured here today, I'll order the grand jury to indict every man who refused to help me stop this war!' But the crowd laughed at him. 'Go to hell, Lowe!' they shouted. 'We came here to see the fight, and we're going to see it!' The sheriff cursed, then pleaded. Finally, with a look of disgust, he shouted, 'You're damned poor American citizens! I'll have every mother's son of you before the grand jury!' "

Li Jin walked to the edge of the gulch and stared across. Ah Toy followed. She stood silently at his side.

After a time he spoke. "When the sheriff galloped from the battlefield, the Hakka leader strode with an insolent swagger to the edge of the gulch and hurled the first insult. The Sze Yup commander responded in kind. Fierce exchanges followed. Then the Hakka leader slowly rolled up the legs of his trousers to his thighs. At this sign, his men yelled savagely."

Ah Toy saw in Li Jin's eyes that he witnessed the moment again now.

"We responded with piercing screams, but I heard the spectators urging battle. Someone said, 'They ain't gonna fight after all!' Another replied, 'The hell they ain't! I come to see a fight!' And the first man said we had just been fooling with all our hollering."

Li Jin looked around at the empty flats. Ah Toy saw him remembering. As he described the impatient crowd, she recognized something familiar in the picture Li Jin painted. It came to her through a fog of memory, the shouting spectators, the snorting bulls with frantic eyes, the bellowing anguish of the grizzly.

"I noticed a commotion among the miners," Li Jin was saying, "and saw forty or fifty of them maneuver to the rear of us. They started shoving the back ranks, hollering at them to fight. 'Come on, you slant-eyed bastards!' they said. 'Let's see you fight!' And then someone else yelled, 'Hell, we'll make 'em fight if'n we hafta!' They scooped up gravel and pelted the China men with it. I heard the stones strike metal helmets and felt the forward thrust. 'That's right!' someone shouted. 'Let's get 'em goin'!'"

Ah Toy hung her head, not to see the fear in Li Jin's eyes.

"The second group's commander, seeing movement, signaled his men toward the gulch. The maneuver excited some miners, who yelled, 'Here they go, boys!' Across the gulch, the Hakkas remained stationary. I heard someone say in disgust, 'Ah, they ain't gonna fight. Them red caps ain't gonna fight on accounta they're outnumbered.' Then someone else yelled, 'Yeah, it ain't a fair fight! Let's make it a fair fight, boys!' And then the crowd moved to block our second group. Across the gulch, the Hakka leader, seeing the advantage, struck his shield with his sword. Giving a yell, he signaled a charge. His men poured across the gulch."

Li Jin hesitated. Ah Toy saw the fearful moment reflected in his eyes.

"I lowered my spear and prepared to receive the charge. But it came slowly, as if through water. Time stopped. I saw the yelling Hakkas as clearly as though painted on bright silk. I thought I could, if I wished, count each red-wrapped head, each beribboned pike and trident, each flashing hatchet and glinting sword. My awareness gathered in the spectators in slouch hats, their mouths opening and closing in a roar for blood. Almost as if it were destined, I saw the Dutchman draw his pistol. I knew the Dutchman, a miner named Malmberg, a crude, squat man with a mean face, always complaining about prices and his poor luck. Sun glinted from the Dutchman's pistol. I saw, through my leisurely vision, the gun in the Dutchman's hand as clearly as if I held the sixteen-inch flintlock in my own. I watched Malmberg lazily raise the gun and fire a ball into the Sze Yups. I saw the Dutchman's mouth slowing forming his words. 'Dere, dat'll get 'em goin',' he said."

Li Jin paused, remembering. Ah Toy shut her eyes against the image he conjured for her. She could almost sense the explosion of the pistol, feel the ball slide past with a caressing breath, distantly hear the choking scream of the China man behind Li Jin. As Li Jin described the scene, Ah Toy saw the Dutchman's mean face stretch a satisfied grin between florid cheeks. And then the grin form a large round *Oohhh,* and the Dutchman's eyes bulge forward, and his hat fly away, and the top of his head dissolve into a scattering red splash of flung bone and flesh and what had been the Dutchman's brain.

"I saw standing behind the slowly toppling Dutchman," Li Jin continued, "a tall man named Diamond Dick, a likable miner known around town. He worked a claim called the Greasy Spoon. In his hand he, too, held a pistol. I distinctly heard him say, 'I bet good money on the Cantons. Don't want no damned fool Dutchman helpin' the red caps lick 'em.'"

Ah Toy watched Li Jin stare into the gulch.

"I saw the red-capped Hakkas flood up the gulch in a flurry of dust and shrieks. And then I was only aware of flashing swords and swinging hatchets, of crashing metal striking shields, of blood and falling men, and gurgling cries. A fierce-looking Hakka ran his spear through a man in the front rank. He withdrew it from the body and plunged it in again. Hakkas crashed past the fallen man, sinking their weapons into his body like forks into meat.

"And then, amid the red cries of pain and fury, the teeth-grinding clash of metal on metal, I heard guns. The Hakkas had concealed pistols on themselves, and I thought, as I thrust my spear into the long thigh of a Hakka man and watched his blue trousers turn crimson, that of course they would, to even the fight. They never suspected the Americans would even it for them. We should all have foreseen that. Americans always favor the 'underdog,' as they say. And these thoughts clustered together in my mind, forming such a perception of clarity as to produce a bright, blinding red of understanding, even as I heard the pistol and felt the ball."

Ah Toy wanted to cover her ears with her hands to stop the words. They flowed over her like a river. She saw Li Jin stare at his chest, reliving the sight of his blue tunic turning red. In her imagination she saw the spreading blood, saw the shield slowly falling from his hand, saw the lacquer-smooth pole drifting to his feet fluttering its crimson streamers. And then, floating gently up to enfold him, the scarlet-spattered gravel once so carefully washed clean of gold by the resolute miners of Weaverville.

As they walked slowly back to town, Li Jin spoke of the long weeks in which his life force vacillated. Throughout the painful recovery from the gunshot, he told her, he had dreamt of home, welcoming the peaceful images of that faraway place like the wound welcomed healing.

"I remember drifting into familiar memories," Li Jin said, stopping in the road to look into Ah Toy's eyes, "remembered the green of rice fields. I could feel the mud sucking at my feet, could hear the sweet flute music of my brother perched on the family's docile water ox, silhouetted by a setting sun. How I wanted to go there."

He looked away, as if seeing the vision now. Ah Toy understood. She kept her dreams, too.

"With memory," Li Jin said, smiling now, "came the fragrant aromas of family meals. I heard the quick harangues of my mother, the chatter of children, the satisfied smacks of the old grandfather enjoying tea. And other memories, too." He put a hand to Ah Toy's face, touched her cheek where the pink ribbon of her bonnet joined it. "Sometimes in imagination I saw the frightened girl on the *Flavius,* wind flapping trousers against her legs and snatching shy English words from her mouth. Time leapt backward and forward again. I was transported to the time before Gum Shan's terrors, tax collectors on dark horses, dangerous mineshafts, dog-tempered Americans, the time before the fear of becoming a hungry spirit and never returning home."

Ah Toy held her breath, fearing his words had a meaning she didn't understand.

"I saw you," Li Jin said, "in the depths of the ship, packing your basket, as clearly as I see you now. I knew destiny had joined me to the slave woman who showered me with English words, the same woman who stands before me now, her beauty sheathed in Gum Shan fashion."

Ah Toy felt tears gathering gladness to her eyes. "Tonight," she whispered, "come to me at the hotel."

In her hotel room, Ah Toy prepared herself for her destiny. Her thoughts a whirl of happy prayers and plans, she dressed her hair in the old way, fastening golden hairpins into black butterfly wings. She put on the red satin dress and around her neck hung the white jade dragon on a black silk cord. She whitened her face with rice powder, darkened her eyes with kohl, rouged her cheeks and lips the color of claret, perfumed herself with sandalwood.

She placed the red envelope on a silver tray and put it on the table. She prepared tea, sat in the oak chair, and waited for his knock. When it came, she heard her voice quivering like a lute string. "Come in please."

The door opened and Li Jin was there, in the arbory room, tall and slender in a green silk tunic.

Ah Toy leapt from her chair like a startled rabbit. She felt herself falling backward in time. In the nervous way of years before, she said, "Come in please, you will sit, please." With lowered eyes, she indicated the chair.

They exchanged formal pleasantries as though they had not parted an hour before. Ah Toy offered tea and watched Li Jin drink. Had he seen the envelope? Did he understand? She watched him place his cup on the table, next to the red envelope. He looked at her, smiled, took it up. Ah Toy knelt before him on the carpet of burgundy roses, her slippered feet beneath her, hands tucked into the folds of her sleeves. She bowed her head and heard him open the envelope. He tapped it against the table, and Ah Toy looked up.

"My wife, Wu-Tze, treasures bitterness like a gardener his flowers."

Ah Toy lowered her eyes and tried not to show disappointment. Of course, there would be a first wife. A good son would not travel the long distance to Gum Shan and leave his family alone. There must be a wife to tend his mother.

"First lady rightful wife," Ah Toy said, adopting the formality her ceremony required. "Second lady respect her, visit only when first lady wish."

Li Jin tapped the envelope against the table again. "Two spoons crowd one bowl."

Ah Toy took his meaning. Theirs was a play of reassurances. The ritual had its observances. She replied in the stilted fashion expected. "Always I wish my own house and courtyard."

She reached beneath the curled iron bed and withdrew her valise. She took from it a red velvet bag and handed it to him.

She saw his surprise at its weight. He clattered the goldpieces onto the table. It was enough to pay their passage home. It was not enough to build a house and courtyard.

Li Jin frowned, and Ah Toy laughed. She jumped up and took the velvet bag from his hands. "This nothing," she said, dropping it into her valise with a dismissive gesture. "In San Francisco I have enough gold to build a fine house for first lady, and fine house for second lady."

"My mother—"

Ah Toy raised her hands, arresting objections. "There is dew for every blade of grass." She laughed with the happiness of her promise.

Li Jin laughed with her as he slipped the red envelope into his sleeve to show his acceptance. Standing, he took Ah Toy's hands in his and drew her to him. She looked into his eyes, saw them study her as if to memorize her. A cooling breeze lifted the lace curtains at the window. Faint sounds of fading footsteps drifted from the boardwalk below. A dog barked in the distance. A mother called a child in from the dark.

Ah Toy bowed her head as Li Jin slowly withdrew the gold hairpins holding the sleek black butterfly at her neck. He dropped them silently into the burgundy roses at their feet. Ah Toy, senses deserting her, felt Li Jin's body hard against hers as he buried his face in the fragrance of pomegranate blossoms.

As-sing closed the door behind him and locked it. A quickening breeze snatched at his New York hat. He caught the brim in both hands, peering from beneath it at the gloom of gathering clouds. He buttoned his coat against the threatening rain and patted his pockets to reassure himself he had remembered the ledger.

At the foot of the stairs, clutching his hat, he turned to admire again the gilded red signboard announcing the Office of the Consul of China. It was a fine signboard.

He looked down Sacramento street. He could follow it to the wharf or take the longer route along Dupont and avoid the worst of the wind. There was no hurry. The ship departed at well past noon, and the captain knew the procedure. A deciding gust whipped at his coat.

As-sing liked Dupont street, Dupont Gai, thick with humanity spilled like rice from a torn sack. China men poured from shops and houses that hinted prosperity, gold, secret lives. Anonymously, they jostled As-sing with elbows and burden baskets.

As-sing dodged a hurrying vegetable vendor stooped beneath his carrying pole, then a farmer carrying a cage of squawking chickens. A green signboard on a storefront caught his eye. He stopped and considered its hopeful message: "Ten thousand profits." As-sing peered inside. A wholesale dealer.

A signboard on a neighboring door read, "Riches ever flowing." A fan-tan saloon. As-sing saw pasted in the window of the fan-tan saloon a familiar red paper card. It promised, "Foreign smoke in broken parcels," for the poor man, who bought his opium in fractional quantities.

These red cards littered the windows of Dupont Gai now, advertising pipes and lamps and the "foreign mud" from Turkey and India. As-sing knew well the promise. Lie back on the wooden platform, your head on the porcelain pillow, the long pipe tended for you, the air sweet with its fragrance. Then no more dragon-filled sleep, only a universe of possibility.

The red cards patched the power leaking from him like tea from a cracked cup.

As-sing continued slowly northward, reading the signboards of merchants vending everything from dried fruit to servants. Their signs announced optimism, not goods: "Everlasting plenteousness," "Eternal affluence," "Glorious abundance."

Useless confidence, he thought, turning up his collar against the chill. He read a sign on the door of a cigar-maker, "Constant increase of wealth," and on another fan-tan saloon, "Riches ever flowing." As-sing suspected his only hope for riches now lay with the red card in the window: "No. 2 opium to be sold at all times." Number two, the second smoke, scrapings from the used pipe, for those too poor to afford the first, the fresh.

All up the street, plastered against the fronts of shops dispensing roasted hogs, clothing, tea, slippers, and tinware, there hung red and green and gilded signboards. As-sing read them with bemusement as he passed: "Let rich customers continually come," "Profit coming in like rushing waters," "Wealth arising like the bubbling spring." How many of their hopeful owners, he wondered, in striving for the mountaintop of riches, had attained unaware the summit of their achievement?

He smelled ginger as he passed a restaurant. "Balcony of joy and delight" proclaimed the signboard at its entrance. A new place, unknown to him. He didn't even know now how many of his countrymen's restaurants jammed San Francisco's Little China. How strange that just five years ago there had been only one, his. Then he had been chief of all the Chinese in Gum Shan. For a year, two years, nearly three, he had stood on the mountaintop of his influence and mistaken it for a stepping-stone. Now his standing slipped from him continually, an erosion, a sliding down of small spills. He wondered, reading the cheerful anticipation emblazoned on doorways, how many hopes had already been realized but not recognized, the height obtained and not to be surpassed.

These signboards struck him as singularly Chinese. Americans never publicly invoked fortune or invited luck. Their signs proclaimed business in forthright announcement, realized and achieved: Dry goods. Hardware. Hotel. Grocery. Ironworks. Always with the period mark, no more to be said, accomplished, completed.

At the corner of Clay street, As-sing turned and surveyed the long reach of his countrymen's enterprise. Dupont Gai was a noisy, crowded Chinese foothold on the Americans' Gold Mountain. Regardless of differences with their hosts, he knew the China men would not leave. This one, that one, yes, but then another would come—a son, a brother, a nephew—to take that one's place, to feed themselves, to feed the family on the exhausted land across the sea, to escape the murderous *taiping* or whatever ill wind blew. The Chinese understood perseverance. Like willows in wind, they would bend their backs on the Gold Mountain to persecution and ridicule. And they would not break. They would endure. A hundred years from now, he thought, two hundred, as long as San Francisco survives, this street will be ours.

Ah Toy woke slowly, reluctantly forsaking the dream. It had come to her first in the curled-iron bed of the Weaverville hotel. In the several weeks since then she had often drifted into sleep seeking its enchantment. In the dream, she sat beneath a tree in a high-walled courtyard surrounded by baskets of rice, filled to overflowing. A fat baby played at her feet, and in the tree two boys climbed and shouted their fun. Beyond the courtyard wall, through which she could see in the strange seeing way of dreams, stretched an endless chain of people walking toward her through bright green rice fields. Beyond the opposite wall, the chain of people extended into the infinite distance.

Ah Toy loved the dream and the contentment it brought her. She knew it represented her place in the long scroll of the ordained order of things.

Chan tapped on the door. "Tea, lady," he said, his voice that peculiar mix of regret and anticipation acquired since her return to the lucky-number house.

Ah Toy rose from her straw mat without waking Li Jin. She rubbed the small of her back, missing her soft bed. Li Jin had said, without pride or apology, that he never slept in *fan qui* beds. Seeing her regret for its feathery comforts, he had explained, not unkindly, that his family's village was not a proper place for foreign affluence. There, surplus rice and abundant fields represented luxury, and Ah Toy added these to her dream.

She sighed now as she padded across the room. The bed would have gone anyway when Li Jin sold the furniture in preparation for their departure.

She took the tea tray from Chan. "Find a drayman to come for the boxes," she told him. Her voice sounded oddly hollow. She thought it must be an echo from the empty house.

Chan looked at her curiously, then turned away with a confirming nod.

Ah Toy placed the tea tray beside the bed mat and watched Li Jin sleep. Husband, she thought fondly. Every morning, she willed herself awake first, that she might gaze upon this wonder of fortune's favor. Watching him sleep, she remembered again, as she often did in her recent happiness, the long-ago time of Willow lane, and Lao Tai Tai's admonition. "You cannot choose your life," the old mistress had said, "but you can choose your dreams."

Ah Toy sat cross-legged on the sleeping mat, a steaming teacup warming her hands, contemplating this wonder of fulfilled dreams. True, Li Jin's acceptance of her red envelope bore no comparison to a ceremonial procession in a red sedan chair accompanied by drummers, but it sufficed. She was his wife. She belonged now to this handsome sleeping man, and to his unknown family.

Li Jin had spoken of her place in his family as they journeyed from Weaverville to San Francisco. They had accompanied a mule skinner on the Indian trading trail leading west from Weaverville through the mountains to the great ocean, to the trading post on Humboldt Bay. By this route they avoided both the heat of the Sacramento Valley and the humiliation of stagecoach travel. Ah Toy had been appalled to learn that in the traditional clothing Li Jin insisted she wear as befitted a wife, she would be required to ride on top of the stage with the baggage.

Instead they enjoyed a respectful passage aboard a boat bringing from the Humboldt forests more lumber for the endless building of San Francisco. Ah Toy had stayed all day upon deck, savoring the passing scene, drinking in the beauty of the wild land dense with trees. By her side, Li Jin had longingly spoken of ricelands, those his family owned, those he would buy. How curious, she had thought then, admiring the exuberant forest, to yearn for obedient land, land that grew what it was told to grow. She nearly confessed that were she a man, she'd choose these magnificent wild woods over tamed land, the lumberman's life over the farmer's. This land promised possibilities, not the dull, repetitive assurance of crops. But she knew she must not speak such thoughts, for she was a woman and these things were beyond her sphere.

Li Jin spoke fondly on the journey, too, of his family, his father and mother, his aged grandfather. Ah Toy recalled old Wang Po querulously demanding tea and rice gruel and pushed the picture from her memory.

From Li Jin's words Ah Toy tried to imagine her mother-in-law, knowing intuitively the life the woman had led, the constant caring for her husband, for his mother, for her children until a son brought her a daughter-in-law of her own. In the ordained order of things, each daughter-in-law eased the mother-in-law's burdens even as she assumed her own.

From Li Jin's description, Ah Toy expected a nagging, demanding mother-in-law. Ah Toy imagined her as a teapot, one hand on her hip, the other pointing an accusatory finger. She buried this teapot picture along with the querulous grandfather dribbling tea into his beard.

As Li Jin described his family's customary days, Ah Toy added herself to his portrayal, in the established ways of families since time began, as obedient second wife. She tried to see herself serving the old ones, bathing the grandfather's feet, fetching sweets for an irascible mother-in-law. The mind picture fit clumsily, like over-size shoes.

She hinted to Li Jin the hiring of servants, but his response silenced her. Her dowry, he said, would buy rice fields for the family, not indolence for his wives.

Li Jin spoke little of his wife Wu-Tze, saying only that she had no talents. Ah Toy understood this statement for the praise it represented. Confucius had declared, "The woman with no talents is the one who has merit." Girls learned this axiom in childhood. It meant submission, docility, the averted gaze, a cool gravity, a demeanor like winter plum blossoms in snow, never the wide-eyed eagerness of sunflowers in summer.

Li Jin spoke of his only child, a daughter, as the "worthless girl." Wu-Tze, he complained, insisted she needed the child to help her with chores and so refused to bind her feet. With Ah Toy in the house, the worthless girl might come to more than a big-footed woman to marry off for a few *cash* to an oil vendor or street merchant. The girl was young and her feet still pliable.

As Li Jin said this, Ah Toy felt again the excruciating twist of binding cloths on her own feet, and then a nausea of remembered pain.

Ah Toy thought of Wu-Tze's child now, watching Li Jin sleep. She could say nothing, it was not her place, but the imagined picture of the little girl screaming in agony, tortured by her deforming feet, saddened her. Ah Toy sipped her tea, feeling nauseated again. She supposed the distressing prospect of the little girl's pain unsettled her. Then Li Jin woke and she poured tea for him and felt better.

The clipper lay moored at the end of Clay street wharf graceful as a captured butterfly. Beyond, gulls wheeled in the gray sky above the jutting masts of anchored shipping. Ah Toy craned her neck, watching the sailors climb the clipper's rigging. She turned to Li Jin to say she thought the sailors looked like puppets in strings, but the watching had dizzied her. She put a hand on her husband's arm to balance herself and said nothing.

Li Jin patted her hand distractedly, absorbed by the last tasks of departure. He opened the money case he carried and took out a double-eagle goldpiece. "For squeeze," he said, giving the case to Ah Toy to hold. She started to protest that San Francisco was not Hongkong, that the clipper's purser expected no squeeze, but she said nothing. Her husband's ignorance of Gum Shan ways constantly surprised her. How little he had learned of this place, she thought, watching him thread through the jostling people and obstructing drays crowding the wharf.

Chan put his valise and sleeping mat down near Ah Toy and began unloading her boxes from the cart. Ah Toy studied him, thinking how confident he looked, this thin-shouldered Hakka boy who had served her so loyally, eager now for his own impending journey. He had devoured Li Jin's stories of the mines like a man starved and begged for more. "You must go see for yourself," Li Jin said, laughing, and gave the boy gold to travel.

Chan and the drayman, grunting from the effort, stacked her six packing boxes on the wharf. Five contained the few Gum Shan acquisitions Li Jin had agreed Ah Toy might take with them: the crackle-glazed statue of Kwan-yin, the screen of the Eight Immortals, the moon-hare god, the *fan qui* clock, her porcelain and lacquerware. She smiled to herself as Chan hefted the last box from the wagon. A chip marked its corner. The treasure box, the great gift to her scholar husband.

Looking at it, she recalled the day she and Li Jin arrived at the lucky-number house from Weaverville, when she had retrieved her concealed money case and given it to him. Li Jin had counted the coins in surprise, impressed by her dowry. She had started to protest then that a thousand dollars in gold was nothing, that she possessed ten times more. At the last she kept silent, enjoying the private pleasure of anticipating Li Jin's astonishment when they reached his village and opened this box. It held fifty pounds of gold, six hundred troy ounces stamped and certified pure by the city's United States mint, wealth beyond his imagining. The gold would buy more than riceland. It would buy Li Jin a scholar's imperial appointment.

Ah Toy, warmed by secret satisfaction, gazed at the box stuffed with newspapers cradling the golden treasure delivered by Wells, Fargo on a morning Li Jin was away. She had chipped the unobtrusive notch herself after Chan nailed the crate shut and lashed it with rope. It pleased her to know which box contained Li Jin's future as a high man.

Ah Toy paid the drayman from the money case. She watched the empty cart rattle up the Clay street wharf behind his patiently clopping horse. She remembered now, through the telescope of time, her first steps upon this wharf and how it echoed the sea, rolling beneath her feet like the ship.

Suddenly she felt the wharf sway again in that old way. How odd, she thought, to induce sensation by recalling it. But the peculiar perception persisted, a dizzying, unsettling feeling. She felt nauseated and light-headed. And then suddenly aware. She sat down abruptly on a crate, the money case in her lap, and buried her head in her hands.

"Are you ill, lady?"

Ah Toy lifted her head to see Chan kneeling beside her, worried. Her head reeled, but she managed to nod an assurance she didn't feel. She needed to think.

"Perhaps I require something to eat." Her words sounded thick to her, and far away, as though hauled up in buckets from a well. Slowly, studiously, she took a dollar from the money case. Her fingers looked odd to her, awkward and unattached, as though they belonged to someone else. She watched her stranger's hand give the coin to Chan. She heard a voice imitate her own. "Find a vendor, Chan, and buy me an orange."

Ah Toy watched Chan elbow his way through a straggling line of blue-coated China men dragging bundles and baskets toward the gangplank. As he disappeared into the throngs of people jamming the wharf, her vision blurred. The blue line of China men frayed, lost its edge, dissolved into a wash of watercolor on wet parchment. She knew neither wind nor salt air caused her tears.

She felt a terrible, deep wrenching of despair, as though a fierce hand clawed inside her, ripping away whole some vital organ. Her throat closed on the suffocating anguish of lost dreams, and the cruel destiny that had erased her from the ordained order of things.

And then Chan was back, an orange in his extended hand, uncertainty in his eyes.

With the sleeve of her jacket, Ah Toy whisked the tears from her face. "Wind," she said softly, and took the fruit.

She knew she must stand, display her strength, exhibit her spirit, for herself as well as Chan. As she dragged her leaden body upright, she felt strangely light-headed again, but in a curious and different way, not from what she knew now, but from the ordinariness of things. It stunned her, as she registered them. The wharf still teemed with people as it had before. The line of blue-coated China men inched on. She saw she held the money case in one hand, an orange in the other. She wondered how they remained firm and unaltered while her body turned to stone and her spirit to vapor.

Slowly, deliberately, she saw herself place the orange on a packing box. She noticed, with no emotion, that the corner of the box was chipped. She turned to Chan and smiled, surprised by the ability. She felt as if she had discovered a secret place from which to inhale correct faces. And now she heard her confiscated voice saying,

"Thank you, Chan, I am well." She saw the foreign hand that was hers placing itself on his shoulder. "We have spoken our farewells. Now you must go or you will miss the steamer."

It surprised her that Chan failed to notice that this was not her hand, her face, her voice, not her at all.

He asked politely whether he should not stay until Li Jin's return.

"Not necessary," Ah Toy's false person reassured him.

And then, through the last of repeated farewells, Chan gathered up his mat and valise, took off his slouch hat to bow to her, and was gone.

"Good fortune, Chan, good fortune," her real person whispered as she watched him go. He turned a final time to wave his hat at her, and she saw through her tears, as he disappeared into the crowd, a stubby queue swinging jauntily at his back.

And then suddenly Li Jin was at her side, and with him her old enemy, leering and clutching a ledger.

Ah Toy whipped her sleeve over her eyes, as if to rid them of wind, and regarded As-sing. For all his presumed authority, he still looked to her like some high man's bond servant. She startled herself with the realization that she felt no hatred for him and recalled her disinterest at learning the courts had indeed indicted him.

Perhaps her happiness, her too-brief happiness, she thought, feeling the painful emptiness tear at her again, had blunted her triumph. Regardless, it was of no matter to her that As-sing, at the last, avoided prison only by the expensive exertions of his attorneys, nor that heavy fines imposed by the courts had broken him.

As-sing smirked and opened his ledger. Ah Toy watched a bony finger leaf its pages, a dirty fingernail skim its scribbled columns. He reminded her of a skittering old cockroach, too messy to smash, too large to ignore.

"Here, you see," crowed As-sing, jabbing the yellowed page.

Beside him, Ah Toy's handsome husband, looking prosperous as a mandarin in his new clothes, said unhappily, "Old debts."

"How much?" Ah Toy asked from the false person disposing of tasks for her.

As-sing grinned. "Also exit fees."

Ah Toy shrugged her indifference. That As-sing survived now on lesser improprieties was beneath her notice. She opened the money case and watched Li Jin count out the double eagles. As-sing grinned, put the money and ledger in one pocket and pulled from the other two crumpled slips of paper stamped with a red seal. He shoved them in Li Jin's hand, nodded, sauntered off.

Ah Toy watched As-sing clomp away in his oversize American boots. She felt a sudden, strange comradeship with the crafty old merchant gripping the brim of his ridiculous hat against the wind. Gum Shan had wrested China from both of them. They belonged nowhere.

"You keep this," Li Jin was saying. "We might become separated." He was handing her one of the red-stamped papers.

Ah Toy stared at the paper in her husband's hand. She made no move to take it.

"Wife, this is your exit paper."

Ah Toy shook her head no, slowly no. Her eyes filled with tears. She tried to speak, to explain, but speech had left her. She felt choked, as if Chan's orange had leaped from the box where it sat and embedded itself whole in her throat.

Li Jin looked confused. "Are you ill?"

Ah Toy tried to speak, but no words came.

"These to go aboard, folks?" A husky man with his sleeves rolled up kicked a boot against the stack of packing boxes. He looked from Ah Toy to Li Jin and back again. "Yes or no?"

Ah Toy dragged the small word up from the well inside her. "No," she said, and bowed her head beneath her crushing sorrow.

"What do you mean!" Li Jin shouted. "What are you saying!"

Ah Toy looked up in surprise. Li Jin never raised his voice, never angered. She saw that alarm filled his eyes, not anger. She felt a tearing grief. He loved her, this good man, this dutiful son, to whose house she could bring no harmony. She saw her dreams splintering into countless fractures, like the glaze of Kwan-yin's statue. "I cannot go," she murmured.

She saw Li Jin's shocked disbelief. She couldn't bear it, this cruel destiny. Were no dreams possible? A person could not choose one's life, the old mistress had warned. But dreams, dreams, Ah Toy wanted to cry out, what of them? She knew she was weeping, that Li Jin and the cargo handler both stood staring at her while tears spilled down her face.

She bowed her head and through her tears saw the box with the orange and the chipped corner. Destiny had denied her dreams, but one dream remained possible.

Ah Toy picked up the orange and offered it to a little boy passing by. He took it and smiled at her. There was this, at least, Ah Toy thought, watching the child skip away with his treat: Gum Shan stole dreams but offered life. She would never be hungry here.

She turned to the cargo handler, pointed at the box, and said, "This one, take this one."

"I don't want your things!" Li Jin said.

Ah Toy took a coin from her money case and put it in the cargo man's hand. "Cabin twelve," she said. He shrugged, dropped the coin in his shirt pocket, hefted the box onto his shoulder, and headed for the gangplank.

Ah Toy watched the box go, feeling a sweet sadness fill the emptiness inside her. "Think of me when you open it," she said softly to Li Jin. "A gift from your Gum Shan wife to your China family."

"You are my family, my wife!"

Ah Toy heard injury in his voice, saw it in his eyes. "I am sorry,

I cannot go." She held out the money case to him. He hesitated, and she put it in his hands. "My dowry is yours, but my destiny is Gum Shan."

She wanted to explain that the life she realized was now quickening inside her might be a daughter, wanted him to understand why she could not return to China after Gum Shan. How could one choose servitude after liberty? And how could she choose for a child conceived in freedom a future of bondage? How could she bear seeing again any young girl's feet crushed into a pulp of collapsed bones however beautifully bound in silk ribbons and satin? How could she bear the child's screams knowing that in Gum Shan women walked free and whole?

She knew she could not, that her anguish over the cruel fate of China's daughters would destroy the harmony of this dutiful son's home. She thought of the daughter waiting for him there, and new tears filled her eyes.

"Give this, please, to your daughter," she said, drawing a silken cord over her head. She pressed the white jade dragon into Li Jin's hand. "For good fortune, tell her, from her auntie in America."

Li Jin shoved the ivory into a pocket and scowled. "Feather beds!" he said, pelting her with the words like stones. "Feather beds and fancy dresses!"

Ah Toy stared at him through her tears and surprise.

"Yes, I see how it is. You cannot leave your rich life in America. You need carriages in which to exhibit yourself, and fancy French dresses. You like now to parade in gold, wear it, eat it from costly dishes and teak tables."

Ah Toy saw his jaw tighten and his hands clench with fury at her betrayal. This is what he thought? That she required riches? Tears spilled down her face. Didn't he realize how she had obtained it? But what could he know of rough men looking and laughing and tossing a coin? What could he know of rank-smelling skin clammy against her body? Of the humiliation and exhaustion behind her smiling invitations with silken pictures, wine, the monk's red powder?

Li Jin and Ah Toy stared at each other in silence for a long moment, and then he turned and headed for the gangplank.

Ah Toy watched him go. "You know nothing," she said softly.

The wind caught her words like a kite and drew them toward Clay street.

HISTORICAL AFTERWORD

On the day James Marshall found gold in the tailrace of Sutter's sawmill, Henry Bigler recorded the event in his diary. The date was January 24, 1848.

Like a pebble tossed in a pond, the news rippled slowly from California's interior. Rumors reached Monterey, on the coast, late in May. Proof arrived in June. On June 20, 1848, Walter Colton, alcalde at Monterey, wrote in his diary, "The blacksmith dropped his hammer, the carpenter his plane, the mason his trowel, the farmer his sickle, the baker his loaf, the tapster his bottle. All were off to the mines, some on horses, some on carts, and some on crutches, and one went in a litter. An American woman, who had recently established a boarding-house here, pulled up stakes, and was off before her lodgers had even time to pay their bills."

The news left California aboard sailing ships. The schooner *Louisa* carried it to Honolulu. From there the word shipped out in ever-expanding circles. Some Hudson's Bay Company men relayed it to Oregon. Mexico heard fairly quickly, and South America. The ripples widened. Within months, the whole world would hear gold, that mystical mineral, beckoning like a siren. And the whole world would answer.

So began the great California gold rush. The legendary forty-niners trudging overland from the States to California would meet in that fabled place their counterparts from around the globe: Mexicans, South Americans, Australians, French, Irish, Germans, English, Russians, Turks—and Chinese.

Among the first to arrive from China was a young woman. Her

name was Ah Toy—with such variant spellings as Ahtoy, Atoy, Attoy, Atoi, Achoi, and Achoy appearing in early newspapers, diaries, and reminiscences. She was not the first Chinese woman in California. That distinction belongs to Marie Seise from Canton, who, abandoned by her Portuguese husband, worked as a servant for Mr. and Mrs. Charles Gillespie and arrived with them in San Francisco in February 1848.

Little is known of Ah Toy beyond her few years as a wealthy courtesan in San Francisco. Contradictory accounts date her arrival there as 1848, 1849, and 1850. Lucie Cheng Hirata ("Chinese Immigrant Women in Nineteenth-Century California," in *Women of America, a History,* Houghton Mifflin, 1979) says she came as a free agent and succeeded in accumulating enough money to own a brothel within two years. Herbert Asbury (*The Barbary Coast,* Alfred A. Knopf, 1933), on the contrary, claims she arrived enslaved and bought her freedom. Her departure is equally clouded. Asbury states she returned to China to spend her declining years in comfort. Curt Gentry (*The Madams of San Francisco,* Doubleday & Co., 1964) asserts that a death notice in the *San Francisco Examiner* of February 2, 1928, for one "Mrs. Ah Toy–China Mary," who "died within a few days of her hundredth birthday," was for the notable Ah Toy.

No contradictions surround her beauty. A reporter wrote of her in 1851, "Everybody has seen the charming Miss Atoy, who each day parades our streets dressed in the most flashing European and American style." Pioneer Elisha Crosby described her in his memoirs as "a very handsome Chinese girl . . . quite select in her associates [,] was liberally patronized by the white men and made a great amount of money." Frenchman Albert Benard de Russailh wrote home, "There are a few girls who are attractive if not actually pretty, for example, the strangely alluring Achoy, with her slender body and laughing eyes." And Charles P. Duane remembered her as a "tall, well-built woman. In fact, she was the finest-looking woman I have ever seen."

And this also is known: Ah Toy was the first Asian woman in America to "go to law," to employ the American judicial system as a means of righting wrongs. Through the courts, she successfully fought off all attempts by Norman As-sing (variants include Ah Sing, A-sing, Assing), de facto chief of California's Chinese community, to control her. Further, she not only brought suit as a plaintiff when her customers cheated her by substituting brass filings for gold dust, but appeared as legal counsel for Chinese women protesting extortion by the tongs. In 1854 she testified against As-sing in a trial that indicted him as a Triad tax collector. The courage and independence exemplified by such actions is remarkable in a young woman whose culture relegated her sex to little more than slave status.

Confucian ideology dictated the place of women in nineteenth-century China as subservient to all men. They were destined to be ruled first by a father, then by a husband, and when widowed, by the eldest son. Because they were of such little worth to the family, in times of famine female children were frequently sold to buy food. When a son married, he brought his wife into the household to help the family; raising a daughter meant feeding a mouth until she was old enough to serve a husband and in-laws. Females were valued, or more precisely, devalued, accordingly.

Despite such societal directives, Ah Toy appeared not to know her place. Norman As-sing did know her place. Their clash was inevitable. That Ah Toy prevailed elevates her from interesting to admirable.

And who was Norman As-sing?

Like Ah Toy's, his history prior to his appearance on the California scene is lost in conjecture. And also like hers, his position in traditional Chinese society was not high. He was a merchant, a lowly station in China. In California, where only money and influence counted, Norman As-sing attained a position unimaginable for himself in China.

Although As-sing declared in an open letter to California's governor that he was "a naturalized citizen of Charleston, South Carolina," and although he may well have visited that city, his claim to citizenship is dubious. His Americanized name he doubtless adopted along with his new country—and its more fashionable raiment. From James O'Meara, who lived in San Francisco in the 1850s, we learn that As-sing's dress was "a singular mixture" of Chinese and American garments, that he wore a "queue and stovepipe hat at the same time."

Early San Francisco newspapers document As-sing as a man of power and influence. On August 28, 1850, he led the procession of San Francisco's "China boys" (as the Chinese were commonly called) in their first public appearance, an occasion for the distribution of religious tracts printed in Canton for the American Board of Commissioners for Foreign Missions. The next day, he led them again in the mock funeral procession the city got up to commemorate the death of President Zachary Taylor, and he would lead them again in Fourth of July parades and the statehood celebration.

As-sing organized a benevolent society for his Chinese brethren and persuaded an important San Francisco businessman, Selim E. Woodworth, to serve as "Mandarin of the Celestial Empire and China Consul." As-sing feted notable city leaders during the first reported Chinese New Year celebration in the United States, and the San Francisco City Directory of 1854 lists "Norman Assing, Sacramento street, between Kearny and Dupont," among "Foreign Consuls in San Francisco." This was the only such listing until 1879, when the first regular official's name appeared.

The clash between As-sing and the Chinese woman who affronted Confucian values and flaunted her independence was inevitable. Corinne K. Hoexter (*From Canton to California: The Epic of Chinese Immigration,* Four Winds Press, 1976) asserts that Ah Toy was one of the two women As-sing attempted to deport through the convenient offices of the 1851 Committee of Vigilance. Gunther Barth (*Bitter Strength: A History of the Chinese in the United States, 1850–1870,* Harvard University Press, 1964) appears to agree. In examining the confrontation, Barth concluded that Ah Toy "scored her greatest triumph when she defeated Assing's intricate scheme, avoided repatriation to China at his expense, and had the merchant bound over in the sum of two thousand dollars to keep the peace."

While Ah Toy and Norman As-sing struggled to establish their hegemony, events of incomparable drama surrounded them. San Francisco in the early 1850s provided a stage for a constant panorama of spectacle: multiple citywide fires, a cholera epidemic, statehood celebration, outlaw gangs, Vigilance Committee hangings—and the continual arrival of more and more adventurers seeking gold. Huge numbers of them came from China, driven by famine and such societal discord as the Tai-Ping Rebellion of 1851.

In 1852, California counted twenty-five thousand Chinese. Consequently, beneath the sounding brass of Ah Toy's and As-sing's battles, larger issues reverberated. The early welcome accorded to the docile, hardworking, and sober sojourners from the Flowery Kingdom quickly reversed in the face of their mounting numbers. The California legislature instituted a Foreign Miners Tax levied primarily against the Chinese. White miners passed resolutions banning Chinese from the mining districts of Marysville, Columbia, Horseshoe Bar, Foster's Bar. Robbers stole their gold, murderers stole their lives. And the state stole their rights: in the courts, Chinese found themselves forbidden to testify against whites.

In time such discrimination would result in the Chinese Exclusion Act of 1882. But that's another story.

For this one, the scattered threads of what is known of Ah Toy and As-sing have been collected and woven together freely on the loom of imagination with the historical events of which they were part. Such is the warp and woof of historical fiction. Did As-sing attempt to deport Ah Toy? Probably. Did the Vigilance Committee brothel inspector both protect and abuse her? Possibly. Did she visit Weaverville? Not likely. Sacramento? Perhaps.

Did the City Hospital burn as described? Yes. And was a young nurse named Sophia Eastman employed there? Yes. Did she solicit Ah Toy's assistance in caring for the injured? No. Did the clipper ship *Flying Cloud* break a record on its journey to San Francisco? Absolutely. Is Li Jin fictional? Yes. Tong Achik? Fictionalized. But his letter to Governor Bigler is verbatim.

And to what purpose is this patchwork pieced?

The story of California's Chinese pioneers is too often overlooked. Their contributions to the state's culture and economy deserve recognition and appreciation. They came for the gold, like all the adventurers, but they stayed to build an agricultural wonderland, construct levees, hurl a railroad over a mountain.

And Ah Toy? Ah Toy's legal battles preserved a fiercely defended independence that made possible a new life in a new land, the opportunity every immigrant seeks. Her achievement of that dream in the 1850s, as an Asian and as a woman, remains remarkable, even in the 1990s. An appreciation of her significance to America's multicultural history has awaited present-day perspective. In the 1850s she was merely an anomaly—a double anomaly: she was Chinese and she was independent of any man's control, including the powerful Norman As-sing's. In the 1990s she rises from anomaly to symbol, a representative not only of the immigrant experience—the adopting of a new home, the making of a new life on foreign soil in a foreign culture—but of female courage. Let us applaud her.